Chapter 1

The cre  ?

Hungerford 1 ' until it

reached abou s

slipped off its ver.

Nobody seeme ..um a

small tousle-hai ....11 looking forward to his
ride on the Lond... ...ye, and had become excited now that he
could actually see the frame of the wheel on the other side of
the river. He clutched the handlebar of his pushchair with his
left hand and licked lazily at an ice-cream cone in his right.
While his mother moved slowly along the bridge walkway
chatting to a young woman beside her, the boy turned and
walked backwards as he squinted at the creature now making
its way slowly northwards towards Northumberland Avenue.
The boy stumbled and fell on his back, and his mother pulled
him roughly to his feet, chastised him, and drew out a
handkerchief from her handbag. The boy's attention had
returned to the ice cream, most of which was now either
spread over his trousers or melting on the walkway.

The drone of the creature's wings was drowned out by
the chatter of a crowd of people who were waiting to cross
Victoria Embankment on their way to the Pride parade in
Trafalgar Square. Some pink and black balloons bounced
gently upwards in the breeze as a seller, who had set up his
stall next to the restaurant ship R.S.Hispaniola, attached a tag
on to another pink one that he'd just inflated with helium. A
young girl eagerly explained what to write as she strained to
pull herself up further on to the barrow. A family on a train
crossing Hungerford Bridge were now staring quizzically at
the creature as it moved away from them but their teenage
daughter stopped pointing as she lost sight of it behind the

group of balloons and the train continued into Charing Cross station.

The number fifteen to Tower Hill was parked in the bus stand on Northumberland Avenue. In its cab the driver stretched forward and craned his neck upwards as he caught a glimpse of something shining in the sky above him, but the glint disappeared as the creature flew out of sight over the horse chestnut trees lining the avenue.

Young, skimpily clad men and women held hands and danced, flaunting their garishly coloured hair and outfits whilst drinking Alco pops and celebrating in the sunshine. Pink Mohican haircuts and tee shirts bearing slogans, some political, some just light-hearted, thronged the pavement in front of the National Gallery at the north end of Trafalgar Square whilst the band on stage at the southernmost end rocked and rolled to the obvious delight of the audience. Admiral Nelson looked on, his column bedecked with ribbons and metallic streamers that fluttered and glinted in the brightness of the July sunshine. All around the Square the six-colour rainbow flags and banners decorated the temporary railings being patrolled by pairs of police constables, each couple made up one male and one female.

The creature continued to fly steadily northwards.

The band ended their gig to rapturous applause. They picked handfuls of badges from boxes at the front of the stage and threw them high into the air above the people in the audience who jumped and grabbed as many as they could catch. The band shouted their thanks and their support to the cause and left the stage to the right as the organiser came back on from the left.

'How about that?' the MC shouted into the microphone. 'What a band!' encouraging the audience to cheer and clap enthusiastically. One or two shouted good-humoured slogans back at him and he punched the air in response. 'Right on people – let's get those messages across. That's what we're here for.' More cheers from the crowd.

A couple of large men in dark suits and ties had positioned themselves at each side of the stage, hands clasped together in front of them, concentrating on movements in the crowd and information coming through their earpieces.

'And now,' the organiser continued. As he said the words, there were murmurings of anticipation. 'Now,' he repeated. 'I'd like to invite someone…' He didn't finish. There was a splash and commotion at the fountain to the right of the stage. Four policemen were pushing through the throng towards the source but they stopped and glared at an entertainer dressed as a long-legged vaudeville dancer who had been on stilts but had slipped and fell unceremoniously into the water. Several people were tugging at the bedraggled man and easing him back on to dry land.

The organiser laughed, pointed at the group and then bent forward, hands on his knees. Eventually he straightened up again, still laughing uncontrollably and wiped tears from his eyes.

'I hope our guest speaker today doesn't fall from grace quite so spectacularly,' he continued, allowing himself a few seconds to regain his composure.

'Ladies and gentlemen - and those of you who are still not sure', some of the audience laughed and cheered. 'Please welcome on stage…the Prime Minister!' The crowd clapped and roared their approval. The MC stepped away from the microphone, and shook the PM's hand vigorously. The PM came to the front of the stage to a cacophony of cheering and shouting. He stood for several minutes, waved a few times, adjusted his cufflinks, and smiled nervously until the noise eventually died down.

The sudden hush after all of the hubbub was electric with anticipation. 'Well,' he started. 'What a great reception

– thanks to you all.' He took a few seconds to look around the audience, smiling broadly. 'It was with enormous pleasure that I found myself able to accept Steve's kind invitation to come here today and share with you this celebration of worldwide love and understanding. I sincerely hope the media today reflect the importance of this event, not just in terms of the obvious wealth of support that everyone has given it but also, and probably more importantly, in the messages that are conveyed here today. As we are all aware, television and newspaper headlines can all too often be dominated these days by bad news rather than good. I sincerely hope that I can add my support to ensure…' the Prime Minister continued.

In the quiet of the Square the murmurings of a few people to the right of the stage caused others to glance across at them. A few were pointing skywards, and a low droning was increasing in volume as its source grew steadily nearer.

'…I feel strongly that it is the responsibility of myself and my colleagues in government to continue to work…' The creature now came into full view of everyone in the Square, and as it did so a communal gasp went up as people stared at the unusual being. The PM's bodyguards caught the sense of the crowd and strained to see the creature. They walked briskly towards the PM, who had stopped speaking and stood looking bemused, first at the audience and then at his bodyguards.

The creature headed for the stage. Groups here and there were laughing and seemed to think it was part of the event although obviously weren't sure what the thing was. Others started to move away from the stage, one or two breaking into a run.

The bodyguards had now pushed the PM down the steps from the stage and the three men were running towards the fleet of police vans parked on the west side of the Square.

The creature veered away from the stage and headed directly towards the three men. As the PM looked over his shoulder one of the bodyguards urged him on, prodding him in the back. The other bodyguard turned to face the creature, planted both feet on the ground slightly apart, and whipped out a revolver firing four shots in quick succession. Two seemed to find their target but ricocheted away.

Many in the crowd were now screaming having realised this was not part of the show after all. A couple of newspaper photographers were running behind the creature taking picture after picture, convinced their bonuses for sales to the Sundays were secure.

Police streamed out of the vans like termites from a mound, taking their guns from around their shoulders. As the PM reached the first van the creature flew over the bodyguard ignoring him completely. Bullets flared into the sky. Still it flew on, as it took hit after hit with no obvious affect.

The driver of the lead van slammed the doors shut and pushed hard down on the accelerator ramming the van through a barrier and into Pall Mall towards Buckingham Palace. The creature accelerated, shooting over the heads of the armed police in the direction of the van.

'Jesus,' the PM stuttered as he caught his breath. 'What the hell is it?'

'Don't know, sir, but I don't think we should stop to find out,' the bodyguard replied looking out of the rear window as he pushed buttons on his phone.

'Is it still there?'

'Yes, sir.'

'But I thought we'd hit it – the bullets bounced off it didn't they?'

'Er…seemed to, sir, yes. Maybe some form of armour.'

'It didn't go for anyone else…even those shooting at it. It seems to want us.'

'Seems that way sir.'

A voice came on the phone and the bodyguard went into a heated conversation. He finished, switched off the phone and barked orders to the driver. The wheels screamed as the van suddenly veered south into Buckingham Gate, sirens blaring. The bodyguard turned to the PM.

'Buckle up, sir. It could get bumpy.'

He went to peer out of the back of the van again but jumped back instinctively as the creature hit the window hard. Its claws grabbed at the rubber around the window and its proboscis started to punch at the glass, retracting it into its head and then punching it out again. After three of four attempts to break the window it began scraping at the glass.

'Is this van bulletproof?' the PM asked, eyes wide.

'Yes. Don't worry – it can't get in.'

The proboscis scratched harder on the glass. Score marks started to appear.

'Shit,' the bodyguard uttered under his breath, and moved across to sit next to the PM, gun pointed at the rear door.

The wheels screamed again as the van turned sharply right, then left, then right again. Those inside were thrown around the van but the creature stuck at its task, trying to cut through the glass.

Suddenly the van shot downhill and over a kerb. It leapt into the air and crashed down again, shaking the creature free. The van sped into a garage area and the creature veered sharply upwards to avoid flying into a concrete wall. A solid metal door dropped quickly from the ceiling behind the van, shutting the creature out.

The bodyguard and driver leapt out of the van and into the building, grabbing the PM and pulling him in after them.

Another solid metal door slammed shut behind them as they stepped through in a room full of banks of monitors and electronic equipment. The driver jumped into a seat and placed earphones over his head as the bodyguard scanned each monitor for activity. He found what he wanted and tapped the screen.

'Camera by the entrance,' he explained as he hit a button underneath labelled 'record'. The creature hovered by the entrance obviously looking for an access point. After a few minutes it flew slowly around the building appearing sequentially on each camera, the bodyguard pressing each of the 'record' buttons in turn.

It continued round. Prodding. Poking. Scraping.

'Where are we? Is this a safe house?' the PM asked.

'Bloody hope so, sir' the bodyguard said, although not able to raise a smile at his joke.

The driver was arranging for backup and some heavy weapons and as he finished the creature suddenly disappeared from the screens. The bodyguard looked intently from monitor to monitor but couldn't find anything. On one, three white vans screeched to a halt and police streamed out in full combat gear.

'Don't know,' the driver was saying over the radio. 'Cameras not picking it up anymore.'

The men studied the monitors as police outside spread out to search the perimeter of the building. Minutes later the driver spoke again.

'Are you sure? Where to? No, we've lost it too. OK. We'll give it a while and move out.'

Chapter 2

Jim Naylor swung his three iron in a wide arc, made the best contact with the ball that he'd managed all round so far, and watched it sail off down the eighteenth fairway.

'Great shot,' Bob Jenkins said patronisingly. 'Definitely your best today. See - you can play this game after all'.

Naylor smiled politely acknowledging the praise but quietly seething inside. Jenkins had played to his usual consistently high standard and he, on the other hand and despite his eleven-point-three handicap, had hacked around like a complete beginner on each and every one of the first seventeen holes.

It hadn't made things any easier that Jenkins had been talking enthusiastically about his firm's involvement in a 'little gold-mine' in his words, 'for a pittance'. Since he owned his firm almost outright, and had now seen its share price almost double since the acquisition Naylor was starting to lose the weekly battle of wits between them. The ten-pound wager on the outcome of the match itself had long since become almost meaningless.

'It's the glory of victory,' Jenkins had reminded him on more than one occasion. But Naylor felt more and more like he was being used as a doormat, and Jenkins enjoyed wiping his feet on people as he moved further up the financial and, as a result, the social ladder.

The two men had once worked together as part of Omni-Digital's management team, selling web-based systems to large corporate customers. They had travelled often together to meet clients and present their proposals and had consequently grown very close, visiting each other's families at weekends and even going on holidays together.

But Jenkins had left the company apparently under a bit of a cloud according to the PA to the Marketing Director, although she didn't know any details and Jenkins had flatly refused to acknowledge any problem at all.

'The offer I got was too good to resist. Besides, Omni was getting too 'traditional'. You need to look forward in this industry and the spark had gone' he had said.

Whatever happened was kept very quiet and had soon been forgotten. Jenkins's new role was in a start-up 'dotcom' and he had quickly amassed a significant number of shares in his remuneration package as VP Sales, a grand title considering the company had only thirty-six employees in total. Funding, like a lot of 'dotcoms', had come from institutional investors wanting 'in' on the boom predicted in Internet services. Jenkins had become well known in City circles, and was covered a lot in the industry press and even, occasionally, on television.

The company went from strength to strength employing whizz-kids straight from University, and in a lot of cases realising graduates were often too old for new ideas, persuading bright young seventeen and eighteen-year-olds with a penchant for mathematics and physics to opt for employment in a leading- if not bleeding-edge technology company, where their future was surely as exciting and challenging as any employment was ever likely to be, and certainly more rewarding than following the herd to a pauper's life for years at University. After all, look how many graduates end up unemployed.

Information was the company's key product. Or rather, software tools to provide information. Anywhere, and via any means - computers, palm-tops, mobile phones, television, car in-dash displays, kitchen appliances, wristwatch displays, ereaders. The advent of satellite positioning systems had given the company incredible new products in 'spatial' technology that even allowed businesses to contact people with news of special offers as they walked past their retail outlets.

'We know you've searched recently online for the latest stereo equipment - why don't you just step inside where a representative will be waiting to take you through all of our new products'.

Vehicle navigation systems were becoming standard in even the lowest model of car in a manufacturers range, so the demand for the company's products had increased dramatically. Executives were getting a verbal update on week over week sales trends for their companies on their car radios on their way to work. They were getting woken up by their bedside radio-alarms that were connected permanently to the Internet and which buzzed out warnings of share price movements or adverse political events suddenly occurring in markets affecting their companies' operations.

Information. Very much in demand. And very much a revenue generator.

And now Jenkins's firm had apparently started negotiations on a joint venture with another heavy-hitter of the scientific world. Obviously one that caused him a good degree of excitement otherwise he would have voted against it and, with his influence, if he had the deal would have been dropped like a shot or at least bound up in so many investigations by the Office of Fair Trading as to effectively be on permanent hold. Already his existing business was one of the few, the very few, dotcoms to have survived the slump and as a result, despite an initial dip in business and share price when dotcoms started crashing, was now a City favourite. So Naylor was intrigued. What kind of opportunity could give Jenkins such a new 'rush' with everything he already had? What angle had he found? A huge new customer base? Probably not. He already had 80 percent of the European, Middle-Eastern and African market. Unless he was getting into the U.S. or Far East? Difficult markets to crack so buying a company already established there was an obvious strategy to go for, even if in the case of the U.S. the economy had been weak following the recent banking crisis leading to a global recession.

If not the market, then maybe the product. But they were already into so many bleeding edge technologies involving information retrieval using the internet, WAP, social networking and satellite communications. Naylor tried to keep up with developments and he couldn't think of anything Jenkins wasn't already into.

Whatever it was, the man was confident but cagey. 'Early days yet', was all Naylor got out of him and there was no way that he'd give him the satisfaction of appearing overly interested. So he'd dropped the subject.

Jenkins took his shot and Naylor groaned quietly once again as Jenkins's ball floated through the air, landed and danced up to and past his own. At least it had finished only a couple of yards past this time.

'Don't you just hate it when that happens.' Jenkins picked up his tee peg and gave a wink.

'It's not how it's how many' Naylor retorted with some degree of aggression before immediately regretting the outburst as he reminded himself of the scores.

Naylor took four more to finish and Jenkins three. It had been a whitewash. After taking a quick shower they moved to the bar and sat quietly for a good few minutes sipping at their beers.

Jenkins broke the silence.

'Jim, I don't want to stick my nose in where it doesn't belong. But you seem a little tense lately. Anything up?'

Underdog. For some reason Naylor could only think of this one word. There was a time when the two of them could have had a close game and he would have won himself on many occasions but it seemed beyond him now. For the past few weeks he had been thinking of excuses for not actually turning up but he did, and maybe always would.

Things were changing for him recently, though. Work was OK, although the money that would have come with a better job would have helped, specially now Jack was seventeen and thinking of college. He did question himself sometimes and wonder whether he should have pushed harder in his career. But then again he consoled himself with the thought that graveyards were full of people that had.

No, the real area of concern for him was Martha. They'd married young and seemed to have had a pretty good life together so far, even when Jack was born and he had needed to travel with his job. He always managed to find time for the two of them to be together without Jack around. Even if the cost of the baby-sitter meant they'd have to have fish and chips and a walk along the sea front instead of a candlelit dinner in a restaurant somewhere.

Now he had moved up to a reasonable position in the company they were eating out fairly often, having one or even sometimes two foreign holidays a year. Maybe not to the U.S. very often, which was their favourite destination, but on European city breaks which they both seemed to enjoy.

They'd also built up quite a few good friends, as many couples do, and saw them quite often at dinner parties, barbeques, or theatre trips. Jenkins and his wife were automatically invited to everything.

Life had generally been pretty good.

Recently, though, for some reason Martha seemed distant. It was as though she was keeping something from him and what kept nagging at him was that she was at an age when women could start to have all sorts of problems with their health. Her mother had died from breast cancer when she was no older than Martha, and Martha had talked about this on several occasions when the subject of health matters had come up in discussions with friends in the last couple of months.

But he'd asked her many times.

No, she was fine. Yes, she had been for a full health scan not that long ago and no there weren't any problems and no she didn't think she needed to go again. He'd even been to her doctor, and felt worse afterwards because he couldn't decide whether he was being told the truth or simply heard what Martha had told her doctor to tell him. He didn't want to push her about it, and certainly felt he'd be on the edge of an argument if he did, so he assumed she'd tell him when she was ready. But he did start to feel betrayed somehow or, at least, not trusted. He wondered whether she had discussed things with her close friends and not with him, although he wasn't sure how to approach them to find out.

When he'd asked Jack he said he hadn't noticed, although he was too wrapped up himself in studies, girls and football to have acknowledged anything outside the small world that he inhabited. The worry had started to affect his concentration and his boss had remarked on it once or twice, although he was too good at his job to let it have any serious impact.

And now, of course, to hear Jenkins spouting off about moving on, doing better, having a great relationship with his wife and kids. Generally being on top of the world.

Underdog.

'No, things are fine,' he tried to sound convincing and managed it fairly well. 'Probably working too hard, but aren't we all.'

There was a silence for a minute or so. Jenkins squeezed his lips together in a smile, obviously thinking things through. Naylor could tell what was coming.

'If you work hard you should reap the rewards. The offer's still there, you know', Jenkins said raising his glass in a mock toast. 'We could be a good team again. You know we could. Come and join me, Jim. We'll make a fortune.'

But Naylor knew they couldn't be a team. Things had moved on and Jenkins had developed a ruthless streak that Naylor could never match. He wasn't sure he even wanted to.

'Thanks, Bob. But I'd rather keep our financial relationship to the tenner bet every week. Which reminds me.' He pushed into his pocket, opened his wallet and handed the note to Jenkins. 'That's cleaned me out - I'll need to go to the cash machine now.'

'And don't forget it's not the money, it's the glory' Jenkins laughed, with a punch to the air.

Chapter 3

As Naylor turned the corner into the High Street a metallic blue Mercedes E-series was parked half on the road and half on the pavement facing him, its engine idling. The driver was alone and had the window wound down, his elbow protruding from the opening obviously waiting for someone. Naylor waited patiently as the oncoming traffic prevented him getting round.

He'd look to find a parking place near the 'hole in the wall', probably a lost cause on a Saturday afternoon. He'd have to pay in the car park instead which always needled him when he was only going to be there a matter of minutes. He decided he'd risk the warden not coming round in the time he was there and not pay at all.

As he waited for a gap in the traffic the sun shone on him like a warm blanket and he listened to the music from his CD player. His eyes were attracted to two young women walking on the pavement towards him. Both had long hair, one brunette the other blonde. The blonde seemed to have just come back from holiday, judging by the olive complexion on her face, arms and long slender legs. She wore a white tee shirt and denim shorts, showing off the tan to perfection. The tee shirt had 'Wild' emblazoned across the front in large red letters, and he allowed his thoughts to imagine that she might well be. Her friend was equally attractive in short figure-hugging floral dress and red sandals.

They laughed and chatted together as they moved closer to him, occasionally bumping into each other as excited girlfriends eager to share their news tend to do. Their hair danced around their shoulders as they bobbed around an elderly woman who was struggling with her shopping. She was round-shouldered and apparently immune to the sun's rays as she pulled her coat around her. As the girls drew level with the Mercedes the blonde giggled loudly when her hair, tossed by the breeze, wrapped itself around her ice cream. Her friend stopped to help her untangle herself.

Suddenly Naylor's mind was thrown elsewhere. In a split second he saw it. Not in reality, but like looking into the near future. He'd experienced this type of thing before. Although he stared into the empty space outside the door to the bank he envisioned three men coming out carrying guns and holdalls. He seemed to have time to watch the action unfold although nothing was actually happening and anyway the experience had only taken a split second so far. *Déjà vu.*

He went to call out to the girls but a gunshot rang out and three men burst out of the open doorway. Suddenly the Mercedes driver was animated, ramming the car into gear and revving the engine. The gang ran down the steps. The girls were screaming now as they found themselves between the men and the getaway car and were frozen like two rabbits caught in headlights.

As the men ran they pushed violently past both girls causing one of them to fall backwards and crack her head on the pavement. Her ice cream somersaulted through the air almost in slow motion and fell on to Naylor's windscreen, splitting and spilling frozen orange juice across it.

Two of the men threw holdalls into the car and started to clamber in. One of them screamed 'Go…GO!' to the driver. Naylor frantically reversed but moved only eighteen inches or so as he hit a furniture van waiting behind him. The Mercedes lurched forward but there was not enough room to get round Naylor's car and it clattered noisily into the front offside light cluster. Glass and rubber spilled on to the road.

A fourth member of the gang, having thrown his holdall through the car window and grabbed the door handle, was now thrown off balance as the car had jumped forward. He had stumbled and was sprawled in the road behind the Mercedes.

The driver threw his head through the open window, looking furiously at Naylor and yelled 'Move, arsehole!' and he slammed the car into reverse for another go. The car shot back, just as Naylor noticed through the Mercedes' rear window that the fallen man had struggled to his feet again. With a look of horror the man suddenly screamed with pain and disappeared. The car thudded and then jolted, as it bumped over him.

'Frank?' one of the passengers yelled, looking behind him. The driver jumped out of the car and ran to the back. The man lay motionless, trapped under the rear wheels. 'Oh shit...oh shit...' the driver was panicking and threw himself back into the front seat. One of the passengers shouted at him to drive.

'I'm not leaving him' the other roared and went to get out. The first pulled him back in.

'The bastard's better off here - they'll get an ambulance for him' and turning to the driver 'Now just go for Christ's sake!'

The oncoming traffic had stopped, not wanting to get any closer to the scene of commotion. A pool of blood started to creep out on the pavement from under the young girl's head and the other one stood stooped over her screaming.

Naylor had grabbed his mobile to call the police but as he fumbled for the buttons he heard sirens. The bank's automatic alarms must have triggered a response he thought. He instinctively forced the gear lever into first to move his car forward to block the Mercedes. But in his eagerness, borne out of something entirely different to courage or bravery, he stalled the car and it jolted forward only a yard or so before coming to a stop.

Having backed up, the Mercedes was now free and started sliding past him. He could see blue flashing lights a few hundred yards up the road, but they were obviously having trouble getting through. He started to memorise the Mercedes' number plate but as he did so a glint of sunlight from inside the car caught his eye. One of the robbers was levelling a gun at him as they now started to speed by, accompanied by a throaty roar of the engine and a squeal of tyres. Blue-black smoke rose in billowing plumes behind the car, and as it drew level with him he saw two barrels emerge from the rear passenger window.

A voice from within the Mercedes shouted out 'No don't, you stupid bastard.'

In the corner of his eye Naylor saw the injured gang member sprawled on the road. Behind him he made out the old woman stood with mouth open, coat done up to her chin, and paper carrier spilling tins of dog food on to the pavement. But his focus was on the contorted face, which now stared wildly at him from the rear window of the Mercedes as it sped past.

He saw the fist clenched around the finger grip of the shotgun. He heard the girl still sobbing as she knelt over her injured friend. He heard the police sirens and the obscenities being screamed at him from the car.

But he didn't hear the shotgun blast.

Chapter 4

The Mercedes screamed round a narrow back street, its rear offside clipping a telephone box, and it shot through a doorway into a warehouse. As it skidded to a halt a cloud of dust floated up around it and settled slowly. Harry Dean, a stocky man in overalls, quickly shut the doors behind the car and slammed both bolts home. Then he hurried over to the car and looked inside.

'Where's Frankie?' he asked.

The driver and passengers jumped out. Bernie 'Jacko' Jackson walked quickly to a rickety table, collapsed on a chair and buried his face in his hands.

'Bernie,' the driver said as he walked over to him. 'You know we had to leave him. The cops were only a couple of minutes away – they'd have got us otherwise. Frankie won't talk …'

Jacko spun round and shot to his feet grabbing the driver with both hands.

'No, he fucking won't talk!' he confirmed forcefully into the driver's face. 'I can guarantee you that. He's my bloody brother and you bastards left him there. But don't worry. He won't shop you,' he said sarcastically. He stared into the driver's eyes, which looked back into his for an instant and then to the floor submissively. Jacko gradually let go pushing the driver away and resuming his place at the table.

Harry Dean stared at the driver. 'Christ, Ray, this was supposed to be straightforward. What went wrong?'

Deano pulled a pack of cigarettes from his pocket, and lit one up shakily.

'Sorry Dad. Some prat parked too close. Nearly stopped us getting away.' He took a long draw on his cigarette and blew the smoke towards the ceiling. 'Frankie fell behind the Merc, and got run over'.

'Got run over? Got fucking run over?' Jacko was up again, face distorted and prodding a finger towards the driver. 'You reversed over him, you stupid bastard'.

'I couldn't help it.' Deano yelled back, angry at being accused. 'I didn't do it on purpose, did I? Oh Christ, what do we do?'

There was a silence for a few seconds and then Harry Dean moved over to the car. 'I'll get rid of this tonight as we planned and then we'll meet up at my gaff. It's safer than here. Frankie'll be OK. He'll be on his way to hospital by now. They'll look after him. Don't worry Bernie.'

Jacko didn't seem convinced. He ran his right hand backwards and forwards over his head, staring at the tabletop and leaning heavily on his elbow.

'Suppose the police get to him before he has chance to think straight? ' Tommy Munroe asked, still clutching a shotgun.

Jacko glared at him. 'Frankie won't talk! What part of that don't you fucking understand?'

Deano turned to Munroe. 'Anyway, it won't happen. Frankie got hurt pretty badly. The hospital won't let the police talk to him until they think he's ready.'

'We'll need to get him out as soon as he's OK', Jacko said more in hope than with any conviction.

Munroe looked at Deano who looked back raising his palms to the ceiling, and shrugging his shoulders. 'Not going to happen Bernie,' Munroe said. 'Sorry mate. The place will be swarming for days and then watched after that, maybe for weeks. Can't see Frankie being ready for visitors before then, even though every bugger in the local force probably will be'.

'We can't just leave him,' Jacko almost pleaded.

'No choice old son,' Munroe replied. 'As you said, he won't talk and he needs looking after. No point in thinking we can give him what he needs now.'

A sudden thought hit Jacko who glowered at Deano again. 'Suppose he's not just hurt, Ray?' His face reddened, and his voice faltered for a second and tailed off. 'You might have killed him.' And then, composing himself, and with reddened eyes piercing the driver's, he hissed 'You better pray you fucking haven't'.

Another minute's silence passed.

'Anyway,' Munroe broke the silence, quietly. 'We've got another problem. If that other bloke pegs it we're on a murder charge.'

'Jesus,' Deano murmured in sudden realisation. 'You got him pretty bad. You think he's dead?'

'What bloke?' Harry Dean interrupted, startled, before Munroe could answer. 'Fuck, what do you mean 'murder'? The guns were supposed to be for show. We agreed. No shooting. What happened?'

'Ray told you,' Munroe said. 'The bloke got in the way – tried to be a hero. That's how come Ray ran over Frankie.'

'So you shot him? What's the matter with you, don't you think we got enough problems? ' Harry Dean asked incredulously.

'You weren't bleedin' well there,' Munroe reacted angrily. And then stopped almost as quickly, as the stocky man frowned at him. 'Sorry Harry. It's all become a bloody nightmare. And there was a girl on the pavement. Fell down and cracked her head. Went down pretty hard.'

'Oh, bloody great,' Harry Dean started, angrily. Then after a minute or so, 'OK, let's think about this. The car needs to go – I'll take care of that. Bernie – your job's to get the money together and get rid of the masks and gloves. Ray – lose the shooters.' He turned to the gunman. 'Tommy, get down to the farmhouse. Make sure it's still all clear down there. Me and the others'll join you in the morning. Call me on the mobile if there's any problem at all. No, better still, call me anyway – good or bad. Let's go'

Everyone started to move except for Jacko.

'Come on, Bernie, get your arse into gear,' Harry Dean called out.

'I got something else to do,' Jacko said, as he started to walk towards the door. As he did so, Munroe grabbed him and pulled him back.

'Don't be stupid. Two things would be top of the list of things to get us caught right now. Number one – you checking out how Frankie is. Number two – you finishing off the bloke I shot, assuming he's not dead already. I don't know which one's on your mind, Bernie, but both are as stupid as each other. Let's try and calm down. Do what Harry says. We'll talk it through at the farmhouse tomorrow. And don't worry. Frankie will be OK. And as soon as he is, if the bloke I shot isn't already dead he'll wish he fucking was'.

Chapter 5

The sunlight shone through the bowl of his John Fuller's glass and cast a bright yellow-white star on to the metal tabletop. He took a sip of his vermouth as he sat dressed only in tee shirt and shorts, letting the warm sun bathe his body. From his hotel-room balcony he watched people playing on the tennis courts below. It was quiet apart from the soft thunk of balls hitting racquets and then bouncing on the ground. The occasional 'good shot' or 'bad luck' rang out across the nets.

The blue sky grew lighter towards the horizon and was dotted with white cumulo-nimbus, whilst the sea in the distance displayed none of the whitecaps thrown up by the winds of the previous few days. Now it was calmer than it had been for a while, both in terms of the weather but also as far as the activities of the Stabu were concerned. As far as he could tell, they had either moved to the north of the island, to another island altogether or back to the mainland.

Fuller used to work for the Security Service, still fondly called MI5 although this had long since stopped being the department's official name. He had grown up and thrived in the world of Information Technology and how gathering it, analysing it and turning data into information could be best used to serve the needs of the people. Gathering it – especially against organisations like Al Quaeda – gave him a quiet satisfaction, especially given the growing availability of satellite and other 'spatial' technologies. As a result of a hastily convened meeting of the Joint Intelligence Committee following the episode in Trafalgar Square he'd now been re-assigned into JTAC – the Joint Terrorism Analysis Centre – and been given the task to lead the efforts to investigate and eradicate the Stabu threat to the UK people, and to the Prime Minister in particular.

JTAC had been established in June 2003 as the UK's centre for the analysis and assessment of international terrorism. The Head of JTAC is accountable to the Director General of the Security Service although it is not part of the Security Service per se. Instead, it is a separate organisation comprised of representatives of sixteen government departments and agencies.

JTAC is responsible for assessing the level and nature of the threat from international terrorism, which it publishes openly on the Security Service and Home Office websites. It had been 'Severe' as a result of 9/11 and the London and Madrid bombings. Since the attack on the PM at the Pride festival in Trafalgar Square it was now at the highest 'Critical' level. Accordingly, the Response Level of 'Exceptional' had been agreed meaning 'maximum protective security measures to meet specific threats and to minimise vulnerability and risk'. Unfortunately Fuller sat sipping at his drink with no idea at all what those measures needed to be. The good thing for visibility and promotion after success was that he had been given a direct line into the PM, which, of course, was not so good if he failed.

He began to think about nature and how wonderful it could be. Or strangely terrifying. Or both. The birds that sang in the branches next to his balcony, the people playing tennis, and even the lizards that shot out from the cracks in the low rock walls and darted back again when he tried to offer them titbits of food. All harmless enough. Most of the dangerous animals now existed in far away, inaccessible places or in zoos, like the lions and crocodiles from Africa, or the pterodactyls and huge sabre-tooth tigers, captured and brought to the zoos regularly from the mountainous regions of Northern Europe. Now these can be strangely terrifying indeed.

He would have loved to have been able to see some of the species 'in the flesh' that were now extinct. Some of the spiders – tarantulas and funnel-webs, for example. They must have been frightening to come across in past ages when they were still around. The dinosaurs must have been awesome too, although in a different way. And apparently the cobra-snake used to rear up to perhaps ten feet off the ground and rain poison down on its victims before opening its gigantic jaws and swallowing its prey whole. Truly remarkable.

But of all the animals in the world – past and present - the Stabu had to be the most dangerous. They preyed on humans, and only humans, and seemed to be fearless. Stabu shelters littered all the larger towns of the world, yet actual human fatalities numbered only hundreds, not thousands or even the millions that they could easily take.

And why they killed still remained a mystery. Crocodiles, sabre-tooths, great whites - all killed for food. Others killed to protect themselves or their young. But Stabu stalked, caught, killed and left, for no apparent reason. Not even in defence, since their metallic-like shells and armoury of weapons afforded them the best defence mechanism in the whole of the animal kingdom. If, indeed, they were animals.

Government cuts in many countries had over the years meant responsibility for protection against the Stabu had been delegated to local government organisations. But these local authorities were recently justifying their lack of spending on maintenance of Stabu shelters on the very low risk to society as a whole. 'If you saw a swarm of Stabu you were safe' went the adage on the basis that they seemed to target one human at a time, and if you had time to see them it meant they were probably after someone else.

Thirty years ago or so, on hearing the first warning siren people would have flocked to the Stabu shelters. Nowadays, some of the older ones would still do so but most would watch to see who the target was, and whether they actually had enough luck on their side to make it to a shelter. Some targets who had made it to a shelter, provided they could afford it, had now armed themselves with an Audio Defence System – or ADS.

For similar reasons, his role in the Security Service had covered multiple sources of threat, and analysis of the Stabu had not been assigned that high a priority, given other terrorist activities and the non-political nature of the Stabu targets in general. This, of course, had changed now that the PM was under threat himself.

In Tenerife, there were several very rich people who had both personal hand-held Audio Defence Systems, and also systems installed in their apartments or villas. One man who had retired eight years ago to Los Gigantes in Tenerife was now suddenly experiencing regular Stabu attacks, and had invested a lot in significant ADS protection. But why was he a target? Why was anyone? Fuller took another sip of his vermouth and prayed silently that he could find out.

He had failed to meet with his previous three subjects. Each had suddenly become a target in the past year, one living in Boston, one in Helsinki and one in Vietnam. Governments were required to keep statistics on new targets so that people were able to either help or avoid them, just on the off chance the Stabu went for the wrong person. They never seemed to. The target was killed and, however messy that process turned out to be, no one else was deliberately harmed. So targets were treated like pariahs, even more than paedophiles returning into communities after being released from institutions. Some targets – especially poorer ones who couldn't afford ADS's – took their own lives as soon as they realised they had been singled out. It wasn't difficult to work out. Assuming you were lucky enough to find a shelter in the first place and to make it there, just walking around the inside walls of the shelter meant the Stabu would hover, emitting their relentless whine and droning of wings just the other side regardless of where the target moved to. Friends you had come into the shelter with would, at best, feel sorry for you, disown you by the time you left, or worst case turn on you themselves to eliminate the risk of the Stabu returning.

The American in Boston was a banker. Fuller had arranged to meet him just down the coast in Plymouth where the banker had to attend a conference. The banker had bought a personal ADS after his experience in a Boston shelter and had successfully used it to repel a second Stabu attack whilst at lunch with a client. Needless to say, the client took his business elsewhere and the banker was now keen to find out as much as he could about the Stabu and how to defeat them before too many clients – not to mention family and friends - jumped ship on him.

Fuller had just landed at Boston airport when he heard that the banker hadn't survived the third attack. He had left his ADS in his car while he bought a newspaper and made it to a shelter next door when he heard the sirens but was horrified to find it locked awaiting refurbishment. He'd even managed to make it back to his car and actually had his hand on the glove box to grab the ADS when the first of the Stabu smashed through his windscreen. Each of the three attackers injected a lethal poison into his body; one into his stomach, one into his chest and the third into his left temple.

Of course there was a big investigation, as befitting the sudden death of an important banker from Boston, and people involved in closing the shelter lost their jobs. But that didn't help the banker, or Fuller who had got no closer to finding out what made a person into a target. However, the banker's family agreed on a sizeable donation towards helping fund Fuller's department's work in the hope he could find a way of being able to change someone from being a target, or to find an effective way of destroying the Stabu. He didn't actually need the money but he would have felt churlish in refusing given their circumstances.

In Helsinki, Fuller actually met the target. She was a woman employed in one of the state-run shops selling alcohol. She'd appeared to have used her own products extensively when they met mid-morning in the Temppeliaukio Church built into rocks in the side of a hill. It had had its windows strengthened to also serve as a Stabu shelter. The woman shook constantly, partly he had guessed from the onset of alcohol poisoning brought on by a significant and continued intake of Finnish vodka, and partly through absolute dread of the Stabu. Unfortunately, she was in no fit state to talk lucidly when they met, so they'd arranged to meet again at seven in the evening at his hotel – which had its own Stabu shelter - when she'd sobered up. He'd lent her a personal ADS and was amazed at the droning that had become unbearably loud coming from below his room window at a quarter to seven, as he got ready for the meeting. He still held his digital audio/video recorder in his hand as he looked out and saw three Stabu, each about sixty centimetres long, pecking at the windows of the shelter, testing the strength of the glass.

They moved around the shelter for three or four minutes, occasionally ramming their rigid proboscis against the windows, walls and doors. Testing, probing. One suddenly stopped and just hovered. The other two joined it. As Fuller watched, dust and small granules of plaster and cement were suddenly spraying backwards from the first Stabu as it bore into the side wall. It took the three marauders less than a minute to break through.

The ADS had not even been activated when the paramedics pulled out the woman's body. Her fingers were clenched around it but the sheer terror in her still open eyes showed she'd simply frozen. Again, an inquiry took place, the weakness in the shelter was rectified and the story was history and forgotten within weeks.

The third case, in Vietnam about two months ago, gave Fuller no chance whatsoever. No sooner had the case come up in government records, than the death of the victim was announced. Fuller suspected that government intelligence was not optimal here and that it was only the death of the victim that got it recorded as a Stabu-target at all. The victim had no real chance anyway. There was no way he could afford ADS, and there was no way local government could afford to maintain adequate shelters or warning systems. The victim was found dead, crouched under the seat of a bus, his body impregnated with acid.

So Tenerife was the location of Fuller's fourth target and his first since moving to JTAC as a result of the threat having shifted from one of targeting members of the populous in general to now targeting the Prime Minister in particular.

He'd already spoken to Bill Goldsworth on the telephone and established that Goldsworth had personal, home and office ADS systems and that he'd used them to ward off the Stabu on ten or eleven occasions. What worried him was that the attacks were becoming more intense, with three in the past six weeks. They had arranged to meet at seven that evening.

Goldsworth opened the door to Fuller in an electric wheelchair.

'Come in, dear boy. Come in. Found it OK then?'

'Yes, no problem,' Fuller said, wondering how he could have possibly missed it. The villa was massive and perched on a hill overlooking the pass down through Masca to the sea. The road was narrow and winding and seemed to have originally led straight up Goldsworth's drive, although now seemed to chink past it and ever on down the mountainside.

As they went through the porchway into the hall Goldsworth turned and closed the door, punching a code into a keypad set into the wall. 'Jenkins Digital – Audio Defence System – Model 112' the plate next to the keypad announced.

'Ahhh, I know the guy whose company make these things', Fuller said tapping the plate.

'I'm glad he does,' Goldsworth replied. 'It's saved my bacon on many occasions. Actually, on too many occasions lately for my liking. Fancy a drink?' Goldsworth slid over to a huge cabinet taking up the majority of one wall of the lounge area. He poured two gin and tonics – in portions commensurate with the dimensions of the cabinet – and they settled into armchairs around a coffee table.

An attractive brunette stepped into the room. 'I'm off, then, Billy,' she started to say and then turned to Fuller. 'Oh, I'm sorry, I didn't realise you'd already arrived,' she smiled. 'You must be John.'

Fuller guessed the woman was forty years younger than Goldsworth, tall, with a tanned complexion that highlighted her large, dark eyes.

'Yes,' Fuller said. 'Just got here.' He turned to Goldsworth awaiting an introduction.

'Apologies,' Goldsworth suddenly started. 'Fuller, this is Julie.'

'Pleased to meet you Mrs Goldsworth,' Fuller said, but before he could continue Julie laughed and started to leave.

'See you later, Billy, I won't be late,' she called over her shoulder as she closed the front door. Fuller turned to Goldsworth, with a puzzled look on his face.

'We're not married, Fuller,' he held his hand up to stop Fuller apologising. 'No need, old chap. My wife left me after the first attacks. Things weren't good between us anyway. Julie's a friend. Well, more than a friend really. She works in one of the birdlife parks. Hence, her interest in the Stabu.'

'My information suggests that Stabu are not actually birds,' Fuller offered.

'I know. But, hey, you think I should send Julie away on a technicality?' he laughed loudly.

'If you don't mind me saying,' Fuller continued, 'you're remarkably calm considering your situation.'

'Oh believe me, after the first couple of attacks I was in blind panic. I was having nightmares and waking up sweating and on one or two occasions actually screaming. But let's face it. I've got the best protection I can get. I have money, so I can afford the best defence systems. Once I knew they worked I settled down a bit.'

Goldsworth paused, and then threw a sideways smile at Fuller. 'And anyway. I'm sixty-seven, Fuller. I've had a great life – no complaints at all – and a lot better than most people have. So what the hell? If I go now, I'll have done OK. Mind you, a few more years would be nice.'

'Well, I'd certainly appreciate it if you didn't go quite yet. I need some time with you to see if we can work out why you're a target.'

'Well, first of all, Fuller old chap, perhaps you'd do me the courtesy of explaining what your interest is in all of this, and maybe then how you think you might be able to help me.'

Fuller thought for a few seconds. 'Bill, you and I need to share absolute confidentiality on this. Believe me, I will let you in on everything I know because quite honestly there is a key driver in finding a way to stop the Stabu. The funds available to me to complete my assignment and the support I can call on are immense. Helping me now can therefore only help you in ridding yourself of this menace. So I need to trust you Bill. And I need you to trust me.'

'Fuller, please don't misunderstand me. I invited you here because you impressed me when we spoke on the telephone with your desire to succeed in this. But I guess I don't know what 'succeeding' means as yet – what your objectives are. I have unfortunately put my trust in certain people in my life – thankfully few of them - that have turned out to be, well, deceitful quite honestly. You say you want me to trust you. I say give me something to place my trust in.'

'OK. You're investing your life in what I'm trying to do so I guess I can share certain things with you. My 'interest' as you say, is that it's my job. I work for the British Government. The reason that myself and certain people in high places are so interested in the Stabu is the events that have recently happened in London. The truth is, the Prime Minister has recently been attacked - twice.'

Goldsworth's eyes widened.

'It's true,' Fuller continued. 'The first happened about a year ago. That's when I was first assigned to the job. The second happened the week before last. Needless to say, we've been keeping it as quiet as possible but there are one or two important people starting to panic since the second attack.'

'Like the Prime Minister?' quipped Goldsworth.

Fuller bit his lip as he reminded himself of the meeting with the man himself. It had been a while since he'd met with the Prime Minister face-to-face. It was a shock to see him so drawn and worried.

'As for what I'm intending to do, to be honest, I don't know at this stage. I need to understand what triggers the attacks and what makes someone a target. Once I've established that then we've got a chance of stopping them.'

'Killing them? Wiping them out?' asked Goldsworth.

Fuller looked at him for a second, not sure what to say. His main aim – no, his only aim - was to protect the Prime Minister by somehow making him no longer a target. He wasn't on a crusade to destroy the Stabu. He didn't think he or anyone else would have much of a chance anyway. And, having thought about things a lot since he was first aware of Goldsworth, he wasn't even sure he was going to be able to do much for Goldsworth either.

'Sure,' he lied. 'But I need a lot more information first. I need to understand them. I need to know why they attack certain people and not others. What is it about you, Bill, that they see as a danger?'

'A danger?'

'Well that's one theory.'

'But I'm not a danger. I'd love to stop them, but I don't have a clue as to how to go about it. And surely there are too many of them anyway.'

'Interesting point. I'm not sure anyone has ever seen more than twenty at a time.'

'But there have been incidents all over the world.'

'Yes, but the Stabu are hard to identify individually. Impossible. You can't tell one from another. And nobody's ever caught one to prove otherwise.'

'You mean there may only be twenty in total? In the world?'

'A possibility.' Fuller had thought about the Stabu and little else over the last year. Theories and counter-theories abounded. Some of these even contradicted themselves. He knew he had very little to go on and was eager to explore Goldsworth's circumstances. How much would they match those of the Prime Minister? Could something obvious fall out? A key common factor. A breakthrough. He desperately needed a breakthrough.

'But we need to talk about you, Bill. Please talk me through what's happened to you. Right from the beginning. I'll make notes on my laptop if you don't mind.' He pulled out the machine and flipped up the screen.

Goldsworth's wheelchair whirled into life and he collected Fuller's glass with his own.

'A top-up first, Fuller old chap. I for one will certainly need it to get through the next couple of hours.'

Chapter 6

The men and women in green gowns and white facemasks worked feverishly below him. He heard orders being barked out and a young woman moved quickly here and there below the bright lights. The operation was not going well. As he looked down he saw the tops of monitors, which emitted intermittent beeps, and the light from the displays glowed and danced on the dishes bearing scalpels and forceps and other tools he couldn't make out.

One of the masks was checking and adjusting gauges on some cylinders next to the patient's head, which was partly covered by a protective sheet, as the surgeon worked inside the shattered forehead. Only one half of the face was visible and a trickle of blood had run down around the eye socket and along the edge of the nose.

'We're losing him', someone shouted.

'Flat-lining!' another urgent voice let out, as a nurse prepared a syringe. The surgeon barked another order and two masks swapped places at the patient's side, one of them passing two paddles on wires to the surgeon as the other stood motionless with his hands clasping knobs on a console.

'Clear!' the surgeon roared as he grabbed the paddles and pressed them to the patient's chest.

The eye opened and the half of the mouth that was visible started to smile as the patient looked directly at Naylor. The procedure continued and the body arced and fell again. Nobody had noticed the patient now seemed to be wide-awake and somehow enjoying the experience.

After a pause there were more bellowed orders that seemed to immediately fade into distant whispers. Naylor was no longer paying any attention. It had now dawned on him that he was staring down at himself on the operating table. As he did so he felt himself rising slowly and he watched as the operating theatre fell away below him. The patient still smiled directly at him as the body lurched and again dropped back on to the table. All the masks were now buzzing around the surgeon like worker bees around the queen, but they gradually faded away as he continued to float upwards through a dark mist getting faster and faster until the scene disappeared completely, much like a passenger on a plane sees the ground drop away as it takes off into clouds.

It was now absolutely quiet in the darkness. Strangely after a while, although he felt he had travelled many miles in his ascending state he had no desire to rush back. He moved from calm to increasing anxiety as he suddenly realised he had no control on what was happening to him and no idea of what awaited him if and when he eventually stopped.

He seemed to be in the mist for only a few minutes more before tiny white lights started to explode around him and vividly coloured forms like tropical fish moved out from the exploding centres and drifted through him. The colours and the explosions made him almost cry out with excitement. He looked with increasing incredulity as the white lights grew bigger.

He was suddenly aware he was upright and no longer stretched out on his front. But he still wasn't walking – although moving slowly forward. The white lights were coming at him from four points aligned horizontally ahead of him a short distance apart.

As the mist cleared further, the two beings guarding a huge wooden door continued to fire the bolts of exploding light towards him from their outstretched arms.

Something carried him closer despite his growing anxiety. The white explosions grew more intense as his eyes fell on a huge glass key hanging above the door. He stopped moving.

The guardians of the doorway were forms he hadn't encountered anywhere before. Very tall and very white with tendrils hanging down from the edge of their mouths the whole length of their bodies. Their eyes were ice-blue orbs set into faces of expressionless marble. The scales around the tops of their legs gave them a lizard-like appearance although they had no visible tails. In fact, as they stood erect, they appeared to be floating in mist so nothing was visible at their bases at all.

They gradually dropped their arms and the explosions stopped. He stared at them for several minutes and then became aware of a voice that seemed to be calling from the other side of the door. It was growing increasingly desperate telling him to grab the key and turn the lock.

The huge key sparkled in the bright radiance emanating from the guardians. His only urge was to open the door, without a thought of what he might find beyond or the possible dangers that might lie there. For some reason he knew it was right to pass through the doorway and his very ambition to do so started to dislodge the key which started to rock to and fro.

The guardians moved laboriously but resolutely reaching up towards the key to stop it falling.

The voice was calling again for him to open the door and he started to drift forward. The guardians replaced the key and turned slowly towards him raising their arms.

The explosions were blinding. As they burst around him he was thrown from side to side and although the sound of the detonations deafened him he still heard the voice urging him on. Courage and determination moved him forward as the key again became agitated and started to jump on its mounting.

As he approached the door the guardians moved together to bar his access still spewing light bolts, their blue orbs now narrowing in resistance.

The key suddenly soared into the air. The guardians turned their gaze upward and the bolts stopped momentarily giving him the chance to move forward. But the key dropped fast, falling in front of the door before he could get to it and smashing into tiny pieces on the ground. Moments later he was stooping at the doorway watching helpless as the pieces started to slip one by one through the mist at his feet and disappear.

The guardians were gone.

The voice still continued, pleading with him to open the door. He didn't know how to stop the pieces slipping away. He was suddenly overcome with a combination of frustration and despair. His mind grabbed the large circular handle on the door and pulled powerfully at it. The door swayed backwards and forwards but refused to open. He went to examine the keyhole and as he did so it closed up, turning into solid wood – just another part of the door now.

The voice continued to whisper forcefully to him.

'Next time - next time. I'll wait for you.' He realised for the first time that it was his own voice calling to him. A feeling of desperation and misery again swept over him but before he could do anything he was suddenly rushing backwards and downwards. The door disappeared.

There was now only the mist he was passing through but which was almost choking him. On and on he sped tumbling out of control and accelerating furiously past the black swirls, which billowed and jetted past.

Suddenly he broke through the blackness and dropped like a stone into the body of the patient, who was now lying with eyes closed and mouth sullen as if nothing at all had transpired.

The surgeon had his right thumb and forefinger on the edge of his watch, wanting to be precise when he announced the time of death. Except now, suddenly, the monitors sprang back into life and started to emit a regular beat.

The surgeon turned, startled, and stared for a few seconds at the screens.

'He's back!' he declared. 'He's with us again. Don't know how we did it, but he's definitely back. Well done everybody.'

Chapter 7

'Guys, I'd like to introduce a new member of our team.' The middle-aged man in the grey suit led in a younger man in tee shirt and jeans. 'Sheena, Tom, please welcome Andy – Andy Forrester'.

'Hi, Andy,' Sheena rose from the table dropping her napkin gently on to the plate in front of her. 'Welcome to the mad-house.' She extended her hand and Andy shook it slowly and cautiously, before glancing at Tom.

Tom continued eating his ham and eggs, and poured on more ketchup.

'Tom, Andy could do with your help getting settled in,' the grey-suit said. Tom continued with his meal, whilst scanning the front page of a tabloid newspaper. Gradually, as the silence became uncomfortable Tom raised his head to look at Andy.

'OK, what are you in for?' he said sarcastically.

Andy looked confused. 'In for?'

'Just a joke. Pay no attention to me,' Tom continued. 'Good to have another person to talk to, I suppose.' He went back to his paper.

'Andy, I suggest maybe Sheena shows you around today. Tom's getting over an illness.'

'Yeah, I'm sick. Sick of this place,' Tom interrupted.

'And besides,' the suit continued, 'Sheena was our first guest here. She's been around long enough to make sure you get the most out of your stay with us.'

'Want some breakfast?' Sheena asked. Andy was still suffering the effects of the drugs and was taking a while to come round fully.

'Er, yes please,' he replied.

'Grab a seat.' Sheena picked up a remote control and pointed it at a wall panel near the door that Andy and the suit had just come through. Within seconds a maid appeared.

'Andy, what's your pleasure?'

'Same as Tom, I guess,' Andy said.

'Mary, bring Andy some ham and eggs please with orange juice and coffee. Thanks.' The maid left. Sheena replaced the remote in its holster and turned to Andy.

'You're still a bit groggy - not been here long?' she continued.

'I've only been awake about ten minutes. They gave me the drugs in Billericay and suddenly I woke up here.' He looked round. 'Where's here?' Andy asked Sheena.

Tom looked up at Andy and then at the suit. 'Didn't they tell you the deal?' he asked.

'Yes, they did,' Andy replied. 'Sorry,' he glanced at the suit, 'I forgot. Still not functioning properly I guess.'

The suit walked to the door. 'I'll leave Andy to you, Sheena.'

'Sure,' she replied smiling at him, and the suit left.

'Come on,' she said, 'sit down. Tell us about yourself.'

'Has it started already, is this part of it?' Andy asked.

'No, no. This is conversation,' she giggled. 'No hassle. There are no cameras in here, no bugs – nobody's watching you.' She stopped for a minute. 'Look, Andy, I'm sure they've told you the deal. It's pretty good – well, I guess you've already decided that otherwise you wouldn't be here. They will be asking you questions, but you'll know when they start. No underhand stuff here. Honest!'

'Yeah, I'm sorry.' Andy yawned and sat next to her. 'I appreciate the welcome,' and he shot a nervous glance at Tom.

'Don't worry about him,' she said. 'Just having a grumpy moment. Come on, give us the story. Tom and I have bored each other senseless with ours. It's good to get something new.'

'Not much to tell, really. I'm twenty-two. I've got – or, at least, I had – an OK job working in a graphical design company as a web designer. Single. Shared a flat with a bloke I'd known since school. No girlfriends. Or, rather, the last one just dumped me last month. No great loss, really. What else?'

'Well, how did they find you? What did you think of the deal? What did you ask for as part of it?'

'I assume you two know why I'm here', he looked first at Sheena then at Tom, who slowly cocked his head and looked back at Andy.

'Let me guess. You've got the gift,' Tom said to him.

'The gift?'

'You see things, or rather, you dream things. You dream a lot, and dream strange things. Things not in the books,' Tom continued.

'Well, yes.'

'And that's why you're here.' Tom lost interest and went back to his newspaper.

'This place,' Sheena went on, 'is a research centre looking into dreams, REM, et cetera, et cetera. The boffins here believe there is another sense which we don't consciously recognise. You know, like a sixth sense. Except we're the subjects and aren't necessarily worthy of sharing their thoughts so we don't get to be told very much. So neither Tom nor I know entirely what they're after.'

'Suits me,' Tom interrupted. 'As long as they keep their part of the deal.'

'Yes, Tom,' Sheena turned to him, 'but don't you just wonder after all the time you've been here?'

'No. I've had seven months of fun so far with no bills to pay and no pain. No needles in my arms or bulldog clips on my privates. That's it. Don't need to know anything else. Not interested.'

'You're so shallow,' she giggled again. 'Anyway, Andy. It's a good deal as far as we're concerned. I don't think you'll be disappointed. They seem eager to please but just don't expect to be given many answers.'

'Probably because they don't have any,' Tom offered not moving his eyes from the front page. 'My guess is we'll be told one day 'that's it', be given the drugs again and wake up back in normal life with not so much as a 'by your leave'. None the wiser. Not a clue. Zip. So, me old cocker,' his eyes met Andy's, 'just bloody enjoy it while you can.'

There was a short silence before Sheena shifted in her seat and turned to Andy again.

'So what have you been dreaming about?'

'Oh, for God's sake,' Tom said angrily. He shook the newspaper and threw it on the table when it wouldn't fold properly. He stood up and went to another door at the far end of the room. 'I'm off for a shower. Leave the questions, Sheena. The poor guy needs to get settled and he doesn't need you cross-examining him. It doesn't help.' Then stopping briefly, 'Sorry', he whispered. 'Don't mind me,' and he shot out a breath and left the room.

'He seems upset,' Andy said. 'I haven't spoilt anything, have I?'

'What by being the gooseberry?' she said sarcastically. 'No,' she smiled. 'Nothing like that. It's good to have you here. Tom feels the same, I can tell. It's just that some of his dreams have started to get pretty intense lately so the boffins are paying more and more attention to him. He's starting to feel under the microscope all the time and I guess it can get to you.'

'Poor guy. What're his dreams about?'

'Hold on, hold on,' she laughed at him. 'You don't get out of it that easily. We haven't finished talking about you yet. So, what happened? How did they get to you?'

Mary appeared and placed a plate with a couple of thick slices of ham and two fried eggs in front of Andy. She filled a glass for him from a jug of fresh orange juice. 'I'll just get your coffee,' she said as she slipped back out.

Andy started eating greedily. 'This is terrific. I didn't realise how hungry I was. Anyway - my story. It's pretty straightforward really. I suppose I've always had dreams going back to my childhood. Some good, some pretty nightmarish. Most people seem to grow out of them as they get older but I just kept having them.'

'Like what?'

'Well one of those I've had the most is me falling from somewhere. Off a wall. Down a well. Over a cliff.'

'Anxiety.'

'Sorry?'

'Anxiety. At least that's what the boffins say. A dream where you end up falling from somewhere means you are tense about something.'

'Well, I guess that's the story of my life pretty much so far.'

'What else?' she asked.

'Well – giants.'

'Friendly?'

'No. Quite menacing really – chasing me.'

'Quarrels with superiors or parents. How do you get on with your Mum and Dad?'

'Dad left us when I was ten, but when they were together he and Mum used to argue a lot. He beat me sometimes. Not badly, but enough to hurt – mentally as well as physically.'

'Case proven,' she announced, satisfied.

'No, wait a minute. The dreams continued after he'd gone – even when Mum had pulled herself together and I started feeling good about life again. Explain that then.'

'I'm not trying to explain anything. Just telling you what the experts say.'

'Yeah, well. I've heard most of this before from the so-called 'experts'. Going to the gallows meant my problems would shortly be over. My dreams of attempting to kill a dog – back to arguments within the family. Seeing myself in a mirror meant a reflection of what a good guy I was. Sheena - I've heard it all before. Few of my dreams went without an explanation and I have to admit most were plausible and fitted my situation. So I'm really not that unusual and so I'm certainly not sure what I'm doing here.' Andy forked another piece of ham into the egg yolk and then into his mouth.

'Well maybe it's just the number rather than the subject of your dreams that interests them.'

'Maybe. Anyway, I talked it through with a doctor at my local hospital and I guess he passed it on to these guys. They offered me the deal – seemed OK and so here I am. So what about you?' he asked. 'Why are you here?'

'Not sure. My dreams have included some of the 'rare' ones apparently. One which I have quite a lot is a witch giving me trinkets – jewels, or fruit - which is supposed to suggest some financial gain on its way. Haven't seen it yet, though. Seeing a dead toad is another 'regular' for me. Apparently means I can resist immorality or dishonesty. Can't say I've had many chances to prove this one way or the other,' she laughed. 'I've had loads of different dreams. Probably been through all the theories and then back again to be honest.'

'Do you believe in it?'

'What – interpreting dreams? Not really. But then again wouldn't it be good to be able to rely on understanding the dreams of the great leaders. In politics. In finance. To be able to use them to predict the next recession, or military coup, or anything.'

'Is that what they're trying to do here?'

'Andy, we told you already. Tom and I have no idea – just guesswork. Really.'

The door opened and the suit re-appeared with some coffee. 'Thought I'd save Mary the walk. Sheena - ready to show Andy around? Here's your key card. All green areas are available to you as usual. You know the routine - take your time. Enjoy the tour Andy. We'll kick off your first session this afternoon, if that's OK.'

'Sure,' Andy replied, and the suit disappeared again. '

'If that's OK'?' Andy said to Sheena quizzically.

'Oh yes. They're very polite here. Seriously – if you weren't up for starting today they'd put it off. No problem.'

'Sounds too good to be true.'

'Come on, are you ready?'

Andy quickly gulped down a couple of mouthfuls of orange juice and a sip of coffee before following her to the door. She was already swiping the card and the door clicked open allowing them to pass through into a short corridor. The card reader on the door at the end of the corridor was made of deep green plastic and again the door yielded as the card was swiped through.

They passed into a large area with an oval-shaped swimming pool at its centre.

Sheena turned to Andy. 'Not bad, eh?'

'Looks terrific. How comes Tom left by the other door without needing a card?'

'That door goes to the accommodation block only. You can't go any further, so it's considered 'free access' - an extension to the dining and lounge area where we had breakfast.'

'And presumably this way leads to some restricted areas?'

'Nothing sinister,' she tried to assure him. 'Apparently, just some rooms containing computers and data libraries that are considered sensitive and therefore 'private property'. Don't know for sure what they contain but I guess it's reasonable if this dream theory does prove out. After all, they'll have a lifetime's worth of dreams for each of us stored away. Remember part of the contract you signed was that no data about you or your dreams would be shared with anyone outside the immediate organisation. I don't know about you but that seems to be a pretty good reason for keeping it all safely locked up.'

'OK by me,' he replied. 'How can you tell where we can go and where we can't?'

'Green card readers OK, red ones not.'

'And how do we get hold of the green cards?'

'Don't worry,' she told him picking up a hint of suspicion. 'It really is above board. They keep the cards because their systems are updated regularly and the cards need patching for the new readers. Ask one of the suits whenever you see them and they'll give you a card.'

'And why do we need cards at all, if the green rooms are not restricted?'

'Honestly, Andy. Chill out. The green rooms are not restricted to us, but the staff – like Mary - are not allowed in. So we get access, and they don't.'

'Sorry,' he said starting to smile again. 'I guess it'll take some getting used to.'

She walked the few steps back to him and put her hands on his shoulders. 'Andy, I've been here for almost a year. I had so many doubts and reservations when I first got here I'm surprised I've lasted the course so far. But they know that. I've threatened to leave, been escorted to the front door and been on my way out before I've changed my mind and decided to stay. There is absolutely no doubt in my mind that you could leave whenever you wanted to. But then again, you'd forfeit the contract and whatever you've negotiated with them in terms of payment...'

Her voice trailed off as she waited for him to tell her what his particular deal was.

'Look, Sheena, I appreciate you looking after me today. I will end up trusting you completely. You and Tom. I love the idea of us living and working together for a while. But I just need a day or two to adjust.'

''Course you do. Sorry, Andy. No problem. Come on. Let's carry on.'

She led him to the far end of the swimming pool and through the changing rooms. The green card got them through two further doors until they arrived in a reception area. A huge glass revolving door went out on to a gravel area that led off down a tree-lined driveway.

'There you go. Whenever you want you can leave.'

He peered down the driveway. 'Where does it go? And why would they get us to accept being drugged on the way here to keep the location secret, if we can just walk out at any time?'

'Psychological.'

'What?'

'It's psychological is my guess. You start to enjoy being here and realise how much you can contribute to their work that you don't feel the need to leave. It certainly worked on me. Anyway we've probably already been through psychometric tests without even knowing it before we even got here so they know we're the right type. Just think of the many people who have dreams – why is it only three have been brought here to take part in their work? Good psychological fit is my guess.'

Andy hadn't noticed before, but the sunlight that shone through the glass now showed the deepness of the auburn colour of Sheena's hair that bobbed from the top of her head down under her cheekbones. Tiny specks of light ringed the slight features of her pretty face, and this combined with her confidence and apparent love of life was starting to put him at his ease.

'OK,' she said handing him the key. 'Where now?'

'I've got no idea,' he said.

'Oh, come on. It must be like a new house for you. Aren't you excited? You lead, I'll follow.'

'OK.' He walked quickly to a door opposite the exit and swiped the card. On the other side of the door was a kitchen and a storeroom containing metal cabinets stuffed with tinned and packet foods. An alcove contained a fridge and freezer. He opened the fridge and saw yoghurts, beer, prawns, and what appeared to be caviar and tiny eggs.

'That's Tom for you,' she said. 'He's ordered 'quail eggs' and I'm almost positive he can't stand the things. Just does it to be obtuse. You'll get your computer access codes later on and you can do your own order. Should be here tomorrow.'

'Great.'

The kitchen had windows out to woodland but no other exit, so they went back to the reception area. Before she could stop him Andy has grabbed at a door handle to his right and pulled. A loud siren immediately erupted with continuous bleeping, and the coving around the ceiling became a bright white strobe light.

'The green readers not the red ones!' she shouted above the noise.

Two doors burst open to their left and three men dressed in white gowns charged through and stood before them. One of them swiped his own card through the reader and keyed a code into a pad on the wall. The noise and the strobe light stopped.

'Sorry, guys,' she apologised. 'Got a new guy here.'

They stood their ground for some seconds looking at Andy with the card in his still upraised hand. One of them took the card and passed it through a mobile reader. He seemed satisfied, passing the card back to Andy.

'We don't have time to waste on false alarms,' one said frostily, and they all returned through the doors they'd just come through.

'Jesus,' Andy exploded after a few seconds. 'That was a bit dramatic, wasn't it?'

'Andy,' she said softly but firmly, 'this isn't a game. They're trusting us to move around where we want to go and they obviously believe in what they're doing and have their jobs to do. If the two can't continue in blissful harmony either our access will get restricted, or those who prove a risk to them meeting their goals will be asked to leave. Neither of these suits my needs at the moment. So let's be careful, OK?'

'Well at least they didn't have guns,' he let out a long, slow breath.

'Don't you believe it. I saw a glint of metal under the gown on the guy who disarmed the alarm.'

'Would they use them?'

'How should I know?' she said. 'I've never done anything to warrant it. But you, on the other hand, nearly achieved it on your first day. Congratulations,' she laughed. 'Ready to go on now?'

They continued the tour passing through a library, a games room and a solarium and sauna.

The final room on the tour, Sheena had informed him, was 'her' room. Her face wrinkled into a mischievous smile as she refused to tell him what it was until they went in. As they did, a cacophony of differently pitched screeching met his ears as a blur of bright colours swept before his eyes. As he became accustomed to the onslaught he realised he was looking at an aviary full of parrots, parakeets, cockatoos and other exotic birdlife.

'Wow,' he exclaimed as he regained his breath. 'It's brilliant. You're an ornithologist.'

'I was hoping you'd like it,' she said. 'Thirty breeding pairs, different species, together with two staff on hand to look after them, access to all the latest information on birdlife research taking place across the globe, and personal one-on-one telephone calls with one of the world's experts. I've died and gone to heaven!'

'It's certainly impressive, and I bet you don't get this as part of your RSPB membership. No need to guess what you asked for as part of your deal then,' he chuckled.

'That's better,' she said. 'You look much better with a smile on your face. Now, this is the one room I can 'redden the green' as part of the deal.'

' 'Redden the green'?'

'Yes. It means I can ask that only I have access without even you or Tom. It would be my private room. I haven't done that – I think it's too beautiful to be selfish with it. You're welcome to visit whenever. On the other hand, I've never been into Tom's room. He won't let me see it. Says it's for my own good.'

'Does that bother you?'

'Not too much I guess,' she said, 'as long as it keeps Tom happy. And now you'll be getting yours. Come on, you've seen my secret. What did you ask for?'

'When it arrives you'll be the first to see it. Promise.'

'OK. Good enough. But I'll keep you to that.'

Chapter 8

Ray Dean passed a can of lager to his father who flipped the ring pull and downed a couple of mouthfuls.

'Cheers Ray. Now. Let's think through this thing. Tommy's gone to make sure the farmhouse is ready for us. We can't stay here long. We'll leave at two. It'll be quiet then – and dark. We'll do the count and work out the shares before we go.'

Bernie 'Jacko' Jackson sat in a corner quietly sipping from a can. He stared at the floor, his face red.

'What do we do about him, Dad?' Deano said quietly, motioning towards Jacko.

'I'll sort him out,' and turning to Jacko, 'Bernie?'

He didn't move.

'Bernie, listen to me. What's wrong with you?'

Jacko raised his head to look at Harry Dean. 'Wrong with me? Are you havin' a laugh, or what? My brother's in hospital in case you forgot. We don't even know which fucking one.'

'OK, Bernie,' Harry Dean continued. 'OK. But we can't help him now, can we? He's in the best place. We'll check it out in the morning so at least we'll know where he is. It's probably Mountfield General. They'll get him right, don't worry.'

'How the fuck do you know they'll get him right? You weren't there – you didn't see him get run over by that fucking idiot,' he bellowed. Deano stood up and started over to Jacko, who jumped up himself to face him.

'Come on, then, Ray,' Jacko challenged. 'You think you can do me?'

'Hold it, hold it,' Harry Dean interrupted. 'Sit down,' he ordered. 'Both of you. Don't be bloody stupid.' A few seconds passed and neither of the men yielded. 'For Christ's sake, sit down,' he yelled.

Gradually both men lowered themselves back into their chairs without taking their eyes off one another.

Harry Dean continued. 'We need to lie low at the farmhouse for a few days and see how the land lies. Then we decide. We can stay in this country or we go abroad. The one thing we do, however, is stay together. I won't allow anyone going their own way. We've talked this through already, so you know this'll work if we stay calm.'

Jacko turned to Harry Dean. 'And what about Frankie? When we talked this through Frankie was supposed to be with us. Things have changed. And there's a score to settle.'

'You know my views,' Harry Dean said. 'I don't want murder on my record. I'll have a word with Tommy about that when I see him. And I don't want anyone trying to finish the job, Bernie. The guy might be dead already. If he is, the heat will stay on us and we'll have to go abroad. In the meantime, none of us are to make any stupid moves. Let nature take its course for the time being.'

'Bollocks. That doesn't answer my question. What about Frankie? When do we get him back?'

'Come on, Bernie,' Deano exclaimed angrily. 'The police will be all over the hospital. We'll need to wait till he comes out. We can't do anything else.'

'That bastard will pay. Tommy should've finished him.'

'He probably did,' Harry Dean said. 'The guy's probably dead. Ray says Tommy blew a hole in his head. And, if he didn't finish him, no,' he told him, 'he won't 'pay'.' He looked Jacko straight in the eyes. 'Listen to me. The way you're going you'll be banged up for life. And probably get us done too. You're not going to do that.'

'You can't fucking stop me,' Jacko hissed under his breath.

'Get the holdalls, Ray.' Harry Dean wanted to change the conversation. He was starting to feel he was losing control and didn't like the sensation. 'We'll do the count. Should be about a hundred grand each if my homework was right.'

Deano and his father spent the next hour and a half counting and re-counting the haul, grinning hugely most of that time. They only stopped from time to time to check on Jacko, who drank steadily and continued to stare at the floor.

Chapter 9

Jim Naylor awoke slowly, turned to look at his wife and belched very loudly.

'That'll be the anaesthetic,' Martha Naylor said and smiled at her husband. 'How are you feeling?'

Naylor looked round and gradually realised he was in a hospital ward. His head ached badly and he could only see out of his left eye so was relieved when he reached up and gingerly felt bandages around his head and right eye.

'They say you'll be in a few weeks before you're OK to go home. You were lucky, Jim. You could have been dead. They even think you'll keep the sight in your eye.'

Martha talked matter-of-factly, displaying hardly any emotion. No sadness, no relief, no tears. But Naylor had got used to this. When people had been together for so long the 'sparkle' was obviously not going to be as bright as it was when they first met. But they still loved each other – just more as companions than lovers. Naylor missed the latter quite a lot though. 'Most men do' was all that she would ever offer when he raised it.

He glanced up over his left shoulder at a monitor that was bleeping quietly and regularly. Over his right shoulder were two bags hanging from a harness and connected to his left arm by thin tubes passing through regulators.

'I told them you've got private medical,' she continued. 'At least they put you in a decent room.'

He surveyed his surroundings. The décor had obviously not been touched since the time the room was NHS and had housed three beds instead of one. Nick-nacks had been brought in. Colour television and a DVD player. Fridge. Some expensive looking prints on the walls. He winced as a bolt of pain shot through his head.

'How long have I been here?' he asked in a whisper.

'Since Saturday afternoon.'

'What day is it now?'

'Monday.' She glanced at her watch. 'Quarter past two.'

He strained to look out the window.

'In the afternoon,' she continued. 'The police came round to tell me when it happened. It scared the life out of me. I rang Bob and he raced round. We came up to see you but you were in theatre. Bob rang your firm this morning to tell them all about it. They said to take your time getting well again. Your boss will probably come to see you tomorrow.'

'What happened to me?'

'You got shot. Don't you remember?'

He struggled but he couldn't recall a thing.

'Shotgun blast to the head. You lost a lot of blood. You almost foiled the raid.'

'Raid?'

'Yes. It was a bank robbery. Three out of the four got away. You blocked their getaway car for a while.'

He still couldn't remember.

A nurse walked in; tall, ash blonde, blue eyes and white uniform. Closing the door behind her, she turned to face the couple. Suddenly, his heart began to race and perspiration appeared on his forehead. There was something very familiar about this scene and although he could only vaguely recall it he knew it was threatening.

'What's the matter?' Martha asked.

He continued to stare at the nurse. Seeing his worried face, she took a step towards him with upraised hands to try to calm him. As she did so he jumped back and let out a cry of fear. She retreated quickly to the door.

His wife grabbed his arm. 'What is it, Jim? For God's sake, you're frightening me'

He continued to stare wide-eyed at the door and the white figure standing guard.

'Mr Naylor. It's only me,' urged the nurse. 'I need to take your temperature. No need to be worried – I'm not going to do anything to you.' She started to inch forward. 'OK?' she asked.

He eased slowly back into his pillow.

'Yes,' he whispered. 'Yes, OK. Sorry. Being stupid.'

Martha wiped the sweat from his cheeks and forehead. 'You're tired after the op. You need some time to get adjusted properly. You've been out a long time,' she said reassuringly.

The nurse took his temperature and made some notes. 'You should take it easy,' she said. 'Mrs Naylor, you've been here a long time. Maybe it would be better if you came back this evening and let Mr Naylor get some rest.'

'Alright. Jim, I'll see you later, yes? Anything you need me to bring in?'

Naylor sat silently and didn't answer. She got her coat, blew her husband a kiss and slipped out of the door behind the nurse.

In the corridor a tall man in a dark grey overcoat turned round as they appeared.

'Nurse, is he awake? I need to talk to him.' She looked harshly at the man but didn't respond. He tried again. 'I'm Inspector Rogers. There's been a serious criminal offence and we need to move our inquiries along. It's been two days already – we'll lose the impetus if we don't move quickly on this.'

'No, I'm sorry – he's not in a fit state to talk to you yet. Anyway, you'll need to get clearance from the doctor.'

The inspector persisted. 'A great deal of money has been stolen, and two men nearly lost their lives. This is attempted murder and I need to speak to Mr Naylor urgently. A couple of minutes. That's all I need, just a minute or two.'

'No,' the nurse insisted, raising her voice slightly to make her point. 'Definitely not. And as I told you, I can't give you the OK anyway. Speak to the doctor and see what he says. But I can save you the effort.' She moved off down the corridor. He turned to Martha.

'Mrs Naylor? Has he said anything? About the shooting. About the man who shot him.'

'No, I'm sorry he hasn't. And he is still pretty poorly.'

'Please tell him he needs to talk to us. We need to identify the members of the gang, and especially the gunman if we can, as soon as possible. Will you do that?'

'I'll tell him tonight, but I'm not going to force him to talk to you if he doesn't want to.' She went to move off.

'Look, Mrs Naylor,' Rogers held her arm gently but firmly and led her into an alcove by a coffee machine. 'Jim – it is Jim isn't it? – Jim is one of the only people who can help us identify the people who did this to him. The longer we leave it the more chance they'll have of getting away.'

She pulled her arm away indignantly. 'Jim is still very sick, Inspector, and he's scared. The shooting obviously shook him badly. I don't want him any more upset than he already is. When the doctor says he's ready, then that's when I'll let you talk to him. Is that clear?'

He glanced out of the window and squeezed his forehead between his thumb and index finger obviously hiding something.

'What is it?' she asked, suddenly worried.

'There's a problem,' he said quietly, and turned to look at her. 'One of the gang members got hurt in the robbery – badly hurt.'

'Yes, you told me that before.'

'But what I didn't tell you is that the guy is dangerous.'

'Dangerous? Of course he's dangerous, he robbed a bank.'

'I shouldn't be telling you any of this, but you need to know and you need to tell Jim. The guy's name is Frankie Jackson. He's got a brother called Bernie. Bernie's not a problem – thinks he's hard but we can manage him once we find him. But it's Frankie who worries us.'

He pulled some change out of his pocket and dropped two coins into the drinks machine. He selected black coffee with no sugar, waited for the drink to finish being processed, took a sip and turned back to Martha.

'Oh, sorry. Want one?'

'No, I'm OK. So, come on, why does this guy worry you?'

He let her continue to look anxiously into his eyes for a moment or two to make sure she was paying attention.

'Frank Jackson is a schizophrenic. Well, actually, a paranoid schizophrenic. He's a killer, Mrs Naylor. We've been looking for him for about two months – since he broke out of Maghaberry prison near Belfast. They were transferring him from their psychiatric unit to facilities outside the prison for special treatment because they could no longer handle him. Two of the three officers accompanying Jackson were killed. Jackson himself pummelled one to death with his bare hands. Kept pummelling long after the guy was dead apparently, according to the guy who survived. We suspected he was being sprung for a job – and Saturday's robbery proved us right. We know there were four of them. We're assuming one was his brother. We're looking for him. But we'll still need the other gang members. Jim could identify the driver almost certainly, and maybe the other one as well.'

Martha listened intently with eyes wide. After a few seconds she cleared her throat. 'You said there's a problem.'

'The problem is Frankie Jackson is here, Mrs Naylor.'

'What, in this hospital?' she asked voice raised, incredulous.

'Yes. He's under guard twenty-four hours and he's still very ill. We can't move him yet but as soon as we can, he'll go elsewhere. The problem would be if he found out Jim was here before we had chance to move him. Schizophrenics can be unpredictable, Mrs Naylor. They have multiple personalities.'

'I know what a schizophrenic is. You're just trying to scare me to get Jim to talk. You must have Jackson under guard, surely?'

'Yes, we do.'

'Well, in that case, put a couple of policemen outside Jim's door, and I'll arrange to have Jim moved to another hospital tomorrow.' She realised this was a bluff. He couldn't possibly be moved yet.

'We've already assigned someone to Jim.' He nodded down the corridor and a stocky man appeared carrying a newspaper under his arm. 'And yes, you could get Jim moved – eventually. But if we can get an i.d. on the gang you won't need to be concerned any more. We can get them all banged up and out of the way.'

She thought for a second. 'I'll talk to him,' she said, and left quickly.

Bob Jenkins pulled up in his BMW at the foot of the steps and Martha climbed into the passenger seat closing the door behind her.

'How's he doing?' he asked as he slipped the car into first gear.

'Generally OK,' she said. 'Very pale and still a bit jittery.'

'Bound to be. He nearly got killed after all. What are the doctors saying?'

'He'll be OK in a few weeks. Ready to come home then probably.'

They drove through the hospital gates to the main road and turned right, away from the town.

'So, golf's out for this weekend then?' he laughed, but she didn't smile. 'He'll need your help to get over this.'

'I know,' she said, still thinking about Jim's outburst and the conversation with Rogers.

'I can stay at your place again tonight if it would help, but I need to get back to the office this afternoon' he offered.

'No. No, it's OK. I'll go back to see him this evening then I'd prefer to be by myself. Don't mind, do you?'

'No, of course not,' he said. 'But call me if you need anything. I'll arrange for a housekeeper if you like, and I'll pop in to see him tomorrow now he's awake.'

'You're a good friend, Bob,' she said.

'I do my best,' he smiled.

Chapter 10

John Fuller took another swig from his glass and hit 'save' on his laptop. His notes he'd taken so far were duly transferred to his hard disk.

'OK,' he said. 'I've got most of your background down. Sixty-seven. Separated. Moved to Tenerife eight years ago. Spend a lot of your time playing tennis – or used to before the attacks. Kept an interest in your old job as investment banker through the financial pages and Internet. Living with 'good friend' Julie in a villa purchased when you came here. One heart attack – otherwise perfect health. 'Comfortably off' – would prefer not to divulge details. Anything else?'

'No. Seems about right.' Goldsworth replied indifferently, as he looked out across the night sky to the two moons moving across the bright golden Emperor Star, now at the closest it had been for months. 'Come here, Fuller dear boy. Watch the Emperor eclipse.'

'Didn't know there was one tonight,' Fuller said as he crossed the room to join him.

'Be a few more minutes.'

The two men stood and watched as the full moons continued to move in unison until the Star was behind and exactly between them, but slightly above their middles nestled in the 'V' shape where the moons met. The brightness of the Star caused two crescents across the tops of the two moons as the rest of their surfaces grew dark.

All of a sudden there was one glowing yellow 'M' shape sat perfectly in the darkness of the sky.

'There she blows,' Goldsworth exclaimed excitedly. 'There'll be some photographs taken tonight. And you have to agree – what an absolutely marvellous idea for a logo!' He turned to Fuller. 'You know the story?'

' 'Moons Restaurants', you mean?'

'Exceptional marketing. Apparently a guy who used to make milk shake machines – name of Kroc if memory serves - got together with some brothers named McDonald to go into the burger business. Stuck for a name and a logo they were watching an Emperor eclipse one night – just like this one – and thought how wonderful that 'M'-shape looked, and they even had a natural meaning for what the 'M' stood for. 'Moons'. And every time kids look into the sky now when there's an eclipse on, 'Moons' has the cheapest and mostly widely available advertising logo. Moons burgers. They've sold billions of the buggers over the years, you know. Brilliant.'

Gradually the twin moons moved away and the light of the hidden sun started to paint their surfaces silver again as the Emperor Star continued to rise slowly.

'So, tell me about the attacks,' Fuller urged, returning to his laptop.

'Started about three years ago I suppose. My wife and I were in a restaurant in Los Gigantes. Foul night for the time of year. November was usually such a warm and pleasant month but it was lashing down so all the doors and windows were closed. She was bleating on about missing her sister back in the UK and was trying to get me to agree to fly home for Christmas. Didn't see any point. We never had children so Christmas was generally a non-event, and her sister and I hated each other anyway. So the conversation was starting to get a bit heated, when I noticed a couple of glints of light coming from outside moving in the street up from the harbour. They seemed to be getting brighter so I stood up and moved to the window. Gradually, over the crash of the rain I heard a droning sound that grew louder until I saw what I assumed to be a big bird flying straight towards me.'

He took a sip at his drink.

'Well the damned thing crashed straight into the window. Luckily, the window held and it just hovered outside for a few seconds in front of my face. I could see it – and can still see it – as clearly as I can see you now. It wasn't a bird - it was Stabu, and it was after me.'

'But it didn't go away?' Fuller asked.

'No, it bloody didn't. It kept tapping at the window with this proboscis thing that must have been pretty tough, because it was scratching the glass but not quite getting through. I was petrified and my wife wouldn't stop screaming.'

'Was there only one of them?'

'Yes, this first time.'

'OK, go on. What happened next?'

'Well needless to say, the restaurant clientele were getting a little nervous and some started to leave when the owner came flying in – from the kitchen, I suppose – with a portable ADS. Well, its light was flashing so I assumed it was on. I'd never had cause to come into contact with one of these contraptions before so I didn't realise the sound of the defence mechanism itself was like a dog-whistle – higher in frequency than a human could hear. The Stabu almost seemed to 'somersault' backwards when the owner got to the window with the ADS and the thing shot off down towards the harbour again. I tell you I was scared. Had the window not held that proboscis thing would have been inside my head. I'm sure of it.'

'So – was the glass toughened. How did it hold?'

'Don't know. Just lucky I guess.'

'How come the owner had an ADS?'

'He bought one years ago apparently when the portables were first out 'in case of emergencies'. First time he'd ever used it. He told me it was a fluke that he could even remember how to switch the bloody thing on.'

'And the Stabu didn't return?'

'No. The owner lent me his portable and within a few days I'd had the villa completely fitted out.'

Fuller pushed his hair back from his forehead. 'No clues whatsoever as to why it came for you?'

'Not an inkling, old boy. Not then. Not now.'

'Was anything strange going on in your life? Did anything happen to you around the time of the attack?'

Goldsworth thought for a few seconds. 'I couldn't have done that much, Fuller, even if I wanted to. I was recovering from the heart attack I'd had a month or so beforehand so I was taking it easy. Besides, I've never been close to any birdlife – looking after it or hunting it. Julie had a job looking after birds but I hadn't even met her then.'

'Could you have had any connections to Julie at all that you didn't know about? Maybe knew her sister. Friends. Did you know her workplace, or anyone that worked there?'

''Fraid not.'

'I still don't believe the Stabu is a species of bird anyway. Not the standard signs. No tearing of flesh with the beak and talons, that sort of thing,' Fuller explained. But he made a note anyway. 'What caused your heart attack?'

'I was told I was still trying to do my job at the same speed I used to do it, even though I was retired. I was running an investment club for ex-pats on the area, mostly those I'd met playing tennis. I guess I was working too hard at it.'

'What sort of companies were you investing in?'

'All sorts,' Goldsworth said. 'Nothing specific to birds. Information technology. Got into dot.coms but got out again just in time. Telecoms. Pharmaceuticals. Defence...'

'Defence?'

'Yes. One or two companies with government contracts in the pipeline seemed worth a punt.'

'What sort of contracts?'

'Mainly armaments. Missiles. Lots of threats in the world at the time, especially in the Middle East and Eastern Europe. What are you getting at, old boy?'

'Just thinking. If the Stabu aren't 'natural'…' Fuller bit at his thumbnail as he thought aloud. 'Suppose they're weapons of some sort. They've certainly got metallic qualities. Remote controlled, maybe laser-guided.'

'So why don't they explode or something? And you don't know they're not natural, do you? I guess what I'm trying to say is that weapons can be natural. There isn't necessarily a clear distinction between natural and not. Dolphins have been trained to fix mines to boats. Is that a natural weapon?'

'Worth a thought,' Fuller agreed. 'Let's carry on. Tell me about the second attack.'

'OK. It was about nine months or so later,' Goldsworth continued.

Ten silver-blue torpedo shapes flew in formation across the small beach and started up the valley towards Masca. The light from both full moons sparkled brightly off their bodies as they whined quietly, but with their wings droning like army helicopters. A stray dog looked skywards at the strange beings and cocked its head before carrying on its scavenge hunt in the darkness.

As a cloud moved over one of the moons the shapes darkened and continued their course up the mountainside towards the villa, whose lounge lights continued to illuminate two men deep in discussion. The high-pitched whining started to grow in volume. Two mating lizards startled by the noise darted into the rocks.

'I was playing tennis at the club. I felt great. Completely over the heart attack nearly a year before, and having pretty much the attitude I have now. No good staying indoors with pipe and slippers, dear boy. Life is for living. So I'd got back into the swing of things. Before you ask, absolutely nothing strange going on to cause the second attack. The wife had almost forgotten the incident at the restaurant – well, had stopped talking about it anyway. I'd even eased up on work for the investment club since the new guy took a lot of it over.'

'And it just attacked you?'

'There were three of them this time. Came over the tops of the apartments and luckily from the direction I was serving to. I saw them just early enough to grab the ADS from my bag. I stumbled into the net and collapsed because the noise they were making was horrendous. They were only about ten feet away as I flicked the ADS on. The result was incredible. If you know the guy who makes these I want to shake his hand. It was like they'd hit a forcefield. Just bounced off at an angle every time they made a line for me. They gave up after about ten minutes. Lucky I keep the ADS charged up. Would have been curtains if the batteries had run out,' Goldsworth chuckled to himself. Fuller found himself joining in the mirth - probably the effect of the drink he thought.

'Trouble is,' Goldsworth continued, 'the wife was playing on the next court. Watched everything absolutely horrified. Well – didn't do much for me either, if I'm honest.' As Goldsworth chortled, a new noise was growing louder alongside the laughter. Droning. And whining.

'After that she told me she couldn't take it any more and so she left me…Fuller – are you listening to me?'

Fuller was already running to the window. His mouth dropped as he saw the horde approaching. Even from inside the villa the noise was like a warehouse full of machinery. The whir of the electric chair signalled that Goldsworth had joined him at the window.

'Don't worry, Fuller. All the villa's ADS are armed. They're about three hundred yards away, I'd guess. They'll make it to about a hundred yards and that will be it.'

'A hundred yards? Are you sure?' Fuller asked nervously.

'Absolutely, old chap. Bounce off all over the place.'

Fuller ran to his case and pulled out a digital camera, flicking on the video and setting the zoom by the time he got back to the window.

'I've got to see this,' he said excitedly, but with more than a hint of anxiety. He took another gulp at his drink.

'Been through this loads of times. Don't worry.' Then suddenly, 'Oh shit, drop the glass!'

'What?' asked Fuller, too late.

Red lights started to flash on panels around the room as the ADS kicked in. Fuller's glass exploded in his hand and a shard shot through the fleshy part between thumb and forefinger. He let out a scream of pain and dropped the stem of the glass and the camera. Blood started to trickle down his arm and shirtsleeve.

'It's the high frequency sound,' Goldsworth told him. 'Don't usually use these glasses – good quality, old son. You OK?'

'Yeah – no problem. Just a shock,' as Fuller slid out the shard and wrapped a handkerchief around his hand.

Sounds of smashing glass emanated from the kitchen and a small ornament in a wall-mounted display cabinet blasted into dust.

'Look!' Goldsworth shouted pointing to the Stabu, which were still flying directly towards them. 'A few seconds more and they'll hit the barrier.'

Fuller grabbed the camera again. He watched their approach through the digital screen and waited for them to come in range of the ADS.

The Stabu moved quickly towards them.

'Christ,' Goldsworth uttered quietly.

'What's wrong?'

'They're not stopping.'

The two men instinctively raised their arms in defence as the flying objects shot towards them. They were only about fifty feet away when all ten suddenly seemed to smash into an invisible wall and were immediately propelled backwards away from the window in different directions spiralling out of control. The men lowered their arms. The Stabu came again with renewed ferocity but were thrust back once more. After the third failure they hovered for a few seconds about fifty feet away and then moved to the left out of sight.

'Looking around the outside for a way in, but there isn't one,' Goldsworth assured him.

The Stabu returned to the window in front of the two men. As Fuller watched taking video footage, there was a loud crack and an immediate bright-green flood of light filled the room. Fuller thrust his camera away to arm's length in surprise still looking at the screen before he realised it was some form of electrical assault from the Stabu. The strike had no effect. They were too far away. As they hovered in front of him Fuller took more pictures and made mental notes.

Jets of liquid were shooting from the proboscis of the Stabu closest to the window, but they too had no real effect. They simply hit the glass and run down to the granite slate patio. Grasses growing in the cracks in the slates crackled and burnt black with tiny plumes of grey smoke as the liquid rolled over them.

The creatures hovered for about five minutes, snouts pointed towards the men. Eventually they gave up, turned and sped off.

Fuller glanced across at Goldsworth. 'That was a damn sight closer than a hundred yards. Have they gone?'

Goldsworth watched as the red lights on the wall panels gradually stopped flashing.

'Yes, they've gone. I don't understand it. In the last three attacks at the villa they've been repelled more than a hundred yards away.'

'Well, it can only mean one of two things,' Fuller uttered, still breathing heavily, his heart thumping. 'They're either getting more powerful, or growing immune.'

As his heartbeat gradually returned to normal, Fuller tapped at the keys and then checked his notes again wanting to make sure he'd captured everything.

'The feathers on the Stabu shimmer silvery-blue, a metallic-like protective covering, maybe carbon based. The eyes are large and on the side of its head like those of a fly. The front of the head is pointed – like a rat's, but without a mouth or a beak, and no teeth. It can apparently give off an electric shock. Bright green lightning bolts emit from two feelers that take the place of ears behind the eyes on either side of the head. Extending from the pointed snout is a proboscis – about six inches long and rigid, like a metal spike. The proboscis can be retracted into the head and be 'punched out', presumably to crack through tough objects. The proboscis is sharp but hollow – acidic-like saliva can be propelled through it. I guess this is how its victims die. Below a double set of bat-like wings are small claws with three hooks on each, presumably for gripping. The tail is whip-like, extending about three feet with two crab-like pincers at its end.'

When he was satisfied he saved his work and walked back to the window. He looked down towards the coast but could see no trace of the Stabu. His hand was still stinging but he politely refused Goldsworth's offer of antiseptic. He hoped the pain might help him to think through the effects of the gin.

He looked up at the receding Emperor Star and across at the twin moons, which were now bright silver in the reflected sunlight. He suddenly swung round and faced Goldsworth.

'Was there an Emperor Star eclipse on the night of the first attack on you – at the restaurant?'

Goldsworth was taken by surprise. 'Er.....yes, now you mention it, I think there was. I noticed after the ADS had sent the thing away and I was looking out after it. Even through the rain the 'golden M' stood out in the sky.'

'And the second attack? I'll need the date from you. And for the other attacks.'

Goldsworth gave him the information, and he also took some dates from his notes on Boston, Helsinki and Vietnam before grabbing his mobile and dialling London. 'I need to corroborate the following dates with Emperor eclipses,' he barked. 'After you've checked, get back to me on this number. I need this tonight.' He gave the dates and finished the call.

'Is there a connection?' Goldsworth asked.

'I'll find out later. I hope so,' he said, trying not to show his excitement.

'What's the link?'

'No idea. But I could really use something to go on. And if the Stabu are growing immune, or stronger, or both, I need to work out how to stop them - quickly.'

He settled back in his armchair to think.

'You and me both,' said Goldsworth taking a large swig from his glass, afraid for the first time in years.

Chapter 11

Sheena's prone body lay on the black leather couch as people in white overalls busied themselves around her. She had been asleep for about thirty minutes and a series of wires criss-crossed her chest and led up to nodes connected to different parts of her head. Three huge screens hung on the wall behind her, and a couple of overalls were switching between tapping into hand-held devices and studying the various figures and graphs as they popped up on the displays.

Sheena walked through hot, sticky jungle. The undergrowth brushed at her sweat-soaked shirt and birds screeched and flew out as she used a machete to slash and cut a path towards something that beckoned her on. Her curiosity and wonder that would normally prevail at the splendour of the shapes and colours of the birdlife presenting itself to her somehow had no relevance here. She crashed on relentlessly.

The graph was steady. No unusual fluctuations or activity. The Climax was still some time away. Of course there was no guarantee there would even be a Climax this time round but the signs were good. Sheena had gone to sleep quickly with no need for drug inducement, and she had been willing. She had steeled herself for the session knowing it may be painful for her, but it was another credit towards her total that she needed to achieve.

As she felled another sturdy bamboo, she instinctively looked down at her right boot which was now pinning down the head of a small python. The snake twisted suddenly and hissed loudly, its body and tail whipping up around her leg. She screamed.

The graph spiked sharply upwards and a warning beep started to sound loudly around the room. All four overalls suddenly looked at the central monitor on the wall. The graph stayed at critical, but below Climactic.

'Not yet,' said the overall-in-charge. 'False alarm.'

Sheena deftly flicked her boot to the side and at the same time sliced off the serpent's head with the machete. The body writhed harmlessly as she moved on.

The darkness of the undergrowth started to recede and the occasional shaft of sunlight shot through the trees picking out the swirls of warm jungle mist and lighting up the debris on the ground. Insects wandered across the light and dived for cover again. Sheena's ears started to pick up the distant sound of rushing water and she hurried on.

Her fingers started to grip the edges of the couch as she walked on determinedly. The overalls noticed this involuntary action and made a note in the hand-helds. Her eyes started to move behind her closed eyelids.

The sound of rushing water grew louder and more and more sunlight cascaded through the treetops. Large brightly coloured butterflies suddenly flew up in front of her and she stopped and smiled broadly excited by the experience. They fluttered upwards brushing her face and flew over her head and behind her. As she turned to watch they continued skywards then disappeared into the brightness.

She turned back, took a step and found air. She tumbled forwards and her body fell down a hillside sliding through mud and then crashing through a spiky hedge on to a grass bank. Small trickles of blood laced her arms.

The graph spiked again, but gradually settled. The overalls studied the read-outs for several minutes, frantically keying and re-keying. Finally, the overall-in-charge made an announcement, having checked the statistics and satisfied himself on his findings.

'OK, people. She's at the Gateway.'

Sheena looked over the edge of the grassy bank. Water from a stream shot over a precipice and down into a pool bathed in hot sunlight. The water in the pool was blue and ordinarily inviting but she was wary. She'd been here before.

Gradually she stood up and gently pushed her hair back away from her face. Her arms were stinging from the scratches and flies had begun to gather around them. They didn't bother her. She peered down at the water in the pool about fifty feet below. Where the cascade from the waterfall met the pool, clouds of steam floated upwards towards her. Her urge was to dive into the clouds but something was holding her back.

'Go on, girl,' the overall-in-charge was urging, peering at the screens and biting his lip. 'Go on.'

She continued to stare downwards into the water, hands on her hips. Her fingernails were almost buried into the leather of the couch and beads of sweat had appeared on her forehead, some trickling down across her closed eyelids.

She took a huge breath and leapt out into space, arms out in front of her. As she completed the arc and started down towards the pool the clouds started to move up towards her. She was suddenly aware the waterfall had stopped. As she plummeted down and the warm air shot past her face she watched in despair as the water in the pool seemed to soak into the earth below it. She hurtled downwards in a matter of seconds until she could pick out the ants on the dry soil just a few feet below her rushing up to meet her.

She jumped violently and woke up.

'Shit,' the overall-in-charge hissed. He went to the wall aiming a remote control and pushing violently at its buttons. The graphs went blank and the room lights brightened.

Her heart pounded as she sat up and looked around. 'Sorry,' she said, gasping for her breath. 'It beat me again.'

A lady overall spoke softly to her. 'It's OK, Sheena. Next time.'

'Which was it this time?' asked the overall-in-charge.

'The jungle pool.' Sheena responded, still shaken.

'Alligators?'

'No, not this time. The pool just…dried up.'

'Dried up? Jesus, you must be getting close again,' the overall-in-charge seemed intrigued.

'I was prepared for the alligators. Even cut the head off a snake along the way to the pool. And getting through the jungle was a lot easier. But there's always something. Something to stop me breaking through again.'

'OK, normal routine. Let's do the de-brief while it's still fresh in your mind. Team – gather round.'

Sheena swung her legs over the side of the couch and sat on the edge, removing the sensors from her head. A lady overall took them from her.

'Firstly, strong motivation?' the overall-in-charge asked.

'Yes. Stronger than ever. As soon as I knew it was the jungle scenario I felt desperate to get to the pool.'

The o-i-c looked over to another overall crouched over some equipment near the wall monitors. The second glanced back and nodded, returning to his equipment for the next question. The o-i-c turned back to Sheena satisfied.

'OK. Obstacles?'

'Er, the undergrowth was easier. The snake was new but not a problem.'

'What did you think of when you saw the snake?'

'I was scared. No, not scared – more shocked, I guess, but only for a second and not afraid to deal with it.'

The second overall nodded over at the o-i-c again.

'Er…can I have some water. My mouth's really dry,' she asked. The fourth overall brought her a glass and she took a long swig.

'Highs?'

'None really. I suppose the butterflies were pretty, and the mud-slide was a bit of a buzz, but no real highs.'

'Lows?'

'Yes. When the pool dried up.'

'How did you feel?'

'Disappointed.'

The o-i-c got a quizzical look from the overall at the wall.

'Just disappointed?' he asked.

'Well, no. Actually desperately sad. I ached. I thought I was there ready for the final stage and when the water disappeared I felt cheated. I really felt this was going to be the one. I was going to be able to cross over. And then the vehicle to do so was taken away from me. So – yes – desperate.'

The o-i-c got a nod from the overall at the wall.

'OK,' he said. 'That's it for now. And don't worry. You're close. Could well be next time.'

She slipped down from the couch and grabbed a towel to wipe her forehead. As she did so, the lady overall gasped as she looked at the top of Sheena's head. The o-i-c saw it at the same time.

'Don't move,' he said sharply, and he reached up and took something into his hand closing it gently. 'Bring me a specimen jar.'

The lady overall did as he asked, unscrewing the lid before offering it to him. He placed his hand gently into the jar and opened it up inside, taking the top with his other hand and putting it on quickly. He held the jar up to the light. Inside, fluttering unsteadily was a beautiful electric blue butterfly.

Sheena stood gazing at the jar in awe with the palms of her hands on her cheeks. She slowly pulled her hands forward until her delicate fingers were over her lips.

'I don't believe it,' she whispered through her fingertips, staring at the wonderful creature. 'Where did that come from? It's exactly like the one in my dream.' She tried to get her thoughts together. She closed her eyes tightly and then opened them again slowly. 'It's obviously flown in here from somewhere,' she decided. 'Beautful thing.'

'You say it's like the one in your dream?' the o-i-c asked.

'Well, yes, but what a coincidence, eh?' She looked around the lab for an open door or window but found none.

'It's not from round here,' the lady overall said. 'It looks tropical. Maybe escaped from your aviary.'

Sheena was struggling. 'Look, this is crazy. I don't keep butterflies in the aviary. The thing has flown in from somewhere. Must've done. You need to check your security. I want all of these experiments to count against my targets. It's no good you wanting to nullify some because of bad procedures. That'll mean I'll never get out of here.'

'It's not a breach,' the o-i-c said. 'The procedures are in place and they're fine.' The overalls looked at each other and then at Sheena and then at the butterfly in the jar. 'I'll get it analysed and let you know. Sheena, don't forget the Non-Disclosure Agreement. What we do here, or find here, and your involvement in it stays between us. You mustn't share this with the others.'

'OK, OK.' Sheena took another long look at the butterfly. Minutes before she was dreaming about one in the middle of a tropical rainforest. She left the room feeling slightly nauseous.

Chapter 12

Jim Naylor lay in his bed thinking. It had been three days now. Martha had been to see him each evening and had appeared mostly distant. They had talked briefly about the bank raid but he still couldn't remember very much so the conversations had dried up pretty quickly.

They hadn't really talked together, much less laughed together, for ages and the two of them sitting, struggling for words that last evening now suddenly brought it home to him.

The fun they had together was always with other people. When Bob and Kate came round, for example, the evening always went well. Bob had a string of stories to tell and the girls always found them funny. Whatever Naylor thought of Bob Jenkins, he was great company. Martha had remarked on it often and now it dawned on him that maybe she wanted him to be the same.

Well now he had a story to tell. Apparently. He racked his brain again but still couldn't remember a thing. His head still throbbed and he had a feeling of foreboding still which he couldn't understand as the whole thing had happened over three days ago.

Was it the dream that bothered him? He had to admit it was stranger than the others he had. As if the injury to his head had somehow taken it out of the unreal and made it so lifelike that he'd actually jumped when the nurse had first walked into the room. And then when Martha had dropped the water jug on the floor the previous evening tiny bright white lights had exploded from the shattered pieces. He had been entranced. He imagined he was in front of the guardians of the doorway again.

His drip was itching and he carefully moved his arm so that he could adjust it with his other hand. As he did so something caught his eye.

He looked sharply towards the door. The handle was moving downwards slowly. He glanced at the clock on the wall. It was nine-thirty pm. There was no-one due in to look at him until the morning now. He looked back at the door-handle. It had come to a stop at an angle.

He reached over and took hold of the alarm buzzer without pressing it. The door moved inwards and came to rest after opening fully. There was a shape in the doorway. A figure, dark against the backlit corridor, gripped a stand with a drip bag hanging from the top and a feed into its arm.

They faced each other for a while. Then the figure spoke as it came into the room and silently closed the door behind.

'Mr Naylor.' It was a man. 'It's good to meet you.'

'Who are you? What do you want?' Naylor was growing nervous. 'I've got the alarm in my hand and I'll press it.'

'They'll be too late,' the man said matter-of-factly. 'I'll have slit your chest from bottom to top and thrown your kidneys out the window before they get to the door.' He turned round and slipped the lock. 'And by the time they break in, of course, I'd have done so much more.'

The man's voice was even. Hardly any emotion. It was as if he was reading a news bulletin. Naylor felt very cold.

'Who are you?' Naylor stuttered.

'Name's Frankie. Frankie Jackson.'

Naylor suddenly felt his heart thumping. He'd read the newspapers. Frankie Jackson had been the guy run over by the getaway car. A nutter the papers had said. He thought about the buzzer again.

'You've caused me some grief, Mr Naylor. I shouldn't be here. I should be with my brother living it up somewhere nice. But you put paid to that, didn't you?'

Naylor wasn't waiting any longer. He was a sitting duck. He'd take the risk and to hell with it. He pushed the buzzer hard. Nothing happened. He pushed again. And again. He saw the shadow of a nurse walking past through the crack under his door.

The figure held up a cord. 'Need this?'

Naylor held the buzzer up. Jackson had cut it silently with a scalpel and now the cord attached to the buzzer was only two feet long. Jackson held up the rest of the cord in his left hand, the scalpel in his right.

'It's OK Mr Naylor. You had no choice but to try it. No hard feelings.' He dropped the cord to the floor.

Naylor had begun to sweat profusely. The light in the room was dim so he couldn't make out Jackson's face. But he could hear him wheezing.

'Chest playing up?' he asked as calmly as he could, as he eased himself up the bed and away from the shadowy figure.

Jackson laughed quickly but broke into a rasping cough. As he fought for his breath Naylor tried to work out which hand he had the scalpel in now. If he jumped out of bed he might provoke Jackson into lunging at him. If he didn't, he figured he was dead anyway. He looked down around the figure's waist but couldn't find any clues.

'How did you get away from your guards?'

'Change of shift and they get sloppy. Always happens eventually. They'll find the two of them in the morning. It'll probably give one of the cleaning staff a bit of a turn. Dumped them in the broom cupboard.'

'But you're in no state to get away.'

'Oh, don't worry about that. My brother is coming to get me. I'll be away from here before dawn.'

Naylor's eyes darted from side to side surveying his options. Then he looked straight at Jackson's head. He moved fast. He grabbed the drip and ripped it from his arm. Blood started running down his left hand. Leaping out of bed he threw his arm out to the right and grabbed the portable television swinging it round as he lunged towards Jackson.

He felt a stinging sensation in the top of his left thigh as the scalpel found its mark, and a jet of blood shot from the wound. At the same time the television came crashing down on Jackson's head. Jackson let out a loud yelp and fell to his knees.

Naylor brought the television round over his head again for another blow but his target was quicker and thrust the scalpel into Naylor's shoulder. The searing pain caused him to release the television which went crashing against the door.

There was commotion outside with people shouting and someone was kicking at the door.

Naylor dived under the bed bleeding profusely. He was starting to feel weak and he seemed to lay there for an eternity. He couldn't see his assailant anywhere. He turned quickly this way and that trying to locate him.

Suddenly he felt warm breath in his face and he realised Jackson was lying on the floor next to him. Jackson seemed able to see him clearly.

'Mr Naylor, you have done well so far but unfortunately lady luck's run out. Goodbye,' and he raised the scalpel over his head.

The door crashed in and light flooded the room illuminating Jackson's face just a foot or so away from Naylor's. They looked at each other for a split second before Jackson rolled back to take a last fatal lunge at Naylor.

He screamed out in agony as he rolled on to Naylor's discarded drip which embedded itself deep into Jackson's side. The delay was just enough for the security guards to grab Jackson's scalpel-wielding arm. Jackson dropped the scalpel and pulled the drip from his side with his free hand.

'It's not over,' he hissed at Naylor. 'We'll meet again,' he said as he was dragged from the room.

Two nurses helped Naylor to his feet but no sooner was he up than the pain from his wounds in his thigh and shoulder caused him to gasp loudly, and he passed out.

Chapter 13

'Are you going to need something to get you to sleep?'

The man in the white overall was addressing his question to Andy Forrester, who was laying uneasily on one of the leather couches in what looked for all intents and purposes like an operating theatre. Out of the corner of his eye Andy had been watching a man and a woman over to his right, both also dressed in overalls and leaning over a specimen bottle studying its contents. Something seemed to dance up intermittently. On hearing the question he instinctively glanced at the clock on the wall. Ten past three in the afternoon.

'Yes, I think I probably will,' he replied, looking a little apprehensive as a young woman continued to fix probes to his chest and head with connections to nearby monitors.

The man nodded to another younger sandy-haired assistant who Andy thought looked about thirteen but hoped was actually considerably older and very experienced at his job. The assistant duly brought over a small hypodermic, rubbed something into the back of Andy's right hand and inserted the needle fairly swiftly.

Andy lay back at the assistant's bidding and wanted to ask what to expect but was interrupted by the man talking again.

'You're bound to be a little nervous. Don't worry. Let yourself go and if you dream, you dream. If you don't, no problem. And remember - there are no prizes for the best. We'll de-brief you when you wake up.'

The assistant whispered a little too loudly to the man 'I'm still not happy Sam. We need to be sure of what happened with Sheena earlier before we do any more.' Andy went to ask what he meant but found his mouth didn't work and he couldn't keep his eyes open any more and anyway he didn't have time to worry about that because suddenly he had slipped into unconsciousness.

He walked fairly quickly through the tunnel, which was dark but warm and he felt completely at ease, actually quite excited for some reason. But then he'd been here before. The light at the exit came quickly. He quickened his pace and then broke into a run in anticipation of the solid steel-barred gate that started to slide down from the ceiling just inside the tunnel. With a mighty leap he crossed the last few yards and rolled into a ball bouncing just under the barrier as it crashed down behind him. He jumped up looking back at the blocked exit and punched the air in jubilation.

'Kick arse, Andy old son,' he yelled loudly and laughed.

The monitor shrieked three times.

'Jesus,' Sam uttered to no one in particular. 'It can't be.'

His assistant pushed a stylus through his hair so it rested on his ear. He kept hold of the electronic pad in his left hand with notes unfinished as he stared at the monitor.

'Shit,' he said softly, repeating it over and over. 'Shit. Shit. Shit...'. Then finally 'Boss – he's through. He's broken through on the first attempt. This is amazing.'

Sam had suddenly become very animated jumping from screen to screen prodding at icons to kick off various monitoring programs.

'Video on,' he shouted. 'Quickly!'

His assistant swung the overhead camera into position and pushed hard at a green button. A screen at the back of the room displayed Andy's prone body at about ten times actual size.

'OK, Eye's on,' the assistant called out towards the screen.

Andy's eyes surveyed the scene ahead of him. The sky was red. Like the sun setting but painted a much more solid shade. The landscape was lunar – similar to that around

Iceland's main airport in Keflavik. Andy had been to Iceland once for a lad's weekend away and had been awestruck at the barrenness of it all driving from the airport to the capital Reykjavik. The Blue Lagoon with its steaming warm sulphuric waters had seemed like an oasis in the middle of a lonely, harsh and eerie landscape.

And here it was again laid out in front of him.

He appeared to be in a valley. The tunnel entrance behind him was part of a ridge of high hills and there was another ridge about a half a mile up ahead. Off to the right was woodland. Although there was no wind where he was standing there must have been a breeze at the edge of the woods because the trees were dancing and twisting.

Rocky outcrops littered his immediate vicinity whilst over to the left appeared to be a large lake or perhaps an inland sea. The ridge of hills ahead skirted the edge of the lake and a waterfall cascaded into it from a sheer drop dug deep into the hills. But it wasn't water – at least not as he knew it. The lake's surface shimmered in the sunlight but was more like moulded glass ridges than millpond-flatness. And where the water dropped from the hillside splashes of gelatinous brown punctuated the local rocks and plant-life. And the lake itself shuddered and wobbled like a jelly as the goo folded and dropped into it.

He suspected the smell came from the lake as well. Like rotting flesh. He screwed his nose up involuntarily as it wafted around him.

He took a step forward and something scraped his right ankle. As he looked he saw small droplets of blood form through his trousers as something slid quickly into the dry undergrowth. He winced as the pain hit him. Crouching down he turned up his trouser leg to see what seemed like teeth marks. He stared into a crack in the rocks into which the shadow had disappeared. Nothing moved.

He pulled out a handkerchief and wrapped it around the small wound. Something howled or cried or both in the distance. An almost human sound but not quite. His excitement subsided as he stood listening. He glanced back at the tunnel, which was still barred. Silence.

'Focus in on the leg,' the man ordered, and the screen was filled with Andy's calf with blood forming in tiny pools in and around the hairs that looked like tree trunks in the magnification.

'What's happening?' the assistant asked.

'He's haemorrhaging. He must be experiencing some sort of strain inside his body.'

'But the monitor shows normal activity'.

The man was staring at the same read-out. 'This is weird,' he said softly.

Andy walked on. The heat was intense and he was gently wheezing. The air seemed thin and his shirt stuck to his body. His eyes were starting to water when his left shin suddenly exploded with pain. Something yellow slid off quickly. He grabbed his leg and noticed torn fabric flapping where his trousers used to be below his left knee. A tiny piece of skin hung limply where the rest had been and the raw flesh underneath erupted with rivulets of red.

'Christ!' he screamed, scrunching his eyes shut as the intensity of the pain flowed over and through him like a massive electric shock.

The screen showed skin missing from the shin over an area about a couple of centimetres square and blood flowing freely. Andy's body on the couch remained completely unblemished.

'What the fuck's happening here, Sam?' the assistant was standing over Andy's writhing body. 'Get him back. We need to get him back,' he shouted.

Sam stared at the screen and then at the monitors. Heart rate up. REM rate up. Theories flowed through his mind. Self-induced injuries? How? Why? May be through mental transference – variation on telekinesis where people can 'will' things to move without touching them.

'No. Keep monitoring.'

Andy grabbed a stout tree branch and ran towards nearby rocks, clambering on top of them. Crouching down, his eyes looked round wildly. The effort had been huge and his chest felt like it would collapse any minute. He stayed searching around below him with his leg smarting intensely.

A shout came. 'Up here, quickly.'

He turned his head. A young woman silhouetted in the bright red sun stood beckoning him to join her. She seemed naked but the sun prevented him from seeing her clearly. Something rustled below him and as he turned back a whistle and rush of air shot downward from behind him and past his right cheek. Instantly in front of his face the head of a yellow and black lizard standing a metre tall on hind legs, gaping mouth displaying a fresh piece of human skin across three of its needle-like teeth, exploded in a shower of yellow gore and pinkish brain matter.

Andy reeled back and pulled his arms across his face to remove the foul-smelling mess. He looked up behind him again. The woman continued to beckon him towards her.

He didn't want to meet any more of these creatures. Suppose they hunted in packs? He scrambled to his feet and hobbled quickly to her.

He was right. She was naked and holding a rifle of some sort with what appeared to be a gas canister behind the stock. Her body was slender and long, light-brown hair draped around and across a pretty face. His dream was getting stranger by the minute as he stared into Sheena's eyes.

'Thanks. Thanks a lot. But what are you doing here, Sheena? This is my dream, not yours.'

The woman spoke hardly opening her lips. 'I am Siren. We need to go. Quickly,' and she turned and ran towards the woodland.

He followed, limping badly.

'His heart rate nearly cleared the scale, Sam. That was some event he just went through. OK to revive now?'

'For fuck's sake, we revive when I say we revive,' the man exploded. 'Something is happening to his body. We need to understand what. Anyway, the monitors are back to normal now.'

The assistant closed his eyes briefly, bit his lip, and then offered quietly 'Sam, he could die. We don't understand this shit. We can't risk any fatalities.'

'But we're not doing anything. They sleep and they dream. That's all.'

'They sleep and they dream at our facilities under our control. Come on, Sam. You know we're exposed here. They've even started bleeding on the 'Eye' for Christ's sake. First Sheena - now Andy. Everything we have ever learned says we bring him out now. Just till we work this out.'

'We need enough to move forward with. If we leave him in his dream he could bring us a lot more. This is the only time we've had anyone break through – and at the first attempt too! What's he seeing? What's he experiencing? No. We leave him.'

As they got to the edge of the woods Andy watched in disbelief as the trunk of the nearest tree heaved and gyrated like a human body. Sheena-Siren stood alongside, turned to face Andy, smiled and drove her feet and lower legs into the soil. The two tree-humans now both smiled at him. Their leg-roots spread out and encircled Andy who stood entranced. The human-tree lowered its branches so that its leaves brushed Andy's face. His skin started to tingle and then go numb from his head downwards.

The hair of the Sheena-Siren tree had become creepers, which at first dangled outwards like stringless arms of marionettes and then danced towards Andy, whose feet were now held fast by the leg-roots.

Fascination had long-since changed to panic but the numbness also seemed to be slowing his brain. He started to slowly drift into unconsciousness as the drugs from the leaves started to enter the pores of his skin.

'REM movement is down,' Sam announced. 'See – it's all working out. We'll bring him out soon.' As he spoke he glanced out of the room to the observation deck. Bob Jenkins looked back and slowly nodded his head. He had been looking and listening to everything and now formed a fist with his right hand and jerked his thumb downwards, like the sign a Roman Emperor would have made to condemn a defeated gladiator to death. He wanted the procedure stopped. Sam jerked his head sharply down and up again to indicate agreement.

'OK – bring him back' he told the assistant. He made a gesture over to an overall standing by the door. The door clicked open and Jenkins walked in and stood next to the couch.

'Stand back', the assistant stated with authority. 'Charging!' He hit a button, which sent a small electric shock into Andy's body. Andy convulsed and then lay still. The assistant checked the monitors, and then looked nervously at Sam. 'Charging again!' he shouted. He hit the button; the body jumped and lay still again.

'Jesus Sam. I'm not getting him'.

'What's happening Sam?' Jenkins asked quickly.

'He's through the other side,' Sam said. 'He might be irrecoverable from there. Out of reach. We need him back over.'

'But if we can't reach him, how do we get him back?' Jenkins said accusingly.

'We don't. It's down to him. He's got to get back through the Gateway.'

'Does he know? Did you tell him before he went?' They both looked at Andy lying on the couch. There was a pause.

'Well did you?' the assistant joined in.

'I didn't expect him to get through on the first attempt. We were going to monitor his progress. There was no urgency to explain all that. But, hell, he must know he needs to return.'

Chapter 14

John Fuller swore at the telephone sitting on a desk in his hotel bedroom.

'Not the bloody eclipses', he hissed, scrunching up his eyes and biting his lip in frustration.

He really thought he'd hit on something when he was with Goldsworth the previous evening. Now he had got the call from London confirming there was no correlation between the dates the Stabu had attacked their victims and the dates of Emperor Star eclipses.

'Shit' he shouted, and started to pace the room.

What the hell was the connection? Boston, Helsinki, Vietnam and now Tenerife. He knew he'd have to report back to the PM today and so far he had no progress whatsoever. He guessed he'd have to just give a status – a report on his meeting with Goldsworth and the latest attack that he had personally witnessed.

But why Goldsworth? He'd had to tell a white lie about his objectives to get Goldsworth to meet with him and open up to him. The truth was he wasn't out to destroy the Stabu. He'd seen these things close up and hadn't got a clue how many of them existed, much less how to get rid of them. Besides, they attacked certain individuals only. A small number of deaths – or was it assassinations? Could that be it? His mind was racing.

And with such a small number of targets, the risk to him personally or to his family, friends or colleagues was minimal compared to the chance he would be taking in trying to find a way to eliminate them. And even though the PM would probably arrange for a knighthood if Fuller could wipe them out the odds against were enormous.

No, he had chosen a different option. He needed to discover a link. A common factor shared between the victims that would give him a basis to defend the PM. An 'antidote'. That would be enough. He'd got the job because he was considered one of the brightest in the Service. Not the most valiant; not the strongest; and certainly not the best at combat planning or strategy.

But he was logical, with a Mensa score off the scale. Honours with everything he did in the academic arena. And a chess Grand Master. He was good at patterns, 'odd-ones-out', algebraic formulae - anything requiring the use of a brain to solve a puzzle.

Brawn was not his style. But then again brains were not even helping him on this one. He looked at the telephone, slowly picked up the receiver and dialled.

'Hello.'

'Hi, it's John Fuller. I'm calling for a status call with the PM. Can you give me a code please'

'Department?'

'JTAC.'

'Mother's maiden name?'

Fuller smiled. This question always amazed him. He was asking to talk to the PM not open a bank account. 'Morgan', he replied.

'Street where you grew up?'

'Eaton Square'.

A few seconds passed. 'OK', the voice came back. 'Your passcode is 33986'. The phone went dead, and he replaced the receiver.

He dialled another number and this time an automatic voice requested his Employee ID and passcode. He entered both and waited. The ringing tome continued for a full minute. He checked his watch – 10.00am Tenerife time; the same as in the UK.

Finally a voice answered. 'Fuller?'

'Yes, sir. Reporting as agreed.'

'We on scramble?' the PM asked.

'Yes, sir. Got a code from Ops.' He gave the Prime Minister a full account of his meeting with Bill Goldsworth and the Stabu attack. He referred to his laptop screen that he had flipped open on his bed, paging down until he'd got to the end.

'I guess that's about it for the time being,' he concluded.

'So no answers for me?'

'Not yet sir.' He said quietly, and winced knowing that he didn't have anything more positive to offer.

'It's been a year, Fuller. I know you've done some good work, don't get me wrong. But I'm close to becoming a hermit. I should be doing public appearances; meeting with important people. And the press won't let up after the Pride event. My career might as well be ended. And worse – I'm not convinced there's enough protection out there to stop these things anymore. Hell, you've just told me in your report that they're getting stronger. Give me some hope, Fuller. Tell me why I just don't set up the military around Goldsworth's place – was that his name? – and blow the hell out of these things when they turn up again?'

'Well, sir. Apart from us not really knowing how many there are – so you may not totally eradicate them in one go - I have a suspicion they are becoming immune to our defences. In fact, they may actually be 'absorbing' power used in those defence mechanisms.'

'Why do you say that?'

'Well, they appear to have got a lot closer to Goldsworth's place last night. The strength of the ADS system hasn't changed and they didn't get anywhere near last time. And if they are somehow using this, just think what energy they might be able to accumulate from military weaponry'.

'But that's conjecture, right? You have no proof?'

'Er, no I don't. But until I know how they are getting stronger it's a hell of a risk to take.'

The PM paused for a moment. 'OK. I know I need to trust you. But we're running out of time. I need you to work whatever hours you can and grab whatever resources you require. If anybody – and I mean anybody – needs an approval for anything you ask for just let me know.'

'I will sir'.

'OK then. Another report the day after tomorrow, right?'

'Right sir.' The phone clicked and the hum of the dialling tone returned.

Fuller put the receiver back in its cradle and lay back on the bed. He looked over at the bedroom walls, which were covered in flipchart pages blu-tacked to the surfaces. Names and dates and events. But no links.

A banker from Boston. Had gained a certain position in life but had no real enemies. His rise to some prominence in the Financial Services sector had never really caused that many problems to people – just right time, right place. Nice family. Good and trusted friends. Nothing to suggest a visit from the Stabu. Probably one of the most vulnerable in terms of his health record, given that he'd already had three heart attacks when they got him. May have had a massive fourth attack even before their poison kicked in.

A Finnish shop-worker. Someone who was effectively an alcoholic but, apart from that, nothing to make her stand out from anyone else in Finland, or the world for that matter.

An ex-soldier who was one of the South Vietnamese working with the Americans against the Vietcong. Biggest claim to fame was almost being killed in 'friendly fire' when an American private lost it on manoeuvres in the jungle. The guy still had the bullet they removed from his brain tied as a necklace round his neck when they found him after the Stabu attack.

He swung his legs over the edge of the bed and sat in front of his laptop. He quickly moved through the records that existed for other Stabu killings over the years. Again, nothing stood out. He slumped back on the bed again.

And now there was Goldsworth. Again – what was the link? He'd originally circled the words 'heart attacks' in red under the Boston banker's name and drawn a line across to the same words under 'Goldsworth'. But he'd made some calls and found that the Finnish shop-worker had no heart problems whatsoever. He'd spoken to her doctor in Helsinki who, now that his patient had passed away, had felt obliged to disclose all the information he had in order to try to help. He had told Fuller that she had apparently experienced very serious and traumatic events under the influence of alcohol, including being hit full-on by a tram during a bender one night, resulting in major injuries. She recovered eventually from these. But she'd never actually suffered with any heart problems.

He couldn't check the Vietnamese soldier – insufficient records – so he chose some of the more recent cases on his 'others' list. Only two out of seven he checked had experienced heart problems. Dead end.

So what else was there? The Vietnamese guy was a soldier, but no armed services links that he could see for any of the others. The banker and Goldsworth had money – but the shop-worker and soldier definitely didn't. Religious tendencies, political allegiances, organisation affiliations – he'd checked them all out and, again, come up with no common thread.

He lay there turning things over in his mind. There was a knock on his door. Before he could answer, a maid walked in and, on seeing him, apologised and went to back out.

'No, it's OK,' he said. 'I need some fresh air anyway.'

He slipped on a pair of shoes, grabbed his wallet and room key from the desk, and grabbed the lift down to Reception.

'Any messages for me?' he asked.

The receptionist checked. 'No sir.' She smiled pleasantly and he caught sight of her name badge.

'Sophia. A lovely name. Italian?'

'Thank you, sir. Yes – er, I'm from Rome originally.'

Sometimes, he thought to himself, he was exceedingly glad at the expansion of the Roman Empire out of Italy in the Middle Ages, and its spread across mainland Europe, especially in relation to the beautiful females the Romans had produced ever since. It was hard to believe that almost half of the total population of Europe, and therefore ten percent of the world population, was actually of Roman descent. Many European males owed a lot to Julius Caesar, even if he did try unsuccessfully to invade England and drowned in storms somewhere off the Essex coast as a result. The story goes that he actually narrowly cheated death when Brutus and other 'so-called' friends tried to kill him on the Ides of March. Hey, a link at last! Shame Caesar couldn't have shared his experience with Fuller's Vietnamese soldier who also had suffered under 'friendly fire'.

As Fuller went to turn away from Sophia, something made him stop in his tracks. He stood – eyes closed – at the Reception desk. Was it 'friendly fire'? No, dammit, he thought. No link to the shop-worker alcoholic. Something else.

He suddenly opened his eyes and after a few seconds ran to the stairs and leapt up them two-by-two to get back to his room. The maid was in the bathroom.

'Oh, I'm sorry sir...'

He ignored her and grabbed his mobile. Checking the address book he found an entry and dialled a number in Finland. The doctor was available and gave him what he needed.

He then called a Boston number, got though to the banker's wife, and again got what he wanted to hear.

Finally he dialled a local number.

'Morning, old boy. Good to hear from you again so soon. I enjoyed our meeting last night apart from the visit by our mutual little friends. Must do it again...'

'Would love to,' Fuller jumped in. 'But I need to ask you a question. How serious was your heart attack?'

'Pretty damned bad if you must know. Almost had my chips. I'm lucky to still be around. But I told you that, didn't I?'

'You actually said you'd had a full life and therefore wasn't too worried about the Stabu attacks. You didn't say how close to death you'd been.'

'OK. But is that important?'

'At a point in your life you were probably as close to death as a Boston banker, a Finnish alcoholic and a Vietnamese soldier had been.'

'So what does it mean? Have you solved it?'

'No, not yet. But it's a start.' Fuller was starting at last to feel hopeful.

'Well, great. Do you want to meet up again and talk it through? I could tell you about my – er - 'experience' when the heart attack happened. Pretty weird actually. And some of the dreams since.'

After they'd finished their conversation Fuller called the PM.

Chapter 15

Jim Naylor's eyes stung and he felt nauseous. His arms ached where the drips were attached. He'd never felt so exhausted. He hadn't slept at all in the last couple of days and conversation with the policeman inside his room had long since run dry. He needed to sleep but couldn't bring himself to do so despite the drugs being pumped into his body for just that purpose.

Inspector Rogers had tried to convince him that Jackson was safely under lock and key in a ward by himself in another wing of the hospital, but Naylor couldn't relax. He'd seen the hatred in Jackson's eyes and recognised the evil fuelling his attack.

And he'd told Naylor 'We'll meet again'. Not the most conducive of situations for rest and recuperation.

He had been sweating for several hours now, brought on by fatigue. The nurse had gone to open a window but he'd jumped nervously and almost shouted at her to leave it firmly closed. Outside was a long drop, but this was little comfort.

He was starting to submit to the influence of the medication, and his eyes closed slowly as his head dropped forward sharply. He jumped up with eyes wide open, and spread his arms instinctively catching the bedside cabinet with a clatter.

The policeman looked up from his newspaper for a few seconds and then went back to the sports pages.

Naylor's head dropped slowly again a few minutes later and this time he was gone. His chest's rhythmic rise and fall made his head move up and down like a lethargic nodding dog. His breathing was easy although punctuated with a slight wheeze from time to time.

The policeman got up and unlocked the door. He poked his head around the corner to tell his colleague sitting outside that Naylor was sleeping at last. His colleague agreed to let them know at the nurses' station and the policeman re-locked the door and returned to his newspaper.

Naylor's eyes, meanwhile, moved behind his eyelids as he started to dream.

He was captain on a spacecraft, in charge of an important mission. He knew this. He didn't know how he knew it, but he did. The craft was small – a 'tender' from the mother ship. Five crew only. A light appeared in the distance and he steered the craft gently towards it. They moved forward gracefully as he gave orders to a computer.

'View one-eighty,' he said confidently.

His screen changed to show where he had just emerged from – a bank of grey-white swirling clouds. He wasn't sure what they consisted of – water like rain clouds, or particles like the dust clouds whipped up by winds in the deserts on Earth.

'View zero'. The screen changed to show the view forward and the light growing bigger and brighter.

He was surprised at how clearly he could hear disks whirring as they rotated in the computer server drives. Monitors on the walls were beeping quietly as graphic displays showed his blood pressure, heart rate, and others he couldn't quite make out. On a larger screen a number in bright amber neon was gradually clicking backwards. This was the distance to the light source although he didn't quite understand why he knew this.

The whole of the cabin was now bathed in bright white light, as he slowly made out the shape of a huge city with buildings lit by lasers, all contained in what appeared to be a gigantic glass bubble. Inside the bubble he could make out some form of vehicles moving constantly between the buildings.

'Steer twenty-five fifteen.' The craft responded by changing direction slightly right and down. A portal appeared – an entrance to the city. His heart leapt in excitement. His mission was nearly over. The craft moved closer. The distance number on the monitor had halved now and was decreasing rapidly as a command came over a loudspeaker.

'Hold position.'

Naylor brought the craft to a stop. He waited for the clearance to move ahead and saw another craft approach the portal from underneath and to the right of him. The other craft moved forward inching towards the portal and stopped. He guessed the other captain was waiting for the command to enter and had been given precedence over his own approach. No problem – he'd wait.

Nothing happened. Naylor was aware he was perspiring slightly and had grown tense although he couldn't think why.

The other craft hung in space pointing towards the portal.

Minutes passed and then the other craft started to turn and move towards his. Something wasn't right. His palms were slippery on the guardrail and he wiped them down his tunic.

As the other craft approached he saw it had two towers, each with something protruding outwards, on its front rim. In the centre of this rim was a clear semi-dome that fitted snugly into the metal of the craft's body. It continued to edge forward.

'Permission to dock?' He intended to make his request with authority, but his voice wavered and ended high-pitched. There was no response. He started to shake as the other craft continued to approach. For the first time on this voyage his confidence in achieving his objective was starting to dwindle. But he didn't know why.

His craft suddenly started to move towards the other.

'Hold position,' he almost screamed and startled himself. His craft didn't stop. 'Steer 180' he bellowed. No change. He started to realise that he no longer controlled anything.

The graphic on his heart monitor was now starting to jump up and down. His blood pressure showed high, bordering dangerous. His craft moved forward.

He stared now at the towers on the other craft. They were emitting tiny white lights that exploded against the hull and cabin of his craft. Coloured indistinguishable creatures floated right through the glass of his cabin and through his own body. He was trying desperately to recall something but it wouldn't quite register. But he knew it wasn't good.

He needed to get into the city. He would fail otherwise. His whole existence depended on it but how was he going to do it?

'Weapons fore and full power.' Two dark rods slid slowly out in front of his craft. He was pleased to get a response. 'Target craft fore'. The rods moved slightly to adjust to their victim's position.

But instead of issuing the command to 'fire' the other craft had come close enough for Naylor to suddenly recognise that it was the guardians in the towers. Recognition made him jump back involuntarily, mouth open and heart pounding. Then his eyes moved to the semi-dome. There was a figure smiling – no, laughing. As the crafts moved even closer he recognised the figure that evidently held the captain's role.

It was Frank Jackson.

Naylor had to do something quickly. His whole reason for being was to gain entry to the city and complete his mission but Jackson's face grew bigger and appeared maniacal as it plainly spat out orders. The hull on Naylor's craft was now melting where the white lights were growing more powerful and striking it hard. The glass on his cabin started to chip away. His crew ran here and there and a young woman stood very animated face to face with him shouting questions at him that he couldn't make out above the noise.

A battery of armaments slid from underneath Jackson's craft and pointed towards Naylor's craft.

Suddenly Naylor could hear everything Jackson was saying over his intercom.

'We meet again,' Jackson cackled. 'I nearly died – and it was you who nearly got me killed. And I can do what you can do now. So be scared, Jim Naylor.'

Naylor didn't need to be told. Blind panic made his body convulse with fear. What the hell was happening? This was too real. His mind drifted in and out. Was this a dream? But how could it be if he had such an important mission to complete?

'Fire' he suddenly bellowed as he remembered his own canons pointing at Jackson, but he heard the same command simultaneously from Jackson. A huge explosion between the two crafts picked his craft up and threw it backwards like a javelin. He was toppling over and over across the deck of the cabin and then across its ceiling. He caught a glimpse out of the craft and saw it was now rushing back through the clouds. There was a monumental cracking sound as the hull split wide open and he screamed as he felt his body start to be ripped apart.

He awoke bolt upright in bed with two doctors and three nurses buzzing around him. A lot of shouting suddenly stopped as they stared at him sitting there, eyes wide, mouth open with pyjamas soaked in sweat and wet hair matted to his head.

One of the doctors was holding two pads wired up to a briefcase on the bed, frozen like a statue. The other was holding up a large syringe filled with a yellowish liquid. The policeman was standing incredulous with his back pressed against the wall, hands straight down by his sides, palms to the wall.

'Jesus,' he said quietly.

Naylor turned to the policeman. 'He's going to get me,' he whispered.

And then from somewhere far away, 'Next time, Naylor. Next time.' And a scream of laughter seemed to echo down the corridor outside.

Chapter 16

'They still haven't recovered him,' Bob Jenkins said to Martha Naylor in the foyer of the Tower Thistle hotel. They waited at a low table for American coffees ordered from a redheaded Irish girl who had appeared very keen to help whilst imparting little impression that she could actually do so.

'Who - Jim?'

Jenkins looked puzzled for a moment. 'No, no. Andy Forrester. They think he went through first time and we weren't ready for it, so couldn't get him back. They're still working on it.'

'So, what does that mean?'

'Well, apart from him appearing to sustain some cuts and bruises showing up on the 'Eye', his legs are metamorphosing very slowly into something we haven't been able to make out yet.'

'No. I mean where is he? Went through where?'

'It's a figure of speech. He didn't physically go anywhere. He is still where he started – on the couch in the lab. We think he and the others in the facility have the ability to do some form of thought transference. He can believe he is somewhere else and can appear to experience it more vividly than in a normal dream. To the extent that he can see – I mean really see – touch, smell, hear and taste everything there is to experience in wherever he dreams he goes to. We have a monitor – a very sophisticated monitor – that our people developed from advanced lie detector technology. It appears to read people's brainwaves when they are in this state, and can translate them into an image of the person as they would appear in the dream. We're working on adding what the person is actually seeing around them and then, hopefully, what they think they are hearing. But that won't be for a year or two yet.'

'But that's incredible.' Martha's face lit up into a broad smile. 'If that's true, you could literally understand every dream that anyone ever had.'

'Well, you could see a representation of them. Understanding them is the next phase. But think of it. All of this data could now be captured, stored and analysed. It could be used to provide an incredible boost to patient care in all sorts of areas of mental stress and illness. Helping people understand exactly what is causing their stress is halfway to curing it or, at least, controlling it.'

'I always knew you were a clever bastard,' she laughed.

'No, don't believe it. Not my forte all this science stuff really. But my company does employ a lot of very intelligent people. For which, unfortunately, we have to pay a lot of very high salaries.'

'And it's worth it?'

'Hopefully. After all, it is information and, believe me, information can be a very valuable commodity. Especially if it is information that lots of people want, and which nobody else can supply.'

'Sounds intriguing. Exciting.'

The coffees came and the young girl placed them on the table. Jenkins signed for them and the girl left.

As he started to pour, Martha Naylor smiled at him.

'I just need to powder my nose,' she said getting up, and headed for the ladies.

Jenkins watched her go and enjoyed the vision until she disappeared into the cloakroom. He had, of course, only told her part of the story. But as he had not much more himself yet he didn't feel too bad about it.

Besides, Martha had started to get very close to him. Hey, no problem with that. But she was an intelligent woman and had begun to inquire more and more as to what he was doing at his 'secret complex' in the country, as she called it.

He would be able to convince her more easily of how important it was not to share any of the information he was giving her if he gave her something to go on. It would also appear he was putting his trust in her – which he wasn't – and this could only help to keep her mouth firmly closed. And giving her that impression could only help him with his other objective too. And he believed the time was about right for that one. Hence the venue.

But the butterfly bothered him. Where the hell had it come from? It had been verified as a native species of South America. What was it doing fluttering into his company's lab in the UK countryside? It was too much of a coincidence for him that the girl had been dreaming of being in the jungle. Far too much.

And then the Forrester thing. Why had they not been able to bring him back? These subjects obviously were the most susceptible to dreaming, and dreaming pretty vividly, but there should have been no problem in snapping them out of it. And where was he supposed to be in his dream? Some strange looking cuts and bruises on the 'Eye' but no clue otherwise.

Once they had discovered the 'Eye' only showed the state of the person's own body, work had immediately started on getting it to provide a view of what the person could actually see. They had even tried to look for reflections in the person's eyes and projections on the back of the eyes themselves. But no luck as yet.

He reached into his jacket and checked that his mobile was on in case the lab called.

Martha returned to the table. She had renewed her lipstick and touched up her eye shadow. She smiled warmly.

'So,' she said sipping slowly. 'Is all this going to make you a multi-millionaire?'

'Well, I guess I'm hoping so. I was given shares in the new research company. It's a subsidiary of the main company at the moment. But it is my baby. The MD of the main company has agreed a nifty little clause that gives me extra share options in the new company depending on performance.'

'Just you?'

'That's the deal. That's the condition I insisted on when I took it on. The fact is I could end up owning the company. And, believe me, that is a very attractive proposition.'

'Oh, I agree,' she smiled.

He studied her face as it shone back at his. Was she teasing him? He changed the subject.

'Er, as far as I know Jim is on the mend. He had a little upset last night though. The doctors don't know what caused it. A bit of a heart flutter apparently, which can happen as a reaction to an operation like the one he's been through.'

'Yes,' she tried to compose herself again. 'Poor man's been through a lot from both a health and a work point of view. Shame he didn't take up your offer of a partnership, Bob. Might've had some real prospects now, eh?'

'Well it wasn't actually a partnership I was offering, Martha. Should I get to own and run the company I would need some good men under me. I know Jim's one of the best.'

'But not very ambitious,' she said quietly as she gazed into her coffee.

'But it's a good job we're all different. Be a boring world...'

He didn't finish. She was staring at him.

'Bob. I know you didn't invite me here to talk about Jim. I have to be back at the office in an hour. If I'm not being too forward, I assume you have a room?'

Chapter 17

An hour later Jenkins was in the shower when his mobile rang. He stepped out, towelled the shampoo from his head and face quickly and hurried over to the dressing table where Martha was combing her hair.

'You OK?' he asked as he grabbed the phone. She nodded and smiled at him.

'Jenkins,' he barked into the phone.

'Bob. It's Chris.' Chris Lambert was Bob's trusted lieutenant at the company. 'Forrester's struggling. He should have been back by now and if we're not careful I'm concerned there could be damage. Permanent damage. There's strange things he's imagining about his body. Hard to believe, but he thinks he's turning into a tree by the look of it. And the press if this got out could damage us too. Very seriously.'

'OK. I'll be there in a few hours.'

'A few hours? Where are you?'

'London.'

'What the hell are you doing in London?'

Jenkins reddened with anger. 'Not your problem, Chris. Just do your bloody job and you'll be OK. If I find out you've screwed up on this I'll have your balls.'

A pause. 'I haven't screwed up, Bob. Maybe we're pushing too hard.'

'Too hard? Too bloody hard? It would take one competitor to beat us to the post, Chris. Just one. And we might as well pack up and go home. You want that? If you let me go, as I said, I'll get there in a few hours,' and he switched the phone off, throwing it on the bed.

Chris slowly put his phone back in his pocket.

'Pushy bastard,' he mumbled under his breath. He turned to look at the 'Eye'.

The image had changed slowly but unarguably to one of a human form down as far as the calves of the legs, and then a gnarled tree trunk after that with tree roots where feet used to be. The monitor displaying mental activity was almost off the scale, as was heartbeat and blood pressure.

The person actually lying on the couch had not changed at all since starting the dream apart from breathing a lot faster now.

Andy Forrester stared at his new lower body as he tingled from head to root as if an electric current had gone through him a few times. It had seemed to nullify the effect of the drugs for the time being. But he started to feel the need to bury his roots into the ground. Sheena-Siren was almost completely back to tree form – something resembling a Silver Birch. Tall and elegant with smooth, attractive bark.

He was trying to work out how she did it. How she transformed. His thought his only chance would be if he could do the same. And he was aware his fingers were getting longer, with green warts starting to appear on them. This was a nightmare, but not a normal one. He knew he could usually wake himself up from nightmares but not this one. It was too real.

He was now about twenty feet tall and still growing. Why did she transform? To lure a victim? Into what? Who cares – he needed a victim. No chance. He was now at forty feet and he could see a long way all around him; but nothing resembling a victim. As he looked down around him he saw an entrance to a tunnel about thirty feet away with a steel-barred gate blocking the entrance. Had he really travelled around in a circle?

His feet-roots had not buried far enough into the ground to support his weight. He leant hard in the direction of the tunnel but swayed back upright. He tried again, swinging backwards first and then throwing himself forward. The earth around his roots was thrown into the air as he broke free and fell towards the tunnel. Seconds later he crashed through the gates.

Andy Forrester's body jumped on the couch. He opened his eyes and gradually eased himself to a sitting position. Chris rushed over to him.

'Andy, you OK? What happened to you? No – on second thoughts don't talk.' The couch was surrounded by now and there were people ripping off leads and helping him to his feet.

'Take him back to his room,' Chris ordered. 'We'll have a de-brief with him later. Look after him.'

Chris looked back to the 'Eye', which had now gone blank. Jesus, he thought, that was close.

A half dozen silver birch leaves fluttered to the floor around the couch.

Chapter 18

The door hissed open. Tom stepped on to a small mezzanine floor and the door closed behind him. Another opened automatically and he walked slowly into the aviary.

Sheena was standing with her back to him. A red macaw was perched on her lower arm and she was feeding it pieces of orange and peach, which it gobbled down greedily. Tom watched for a minute before stepping up beside her. She didn't acknowledge him.

'Heard the latest', he said softly. She didn't respond, but continued to hold a piece of fruit as the macaw pecked little chunks from it. A parakeet squawked somewhere across the room as wings fluttered above them.

'Sounds tough,' he continued as he watched the bird eat. Again no response. 'I'm going for my next session myself tomorrow. Not sure I'm looking forward to it.'

He turned to her and watched as a tear ran down her cheek. A few moments passed in silence.

'I was so close', she said finally.

'I know – I heard. But you'll get there. Don't worry about it.'

'I'm not sure I will. That's what concerns me.'

'Jesus, Sheena. With all due respect they've got you brainwashed. When it comes down to it so what if you don't get there? What's the hassle? Problem is after a while you start to feel you owe them something. And if you don't get through you've failed. You haven't, believe me. And you owe them nothing. You've had a year in here – given up a year of your life for them in fact. So they owe you if anything. And think of poor old Andy.'

She turned to him and wiped the tear away. 'What about Andy?'

'I suppose you've not heard yet. He got through today.'

'What, first time?' she asked incredulous.

'Yep. And a fat lot of good it did him. Right state apparently.'

'So tell me,' she said eagerly, concern etched on her face.

'That's all I know so far. He's in recovery.'

She started to walk through the aviary. He joined her, glanced around at the colours of the birds and the foliage.

'I'm thinking of giving it up,' she said.

'Your choice. But wouldn't blame you if you did. You've been through a lot.'

'I know you don't care so much, Tom. But if I can't break through, I can't move on. And if I can't move on then what's the point?'

'This is very unlike you. You're normally so positive.' He continued to look around, his eyes probing the grasses, and trees and wildlife.

She smiled nervously. 'I know. The funny thing is I enjoy the dreams. But there always seems to be a barrier to me taking the final step.'

'And if you did?'

'Did what?'

'Did manage to make that extra step. What do you expect to find? What makes you think it's worth it?'

'That's what we're here for, isn't it?'

He laughed loudly and some birds squawked. 'Brainwashed – I told you. Sheena, it's become what they want not what we want. What do **you** want?'

They walked a little more before she offered the macaw up to a branch where it carefully stepped from her arm. She turned to face him, and he was peering into some greenery.

'You got any other stuff in here?' he asked still searching.

'Like what?' and then she realised. 'Ah, so you've heard. About the butterfly. How come you know so much?'

'I've got my contacts,' he winked at her. 'And?'

'It's the first thing I thought of too. But no. It didn't come from here. I've had a good look round. No moths, butterflies, insects or anything else other than plants and birds.'

'Weird' he gave her a quizzical glance. And after a few seconds 'Anyway, you didn't answer my question.'

She started to walk again.

'It's OK,' he said to her back. 'We've all got things we want to keep private. No probs. By the way, I've gone red to green on my room. Just visit when you want to. If you want to that is.'

He turned to go, but she turned to look at him. Tears streamed down her face. She took two steps towards him and threw her arms round him.

'Please just hold me, Tom.'

Surprised, he slowly put his arms around her awkwardly but caring. She cried on his shoulder for a long time, neither of them talking. He eventually put his hands gently on her shoulders and eased her away to face him. He had a question in his eyes and she responded.

'I killed my father,' she blurted out and stared deep into his eyes.

'What?' he gasped.

'Not murder or anything like that. A car accident. I was driving.'

'What happened?'

'My mother was ill in hospital. I'd arranged to drive my father to see her because I'd borrowed his car the night before to go out with friends.' She sobbed for a few seconds, before continuing. 'I was late picking him up after partying most of the night. So I guess I drove a little too fast to get him to the hospital as soon as I could. I didn't see the lorry reversing out of the factory.' Her knees buckled and she dropped to the floor.

'Oh God,' she blurted and buried her head in her hands. He knelt beside her and held her.

'Jesus,' he said, 'you poor girl.'

Between sobs she finished. 'It gets worse. I was over the limit. My mother later called me a drunken bitch. We haven't spoken since. The funny thing was that I nearly died too. But I lived and he didn't. How come?' She looked into his eyes and he felt himself welling up.

'How long ago was this?' he asked awkwardly.

'Just before I came in here. The court let me off lightly and I needed to get away from things.'

'And that's why you're here?'

'Partly.' She continued to look straight into his eyes. 'Please don't think I've lost it when I tell you this. I want to see Dad again.'

He moved back slightly surprised. 'What makes you think..?'

'Not sure. But I saw him and talked to him in hospital. He said we'd meet again soon.'

'I know, Sheena, but you have to be strong. People say strange things when they're dying. You shouldn't count on things like that.'

She stared at him and started to smile. 'No, Tom, you don't understand. Dad died in the crash. I spoke to him afterwards. When they were trying to save me on the operating table I had a strange experience. They call it 'out of body' or 'near death' or whatever. I floated away, Tom, literally and met up with Dad. But I was so surprised I didn't get chance to say sorry. I need to break through, Tom. I'm desperate. He needs to know.'

Chapter 19

'Can't talk to me now? What does that mean?' Fuller was indignant and therefore loud. This was the PM's top priority as a matter of national security. Why the hell wouldn't he talk?

The girl on the other end of the phone stated calmly 'He cannot be disturbed, sir. A matter of grave concern has arisen to which the PM has to attend.'

'Did you tell him it was me?'

'Yes, sir, but the PM asks that you call him very shortly. He's having to deal with an emergency.'

'What sort of emergency?'

'The PM simply states…' then a crackling and the PM's voice.

'Put him through, dammit. Fuller? That you?' The PM was shouting to be heard above the shrieking of the ADS alarm and crashing noises.

'PM? What's happening? Sounds like a war zone.'

'It fucking is. They've broken through the outer security glass – it's shattering all over the place. The inner's holding, thank God. How do you stop these bloody things for Christ's sake?'

'Sorry - don't know yet, sir.'

'Suggest you find out pretty fucking soon, Fuller. The army are in here trying to save my arse and not, as far as I can see, very confident of success. These things are scary. Why the hell are they after me? What have I done?' He stopped as another crash interrupted his flow.

'Sir?' shouted Fuller.

'It's OK – just another outer wall gone. They're bouncing off the inner walls. But the soldiers' bullets are bouncing off them. This is not good, Fuller.'

'It's death, sir.'

'What?'

'It's death, sir. It's something to do with death – the reason they're after you.'

There was a long pause and Fuller could hear the noise dying down when the PM responded.

'They've gone,' the PM said sounding relieved. 'The Stabu have turned tail. Getting a second wind or reinforcements or both. You need to solve this, Fuller. Quickly. What's this about death?' In the background someone asked the PM if he was OK. 'Yes, yes – get me up.'

'I met up with Goldsworth again after I spoke to you last. After his last heart attack he had an 'experience' in the operating theatre. Saw himself lying there – started to float towards his maker, or so he assumed at the time.'

The PM took a sharp breath. 'But was stopped.'

'Er, yes.'

'By locked doors? Guards? Gates? Forcefield?'

'Well, some sort of net apparently. But he's had some strange dreams since, and come up against all of these - and more. How do you know?'

After a few seconds, 'Same here. Been there myself.'

'What?'

'I live in a big old house, Fuller. In the country. Helps get me away from the pressures of London and helps me relax. The wife's idea. Works well but an old house needs looking after and a bit of DIY can be very therapeutic. About a year ago I decided stupidly to sort out a bit of re-wiring myself rather than get a man in. Bloody electrocuted myself. Got pretty badly burnt as it happens and it was touch and go for a couple of days as to whether I'd make it.'

'The sudden vacation last year?'

'Yes.'

'And no newspaper coverage,' Fuller suddenly realised.

'See why now? Anyway, I lay on the floor of the lounge pretty badly shocked, and was actually watching myself at the same time. It was the strangest thing I'd ever experienced. And then suddenly I seemed to be in another world – like a dream but not really.'

'What sort of other world?'

'Only one moon, for example. And other strange things. Cars with only four wheels instead of six. Birds with two wings instead of four.'

'Wow. And what were you doing?'

'I remember I had gotten the country involved in a war in some place called Iraq. In this world it was a separate country and not part of Syria. But it was as if I'd suddenly gained a whole new life – new memories, new knowledge and skills. I felt I knew this place. And I felt I knew my life history in this place. And my friends and family. Very disturbing and very weird. I felt my mind almost couldn't take this sudden and colossal amount of new information. I remember feeling nauseous as hell.'

'And then you woke up?'

'That's just it. It didn't feel like waking up but I obviously did. It felt more like …'returning'. I 'returned' to the floor of my lounge to find paramedics reviving me.'

'And you've had dreams since?'

'Yes, but never managed to go back to that other world. Same sort of things as Goldsworth. Locked gates and doors stopping me all the time.'

Both men stayed silent for a few seconds, before the PM picked up again.

'OK, Fuller. So there are similarities with Goldsworth's situation. But what's it all mean? What's the link with the Stabu?'

'Not just Goldsworth, sir. I checked with the banker's family in Boston. He told them he went through similar experiences. And a doctor in Helsinki is saying the same about the Stabu's victim there too.'

'And?'

'Don't know, sir. I'm close. But I'm not there yet.'

'Any more known attacks?'

'Just one.' Fuller had found out a restaurant owner in Rome was now a Stabu target. 'I'm flying to Italy in the morning. Arrive in Fiumicino airport at 10.15am and meeting this guy at his restaurant for lunch. At least I know what questions to ask now.'

'Ask them quickly, Fuller.'

'OK, will do. Meanwhile, I'm going to cross-check Goldsworth's recollection of events with his partner in case he's missed anything. I'll get back to you later.'

A short while afterwards he was in ParrotWorld.

'Thanks for agreeing to see me.'

The young security guard left the room and closed the door behind him. Julie Furness looked up from a folder on the desk and smiled broadly.

'That's OK, Mr Fuller. It's nice to see you again. Your call earlier certainly left me intrigued. Please sit down, if you can find a chair.'

Fuller looked round the small office, moved some files from a plastic chair on to a filing cabinet and drew the chair up to Julie's desk.

'Getting a bit scary,' she continued, 'all that stuff at the villa the other night. Bill was a bit shaken up.' She finished writing a note in the folder, closed it up, and put the pen down. 'Drink?' she asked.

'Er, yes. Please. Got anything cold?' This was late morning and it was hot and sticky outside. He noticed the airconditioner was humming away but it was still uncomfortably warm. Julie had some tiny beads of perspiration on her tanned forehead and cheeks.

'I know what you mean. Trouble is we're quite a way inland here. It's cooler down by the coast. Diet Coke OK?'

'Fine.'

She stepped over to a small fridge on the floor in a corner of the room. Julie was a slim woman who obviously did something to keep her figure. Either work-outs in the gym, swimming or aerobics Fuller guessed. Or maybe all three. She had pinned her hair up in an attempt to keep cool, which emphasised the olive complexion in her oval- shaped face. She wore a white T-shirt that showed off her midriff. As she bent down to retrieve the can from the fridge the top of her thong was visible above the waistline of her khaki shorts.

Bill Goldsworth was a lucky man, Fuller thought.

She handed him the can. 'Need a glass?'

'No. That's fine. Thanks.' He gratefully pulled the ring-pull and drank about half the contents. He wiped the sweat from his forehead with his arm. 'Jesus – that's better,' he smiled.

'So,' she said. 'What brings you to ParrotWorld?'

'I guess I just wanted to talk through with you what's been happening to Bill lately. Get a second opinion. Maybe a different angle that we haven't thought of so far. That sort of thing.'

'Fine. Where do you want to start?'

He took a couple more sips from the can. 'I need patterns, Julie. Er – OK to call you Julie?'

'That's my name,' she smiled.

'Patterns tend to suggest reasons or clues for things happening. I can't find any at the moment. I thought I'd hit on something with the eclipses but it wasn't consistent. Is there anything unusual that happens when the Stabu try to get to Bill? Maybe just before?'

She thought for a few seconds. 'No, I can't think of anything. The attacks have seemed to come out of the blue.' She busied herself making notes in another folder. 'Do you mind?' she asked pleasantly.

'No, please carry on – I just appreciate you being able to give me some of your time today,' he was being absolutely honest. She returned to her scribbling and he continued 'What about Bill? Why him?'

'No idea. We've been racking our brains about this for quite a while now, as you can probably understand. Bill's a good man. He doesn't have any enemies. He may have had some in the past. You know – when he was working. But now he's retired we can't think of anyone who would want to hurt him.'

'Any reason to believe the attacks might have been arranged by someone?'

'It was a thought we had. It's reasonably easy to train birds, or animals, or whatever these things might be. I should know. I used to be out there,' she nodded towards the window, 'training the parrots, parakeets and cockatiels. Used to have my own act. Did stints in nightclubs and bars down on the coast for tourists to make extra money.'

'Did you enjoy it?'

'The tourists? No.' She frowned and tutted like a little girl as she wrote, which Fuller thought only made her more alluring. 'They had no real interest in the birds and, to be fair, I always felt saddened to have to 'use' such lovely creatures in that way. Used to kid myself that I'd make it up to them somehow but, of course, I never really did. I do care for them though. I rescued many of them from cowboys who were doing the same sort of act that I did in different resorts on the island but didn't care half as much. Some of the birds were in a terrible state when I bought them and took them in.'

'You're obviously pretty fond of them.'

'They don't screw you around like people do.' She stopped writing with a jolt and looked at him quickly. 'Oh, I'm sorry,' she blurted, embarrassed. 'I don't know where that came from.'

'Hey, don't worry about it. I know exactly what you mean.' They looked at each other a little awkwardly for a second. 'If you like,' he continued, 'you can borrow my shoulder sometime...' and regretted it as soon as he said it.

Shit, he thought. What a crass thing to say. She continued to look at him. *You arsehole. She's going to tell you to get out.* It was his turn to redden.

But instead she just smiled slowly. 'You look like you have a story to tell yourself. Maybe we can borrow each other's.'

He felt suddenly very warm again and was aware of a wet patch between his shoulder blades. It wasn't just the heat making him perspire. He managed somehow to compose himself.

'And in the meantime, we need to get Bill sorted out,' he offered as a way to move the conversation back into the safety zone.

'Please pass me that briefcase,' she motioned to a slim leather case sitting on top of a filing cabinet. As he grabbed it to pass to her he noticed the inscription 'J. S. Furness'.

'What's the 'S' for?' he asked as politely as he could, mind still racing with excitement at the fact that his attentions were being returned.

'Are you always so nosey?' her eyes seemed to sparkle.

'I'm sorry. I guess I'm just interested in anything that could help Bill's situation.' *Weak he thought. Very weak. He was definitely losing it.*

'Maybe I'll tell you one day,' she said as she opened the case. She placed a diary on the top of the desk and put the case on the floor. She started leafing through the small book.

He wanted some information but it wasn't necessarily in Bill Goldsworth's best interest. 'So how far do you and Bill go back?'

She looked at him quizzically, but then saw he was motioning towards the diary. 'Oh I see – quite a few years. I've got notes from before the attacks started. I've been going back through them to try to find some clues.'

He thought to himself that he'd love to have an hour with that little book. He needed some clues himself. 'So you guys have been an item for a while? Living together here?'

Her eyes lifted from the diary and gazed into his. 'Bill and I have been together for several years. I owe him a lot. Sort of revived my faith in human nature.' A few seconds' more awkwardness. 'God,' she laughed. 'I haven't got a clue why I'm telling you all this. Yes, we've been together for quite a while and, yes, everything he's been through is in these pages.'

The door suddenly burst open. A teenage boy with ginger, tousled hair and wearing green overalls and Wellingtons stood in the entrance with a red face, breathing quickly.

'Julie, come quick,' he blurted. 'One of the African greys has had an accident. I think it's broken its wing.'

She ran after the boy and Fuller followed. They heard the squawking before they got to one of the large cages where a parrot was in obvious distress running backwards and forwards across the floor. Birds in other cages were shrieking and calling in response.

'What happened?' she asked the boy.

'Dunno. I didn't see it. Just heard the commotion.'

She carefully opened the cage. The parrot darted away from her as she went in but kept running around the edge of the cage, screeching loudly ad dragging its damaged wing along the ground.

She went to one corner of the cage, turned and crouched down. She followed the parrot around the cage with eyes opened wide just staring at it for a few moments and then slowly raised both hands just below her chin and opened the fingers to form two fans.

The parrot stopped dead in its tracks and slowly rolled over on the floor motionless. She walked over to the bird and gently cradled it in her hands.

'I'll need to try to fix its wing,' she said to Fuller. 'Meet you back in the office in ten minutes?'

He just stared at her for a moment, amazed. He eventually muttered 'Yes. OK. Fine.'

'How on earth did you do that?' he asked incredulous as she arrived back in the office.

'I don't know why it works, but it works,' she laughed. 'A kind of hypnosis. Helps calm them down when I need to move them or operate on them.'

'That's incredible.'

'Well, not really. Did you know that if you hold a chicken down on its side it goes into a kind of hypnotic state and can stay that way for hours?'

'Well, maybe that's true,' he said, 'but you didn't even touch that parrot.'

'Or that in the late 1800's a guy once hypnotised all the animals in the Budapest Zoo? There's a lot of sceptics who poo poo the idea of hypnotising animals and birds but I seem to be able to hypnotise just about any of the birds in here. With some of them I need to use my hands and with others I have to talk – or make certain sounds - but, like that parrot, lots of them respond just to certain gestures. Not a big deal really.'

'I still think it's cool. How on earth did you learn to do it?'

She smiled her appreciation. 'Mostly by accident. It worked the first time when I was talking to a parakeet and trying to imitate birdsound to calm it down. It fell into a trance almost straight away. The other stuff just came through trial and error. Maybe I've got a gift for it.'

'Ever tried it on humans?'

'No,' she laughed. 'But next time I come across someone with a broken leg…Anyway, enough of that,' she was starting to feel embarrassed. 'Are you still interested in the diary?'

'Yes. Especially if there is anything that might help.'

She nibbled the corner of her lip for a second. 'Well, it's just the dreams Bill has. They're sort of strange.'

'In what way?'

'I don't quite know how to explain it. He says they aren't dreams.'

'Oh?' Fuller was intrigued. 'He didn't say anything about this to me.'

'I'm sure he wanted to. But he feels people will think he's going senile. I think he worries a lot about that. I think he worries that I would leave him.'

'And would you?'

'We've been through a lot together.'

'You certainly have. But that didn't answer my question.'

She flicked nervously to a page she wanted to read from and repeated it aloud. '*March 19. Breakfast took a long time today – Bill woke up sweating again and needed to talk. He's still saying these dreams he has are real. I don't know how to help him. He is starting to frighten me. Maybe I should get him an appointment with Dr Wood. He says he went somewhere last night. Finally found a way there apparently. I know he's not sleepwalking. Poor Bill.*' She looked up from the page. A small tear traced a line down her face as she reached for a handkerchief.

Fuller moved over to her, took the handkerchief from her hand and gently dabbed her cheek. She hesitated but then reached up slowly and held his hand. She noticed him glance at the white linen of the handkerchief where her initials appeared in the corner in pink. JSF.

'It's Sheena. Julie Sheena Furness,' she whispered as she kissed him gently.

Chapter 20

There was a large queue for the official taxis at Fiumicino Airport, and Fuller didn't fancy getting ripped off by the unofficial ones so he took the train into Rome Termini station. The journey was comfortable and quick and for twelve and a half Euros' was pretty good value too, even though the air conditioning left something to be desired. He couldn't get Julie out of his mind for the whole of the journey. Nor the weird entries in her diary that she'd read out to him after they'd made love in his hotel room the previous evening.

He tried to think of something else. He remembered staying in Ostia on the coast, close to the airport, for a holiday once and had enjoyed everything about it. The food, the people, the climate and the culture were all very much to his liking, and as the train drew closer to Rome itself the grandness of the architecture evoked stories of epic battles involving Caesar's legions and riches gained from the spoils of war. He was only sorry that the Coliseum had been completely destroyed in the Second World War. A huge crater was all that was left with the obligatory glass-encased notice boards scattered around telling tourists of this and that noble and heroic deed. He would have loved the opportunity to have stood where the gladiators had done when facing the lions, or worse, whilst fighting for their lives and for freedom.

But then came images of Julie again. Slim, naked and wet as they showered together. So lively. So much relief now that she could share her concerns about a man she cared deeply about but didn't love. But her account of Bill's dreams had been disturbing. No wonder she was at the end of her tether.

He got out of Termini station and grabbed a taxi to Piazza Navona where Ristorante Napoli sat proudly on the east side of the square. The sky was a bright powder blue and the sun shone its warmth on the crowds of visiting tourists who milled around the artwork in the centre of the square and sat in the bars and restaurants surrounding it. A piano-accordion player passed from restaurant to restaurant entertaining customers further down the square.

Fuller paid the taxi. He slipped his jacket off and carried it along with his overnight bag to the Napoli where Julio Rossi met him with a strong handshake and huge grin.

'Thank you for coming, Mr Fuller.' Rossi exclaimed excitedly as his personal ADS strapped to his belt glinted in the sunshine. Fuller looked at the restaurant entrance which appeared not to have any protection. Rossi picked up Fuller's nervousness.

'Please don't worry, Mr Fuller. There are all these people every day in the square and the Stabu only have eyes for me. And this is my guardian angel,' he said patting the ADS and laughing.

'Well you're pretty cheerful for someone risking death every day.'

'Of course. Because now you've come to help me and to destroy the Stabu,' he smiled.

Something had definitely got lost in translation Fuller thought, but decided not to take it further at this point.

'Please,' Rossi showed Fuller to a table shaded by a huge parasol. 'Let us sit and discuss the future – now that I have one.' Rossi laughed out loud and slapped Fuller firmly between the shoulder blades.

'So how close to death have you been?'

'Well they have attacked only once, and the ADS....'

'No. I mean before that. You nearly died didn't you.'

'How do you know this?' Rossi was puzzled.

'Wild guess.'

'One night a couple of weeks ago some young men had too much to drink and wouldn't pay the bill. When I insisted the tall one pulled out a knife and stabbed me in the chest and stomach, and then they all ran off. They nearly got my heart. A close thing, Mr Fuller.'

A young waitress with 'Adrianne' on her name tag brought up a bottle of Chianti and some mineral water. Rossi offered Fuller a menu as he sat down beside him.

'Hope you don't mind me choosing some wine for us,' Rossi continued as he started to pour for both of them.

'Why should I? You're the restaurant owner. I'm guessing you might know a little more about nice wines than I do.'

'I know this one is called Mianni and not Chianti in my other world.'

Fuller stopped looking at the menu and stared at Rossi. 'Your other world?'

Rossi was no longer smiling. 'Mr Fuller, it is good that us Italians enjoy a long lunch because I have a lot to tell you.'

Chapter 21

Jim Naylor sat in his dressing-gown in his lounge at home opposite his long-time friend and colleague Bob Jenkins. They had been talking about developments in the neighbourhood since Naylor had been in hospital; or rather Jenkins was talking at Naylor but not quite sure whether any of it was being heard. A new mini-roundabout at the end of Naylor's road which Jenkins described as a 'total and complete waste of taxpayer's money'.

'Something about improving road safety in the district which no doubt was intended to earn the Borough Council a few brownie points with the local residents until Harry Cousins' Mini ploughed into an old dear's shopping trolley. She was carrying her two Pekinese dogs in it at the time and they apparently shat themselves all over her husband's steak and kidney pie. He happens to be a County Councillor which is obviously higher in the pecking order than anyone in the Borough Council and this lead to a rather larger group shitting themselves.' Jenkins laughed raucously. Naylor seemed largely uninterested.

'And then the Golf Club. You know the Captain got thrown out?'

Naylor sat silent.

'Apparently got caught with the Lady Secretary in the back of the Pro Shop going for a hole-in-one.' Again Jenkins bellowed. Naylor again didn't react, buried in his thoughts.

Jenkins sat for a while looking at Naylor. He gradually leant forward, his whiskey cupped between his hands. He stared into the drink and spoke quietly.

'Look. Jim. I know this is difficult for you. You nearly died for Christ's sake. It's really great to have you out of that bloody hospital and back home. Martha and I would do anything for you, you know that don't you?'

Naylor's drink was untouched. He'd always loved Lagavulin so the full glass told Jenkins his companion was still suffering.

Martha Naylor came in with some coffee. She stopped in front of her husband, registered his remoteness and then brushed her thigh against Jenkins' outstretched hand as she put the hot drink down on the coffee table in front of them. Jenkins reacted quickly and angrily, motioning her to sit down. A mischievous smile crept across her face. Jenkins grimaced at her trying to warn her to be careful. Her husband still stared into the distance.

'Jim,' Martha started. No reaction. A glance at Jenkins then back to her husband. 'Jimmy. There are things that need to be discussed.'

Jenkins turned sharply and glared at his lover. 'Not now,' he hissed almost inaudibly under his breath. She returned his look and smiled again. Bitch, he thought.

'Bob's still offering you a position in his company. A good position. We should thank Bob and give it some thought. The company's doing well.'

Jenkins heaved a sigh of relief, and then followed the theme. 'That's right, Jim. But let's not worry too much about it now. We can talk about it when you're feeling fit again.' He wanted time to think about this himself. Naylor was showing signs of stress. He knew he'd been through a hell of a lot with the shooting and the bank robbery and the attack in the hospital by some nutter, but he still had to have someone he could rely on. He was on the verge of something pretty important – he knew it. Even if his team couldn't help him work out what it was yet. But what sat in front of him now was a shadow of his former friend. An apology for the strength and energy and vitality that had gone before. Sorry Martha. This might not actually work out.

Naylor suddenly lifted his head and glanced first at his wife and then fixedly at Jenkins. Jenkins was a little uneasy. Naylor spoke quietly but firmly.

'In the last few weeks,' he announced, 'I have experienced many things. Things I haven't experienced before and hope I never do again. Being shot at such close range was horrible. No - cataclysmic. Life-changingly awful. The sort of situation that no-one should ever have to go through but which, inevitably, means you'll never be the same again.' He lifted his eyes and glanced quickly into the other two faces realising what he'd said. 'Yes, I know,' he smiled wryly to himself. 'The ultimate cliché. But it's true.'

'You've certainly been through a lot, Jim, and let me say…'

Naylor interrupted. 'No, let me continue. Please.' He was insistent. 'You know all about the hospital attack.' His wife and her lover nodded attentively. 'The guy is obviously a schizo. You know what a schizophrenic is?'

''Course,' Jenkins offered. 'A complete nutcase and dangerous with it.'

Naylor glared at Jenkins.

'And,' Jenkins continued a little weakly, 'someone who has a split personality.'

'Exactly.'

'So what's your point?' Martha Naylor asked.

'I'm thinking aloud. But what if the second personality comes from somewhere else?'

The other two looked at each other, and Jenkins shrugged his shoulders. Naylor continued 'I went somewhere else. I went to a place I didn't recognise. It wasn't a dream. I know what a dream is and what it isn't. I know also that 'the mind plays funny tricks' et cetera et cetera when you're in stressful situations.'

The other two were nodding as if in agreement. Naylor stood up, plainly agitated.

'But I was there. I was there.' He said more forcefully the second time. Then realising he was not making any sense. 'In the spacecraft fighting Jackson.'

'Whoa there!' Jenkins got to his feet too. 'Jim, for God's sake. Listen to yourself. You're starting to scare Martha.'

'I'm scaring myself!' Naylor continued, and downed the whiskey in one enormous swallow. 'But it's reality. I wouldn't have believed this shit myself beforehand - but I'm telling you it was not a dream. Bob, Martha. Believe me this was not a dream.'

'Jim,' Jenkins cut in. 'Calm down and think through this rationally. You'd been in hospital after a near-fatal shooting and this nutter, Jackson, attacks you in your bed. Then you go off into a... well, let's not call it a dream if you insist, but something happens to you while you are asleep. Who is uppermost in your thoughts? Not me. Not even Martha. But Jackson. Stands to reason. Logically, Jim, he's on your mind. Has to be. And everyone would understand that. If he wasn't there would be something wrong with you. And obviously you're wary – no – frightened, maybe even terrified, that he'll attack you again. Come on, Jim. You dreamed it. Or nightmared it, or whatever the correct verb is. But it is not real. You cannot expect not to be affected. The guy needs to be hanged or put in the electric chair or something similar when he is allowed to have this sort of affect on someone. But, Jim, believe me. If you don't want to call it a dream than OK, but don't start to believe it is real. I have people who help my research team out all the time and you should hear what they have to say. In fact, when you're a little fitter I'll invite you along. I'll get my team to do some analysis on you. Then you'll see.'

In this short time Jenkins had now made a mental note that Naylor would never be invited to join his business.

Naylor stood motionless. Apart from a slow movement of his left hand into his dressing-gown pocket. 'Bob, unfortunately you've turned into the worst kind of shit.' Jenkins mouth dropped open, and Martha Naylor was reminded that she'd only ever seen this in films or comic books. 'I've tried not to believe you're deliberately making me look small in recent months, so I was really hoping you would give me some degree of respect and be prepared to understand what I was trying to tell you tonight. That plainly is not going to happen. So, I assume you two want to carry on screwing…,' his wife dropped her coffee cup in surprise which smashed through the glass-top table. 'In which case I'd appreciate it if you'd do it other than in my house. Martha, I need you to pack your bags tonight. And as for analysing me, Bob?' he spoke quietly. 'If you are going to analyse anything, analyse this.' He withdrew a small piece of a metallic substance that came from a spacecraft's control deck as it crumbled under attack. He held it up to the light in front of Jenkins.

The thinness and blueness of the jagged scrap of metal reminded Jenkins of a tropical butterfly.

Chapter 22

Bob Jenkins leant back in his leather upholstered chair inhaling deeply on a Cuban Montecristo cigar studying the file on his lap. Chris Lambert sat on the opposite side of the desk waiting patiently.

Finally Jenkins closed the file and tossed it on to the desk. Looking straight into Lambert's eyes he let out a huge puff of smoke, sat up, and smiled broadly.

'The project's changed,' he said, almost triumphantly. 'What do you see on the desk?'

Lambert hesitated for a second. 'The file on Project Evolution. What do you expect me to see?'

'No, that's quite right Chris. It wasn't a trick question. Evolution. From the Latin for 'unrolling'. And what we're starting to 'unroll' now is pretty exciting, isn't it.'

'And we're making progress – aren't we? These latest stages in the tests have given us much more information than we've had before. We've got a programme mapped out for the next few months that will give us even more. And the quality of the subjects is beyond question. The MoD must be over the moon with us.'

'Oh, they are, Chris. They are.'

Lambert was still confused. 'So what did you want? Why are we meeting now? The funding's still OK, right?' He was suddenly concerned.

'Yes, no problem at all with the money. The budget extension was approved and we've got a contract signed off that'll take us well into next year.' Jenkins puffed again and let his eyes move up to the ceiling, a smile drifted across his face.

'OK, I give up. What is it?' Lambert was getting irritated.

Jenkins looked at Lambert and picked up a jar that had been sitting behind a photograph of him and Bill Gates at a charity dinner event. He placed the jar in front of Lambert. 'This butterfly changes everything.'

Lambert angrily rose from his seat. 'Christ, Bob. You've been dancing around that bloody insect for days. What does it change? We don't even know where it came from. I need to get the last data into the report for our 'sponsors' by first thing tomorrow and I'm behind.'

'Chris – sit down please. We've been friends for a long time now. You don't think I'd mess you around if I didn't think there was something in this, do you?'

Lambert took his seat again slowly, becoming intrigued. 'So we know that butterfly got into the facility about the same time that Sheena came back this time round. Have you found out where it came from? Why is it so important?'

'There are a few things going on. No – I can't explain them all but maybe they are linked and, if so, things could get very interesting indeed. Sheena comes back and a butterfly appears. At the same time that Andy came back from his latest experience we suddenly had leaves piling up on the floor. Where from, Chris? The doors and windows were closed. Nobody had walked in. Nobody had noticed them before and Andy didn't have them before the test. So?'

'Ok, so I don't know. But I'm still lost here. The project gets us to a place where we can hopefully find a way to actually read people's minds. Read their dreams first - then read their minds. A logical progression that should reap us some pretty decent rewards from a lot of potential clients. So again at the risk of repeating myself, Bob, why is the butterfly so important?'

'I didn't have any real answers to that question until I spoke to Jim Naylor yesterday.'

'Spoke to him? I'm surprised he didn't take your head off. It's so obvious you're screwing his wife I can't believe he hasn't found out.'

'Oh, he has found out. Didn't take it well. But that's not important now. The point is he told me about a piece of metal he'd got hold of. Or rather how he got hold of it.' Jenkins eased himself out of the chair and started to slowly walk around the office. He continued by pointing his cigar towards Lambert. 'Now keep an open mind here, Chris. Believe me when I say I'm not losing it.' He took a long draw on the cigar and exhaled slowly before retuning his gaze to Lambert. 'Supposing that when people – no, let me say maybe just *some* people - go into their dreams that they actually do *go* into them. It can't be a physical thing, or at least I don't think it can, because they obviously stay in their bed or, in our case, on the couch in the lab. But suppose they, or clones of them, or clones of their metaphysical beings – whatever – can actually travel somewhere. To the same place that their dreams take place.'

'So, to the jungle in Sheena's case? To the forest in Andy's case?'

'Exactly.'

'Well, OK but why only some people. Why not all people? Bob, this isn't…'

'No, please. Indulge me,' Jenkins continued. 'Let me finish. If they could do that – travel to other places – just maybe they could get so 'involved', so 'integrated', that they could interact with that location. They could feel the sensation of being there and they could see, hear, smell, touch things that were there. They could hold things, and could maybe even bring things back from there. A butterfly, for example. Leaves, for another. A fragment of metal.'

'Metal?'

'From Naylor.'

'Ah. But you're suggesting they travel without leaving their current location physically? That's against every law of nature, Bob. Unless you're into quantum physics – parallel worlds and all that. But those theories revolve around the concept that one person can exist at the same time in different universes. So someone is not travelling anywhere. They already exist there. Or maybe in hundreds of different universes, at the same time doing the same or different things. I'm a little rusty on all this stuff but I'm pretty sure this is not about moving from one location to another - from a laboratory couch to a jungle or a forest. It's about existing in different places not moving between them.'

'Accepted, Chris. I've been reading up on all of this myself.'

'And what was it that Naylor told you he brought back – just a piece of metal? Where from? Why did this convince you?'

'A spaceship.'

Lambert sat staring at Jenkins. He suddenly laughed loudly. 'A what?'

'That's right – you heard me correctly. He was in his hospital bed and found himself transported to a spaceship. The piece of metal he gave me? Nobody knows what it is. A couple of the lab guys have spent hours on it. Got them completely foxed. It's nothing we've come across in this existence, Chris. Suppose the jungle that Sheena goes to, and the forest that Andy went to…' Jenkins could hardly hold back his excitement. 'Suppose they don't exist in our world. Suppose all three of them are actually travelling to a parallel world. Andy says he turned into a tree and it was real. Sheena has been in this jungle a few times now. She says it is not a dream. She was really there. And Jim Naylor – was on a spaceship. The piece of metal is made up of elements we don't even know - that don't even exist. Think about it, Chris. It makes sense'

Lambert was still sat, staring. 'Bob – believe me, it makes absolutely no sense at all. If Andy turned into a tree, why didn't Sheena? She was in the middle of a jungle for God's sake. And even I know that the parallel universe theorists agree that two people cannot exist in the same universe. The proposition collapses around your ears for all sorts of reasons I can't pretend to understand. One person, one universe.'

'Andy and Sheena were in different universes – different laws of nature. That's why they experienced different things. One person – one universe. Yes, I agree. That's the one that's been bothering me. But if the universes exist why could you not cross them? Parallel universes exist – at least the theories go - because every time a decision is made where there could be two outcomes another universe is created such that both outcomes become reality. Millions of parallel universes, not just one. New ones all the time. You know we have moved on in leaps and bounds on our work around dream-reading. We have learnt things that 99.9% of people will never know exist. Ways of monitoring progress through people's dreams - on recording feelings and what they are seeing, smelling, feeling. And the potential to actually see it – on a monitor to show the world. And if you can smell and feel in dreams, to eventually smell and feel with them. This is all a potential reality, Chris, as you know from our work.'

Bob walked back to his desk and took out a bottle of Laphroaig and two glasses. He poured one for Lambert who drunk it eagerly. Lambert was deep in thought and Jenkins left him there as he stared out of the window at the rain that blackened and slickened the car park tarmac below. Rivulets ran down the window glass – ran, stopped, then ran, joined others and continued down the glass.

'So what if there is something in what you say, Bob? There are a million questions.'

'Yes, there are,' Jenkins agreed.

'What triggers the cross-over? Why some people but not others? What guarantees they come back? Shit, what happens if they don't?'

'Correct,' Jenkins agreed again. 'All good questions. I may have an answer for one of those. I've checked the background to Sheena, Andy and to Jim Naylor. They're all in the file,' Jenkins nodded towards the blue folder on the desk. 'All three nearly died. At some point in their lives they came close to death. If you were going to experience something extreme – like having the ability to cross over to another universe – then couldn't a near-death experience be the trigger?'

'But it still leaves the biggest 'no-no'. Even if parallel universes do exist, then two occurrences of the same person in the same universe cannot. It's completely against the laws of physics and of nature. Doesn't this alone completely blow your theory away?'

'Maybe. Maybe. But that's what I mean, Chris. We need to spend some time on this. Suppose it's true. The project's changed, Chris. We can't afford to ignore this. The project's changed.'

'You going to tell the MoD?'

'Shit, no not yet. Think of the potential impact - the ability to go to a parallel world and change their history and come back to avoid detection. Ending the lives of potential tyrants. Introducing cures that haven't been discovered yet. Good, noble ambitions. But in the wrong hands?'

'Hold on, Bob. When we hand over the final project deliverables from 'Evolution' were you going to worry what the MoD did with it? Do me a favour. We are doing this for the money and only for the money.'

'True. True. But until we understand what we have and what potential value it could give its eventual owner how can we possibly put a price on it?' Jenkins smiled.

'OK, Bob. I'm sort of with you. If it pans out this could be worth a hell of a lot more to us than 'Evolution'. But I've got another question for you.'

'OK, go on.'

'If those with near-death experiences in this world can cross over to others, can't those in other worlds cross over to ours?'

'Chris, you're finally getting this. Think of the implications! But there could be a problem for us. An obstacle stopping us meeting our full potential and realising the rewards for all our efforts.'

'What?'

'Jim Naylor. He's an intelligent guy. He's thinking through what his own experiences mean – the spacecraft and the piece of metal. If he stumbles across the same potential solution he may decide to go public. We can't afford the risk, Chris. We'll need to do something about him.'

'I can arrange an accident, Bob. You know that's not an issue.'

'Meet up with him, and let him know I sent you. Get him in here. Give him a flavour of what we're doing here. He won't be able to resist an invitation to poke around. He can have his accident out of sight of prying eyes.'

'By why hasn't this happened up to now? Why have we not heard of people transferring across the parallel universes before? Why is it starting now?'

'Chris, I don't have all the answers,' Jenkins said.

'The implications are horrendous. Two of the same person – or more? – in the same world at the same time? No

Bob. You can't be right on this. It's unnatural. It's messing with the balance of Nature. Parallel universes maybe. There's billions of dollars being spent researching into that subject and some pretty convincing arguments supporting their existence. But travelling between them? Not a chance. Couldn't happen. Wouldn't happen.'

'Why not? What is there to stop it?'

Chapter 23

The mobile rang loudly in Fuller's room and he opened his eyes, startled. His heart beat ferociously as he lay rigid staring into the blackness. The phone rang again and as he realised where he was he turned his body so that he could see the digital bedside clock. It read half past midnight.

On the third ring he fumbled for the mobile, eventually found it and put it to his ear.

'Hello...' he managed to croak. He was listening to mayhem. Glass was breaking somewhere, a man was screaming and a gunshot rang out. He jumped to the sitting position as Julie sobbed loudly into his ear.

'John, they've come. They're in.' She was hysterical and her words were almost being drowned out by the alarm screeching in the background. 'I've just got home. They were already here. We can't stop them. The police are shooting at them but it's useless. There's no effect. What do I do, John, what do I do?'

Bill Goldsworth shouted loudly as something crashed and splintered. 'Shoot the buggers, shoot the buggers! They've smashed through the door – quick get them, for Christ's sake.' Shots rang out again.

'Julie,' Fuller shouted so she could hear him. 'Get away from Bill. Let the police handle it. There's nothing you can do.'

'But the creatures are closing in. They'll kill him,' she sobbed, 'Please help us.' Then 'Bastards!' she screamed. There was a clap as her mobile hit the floor followed by a loud crack. Fuller guessed she had hit out with something. There was a fizzling and crackling like the sound of an electric train's pantograph in winter as it slides along the overhead wires and hits ice.

Then the line went dead.

Chapter 24

He'd got the earliest flight possible out of Rome and arrived in Tenerife at 3pm having had to change in Barcelona. He'd spoken to the Tenerife police before leaving Rome but only managed to talk to Julie on her mobile during the stopover. He had persuaded her to meet him at the airport when he arrived.

As he passed through the other side of the Customs Hall he saw her standing quietly with a policeman. Her eyes were red and her hair dishevelled. She watched him approach without changing her expression. As he reached her she put her arms around him and buried her head into his neck, crying quietly. He held her tightly and let her release her tears.

The policeman stood silently making only a slight nod to Fuller to acknowledge his presence. Travellers arriving off the flight passed and sometimes brushed the three of them with their baggage trolleys. For many minutes the three of them didn't move.

Eventually Julie slid her arms from around Fuller's neck and they looked at each other for a few seconds. 'Come on,' he said. 'Let's go and talk.'

The policeman led the way out of the arrivals lounge to a waiting police car. He opened the rear door and let the two slide in before closing it after them and climbing in the front beside the driver. The car sped off towards Fuller's hotel.

When they arrived Fuller agreed to bring Julie to the police station later to complete formalities. The car disappeared as they entered the hotel foyer.

'Message for you, Mr Fuller,' the receptionist piped up as they collected the room key from the front desk. Fuller took the envelope and the key, and guided Julie gently to the lift area.

In the room he helped Julie over to his bed. She slipped off her shoes, and slid under the covers and went almost immediately into a deep sleep.

He unpacked quietly, poured a gin and tonic from the mini-bar and went outside to slump into a chair on the balcony. He flipped the envelope on to the table and allowed himself a few minutes to gather his thoughts as he sipped gently at his drink letting the warm sun bathe his body. He closed his eyes as he thought.

His trip to Rome had started to give him some answers but he was – even now – struggling to believe what he'd heard from Rossi. The restaurant owner and his brother were at one point running the restaurant together. But they had a few years previously had a serious argument after Rossi discovered his brother and his wife in bed together one day. They had agreed never to see or talk to one another ever again, and Rossi bought his brother out.

Rossi went on to tell Fuller that since the attack on him by the guys trying to avoid paying their bill, he regularly visited his 'other' restaurant in his sleep, but this other restaurant was run by his brother, not him.

The 'other' restaurant served a wine called Mianni – Rossi was adamant this was Chianti in his normal world, and the labels on the bottle were identical apart from that. His brother went for him with a meat cleaver the first time it happened – more out of fear than anything else trying not to believe that Rossi had risen from the grave.

Fuller had asked whether Rossi had ever 'met himself' in the other world. The answer was 'no'. Apparently Rossi had died in his 'other world' in an attack by some youths one night as he defended his brother when he approached them after they refused to pay their bill.

Fuller pressed Rossi on his story telling him that it was probably a vivid set of dreams brought on by the stabbing and his 'near-death' experience. Rossi had flown into a rage and accused Fuller of being narrow-minded and stupid. He insisted he was actually there at his 'other' restaurant – could see it, feel it and smell the cooking for God's sake. Finally he had shot into his cellar and returned triumphantly placing a bottle of wine bearing the Mianni label on the table in front of Fuller.

He sipped again now at the gin and tonic thinking through the possibilities. He recalled Julie's diary entry on how Bill had been scaring her '...*He says he went somewhere last night. Finally found a way there...*'.And now he was dead.

All of the people attacked by the Stabu claim they had been to 'other worlds'. Including the Prime Minister. Some travelled easily to these worlds – others met obstacles and couldn't get through to start with, or at all. Is it possible the Stabu wanted to stop the people being able to have these experiences? But how did they know who was having them? How did they know where they lived? And why would they want to stop them anyway?

It was no use. He couldn't see the connection. Too many questions flooded his mind and he sunk the last of his drink. He reached for the envelope and opened it removing the single sheaf of paper, dropping the envelope back on to the table. He read the first couple of lines and sat up quickly. He glanced at the signature and then grabbed the envelope from the table. He hadn't noticed before but it was addressed for his attention with the name of his hotel and its address. It was a letter that had been hand-delivered, not a message taken at the front-desk as he had first assumed.

'*Dear John,*

*It was good to meet with you the other day, old boy –
those creatures certainly gave us something to worry about,
don't you think? Hope your hand is getting better.*

*It might interest you to know that I've now got a theory
that I want to share with you. Julie helped me come up with it
actually although I haven't told her my thoughts just yet - in
case she thinks I've finally gone over the edge.*

*I'd really appreciate the chance to talk to you about it
though so give me a call when you can.*

Kind Regards'

It was signed 'Bill Goldsworth' and dated the previous
day. He must have had it delivered only hours before he died.

Fuller read it again but couldn't imagine what
Goldsworth had come up with. He looked quickly at his
watch and called the PM's office to give an update. Yes,
things are progressing. No, no answers as yet.

A noise behind him made him wake with a jolt. Since
the call from Julie late last night he hadn't had chance to
sleep and had dozed off in the afternoon sun. The light was
fading now as he turned to see Julie brushing her wet hair as
she sat in a robe in front of the dressing-table mirror.

He got up still clutching the envelope and letter and
went inside.

'How are you feeling?' he asked.

'A bit better,' she replied softly. 'The shower helped.'

'We need to go to the hospital. They want us to formally
identify Bill's body.'

She bowed her head and closed her eyes. 'Surely that's
not necessary. The police were there.'

'Unusual circumstances. It's OK,' he offered. 'I can do
it. You don't have to see him again.' He imagined what it
must have been like for her to watch as the Stabu attacked
and killed someone she cared so deeply about.

'Thanks,' she said as she continued brushing. 'I'll come with you though. Give me fifteen minutes.'

Fuller left Julie and walked quickly behind the pathologist towards the morgue. He had insisted on a full autopsy and asked for the report to be delivered to him at his hotel as soon as possible. He was glad the Spanish and British governments were co-operating so smoothly on this.

The pathologist had already tried to warn him that there were serious injuries to the body, and he had insisted on going ahead.

As the sheet was removed from Bill's face Fuller jumped back, just making it to the sink before vomiting noisily.

'Jesus,' he hissed eventually, blowing out his cheeks and walking back slowly to the body.

Most of Goldsworth's lower jaw was exposed with bits of brown flesh around his lips and nostrils caused by acid burns. A reddish-brown circle surrounded a puncture through his forehead just above the bridge of his nose. His hair was black and powdery, and small piles of black dust had settled around his head. His eye sockets contained shrivelled crusts that once could see.

Chapter 25

Jim Naylor read the note again as he sipped his drink at the bar of the Marriott. Bob was apologetic and begged to be forgiven for having an affair with Martha behind Jim's back. It just happened, apparently. Nothing personal. Bob hoped that he could in some way atone at least to some degree for the hurt he had caused. He was sending his man to pick Jim up and bring him to the Research Centre. Let Jim in on the work that was exciting Bob so much. Might help explain Jim's spaceship adventure. Even have Jim re-consider coming in with him if he could ever find it in his heart to forgive and accept that Bob and Martha were meant to be together. If Jim could put the episode aside Bob promised that what he was to see would amaze him.

'Arsehole,' Naylor whispered as he crumpled up the note and threw it into a waste bin. But he had to admit to being intrigued.

'Jim?' A voice behind him inquired.

He turned to look at Chris Lambert in dark, pin-striped suit who offered a handshake and smiled at him gripping the keys to a Mercedes 'C' class in his other hand. 'Are you ready to go? The car's outside.'

Naylor finished his drink, dropped some coins next to the glass on the bar, and followed Lambert out.

Lambert didn't give anything away in the car. Apparently Jenkins wanted to give Naylor the star treatment, to personally show him around the facility and explain what was going on.

Sure enough Jenkins stood at the entrance to the building as the car pulled up outside.

'Jim, hello. I'm really pleased you accepted the invite. I've got lots to show you.' He went to put his arm around

Naylor's shoulder but retracted it on being returned a frosty glare.

'This doesn't change anything,' Naylor said icily.

'Of course. I can understand that,' Jenkins replied. And then with a smile, 'but you do want to see, don't you? Otherwise you wouldn't be here. Come in, come in.'

As they walked through the double doors Jenkins looked over his shoulder at Lambert who had a quizzical look on his face, both hands palm up in front of him. Jenkins turned back to face the entrance and with his hand furthest from Naylor and out of his sight made a gesture patting the air three or four times. *Stay calm. Don't worry, you'll get your chance.*

Jenkins and Naylor walked into the small dining room. 'Thought I'd introduce you to the important people first,' Jenkins quipped.

Sheena turned her head towards the men as she filled her cup at the coffee machine. Tom and Andy looked up from reading different sections of the Sunday Times. The man in the grey suit introduced the stranger.

'Team,' he announced, 'this is my good friend Jim Naylor.'

Tom blinked a couple of times. His face was white with redness around his eyes. Naylor thought he looked distinctly vampirish.

'Jim. This is Sheena.'

'Nice to meet you, Jim,' Sheena beamed. 'Are you joining us as another guinea-pig?' she asked playfully.

Naylor flashed a glance at Jenkins. 'No,' Jenkins said. 'And please don't frighten our visitors, Sheena. You are not 'guinea-pigs'. You are being compensated well for contributing to humanitarian research.'

'Oh yes, I forgot,' she laughed. Naylor was warming to her already.

'They've delivered the wrong guitar,' Tom piped up, angrily.

'Sorry?' Jenkins said as Lambert came through the door and took a position slightly behind him.

'I asked for the Gibson Les Paul. They brought me the Firebird,' Tom continued to complain.

Jenkins turned to Lambert, 'Chris, please sort this out for Tom would you?' and then back to Tom, 'No problem. Keep the Firebird as well. The upgraded sound-proofing works well, Tom. Right Sheena?'

'Yep, can't hear a thing now. My feathered friends are all a lot happier.'

'Are you OK?' Naylor was asking Andy.

Andy had bowed his head slowly into his hands. He jerked it back at the question and faced Naylor, bleary-eyed. 'Oh yeah,' he mumbled. 'Just a bit tired,' and rubbed the back of his neck as he stretched his face towards the ceiling.

'Andy's been working very hard for us,' Jenkins offered. 'Given us a lot of interesting new data to move the project forward. Come on, Jim. Let's give these good people some peace and take a tour around the place.'

'Before you go,' Sheena was stirring the coffee. 'I really think you guys need to do something for Andy. He's not right.'

'No, he doesn't look too good,' Naylor chipped in. 'What are you doing to these guys?' he addressed his question to Jenkins as he put his hand on Andy's forehead. 'He's got a fever.'

Lambert was pressing buttons on his mobile. 'I'll sort it,' he said.

'Well please do it quickly,' Sheena pleaded as she placed the cup to Andy's lips. He took a sip but spat out the steaming hot liquid, screwing his eyes in pain.

'Here, let me,' Naylor took the cup from her hand and went to the basin to add some cold water.

'Thanks,' she smiled as she took the cup back from him and offered it to Andy. 'Maybe see you later?'

'Hopefully,' he said as he walked over to Jenkins and Lambert. The three left the room and Jenkins led them towards the main laboratory. They stepped into the large room, stacked with electronics with a leather couch 'centre-stage' and a huge screen along one wall.

Naylor tore into Jenkins as Lambert moved across the room and undid the straps on the couch. 'So. Can I assume this is where you wallow in self-satisfaction and tell me what terrific progress you have made towards your ambition to be one of the richest men in the world? Does Martha realise you'll drop her like a hot brick as soon as your new-found wealth takes you into the highest social circles? That guy in there looked like shit. Do you care? I suspect not.'

'Oh, come on Jim. The three in there have everything they could possibly want in return for their services. Tom's got his recording studio. His band's a bit light on numbers but he's happy. Sheena has her aviary. Studying and looking after her exotic birds. This has been a great opportunity for her and she's taking full advantage of it. Let me tell you – none of them have suffered any physical pain other than the fact it can be a tiring process. We'll sort Andy out. We have access to the best medical people available. No problem. And as for Martha, well, I'm sorry. Truly. It wasn't to get at you – it just happened. And as for the future I've got no plans to change anything. Other than to get over the obstacles we're currently experiencing on the project and to succeed in delivering on the final objective.'

'Which is?' Naylor asked bluntly.

'Bob!' Lambert called out. 'We need to be careful. Our client expects us to keep things confidential. We have a non-disclosure agreement, remember? We need to get this done.'

'Get what done?' Naylor asked.

'Take a seat, Jim. It's not a problem Chris,' Jenkins said firmly. 'We can trust Jim.'

Forty minutes later Jenkins had finished taking Naylor through their theories and how the three subjects were helping them prove them out. It was a long forty minutes for Lambert who had shaken his head and tried to stop Jenkins at several points. But Jenkins was enthusiastic, relishing the opportunity to proclaim not only the possibilities in terms of scientific and technical advancement but also, and Naylor took this second piece as of massively more importance to Jenkins, in terms of value to potential customers.

Finally, Naylor put the fingertips of both hands over his mouth as he stared across the room and took in the implications of what Jenkins had shared with him.

Jenkins broke the silence. 'They are experiencing parallel worlds, Jim. Think of it.' Jenkins eyes were alight. 'They are somehow travelling outside of the world that we know. Like you did in your spaceship.'

Naylor broke out of his trance and stared at Jenkins. He somehow knew Jenkins was right, even if he was struggling with explanations for most of what he'd just been told. But, yes, he'd had an out-of-body experience – nearly died. So had the three subjects.

'And you can measure this activity?' he asked, and then looking at the screen. 'And see it?'

'Well, to some degree Jim. But we need more experiments. Test out the theories. Develop a test bed of sample scenarios and try them out on the different subjects until we get a consistent result. When we do we can move on.'

Lambert was now glaring at Jenkins and revolving his hands in the air, out of sight of Naylor, urging Jenkins to the next step in the plan they'd agreed earlier.

'And you could be part of that plan, Jim. You have almost been there yourself. If we're right, with our help you could experience a parallel world. A parallel world, Jim. Just think about it. What an opportunity.'

'And if your theories are wrong?'

'Well, if we're wrong, we're wrong. But what do we have to lose? The important thing here, Jim, is that we could be right. Stay with us Jim. Help us on this.'

'What?' Lambert started to protest, realising their plan was taking a different turn. 'Bob, I think we have all the subjects we can handle currently. We can perhaps offer Jim a 'one-off' – the opportunity to enhance his existing experiences, and no doubt the data we record from his working with us for those few hours will be gratefully added to what we have built up already. But our client would not support additional full-time subjects on the programme. You know that.'

Jenkins' exuberance ended abruptly and he walked to the couch. 'How about it, Jim. Want to try it out? I can get the team together and try to help you get there. Now?'

Naylor had to admit that he was excited. Jenkins had told him he would be, and he was. He remembered the gatekeepers who stopped him on his first attempt to get through to another world. An attempt he had made without even realising that was what he was doing. And the spaceship. But then suddenly the face of Frank Jackson was in front of his, laughing hysterically as Naylor's craft started to crumble around him. He grew cold.

'There's a problem,' he announced. 'There's someone I don't want to meet on the other side. At least, not until I'm ready for him.'

'Who?'

'I'm not sure,' he lied. 'It's just a figure in my dreams.'

'It's OK. We can bring you back whenever the readings show you under any kind of serious stress,' Jenkins assured.

'But what if I don't dream? What if I don't even sleep?'

'We use an accelerator that we've developed,' Lambert was holding a hypodermic containing a bluish liquid. 'It's not a guarantee but as a relaxant it acts as a catalyst in the process. We'll inject you on the couch, get the lab team in and start you off.'

As Naylor lay down, Jenkins exclaimed excitedly as he did up the restraints, 'It's an adventure, Jim, and an experience you'll never, ever surpass in anything else you ever do. It's also a privilege that life's presented to you. Not to me. Not to Chris. Not to the vast majority of the people in this world. And, presumably, in other worlds.'

But the speech wasn't for Naylor. The plan for Naylor had already been made and it didn't include being able to look back on his experience. Lambert injected some of the liquid into his vein and placed the hypodermic back into its container. He called the Programme Head and told him to get the team together. They had another subject.

A few minutes later the room had seven additional people in white coats all purposefully attending to machines or charts or writing notes.

Naylor was trying to relax. His eyes were closed but he could see Jackson too clearly for him to drop off to sleep straight away. He really hoped they could bring him back if he came across that psychopath on his travels. A young woman was attaching sensors around his head but he realised momentarily that he wasn't feeling anything and was just really focussing on Jackson's face that he hoped not to see until he was ready to deal with him and he found himself swimming around in a warm, dark mist the focus of this activity overturning the importance of events in the lab except for a far away woman's voice which was saying that the accelerator was developed to help him sleep and move into a dream state and she would be giving him the maximum safe dosage to ensure the process went perfectly and that he would only feel a slight pinprick and he felt he should perhaps tell her that he'd already had the maximum safe dosage from Lambert except that the mist had got lighter and he wasn't spinning quite so quickly anymore and something started to appear in front of him which sent a wave of apprehension through his being.

Tiny white lights started to explode around him and vividly coloured forms like tropical fish moved out from the exploding centres and drifted through him. The colours and the explosions made him almost cry out with excitement, and looked with increasing incredulity as the white lights grew bigger. He knew he'd been here before but was powerless to change it. Neither did he want to.

He was no longer swimming. The white lights were coming at him from four points aligned horizontally ahead of him a short distance apart. As the mist cleared further, the two beings guarding a huge wooden door continued to fire the bolts of exploding light towards him from their outstretched arms. The large glass key was there again above the door.

The guardians gradually dropped their arms and the explosions stopped. The key sparkled in the bright radiance of the guardians' light. This time he felt he knew that there would be something beyond the door for him and the key leapt from its perch, flew through the air and landed in his hand.

The explosions started again - they burst around him and he was thrown from side to side. Although the sound of the detonations deafened him he approached the door as the guardians moved together to bar his access.

The voice that had been there the first time had gone.

His mind grabbed the large circular handle on the door and pulled powerfully at it. The door swayed backwards and forwards but refused to open until he slid in and turned the key. The door moved slowly. The explosions stopped and the guardians disappeared. He moved through the doorway into a new world.

Julie Furness' face was set a metre in front of their own. She had both hands cupped around her mouth and her eyes wide open shaking with fright just staring at them as Jim Naylor and John Fuller peered out from a single body, screaming loudly.

Chapter 26

Fuller and Naylor read each other's thoughts whilst standing there in the same body.

Fuller now remembered making love to a woman called Martha Naylor who was the woman who was the same person as his ex-wife called Liz Fuller except Martha and Liz had different tastes in clothes and he and Liz had always wanted a child but she miscarried and the child she lost was a boy and would have been the same age now as his son, Jack. His mind shifted suddenly as he struggled to work out how he had gained his vast experience in IT or how it tied in to his work for the Government and as he tried to trace his career back to his university days he realised he'd attended two universities and these were the two choices that his father had tossed a coin to help him decide between. He'd got his BA after studying Economics with Russian at Nottingham whilst in his alter ego Naylor received his BSc through studying Computer Science at Loughborough over the same period. They shuddered as they remembered the news of their father dying of a heart attack a year after they started university and them making the trip home to attend the funeral. Their mother stood at the graveside in a long black dress but also in black jacket and skirt – which outfit? – both outfits. One of their uncles saying some words and inviting their friends and family to toast their father's memory. Their sister bursting immediately into tears. Their niece bursting immediately into tears. Which one? Both. Their determination afterwards to finish their studies and get their qualifications 'for him'.

The memories continued. Some perfectly in synch, others slightly out. Exactly the same girlfriend at university. They met her at a pub in Ruddington, a village close to both universities. Same sexual experiences. Naïve early fumblings at bra straps up to finally 'doing it' in a park under the moonlight – under the 'moons' light - leading to the same feeling of exuberance. Same feeling of dejection when she went off with some idiot who worked out and played rugby. Same tutors – lecturing on different subjects – but same people. Same first cars after finishing university with the same registration numbers but one car with four wheels and the other with six.

At exactly the same time Naylor had exactly the same thoughts as Fuller but the main one they couldn't reconcile was that they had different names and nausea suddenly swept their body. They collapsed to the floor throwing up violently.

They crouched on all fours for several minutes before their eyes slowly started to focus again. Naylor strained hard and targeted his mind towards union of the two men into one and the one was John Fuller. The life, the attitudes, the beliefs of Jim Naylor still existed. But the body and the mind which was slowly assimilating the two lifestreams was John Fuller's. And Fuller was now thinking of the merger of two large organisations with equal lifespans that had existed in a similar industry with similar products, similar customers and suppliers, but that had developed on slightly different lines, with unique events causing high and low performances towards ultimately similar strategic objectives. The merger would be a sensible move for many reasons and a lot of the values would be combined, and the skills and experiences of the combined workforce would be greater then the sum of the two parts, but there would be challenges in the integration process. And maybe there would be some surprises – good and bad – in what was now the combined knowledge-base of the new organisation. And there would continue to be challenges as personal agendas didn't match – or worst case were contradictory to – the goals and objectives of the new organisation. But things would sort themselves out. And the

John Fuller Corporation Limited was starting to sort himself out.

Julie stood both entranced and scared as John Fuller's obvious confusion had his wide-eyed facial features dancing like fireflies. Jim Naylor was an apparition, merging and then demerging with Fuller's body as in a heat haze. Naylor's face on Fuller's body, then vice versa, then Fuller disappearing leaving Naylor in full and solid view and then vice versa.

Julie held her hands on the top of her head as she tried to make sense of the scene. But she struggled. These men were twins and then ghosts and then real and yet swapping and alternating like those jelly-form sea creatures that live in the dark ocean depths until disturbed when their bioluminescence would light them up in electric reds and greens and blues. Julie stared at the men's faces. They were the same person. She could see that. One with a more receding hairline, the other with a five o'clock shadow but both the same. Two John Fullers fighting to inhabit a single body. Eventually one man stood in front of her and the outline of the other bathed the first in wisps of fading colours and hues until that form drifted shrinking into the man's body and disappeared.

'John?' she asked. Quietly. Tentatively.

He took a few seconds to answer as he pushed his fingers roughly through his hair, beads of perspiration on his forehead.

'It's OK – let me think for a minute,' he answered a little abruptly before pulling his laptop from its case and flipping the lid. He'd been the invader as Naylor and the invaded as Fuller. Realities were flooding his mind. Input from the two brains were slowly resolving each man's questions as they arose. But he was having problems enough dealing with the merger. He certainly didn't need two names. John Fuller. He'd stick with that.

Logging on he searched for 'bank robbery London' and found it quickly. It was a BBC News article from a couple of weeks ago and he read through it eagerly.

Three men and a getaway driver had robbed a bank in Central London. A young girl had since died after being brutally pushed to the pavement out of the way of the escaping men and suffering serious head injuries. The gang had escaped in a blue Mercedes. The police had identified one of the gang as Frank Jackson from DNA in some bloodstains he'd left when the car had accidentally reversed into him. Jackson had managed to hobble into the Mercedes and get away. According to onlookers the car was trying to avoid being blocked in by another car that had recently pulled up in front of it. Police were looking for clues as to the identities of the other three gang members and as yet all four still eluded capture.

'That was me,' Fuller suddenly said aloud.

'Sorry?'

'This news story about the robbery in London. It was my car the gang was trying to avoid. I'd parked to meet up with one of the PM's team in the offices next to the bank to give him a heads up on progress. Perk of the job to be able to park where you like. How could I have missed all of that going on?' He stared at the screen.

Julie stood silent for a moment and then spoke to him almost in a whisper.

'I think I've seen a ghost.'

Fuller turned to look at her, quizzically at first but then closing his eyes wearily. 'No it's alright. There's a ton of stuff I've got to tell you but not now, OK? I've just been to hell and back – don't expect I look so good. Probably deathly, to be honest. I'll explain it all. Soon. I promise.'

'Yes John, you're white – no question. But listen to me. I've just seen a ghost. An apparition. The ghost was of you.

Identical almost. Some sort of shape dancing around you for a long time. Then it disappeared. And you stopped screaming.'

'Screaming? Was I screaming?'

'You both were. You and the ghost. It was horrible. Tell me what's going on. Please,' she begged, tears forming in her eyes as she struggled to take it in.

Fuller's mind still raced. And now he was wondering about ghosts. So they do exist and here was the reason, or at least one of the reasons. He gently pulled her towards him and put his arms around her. She listened intently as he explained what he now knew to be true. The existence of parallel worlds with parallel lives. How one of her alter ego's was Sheena, a guinea-pig in Bob Jenkins' research facility, whose love of birds matched her own and whose first name matched her second. And another - in yet another world – was called Siren and could actually turn into a tree. Julie let out a nervous laugh which she cut short as she realised he was serious. He told her all about Jim Naylor's life. She knew the John Fuller story already. Finally he explained the theory behind Nature stepping in to correct things and to prevent the crossing over between parallel worlds. And the creatures that had developed - had evolved - to stop it. Specifically to stop in the most absolute way those people most likely to cross over. Bill Goldsworth had died because of it. Darwin would have had a field day. Fuller's eyes glided back to the news article on his laptop screen and he craned his neck to get closer as he read the last couple of sentences.

'One of the gang members fired a shotgun in the direction of the second car as the Mercedes sped away, but they missed the vehicle. Police believe the gang may have thought the driver was still inside and therefore able to provide descriptions of the men. When police arrived at the scene the second car had disappeared. None of the witnesses

*could provide the registration number, and CCTV footage
was limited. Police are asking for the driver to come forward
as a matter of urgency.'*

Fuller sat Julie down gently and turned to the laptop. He
searched for an update and found it. A news item dated a
week later.

*'...and police believe the driver may be reluctant to
come forward for fear of reprisals from the gang led by
Frank Jackson, a known psychopath.'*

Julie's eyes followed the same words on the screen then
she said confidently 'You weren't even in the car so you
couldn't give the police any descriptions anyway. Jackson
doesn't know it's you. If the police don't know then he won't
- right?'

'Wrong,' Fuller said, convinced. 'Jackson knows. Don't
ask me how, but I know he knows.'

Chapter 27

'I'm sorry Mr Fuller, I still don't understand why you took so long reporting this. You must have known we were looking for you,' Inspector Rogers barked as he marched ahead of Fuller to an interview room. He pushed the door open and Fuller awkwardly eased past his bulk, almost gagging at the smell of stale cigarette smoke, into the poorly lit room.

'I've been travelling. I've only just heard about it.'

'Just heard? It's been all over the media here in the UK as well as most of the rest of the world. Where have you been – Mars?' He ignored Fuller as he positioned himself at a table facing away from a large mirror on the wall. Fuller guessed it was two-way for the more interesting interviews. He doubted his own justified any special attention.

The inspector motioned Fuller to sit on the opposite side of the table, where a couple of ballpoint pens and a sheath of paper lay waiting.

'OK. So tell me. What happened that afternoon? Oh, and I have to tell you this interview is being recorded. Nothing sinister. Just procedure.'

Fuller looked around and guessed that there must be at least one person on the other side of the glass operating the recording equipment. The inspector sensed his question before he could ask it.

'Only one operator. Nothing to worry about. So?'

'I'm sorry but there won't be a lot I can tell you.' Fuller almost laughed out loud at the absurdity of that statement given the events of the last twenty-four hours or so. He had become twice the man he used to be and actually had loads to tell people. But not yet. And certainly not to this guy.

He searched his memories as Fuller. 'I'm employed by the Civil Service and was scheduled to deliver a report to a colleague in the office building next to the bank that was robbed. I arrived about five to three I suppose and left my car running. I wasn't planning on being long but I'd already gone in when the robbery took place and the men made their escape. I saw and heard nothing.'

'You seem not to see or hear very much at all these days Mr Fuller,' the inspector offered sarcastically. He was really not sure from the start that he would get much from interviewing the man sat in front of him and to begin to have that confirmed was irritating him.

'I came out from giving in the report, got in my car and drove off.'

'And what time was that?'

'Around five past. I wasn't more then ten minutes.'

'The robbery took place just before three. The gang was in the bank for a little over three minutes and left at a couple of minutes past. You must have seen something? The police got there only a couple of minutes after you said you left, which means you took off after the robbery but before the police arrived.'

'Well, I guess there were a few people standing around but I didn't think much of it,' Fuller answered weakly, struggling to control the thoughts of his 'other' self Fuller. And anyway, he didn't appreciate the fact that he was apparently being accused of something.

'And the poor girl dying on the pavement with people trying to give her the kiss of life?'

'Didn't see her. What I've been working on is pretty important stuff.' Even as he said it Fuller felt stupid, especially as he obviously couldn't share any of it with the inspector who was reddening now.

'What about the car?' he almost shouted. 'Blue Mercedes – screeching up the road. Didn't hear that I suppose.'

'Look,' Fuller said indignantly. 'The timing was unfortunate. But that's not my fault. A few minutes either way and maybe I could have helped. Yes, I may have heard a car screeching but so what? There are boy racers all over the place any time of day or night nowadays.'

The two men sat looking sternly at each other for a few seconds. Eventually the inspector continued, more calmly.

'Jackson thinks you clocked them – can give us descriptions. You know who Jackson is, right? Seen it in the news? The windows of your car are tinted apparently and the engine was running. He couldn't see inside. Doesn't know you weren't at the wheel. We don't want to dispel that belief because, quite frankly, we need to identify the rest of the gang.'

Fuller shifted nervously in his seat. 'You've got Jackson?'

'Yep. Picked him up this morning as it happens.'

'And where is he now?'

'Safely tucked away in a cell down the corridor. Don't you worry about him.' The inspector was obviously starting to get bored. 'OK, complete the statement and then you can go. I want to know when you arrived, which office you delivered your package to, who you gave it to, when you left, where you went afterwards. I need an address and contact number. We may need to chat again. Buzz me when you're done,' he said pointing to a button on the wall. 'Susie – we're done,' he called in the direction of the mirror and got up and left, closing the door behind him.

Fuller's thoughts were not on the robbery but on a stay in a hospital.

He shouted after the inspector, 'Jackson's not in his cell any more and the policeman guarding him is dead!' How did he know? He stood up quickly glancing at the door and at the same time the lights in the room went out. Shit.

He knew going for the door would be too late so he leapt towards the buzzer and pushed hard. Nothing. He turned and spoke to the shadow in the doorway.

'Knocked out the buzzer as well as the lights, Jackson?' He tried to sound calm.

'Clever boy. I knew you'd be able to help identify me.'

'But I didn't. I wasn't even in the car.'

'I know. How's the ship, captain? Heard you brought a piece home.'

Fuller shuddered. He didn't understand. His mind tried to piece together what was happening, what he knew and what he thought Jackson would know. He finally realised. Jackson must have done what Fuller and Naylor had done. He must have merged with one or more of his alter ego's in other worlds. Including the one where Jackson had blown his spaceship to pieces. Jackson's schizophrenia must be the key to have helped him do it. And he continued to want Fuller dead.

He was slowly moving to the corner of the room so he had little or no light now on him and blackness behind. He needed to disappear within the room for a few seconds more to give himself time to think.

'So how do you do it – move between worlds?' he asked the darkness.

'Doctors tell me I'm ill,' Jackson chortled like a five-year-old. 'Well if that's being fucking ill, I don't want no treatment. It's great - just leave me to suffer.' He chortled again. 'I've seen more things than anyone ever has, and I've only scraped the surface. I'm enjoying it and you're the joker who could put a stop to it.'

'But I don't want to. I'm happy to live and let live.'

'Oh but you're not, Mr Fuller. And now that you other half Mr Naylor has joined you, so to speak,' he smiled wryly, 'you still need to find a way to save the Prime Minister. And if you do, then my fun ends. Because there's only one way to stop all of this and if either of you find it then I'm dead.'

Fuller clenched his fists to try to stop himself shaking. He noticed a slim strip of light under the door indicating the hall lights were still on. Jackson had just killed the lights in the interview room. The glow under the door flickered as someone walked past outside.

'Been in this position before, Mr Fuller. Right? Or should I say Mr Naylor? Remember what I told you then? In that hospital room? I said they'd be too late. I'll have slit your chest from bottom to top and thrown your kidneys out the window before they get to the door. And by the time they break in I'd have done so much more. Well, no window this time and the door's not locked. But even so let me assure you the sentiments are exactly the same. And no television to break over my head, nor any needles to stick in me. What are you to do?' He chortled so long and loud that Fuller was sure someone would hear and come in. They didn't.

'So what have you seen? On your travels,' Fuller asked weakly.

'I have seen things that would turn your head and many that would turn your stomach. But Mr Fuller, enough talk. I have business to finish with you.' A tiny dart of light danced from the blade in Jackson's hand.

'But can't you bear to share one piece of information as the last request of a dying man?'

'What information? You should be aware, Mr Fuller, that neither respect nor sentiment lie easily with me. Last requests just delay matters.'

'No, really. Let me die knowing how you do it. How do you move between the different worlds and how do you guarantee getting back to the one you left?' Fuller moved gingerly towards the table.

'Mr Fuller, should you have lived a little longer you would no doubt have discovered for yourself. As it is…'

'Have you finished that bloody statement yet?' the voice of the inspector boomed across the room as he flung the door open and reached for the light switch. 'Why's it so dark in here?' But before he could discover the answer to his question his chest and throat had been slashed deeply and he fell to the floor gurgling blood.

At the same time Fuller had grabbed the two pens from the table now illuminated by the light from the hallway and leapt at Jackson jamming both into his face. One found soft eye tissue and sank into his head. Jackson screamed and reeled back slashing wildly and blindly back and forth but Fuller had retreated to the corner again. Jackson banged into the table and then buried the knife into the wall as he fell to the floor before he disappeared under the bodies of four of the inspector's colleagues. He was dragged off screaming obscenities and trailing blood. A woman PC was shouting to someone down the hall to call for an ambulance as she tried to stem the flow of blood gushing down the front of the inspector's shirt and trousers. His head lolled to the side and he was gone. His attendant screamed and started to sob.

Chapter 28

'So what are we looking at? Sam? Chris?' Bob Jenkins stood in his laboratory staring at the 'Eye' trying to decipher the shapes.

Lambert focussed hard but didn't answer.

'I think I see two men, Bob,' Sam offered weakly.

'OK so what does it mean? Naylor's obviously succeeded in going across but where is he, and what changes is he seeing in his body as a result?'

'He appears in his dream to initially be in some place where he is struggling to share a single body with someone else. Having played it back again – it shows that he eventually succeeds,' Sam concluded.

'OK,' Jenkins agreed, 'so who is the other man and which body do they decide to share?'

'Well, that's the strange thing. If you look at the limbs and the overall shape of the body they are very similar,' Sam went on, and then shouted over to one of the technicians. 'Can you magnify the faces please?' After a couple of seconds. 'See there – the features are the same down to the colour of the eyes. Magnify the fingers now, and focus on the right index. OK – now the right thumb. And now the left index please. See – the prints are identical. We can't get hold of the actual DNA but I'd swear these two men are the same one.'

'He's met a twin?' Jenkins asked.

'No,' Lambert joined the conversation. 'I think what Sam is saying is that he's met himself.'

'Seems to be,' Sam confirmed.

'Jesus. Must have shook him senseless. But are the other readings OK?'

Sam checked the monitors. 'Yeah OK now. But when he first met his other self his heart rate was dangerously high.'

'I'm not surprised. OK thanks Sam.' Bob dismissed the man and turned to face Lambert. 'Why is Naylor not dead?' he asked firmly but quietly. 'We gave him two full doses. Should have gone hours ago.'

'I don't know,' Lambert replied. 'I'll give him another dose.'

'No! Not now. Might raise suspicions and in any case I want to understand what's happening to him. If he's crossed over to another world could he really have met and merged with himself? Fascinating. Absolutely bloody fascinating. Chris, you know this could be the answer to the question of how the same person exists twice – or more times – in the same universe. We need to be able to get him back. We need to question the guy. How do we do it, Chris?'

'Could use the defibrillator. No guarantees though. Could fry a weakened body like his after the dosage we've given him. And if he's merged with himself on the other side he's unlikely to come back of his own accord. A homing pigeon is set free to return home. He, on the other hand, appears to be trapped. Of course, the other issue is that – assuming we haven't given him brain damage – he may not take kindly to us having tried to kill him, assuming he's worked that out.'

'Sam,' Jenkins called out. 'We're going to need to shock him. Bring the equipment to the couch.' And then to Lambert. 'We take the risk. We didn't expect this to happen but now that it has it could give us the answers we're looking for to move forward. And if that doesn't work we'll need to find him and bring him back. Andy has been over, and Sheena went close a couple of times. We could send one of those two to retrieve Naylor. But how do we get them to the same place that Naylor is?'

'Could try wiring them up in parallel. If they are connected in this world maybe they still would be when they arrived the other side?'

'Worth a try,' Jenkins said.

'It's all we've got,' Lambert pointed out. 'Let's start with Forrester. He's actually been there.'

The men gathered around Naylor's prone body. Most of his skin was white and his lips had a bluish tinge, but around his eyes the skin had reddened and two tear tracks traced themselves from the outer corner of each eye around and below his ears on to the surface of the couch. Underneath his closed eyelids his eyes were darting around clearly agitated. The little finger on his right hand made small flicking movements.

A door opened and an overall stood next to Andy and Sheena at the entrance. The overall beckoned them towards the couch with his clipboard and Andy walked over eagerly. Sheena hesitated at the doorway, but then slowly moved to stand next to Jenkins.

'Guys, thanks for joining us,' Jenkins said as a smile suddenly came back to his face. 'I wanted you to witness this. No point in keeping you too much in the dark.'

Lambert guessed that Jenkins had summoned them in case the shock to the heart didn't bring Naylor back. He'd need to persuade them to act as messengers – captors almost – to get to Naylor, wherever he was, and bring him back.

'We want all of our subjects to be safe,' Jenkins went on. 'But sometimes, especially when they are new to the procedure, one or two suffer difficulties and Jim unfortunately has hit a problem. He's in no danger per se, but he's having difficulty coming out of his dream state. We're concerned that the longer he stays where he is the more his body may react badly to it, and we obviously want him to stay healthy while he's helping us here, so we're taking some pretty routine measures to help him back.'

'That's a defib unit,' Andy protested pointing at the machine next to Sam. 'Not sure that can be called a routine procedure in any situation. And it didn't work on me, did it?'

'Well, OK, not exactly routine, but we have found it to be effective before. It's perfectly safe. It didn't work on you, Andy, simply because we decided to stop the procedure and allow you more time to find your way back of your own volition which, of course, you did with absolutely no side effects. If it doesn't work in Jim's case – as he's been gone for longer than you were now - we will obviously escalate a solution.'

Escalate a solution – Lambert expected the obvious question from one of the two but it didn't come as Sam started the procedure. 'Stand clear!'

Each of the group moved backwards automatically even though they were not in contact with Naylor or the couch.

Sam pressed the paddles to Naylor's chest and pushed the button with his thumb. A small thudding and Naylor's body jolted and returned to its prone position. There was no other reaction. Naylor's eyes still darted and his little finger still twitched. Sheena watched but placed her hand on Forrester's arm for comfort.

'Charging again,' Sam announced. 'Stand clear!'

A few seconds later there was another thudding and another convulsion from Naylor but with the same result. Sam looked over nervously at Lambert.

'Increase the charge,' Lambert ordered.

Jenkins shifted from side to side.

As the shock hit Naylor's body he jumped about six inches and fell back motionless. For a full ten seconds there was no eye movement and no finger movement. Nothing.

'Is he dead?' Sheena asked to nobody in particular.

But then as they all watched intently the darting and twitching slowly started again. Sam again looked at Lambert but Jenkins stepped in.

'Stop. Let him rest. Andy, Sheena - this is where we may need your help.'

'OK,' they said slightly hesitantly but in unison.

'Jim's been dreaming for a long while. We've tried drugs and now, as you've seen, our efforts to shock him back have failed as well. You both know how intense these deep dives into your subconsciousness can be, and it looks like Jim's has got pretty severe. We need to help him back and one way to do that is for one of you to go and find him.'

'Find him?' Sheena asked with a frown. 'But he's in a dream. Or that's what you tell us, even though mine always seems very real to me.'

Both Jenkins and Lambert looked at her without saying a word.

'Do you mean,' she struggled for the words. 'Do you mean it's something else? He's not in a dream?'

'I knew it!' Andy blurted out and spun round excitedly. 'This is something better. Something more important. Something really worth investing the millions in. Look at this place.' He waved his outstretched arm around the room and continued. 'Who's paying for all of this? What's in it for them? OK, what do you want me to do?'

'Wait.' Sheena had her head bowed, staring at the floor. 'I want to do it.'

'Well that's fine, Sheena,' Jenkins stepped in. 'You'll get your chance. But as you know Andy has got through already. He's a natural at this.'

'But Sheena needs to do this,' Andy pleaded. 'She needs the chance to find her father and try to sort things out with him.'

Jenkins hesitated, but Lambert made a shake of the head to Jenkins. No – Forrester needs to go so things stay objective. Besides he's the better bet for getting through.

Ten minutes later a second couch had been positioned next to Naylor's and Andy Forrester lay on it, back-to-back with Naylor.

Lambert stood over him. 'So you know what we want you to do?'

'Yes,' Andy answered. 'Being connected to Jim this end will give me the best chance of finding him on the other side, and when I do find him I need to try to find a way to connect us so you can bring us both back.'

'That's it. It's a rescue mission. But don't hang about. We need you both back here asap. Oh, and double credits for this trip, right?'

'OK. Let's do it.'

The monitors clicked into life. Jenkins and Lambert stood next to Sheena in front of the 'Eye' watching and waiting.

An overall carefully brought a length of cable to Forrester's couch and connected one end to the wiring loom on his head. He let the other end drop to the floor while he administered the injection to send Forrester to sleep. As Forrester started to drift off he was aware that the overall was walking back to the monitors with the syringe in a dish. In his drowsy state he started to panic as he tried to call out for the other end of the cable to be connected to Naylor, but he found his mouth wouldn't work and he was sinking into mist.

The overall suddenly realised his error, turned and rushed back towards the couches.

'Forrester's definitely a natural,' Lambert announced, unaware of the problem. 'Look at the graph. He's over already,' and he turned quickly at there was a crash behind him. The two couches were now in a V-shape with an

overalled technician crumpled between them unconscious,
and a syringe smashed next to him on the floor.

Chapter 29

The jeep sped across the terrain jolting left and right as the driver swung the wheel to avoid pieces of burning wreckage and bodies strewn across the landscape. Army ambulances littered the scene and paramedics ran backwards and forwards to their vehicles piling in stretchers bearing the injured and dying. Small, random fires reached into the distance all around for hundreds of yards and smoke and the acrid smell of burning rubber choked the jeep's passengers as they tried to take in the scene before them.

They swerved around a charred and burning Rolls Royce RB211 engine which sat upright and partly buried in the earth as an army helicopter whirred overhead whipping up the swirls of smoke into crazy, flowing patterns.

The jeep stopped suddenly next to a hole in the ground about fifteen feet across guarded by four rifle-bearing soldiers who stood erect at the four points of the compass around the hole.

As they clambered out of the vehicle they stood and took in the scene.

'So what's the story?' Fuller asked as he tried to catch his breath.

The PM's call had interrupted one he was having with Julie to tell her about the police statement and the visit from Jackson. A plane had just crashed that morning in a remote area in the Yorkshire Dales. Tragic, but nothing necessarily worthy of Fuller's attention except for the fact that the cause of the crash appeared to be a huge surge of electromagnetic activity in the area. He promised Julie he'd get back to her later.

'757 came down en route to Heathrow,' Colonel Hilton offered. 'We'll know more when we analyse the black box but we suspect the crew had no chance. The electromagnetic pulse would have caused massive current and voltage surges which would have taken out the engines and rendered the instruments useless as they tried to regain control.'

'Electromagnetic pulse?'

'First thing we found after we initially thought it was terrorism. Like the E-bombs the U.S. were suspected of dropping on Iraqi TV during the 2003 invasion of Iraq. Pulses take out transistors, integrated circuits, motors and so on. It happened so fast. Not even a mayday call. The plane was banking so didn't have the speed or direction to glide anywhere– it just dropped like a stone. Poor bastards. The pulse has stopped now, but as we moved into the area the dials on our vehicles went crazy. We brought in the magnetometer. It was still off the scale.'

Fuller shone a torch into the hole but couldn't see more than about twenty feet down through the swirling smoke. 'Anyone been down yet?'

'No, we were just about to rope up.'

'I'll go down,' insisted Fuller not expecting nor getting any objection. It was clear when the Prime Minister's office had given clearance for him to be onsite that this was bigger than just a plane crash, and it wouldn't help for the army to start asking too many questions.

Fuller removed his jacket and motioned to one of the men to bring over the climbing gear for him. The two of them then clambered into their safety harnesses and Fuller quickly declared himself ready. He stood at the edge straining to see into the gloom. There seemed to be a faint humming from far below him and his questioning look at his companion was answered with a simple shrug of the shoulders.

The ends of their ropes had been shackled to the jeep. 'Follow me in,' his companion instructed as he started to reverse into the hole, 'and use your oxygen mask if the smoke gets too much.' He disappeared. Fuller hovered over the hole for a few seconds then he too backed over the edge and into the crevice.

A warm current of air engulfed Fuller and moved skywards as he descended, his heart beating faster now. Clouds of smoke surrounded his face and the light in the entrance above got smaller and dimmer as he moved down and away from it. Almost total darkness moved in around him. He struggled to keep a foothold as loose rocks fell away or crumbled beneath him. He suddenly slipped and cried out as his right knee struck the hard face of the crevice.

'You OK?' The words hissed close in his left ear and made him jump. The beam of his companion's torch played into his eyes and he winced.

'Yes, fine,' he whispered. 'Can you see anything?'

'No - not yet. Reckon we're about eighty or ninety feet down or so. Wait,' he said suddenly. A few seconds passed as the torch beam danced up and down the hole and then clicked off. 'There's a light.'

Fuller turned to see where his companion was looking. Slowly his eyes focussed and he saw a faint glow of bluish light about a hundred yards away along what appeared to be a tunnel into a cavern. Plumes of smoke still rose from pieces of metal scattered around and soaked in burning aviation fuel sitting on the tunnel floor immediately beneath the hole that they had just came down. They were hanging about three or four feet above the floor, and so let themselves down slowly until they were standing again carefully avoiding the bonfires. Fuller rubbed his knee and could feel a slight swelling around the soreness. They both stared towards the light. The humming had grown louder.

Fuller whispered 'You got a radio?'

'No – didn't think we'd need one'

'Can't get any weapons sent down then?'

His companion stared at him, a worried look on his face. 'Why do we need weapons? What's going on?'

'Probably nothing. Anyway I'm not going back now. Let's take a look,' and he started to limp towards the source of the light.

A couple of minutes passed as they edged forwards and finally reached the end of the tunnel rounding a corner of the entrance to the cavern and the light. They both instinctively jumped back and hid behind a boulder. They crouched with hearts beating crazily as they took in the scene before them. Fuller recognised the creatures immediately.

A huge stalactite of silvery metal hung down from the centre of the cave and swayed and gyrated in time to the motorised droning and humming. A thousand wings beat in eerie unison, the claws of the creatures on the outside gripping tightly to the bodies underneath. Bright blue light emanated from the mass and danced and shot out from time to time as electricity crackled noisily in the enclosed space. Small streams of acidic steam rose from the floor beneath as droplets of liquid fell from the creatures' pointed, lance-like snouts. From time to time one of the Stabu would drop from the stalactite, hover for a few seconds and join the swarm again further up the structure.

'Jesus,' Fuller's soldier finally whispered. 'There must be hundreds of them. What are they? Why are they here?'

Fuller couldn't answer the questions, at least not fully with any degree of confidence, so didn't bother to respond. He thought back to his – Fuller's – meeting with Goldsworth in Tenerife, and the belief then that there might only be twenty Stabu existing anywhere in the world. How wrong can you be? Instead he looked around the cavern noticing the smoothness of the walls and floor. They had been fashioned – could he suggest 'designed'? – such that the whole of the space was like the inside of an almost perfect dome. The walls seemed wet, but as he tentatively stretched out a hand to examine the rock face his fingers instead sunk into a thick, clear membrane. He jumped at the unexpected sensation and withdrew his hand quickly. The soldier jumped too, and at the same time the droning from the stalactite grew quiet. The two men looked nervously at each other. But after a few seconds the droning resumed its regular beat.

Fuller examined his hand. There were no marks or obvious effects of contact with the wall although for a split second, as his hand had been engulfed, he had felt as though he had lost it. As though it was detached – in another place altogether. He passed the tip of his thumb across the tips of his four fingers and then made a fist a couple of times to confirm he'd regained the feeling in his hand. Had he really felt someone grab his hand as it passed into the membrane? He was aware again of his heartbeat, rapid and heavy.

'Look,' the soldier pointed at the structure. 'Something's happening.'

Six of the creatures dropped, turned towards the two men and hovered. The soldier grabbed Fuller's arm. 'We gotta go – now!'

'Wait,' Fuller hissed. The creatures started towards them slowly. Had they been discovered? If they had it would be no use running - they'd never get away in time. But the creatures arched towards the far wall. As they accelerated away from the two men they passed into the membrane and the wall and then were gone.

The soldier's jaw dropped as he stared at where the creatures once were. 'Did you see that? They just disappeared!'

Fuller pressed his hands together in thought. 'Someone, somewhere has just had a visit. Hope they've survived, the poor bastard.'

Chapter 30

Andy Forrester stood in a room in a house in front of the fireplace. A threadbare rug was covered in soot, and logs were strewn across the floor with an overturned, rusty scuttle nearby.

'I certainly enjoy making an entrance,' Forrester said to himself, brushing his clothes down.

On the floor were bare boards, some broken and some completely rotted away. As he looked around the room he realised the last occupants of the house must have left years ago. Some of the wallpaper hung from the tops of the walls in strips, and a brown stain a couple of inches wide circled the room where the walls met the ceiling. Where windows once were mainly broken glass, with shards in piles on the floor and on the windowsills. A remnant of cloth that once was a curtain fluttered in the breeze. Above the fireplace an old 'art deco' style clock sat on the mantelpiece having long lost the ability to give the time, both hands stuck pointing to the Roman numerals for 'two' and its electric flex dangling below it, its scraggy end made up of worn cord and wire left hanging about six inches above the floor.

Two armchairs and a sofa were covered in thick dust, the pattern of the material almost obliterated.

There were no pictures in the room. A single frame on the windowsill bore no photograph although around the walls there were perfectly formed rectangles of lighter colours highlighting where pictures of some form used to hang.

Forrester could see through to the kitchen. There was a rusty kettle on the stove and faded packets of cereal covered in cobwebs sat on the shelf above. A carton of what must at one time have been milk was on its side on the work surface next to the stove.

This family must have left in a hurry, he thought and started to brush away the soot that covered his clothes.

He moved over to the staircase in the corner of the room when suddenly a loud crack gave out as a floorboard broke and he almost lost his balance as his right foot disappeared into the floor. He retrieved his foot and moved forward carefully.

The stairs creaked as he went up. It was narrow and he had to negotiate a half-landing covered in broken pottery from flower vases. At the top of the stairs he could see three doors. He went into the first. A reasonably sized bedroom with a bed, again covered in dust, with a wrought iron bedstead. A book lay on the floor by the window. As he picked it up the cover and most of the pages disintegrated and fell in a cloud to the floor. Only three pages from its middle were still intact in his hand. He tried to read them but didn't recognise the language. He carefully folded them and put them in his pocket.

The second room was a bathroom. There was a large brown stain in the basin and he tried the taps but no water came out.

A loud squawk from outside, like that of a parrot, made him move to the window. He couldn't see anything apart from the redness of the setting sun.

The third room was obviously the master bedroom. It would have been light and airy at one time with light-coloured wardrobes along one wall. He tried the drawers in the dressing table but they were all empty as were the wardrobes themselves. The mirrors on the wardrobes were dirty and covered with cobwebs.

Another squawk, followed by another. He went quickly to the window but again saw nothing. The gardens were overgrown with long grass all around, and ivy had grown up around the window frames. The house was situated in a clearing in a forest so beyond the gardens were only trees.

Forrester sat down on the bed. Why on earth would Jim Naylor come here? There was obviously nobody there now and didn't seem to have been for years. Was this where he used to live when he was a boy? He looked around for clues but found none. Maybe this was his parents' room. But that would mean the book in the other room could have been his. What language was it in – Arabic? Russian? Did Naylor study languages? Or maybe this wasn't even his house. Maybe he just wanted to visit it again – maybe a friend's or relative's.

Another squawk but louder. Nearer. And didn't sound quite like a parrot now.

He went downstairs and through the kitchen into the garden. The air was warm but humid. And a smell hung in the air like rotting vegetation. No, like rotting flesh. Some plants smelled like that. He seemed to remember that one was called the 'dead horse' arum and specifically let off the smell to attract pollinators like flies and other insects. But these were grown in tropical climates. And he was suddenly desperate to know where he was.

'Jim!' he yelled. 'Jim Naylor!' The forest seemed to echo his shouts but no response otherwise. Over to his left the tall grasses moved as a small animal blundered its way through in Forrester's direction apparently unfazed by his shouting.

'Jim, can you hear me?' he bellowed into the forest. No response. He lifted his face to the sky and as he shouted Naylor's name again the grass to his right started to rustle. He didn't notice it. His focus was on the sun that was high in the sky. The redness wasn't a sunset. It was the colour of the sky.

A memory – as if of decades ago – came to him. Of an overall reaching to connect a cable to Naylor's head. Of the overall falling to the floor. Of panic as he had slid away from Naylor's body and slipped through the fireplace to where he was now.

Suddenly the grass at his feet danced around and something scraped his right ankle. As he looked he saw small droplets of blood form through his trousers as something slid quickly away into the grass. He winced as the pain hit him. Crouching down he turned up his trouser leg to see what seemed like teeth marks.

Then he slowly began to realise. He'd been separated from Naylor in the lab and he wasn't where he was supposed to be. In fact, he was where he definitely didn't want to be. Siren-land.

He made a dash for the house. As he crashed through the kitchen the heat from the fire in the living room made him stop in his tracks. He stared at the three creatures standing on their hind legs on the hearth as blood trickled into his shoe. Lizards standing a meter tall with yellow and black markings bared their teeth and squawked.

'What's that on the screen?' Sheena asked urgently. 'Looks like blood on his leg.' She turned to look at Forrester lying on the couch. He was perspiring but no signs of blood.

Jenkins threw a glance at Lambert. 'He's in the wrong place. He's back with the lizards and the trees. Shit,' he hissed. 'Get him back.'

Forrester looked around the room and spotted an old bedpan rusting in the corner. He made a lunge for it and one of the lizards jumped at him catching his face with its claw.

The face on the screen exploded with blood and Sheena jumped back and screamed putting her hands to her mouth in horror.

Forrester swung the bedpan smashing it into the side of the lizard's head, sending it sprawling across the room dazed. He wiped the blood from his right eye in time to see the second lizard come at him. Before he could swing again the creature had leapt on him knocking him to the floor and he instinctively grabbed it around the neck and pushed its head away hard to keep it from his face. Its short claws were slashing in the air trying to reach its prey. Out of the corner of his eye Forrester saw the third animal start to circle around the back of him and between the second's legs he saw the first start to get to its feet again, shaking its head from side to side. It turned to face him and bared its teeth in a snarl. From behind him Forrester heard the third creature do the same. He looked at the fireplace where flames still leapt up preventing him from returning to the laboratory. He cried out in desperation.

'Sheena! Help me.'

The monitor showed Forrester's heart rate racing. Sam was already placing the paddles on his chest and shouting 'Clear!' Forrester's body spasmed and fell back.

Forrester felt his heart almost coming through his chest. A sudden sharp pain shot through him but then it was gone as quickly as it came. The beast on top of him was still struggling despite Forrester's hands gripping tightly around its neck trying to squeeze the life out of it. And as he squeezed harder the thing exploded, skin and flesh and sinew and brain splattering against the walls, against the other two lizards, against Forrester and against the beautiful woman standing in the corner of the room, her legs reaching down beyond the floorboards buried in the earth below.

The other two lizards turned briefly to face the new adversary and then they too exploded across the room, one after the other.

Forrester was still on his back, gore now dripping from his hands. He jumped up quickly to face Sheena-Siren.

'Remember me?' she asked, provocatively. 'You left a little quickly last time. I was quite offended. I thought you were going to stay with us.'

'As a tree? I don't think so,' and he looked quickly at the fire. Could he push through the flames without getting burnt alive? The fire raged. He didn't think so. He needed to quell the flames – he needed water. He ran through the kitchen and back outside towards the woods. He pushed through the first fifty yards, low branches and undergrowth tripping him as he went. He turned to face the house as Sheena-Siren called after him to go back. As he turned his jaw dropped.

Now, between the house and where he stood, four of the trees, two large and two no more than saplings, stared back at him. The faces of a man, a woman, and two young girls were unmistakeable in the bark. He guessed that they had been there for quite a while. He guessed they'd been there since they'd all run from the house, their belongings under their arms, several years ago. In the undergrowth Forrester picked out a couple of photographs that had fallen from two suitcases that were now open on the woodland floor, damp and covered in moss and lichen.

Chapter 31

Temporary fences had been erected all around the hole about a hundred and fifty yards away from it, and soldiers guarded the single gap where army vehicles were steadily rumbling in. The wreckage from the 757 was strewn for hundreds of yards further to the north but the erection of the fence had aroused the curiosity of news reporters. Most were firing questions on the eastern side of the perimeter through the fence to some high-ranking army officers sitting with Fuller in a jeep on the inside.

'Colonel Hilton, what caused the crash?'

'We are not in a position to say for sure. The Flight Data Recorder will be sent for analysis when the experts from the Air Accidents Investigation Branch get here shortly.'

Inside the fence an ambulance suddenly bolted towards the exit, the driver skilfully manoeuvring around patches of burning debris. The other army vehicles stopped to make way.

'How many on the plane?' the journalists continued. 'Any survivors?'

'The plane was almost full. We understand there were two hundred and thirty-two people on board, including the crew. We are still searching for survivors as you can see,' Hilton waved his hand in the direction of the wreckage. 'But we don't hold out much hope. There seemed to be little warning – no mayday calls – and out here in the Dales there was never much chance of the pilot being able to make a successful emergency landing.'

'And why the fence?'

'Some sensitive documents on board, government material being carried in the cockpit for security reasons. We obviously need to cordon off the area until the documents are found and returned to a secure place.'

'What sort of documents? Are these related to the upcoming election?'

This last question came, of course, from someone planted by the army to ask just that, so that Colonel Hilton could confirm, as he did, that he was unable to provide any further information save that, should the journalists be able to read between the lines, that the Conservative prime ministerial candidate would not be too happy if the documents were not found quickly.

The truth was, of course, that John Fuller had got approval for the area to be cordoned off after emerging from the cave. The Stabu seemed stable where they were and at a distance of a hundred and fifty yards the glow from the hole was not visible nor the humming audible, especially given the winds gusting across the moors.

As Fuller also thought to himself the other truth was that the upcoming election might be a candidate short if he couldn't find a way to stop the Stabu.

Colonel Hilton finished the interview with the journalists by telling them again that the experts from the AAIB would be arriving shortly with the Secretary of State for Transport, and would give a detailed statement to the media. He didn't really care if this was true or not at this point. His jeep sped over to a small green marquee, where he and his men jumped out and gathered inside with Fuller around a table in the centre of the tent. One of the soldiers served up steaming mugs of tea as the men shook their brightly coloured cagoules to remove the wetness from the drizzle that had fallen all day and hampered the rescue operation. They hung them on makeshift coat hangers and sat at the table.

'You know about Stabu and how they operate?' Fuller asked Hilton after the two had taken a couple of sips from their mugs.

'Never seen one,' Hilton admitted, 'but, yes, I know what they can do.'

'And as you are now aware we have a cave full of them underneath us.'

'Got orders to assist you in whatever way you feel is appropriate, Fuller. I obviously have to abide by army regs and protect my men but other than that. What do we do?'

'We need to find out what these things are so we can stop them. We need to capture one.'

'OK, I understand. But I thought you said earlier there were hundreds of them. Why not just seal the cave and bury the lot of them? I've had explosives ferried in and our experts are on hand.'

'Because,' Fuller raised his voice a little, slightly exasperated, 'we firstly don't know whether these are all there are, and secondly whether crushing them is a solution anyway, especially given that they appear to be able to pass through the walls of the cave. We'd never know whether we'd destroyed them all or not. No – we need to be able to disable one and study it to find a way of dealing with them effectively and permanently.'

'OK. So the container has arrived; acid-proof at least against all the ones we are aware of, and made of non-conducting material as you requested. The steel net's loaded into the launcher. What's next?'

'We need to get them down into the cave and hope the Stabu don't work out what we're planning, or if they do, pray to God they're not interested. The net won't last long – the Stabu's acid will eat through it quickly. We need to wait for one to separate from the pack, net it, and then get it into the container. So as soon as we have it in the net, unhook this end of the cable and feed it through the aperture in the side of the container. Dragging the cable back through we can get the net and the Stabu into the container, the bung screwed back into the aperture, and the lid sealed.'

'And what if the other Stabu don't like what we're doing and decide to attack?'

'Then, I guess, we're back to your idea. We get out quick and we blow the cave and hope it does the trick. But you know that the cave system around here is supposed to be the biggest in the UK?' Fuller opened out a large piece of paper in front of him and spread it across the table, smoothing it out with his hands. 'Now,' he stabbed with his index finger at an area in red ink on the paper. 'This is in red because I've had it added to the original map of the cave system. Where the Stabu are now is a new discovery. Something opened up by the crash. It looks like it might join up with two other, smaller caves here,' he pointed to its northern boundary, 'and here.' He pointed south-east.

'Then I'll have my men place their charges so as to ensure these are sealed in the explosion,' Hilton said confidently. 'They won't escape, believe me.'

Thirty minutes later they were assembled at the cave opening.

'So don't forget.' Fuller spoke to the small group of soldiers with cables clipped to their waists, the ends tied to vehicles' winch mechanisms. 'We ease down on to the floor of a tunnel that leads into the cavern where the Stabu are. Lay the charges around the cavern. If we need to blow up the place then that order comes from me.'

Two of the soldiers looked at Hilton who nodded back his agreement. Fuller continued.

'Direct the launcher at the group of Stabu. When one breaks away the order will be given to fire the net. Again that order comes from me. I'm guessing you will have a little less than a minute to get the creature into the container before the acid burns a whole in the net and the Stabu gets away. Or gets us. Either way – don't let it happen. And don't go near the walls in the cavern. And if there is any threat of attack from the Stabu just get out. Any questions?' he looked around the group. Nothing. 'OK – let's go.'

The smoke had long cleared and the faint glow from the Stabu below was illuminating the entrance to the cave. Hilton had wanted to place a steel cover over the hole to stop the Stabu escaping but Fuller had rejected the idea. If they needed to get out quickly he wanted the exit clear, and besides the Stabu were not going anywhere. In fact, if they did they could go through the walls anyway.

The cable winches clicked on and whirred into motion slowly lowering five solders and Fuller into the cave. A minute later they stood on solid ground again.

The tunnel floor was damp and slippery, and greenish in colour. There were rivulets of rainwater running down the walls from pools formed high on ledges, where the drizzle outside fell and came together in crevices in the earth, permeating through to the cave below. As the men stood in silence they listened as droplets of water fell into a puddle somewhere in the darkness. The glow from the cavern threw light on to some stalactites and stalagmites and their shadows together with the shadows of the men danced as the horde of Stabu swayed together from side to side. The humming droned on.

The men unhooked the cables from their harnesses and from the net launcher and container, and moved towards the cavern. Two moved off in front to place the charges and two eased the launcher forward, carrying the container between them. One walked behind the launcher with Fuller. All except Fuller were armed with L85 rifles, the soldier walking with him having an Underslung Grenade Launcher (UGL) mounted beneath the barrel of his weapon which he held loosely in front of him as he moved forward. The UGL was designed to fire 40mm high explosive, smoke and illuminating rounds out to a range of 350 metres to destroy, obscure or indicate enemy positions. In this case the group had no idea what it would take to hold these creatures back if things went wrong and they needed time to escape. Whoever fired off a grenade would need to be accurate. Hitting the stalactite of Stabu was one thing. Missing it and setting off a rock fall blocking their exit or, worse, bringing the cavern in on top of the men was another.

Fuller's group reached the cavern and the horde of shimmering silver went quiet for a few seconds, and the soldiers froze. But the humming soon continued. The net launcher and container were set in position and the men watched the mass of creatures, waiting for their opportunity.

The closest Fuller could get to likening the creatures to those he and others might recognise was to bats, and he wondered whether the Stabu had the same radar-like sensory skills for moving around the cavern or whether they navigated by sight given the glow from their bodies would light their way. He watched as bat-like one of the creatures hovered a couple of feet from the bottom of the group and then scrambled up towards the top, merging again into the mass. The soldier with the UGL instinctively tightened his trigger finger but eased it again as the creature settled back.

A bright wide crack of whitish-blue electricity arced from top to bottom of the stalactite, and two smaller jagged arcs shot across from right to left, and then top-left to bottom-right. The two soldiers with the net launcher jumped but then relaxed again after a few seconds.

The air was cool but not cold. Fuller allowed his eyes to drift around the cavern, and he could see the outlines of the two soldiers on the periphery of the darkness laying their charges. He looked up and could see the bulbous bases of some stalactites lit up by the glow from the Stabu but the tops disappeared upwards into the black. Other needle-thin formations cast wand-like shadows, which danced across the walls. Oranges and yellows and reds with tiny hints of blue and green here and there were illuminated on the ceiling, on the walls and on the ground around the Stabu. Elsewhere there was just darkness. His gaze fell across a face in the cave wall. He found himself wondering why there was always a face to be found in cave walls – whether or not anyone else could see it. Crevices and holes and protuberances making up mouths and eyes and noses. The face stared back at him defiantly until a tap on his shoulder returned his gaze to the Stabu, and he watched as one of the creatures hovered around ten feet from the group slowly moving further away.

'Is it going through the wall?' the soldier with the UGL whispered in his ear.

'Probably,' Fuller whispered back.

UGL crouched behind the men with the net launcher. 'On Fuller's orders…' he said to them, turning to look at Fuller.

'Wait,' Fuller hissed. 'Wait.'

The creature continued to hover, slowly revolving so that its snout started to describe a circle around the walls of the cavern.

'What's it doing?' UGL asked.

'Not sure,' Fuller responded. 'Maybe it knows we're here. Keep still. Can they get a shot?'

'Yeah – no problem.'

The creature was still revolving appearing to survey the blackness until it came to a stop facing the men laying the charges. There was a crackle on UGL's radio. 'Sir, the thing's staring directly at us. What should we do?'

At the same time Fuller saw one of the two raise his rifle towards the creature.

'Tell him not to shoot,' Fuller told UGL urgently. Too late.

Ten or twelve loud cracks thundered across the cavern accompanied by a huge flash of light as shots ricocheted off the cavern wall. From the base of the mass of creatures to the top they fanned outwards like the plume of an atomic bomb. The cavern was completely illuminated now as the Stabu filled its space like locusts.

'Get out!' Fuller stood and shouted. 'Get out!'

One of the creatures rained acid on the soldier who had shot at it and the smell of burned flesh and acrid smoke filled the air as he screamed out in pain and dropped to the floor, writhing in agony. His buddy grabbed the collar of his uniform and started to drag him towards Fuller's group, finger on the trigger of his rifle shooting randomly into the air around him. Fuller ran to help but before he could get there white light arced around the soldier's head as a bolt of electricity streamed through him and he was dead before his charred body hit the ground.

Fuller continued his run towards the injured soldier. From behind him he heard screams of pain as the Stabu pressed home their attack on the soldiers with the net launcher. One of them triggered the launcher as blinded by acid he reached out for something to cling on to. The net slithered out, the metal of the net scraping against the barrel of the launcher, glanced off a creature on its sweep across the cavern and then falling to the floor empty.

UGL shouted at Fuller. 'Leave him - we need to blow the cave. Now!'

Fuller reached the soldier who was clutching his face with both hands, writhing on the ground screaming. Blood poured through his fingers. Fuller grabbed his lapels with both hands and started to lift him on to his back. A bright green flash and a sharp pain made him jump and drop the soldier, who was now dead with a hole in his chest surrounded by charred flesh. The arc of electricity projected by the creature had glanced Fuller's right shoulder on the way through to the soldier and now Fuller turned to face the attacker. It hovered in front of his face. Fuller could almost believe the creature recognised there was something special about him. Large, dark, fly-like eyes sat either side of its head far behind its long snout. Out of its snout the creature had extended its proboscis, which had the appearance of a sharp metal tube and out of which acid dripped and steamed on contact with the floor. Behind the creature the other Stabu still flew about crazily searching for more intruders. Fuller heard UGL's desperate voice again from fifty yards away.

'Fuller? I need to blow the cave. Run for God's sake!'

Fuller knew running wouldn't help despite his urge to do so. He held the soldier's L85 in his hand but shook involuntarily as he realised just to raise it would be suicidal. The creature continued to stare at him as he very slowly backed away, allowing the rifle to slip quietly to the floor. From the corner of his eye he realised another Stabu was hovering to his right, also apparently examining him. Then two more glided in from the left. And another from above. And another. All hovering and humming close to his head. He took another step backwards but stumbled. As he tried to regain his footing he fell back heavily. He screamed in pain as he hit a mound of rock making contact with his damaged shoulder which he grabbed with his left hand, his right hand flailing backwards and passing through the wall of the cave.

As his mind raced his body suddenly jolted towards the wall. His eyes widened in surprise. Something or someone had gripped his hand on the other side and tugged it. He could feel another warm hand clenching his firmly. He tried to draw his hand back but it was held fast. The Stabu's humming suddenly grew louder and it lunged at him at the same time as a fiery light engulfed ten or twenty of its brethren, thunder boomed across the cavern, heat seared his legs and dust clouds swirled around him. At the same time he was heaved bodily through the wall by a strong force the other side and then found himself on that same side staring back from where he had just come from fully expecting the Stabu to pass through the wall and kill him. He stood up and stared, fully prepared to try to run, for a full ten seconds. Nothing happened. No Stabu appeared. Another ten seconds. Nothing. Whoever was holding his hand now released it and he turned quickly to see who had saved him from a painful death.

Chapter 32

Andy Forrester stood staring at the faces for a long time. They had long since lost their human form and become part of the woodland habitat but their features were still clear. The man's expression was defiant but frightened. He had obviously struggled against the transition until the end desperate in the knowledge that his family had been plunged into the earliest, slow stages of a bizarre form of fossilisation. The wife was weeping; the two girls wide-eyed, terrified with their sapling trunks entwined with their mother's.

Within the trees the skulls, teeth and bones remained, their calcium perfectly formed within the wood, but the remainder of their bodies had turned into the tree materials themselves. Veins and arteries had become the phloem and xylem carrying nutrients and water around the organism, skin had morphed into the outer layer of the bark, and flesh, muscle and sinew had become the wood itself. And in this new tree form, boughs, branches and leaves had then developed and photosynthesis now took over to provide food. Some of the knots in the trunks of the trees were hand- or foot-like.

At some point in the future the trees would fall and rot. The skeletons of the family would become exposed as weird fossils.

Forrester didn't want to become a fossil. He turned again and started to run. He needed to find water to dowse the flames that raged in the fireplace so that he could get back to the lab. Undergrowth snapped and cracked under his feet as he bounded over ferns and bushes and fallen branches. He made a mental note of his way back to the house and turned from time to time to remember the way, and to check she was not following him. No sign.

Suddenly he could see sunlight glinting on something shiny up ahead. He raced on but then stopped suddenly as, looking down, he saw his foot had crashed through someone's skull. As he surveyed the scene around him he picked out the whiteness of more and more bones on the ground. Human bones. There was a stench in the air.

He slowly raised his eyes with grim anticipation and gasped audibly as tens of lifeless frightened faces stared down at him. From some of the trees the shapes of arms and legs were clearly visible making up macabre branches and roots, covered in bark but unmistakeably human limbs underneath.

How could Nature let this happen he found himself asking. It was grotesque.

Something snapped behind him. He turned, saw nothing, and ran on towards the sunlight. Every third or fourth step now snapped bones, or kicked or cracked skulls.

'Anything more?' Jenkins demanded. 'His legs OK?'

'Nothing, apart from his heart still racing wildly,' Sam replied, intently staring at a couple of monitors and then back to the 'Eye'. 'He has some cuts to his legs – teeth marks on one of them – but otherwise no damage. Or change.'

The technician had returned to the couches and was sweeping up the broken syringe with a dustpan and brush as he looked sheepishly in the direction of Jenkins and Lambert.

'Jesus,' Lambert hissed at him, red-faced. 'You fucking moron!'

The technician quickly finished sweeping then moved towards the door of the lab and was gone.

'He's obviously returned to where he went before. Presumably nowhere near where Naylor is and probably not even the same world.' Lambert whispered to Jenkins.

'When he gets back we'll try again. But this time you do the prep,' Jenkins ordered.

Forrester leapt over another bush towards the bright sunlight and suddenly stopped dead. He stood on a precipice in a clearing about thirty feet from the shining surface below. A huge lake spread out before him and he squinted as reflections dazzled and partly blinded him. He needed to get down to the water.

'Shit,' he said loudly. He had nothing to carry it in. He looked along the edge of the lake to his left and picked out three log cabins five or six hundred yards away.

The drop to the lakeside was fairly steep but with outcrops of stones that gave him purchase as he squatted and gingerly eased himself downwards. He stopped briefly as a few stones crumbled away under his right foot and fell to the beach below. He sat for a few moments removing the belt from his trousers and looping it around a small rock to mark his way back.

He continued downwards, heat starting to make him sweat. Then, with fifteen feet to go his left foot kicked into the air as the ground beneath it gave way. He started to fall and instinctively grabbed at a thick knobbly stem growing out from the overhang, his body swinging underneath it. As he looked to see what had saved him he saw his thumb inside the woody mouth of a baby's screaming face. He drew his hand away in terror and fell backwards, tumbling on to rocks and stones and falling heavily on to the packed sand. He sat upright and grabbed at his chest as pain shot through his body.

'Two cracked ribs,' Sam announced, staring at the 'Eye'. 'Someone's hit him or he's fallen or something similar.'

'How bad?' Lambert demanded.

'Can't tell. He's still breathing and no broken limbs. His legs are badly bruised. Small cut on the back of the head.'

The smell was stronger now and rank. As he sat there, wincing with the pain and with teeth gritted, he could hear a slapping sound. The source of the sound was a waterfall in the opposite direction to the cabins cascading from the top of the rock face to the lake below. The ground and shrubbery around the foot of the waterfall was covered with a brownish, gelatinous goo and as he turned to look at the lake itself it was smooth, but not like a millpond as the surface of water would be, but like treacle.

There was no way this was going to put out the flames. Judging by the nauseating, gaseous smell he thought to himself this was more likely to turn the fireplace into an incendiary bomb and he'd never get back.

Maybe one of the cabins still had a supply of real water. Obviously humans lived here – at least once upon a time – and they must have had water.

He eased himself up using one arm as he still clung to his chest with the other. He limped hurriedly towards the cabins taking a full ten minutes to get there, stopping often to catch his breath.

Further away from the three cabins down the beach stood a group of nine trees, six fairly large and mature, one smaller and a couple of saplings. Forrester was happy that their faces were pointed in the opposite direction.

In the first cabin he tried both taps in the kitchen. Brown, pungent goo slopped into the sink. He tried the tap in the bathroom with the same result. He lifted the top of the toilet cistern but the inside was empty and dry.

The second cabin was next door to the first and of exactly the same design. Again, normal sources of water within were either emitting the goo or were completely dry.

The third cabin looked older and was set back towards the woods. He went up to the door but realised when he tried it that the previous occupants must have expected to come back one day as it was locked. The timbers of the door were old and some had started to rot. He shoulder-charged the door without thinking and screamed as he fell to his knees clutching his chest again. His breaths came is short bursts.

He eventually stood slowly and faced the door again. He kicked with his left foot catching the door hard with the bottom of his foot near the latch. The frame split slightly but nothing more.

He kicked again, harder this time, and the latch splintered and exploded as the door flew open into the cabin and bounced back off the wall, hanging ajar. Forrester eased into the cabin. It was a different layout to the previous two, and obviously older. Exposed metal pipework led out upwards from the bath and basin in the bathroom and from the sink in the kitchen. He tried the cold tap in the kitchen and was dismayed to see brownish liquid drip from it. But after a few seconds the tap coughed and spluttered out brown, brackish water and after a minute more there was clear water gushing into the sink.

He hurriedly scoured the cupboards and found a metal bucket under the sink which he pulled out and placed on the floor. He searched again but found nothing suitable. He eventually recovered a plastic bucket from the first cabin, and also grabbed the flex from the clothes line. Tying the buckets together he filled them with the water and eased the flex across his shoulders. Lifting the full containers made him wince again but gradually he could stand upright and he headed outside.

Behind the third cabin was a set of wooden steps leading to the top of the rock face. He couldn't imagine not being able to find the house again from the top, and struggling anyway to think of how he was going to climb up the slope that he came down, he decided to go up the steps.

The climb was arduous, and sweat trickled down his back under his shirt and off his forehead into his eyes. He stopped several times to wipe his face. The smell got bearable again as he reached the summit and he bent to place the buckets carefully on the ground to rest.

He didn't move from his stooped position. He looked in horror as tree roots started to curl themselves around his feet and ankles. As he watched he felt from over his shoulder strings of creepers drop lightly on to his body and then leaves gently brushing his face. He felt a tingling on his forehead and cheeks as the drug from the tiny barbed hairs on the leaves started to kick in.

He knew he had to get away quickly. He propelled himself forward out of the coils that snapped tight just as he freed himself, and rolled on the ground. He picked the buckets up, one in each hand, and headed diagonally into the woods, bones and teeth and skulls crunching beneath his footsteps. After a few hundred yards he dared to look back and saw that she was following him in human form, slim, beautiful but lethal. He'd still managed to keep a lot of the water in the buckets by the time he got sight of the house through the trees and he was feeling sick but relieved. He stopped briefly to confirm that she was still following, but not gaining on him. He could see the glow of the fireplace in front of him, which now spurred him on.

As he went to move again he found his right foot wedged in a rabbit-hole. He tugged his leg but the foot wouldn't budge and he'd started to feel weak and light-headed. He could hear snapping from a distance somewhere behind him as Sheena-Siren closed on him. He quickly put the buckets on the ground to free his arms to pull his leg from the hole, almost throwing up as he did so. He grabbed at his ankle but felt wood where flesh should have been. He instinctively felt his other leg which was now the same, with roots splaying out from his feet tearing through his shoes and into the ground.

He screamed as he looked towards the house and the glow of the fireplace and as his skin started to turn to bark he realised that the fireplace – his gateway back to the lab - would be the last thing he would ever see.

Chapter 33

Julie Furness released Fuller's hand and he turned to face her.

'You…you just came through that rock face,' she stuttered incredulous.

'You pulled me through?' he asked. 'Where is this? Tenerife?'

'Well your arm suddenly appeared. Over there,' she pointed to the wall of rock leading down from the top of the cliff. 'Bill and I often sat here looking out at the whales and dolphins so I just thought I'd spend a little while here again when your arm suddenly appeared. I thought I was going mad. Again.'

'Again?'

'It happened earlier. Your hand appeared and I held it but you must have pulled it back.' She slapped at the rock face. It was solid. She tried harder but it didn't budge. Her legs suddenly gave way and she found herself in a squatting position, holding her forehead and sobbing.

He moved quickly to her. 'No, don't worry. We'll figure this out. You're not going mad, trust me.'

He held her tightly while he looked back at the rock. He reached out and touched it very slowly and it started to give way as he pulled his hand back quickly. He found himself wondering if the Stabu could or would follow him through. He became aware of the pain in his feet. His shoes were charred and he kicked them off to reveal burns on his socks and blisters on his ankles and heels.

'That must be how the Stabu travelled to the island when they attacked Bill. They used a portal. But that was close,' he said to her. 'If you hadn't pulled me out I'd be dead. They blew up the cave. We need to get to the villa and make a phone call. Is the ADS on? It might give us a little time,' he said but then remembered that it hadn't helped Goldsworth in the end.

'Colonel Hilton? John Fuller,' he said into the phone. 'What happened in the cave?'

'Who is this?' Hilton demanded.

'It's really me – John Fuller. I escaped.' Then realising the portal story could take some time to explain, 'Some people found me and have taken me to their house not far away.'

'It's a bloody miracle, Fuller. How the hell did you get out? No other bugger did as far as I know. Corporal Riley blew it to pieces – brave man. Took his own life in the process. Obviously decided he couldn't let those things escape and couldn't wait any longer.'

'Are they dead?'

'Almost certainly. Explosion was enormous.'

'Almost? Have you seen them?'

'We've got people hacking their way through to recover the bodies of our soldiers as I speak. They should be able to confirm soon. But if any of those creatures are still alive they're certainly not going anywhere – no way in or out.' *That's what you think, Fuller thought.*

'Colonel, please call me back on the mobile when you get more news,' he beckoned Julie over, and as she whispered her number he repeated it aloud to Hilton before putting the phone down.

Hilton frowned in confusion at the scrap of paper on which he'd just scribbled the information from Fuller. Looks like a bloody foreign number to me, he thought.

'How did you know it was me? I mean it could have been anyone you were pulling through,' he asked.

'Recognised the watch,' she replied. 'I noticed how nice it was when you came to see me in ParrotWorld. Kind of hoped it was you even though it scared me to death when it happened the first time.'

Fuller had sent Julie back to Tenerife when the PM called him about the plane crash. She'd only been home a few hours.

'The Stabu are in a cave in England. Yorkshire. Hundreds of them.' He switched the radio on in the villa to catch the 6.00pm news which was always broadcast in English for the tourists and ex-pats.

'An underground explosion has been reported at the scene of the plane crash in the North of England. It is thought that aviation fuel may have escaped from the wreckage, seeping into the cave system and somehow igniting. Some soldiers who were in and around the caves looking for missing classified government documents lost their lives in the explosion. We go to our reporter at the scene...'

'If those creatures that killed Bill originated from that cave, they must have travelled through some sort of portal. The same one you pulled me through. So theoretically they could follow me here.'

'A sort of gateway? Like the one you came through when you – er - came together?' She couldn't think of another way of putting it. Fuller had explained to the best of his ability what he thought happened between Fuller and Naylor. He'd told her he felt strongly there was a reason, a purpose, but didn't know what it was yet. That living in this world – in her world, with twin moons and Stabu – was difficult and exciting at the same time for that part of him that was Naylor. But the feeling that the two men – or the two versions of the same man - would never separate again was nagging at him, as was the fear that Naylor would never be able to return to the lab and to his world.

'But I came through a gateway between parallel worlds. The Stabu move geographically within the same world. This one. They're not fast. Deadly, but not fast. Creating a portal obviously gives them the means of getting close to their victims quickly. And it seems that I now have the ability to travel through the same portals.'

Then a thought suddenly dawned on him. Fuller had known for a while that those in this world who have had near-death experiences and were apparently able to go through gateways to visit other worlds as a result – Goldsworth for example - were being targeted and destroyed by the Stabu. So what about those who'd had similar near-death experiences from other worlds that came to this one? Naylor when he transitioned into Fuller, for example? Is he a target now in this world because he may be able to travel back? Is this nature's way of stopping people crossing over from one world to another – the Stabu?

His throat tightened and he started to perspire. If Stabu were put on this world – in Fuller's world - as Mother Nature's caretakers to prevent movements to other parallel worlds, but they can't stop movements from other parallel worlds – like Naylor's - to this one, then what does She do about that?

Maybe he'd now committed the ultimate sin. The question of what happens when there are two occurrences of the same person in the same world had been answered now - or at least experienced. And he couldn't help thinking that the punishment for the ultimate sin was probably pretty harsh.

'We need to go,' Fuller said sharply and pulled her to her feet. He borrowed a pair of Goldsworth's shoes that Julie had just packed and they were soon driving quickly towards the airport.

'In Naylor's world I was on a couch in a laboratory in a Research Centre. It was a different world to this one but not by a lot. So the Research Centre must be here as well. In this world I mean. In England. Maybe run by a guy called Jenkins and his sidekick Lambert. With some subjects – 'guinea-pigs' - but they obviously don't have you as one of them.'

'Me?' she asked. 'Why would I be in a Research Centre?'

'In Naylor's world there is a woman called Sheena. Your middle name, right? She's a subject in Jenkins' facility. She is you. I'm convinced of it – same looks, same hair, same physique. She's identical. Even likes birds – she has an aviary there. I wouldn't mind betting her middle name is Julie.'

'She sounds cool. I'd love to meet her.'

Fuller gave her a disapproving look.

She continued. 'But if we go to England, what about the Stabu? You're presenting yourself to them on a plate. And anyway, suppose it doesn't exist here your Research Centre. Do you have a number for them?'

'Got to take the risk. I need to understand more about what these guys are trying to do. And I need to find a way to get all what I've learnt back to Naylor's world. We need to stop them doing more experiments until we can find a way to stop the Stabu. And, no, this isn't the sort of place that gives out telephone numbers so I can't call them.'

'Stop the Stabu? But I thought Colonel Hilton just told you they were dead.'

'They're not.'

'How do you know?'

'I just do.' He said bluntly, and drove on quietly.

Four and a half hours later they were leaving Gatwick in a hire car. It was dark and he had difficulty remembering the route but eventually arrived at the site of the Research Centre.

But it wasn't there. They both stood and stared across a leisure park that held a couple of cinemas, a bowling alley and various eating places. A group of half a dozen teenage girls screamed with laughter as they bumped into each other coming out of a Wetherspoons pub next to the cinema. Couples walked quickly clutching their collars around their necks or huddled under umbrellas. A young man shouted obscenities to his friend across the car park then laughed and ran to his car. Neon signs glowed and their reflections wobbled in the puddles on the ground as the rain fell. Moons, Starbucks, Chili's, Nando's. But no Research Centre.

Fuller turned ninety degrees and stared. And then again. And then twice more. He recognised nothing.

'This is definitely the place?' Julie asked, hands clasped tightly in her pockets, hair bedraggled and rivulets of rain running down her face.

'Definitely. Right town. Right street. But wrong result.'

'Maybe it wasn't built in the same place,' she offered. 'Maybe Jenkins lost out in the race for planning consent and the leisure park won. Maybe his facility is somewhere else.'

'Maybe – but where?'

'Surely you know the right people to ask in your position. You report to the Prime Minister for God's sake. You said Jenkins was doing work for the government in Naylor's world – the MoD you said, right? Can't you check with them? If it's the same in this world then they must know him.'

'Good girl,' he said excitedly. 'Pass your mobile.'

He dialled a couple of numbers before finally locating who he needed. When he finished he closed the mobile and passed it back to Julie.

'Well,' he started with a satisfied smile on his face. 'Mr Robert Jenkins heads up a facility about three miles from here.'

'Great,' she enthused, shivering slightly. 'But it's 11.30pm. It's dark. It's raining – hard. The likelihood of finding him there now is pretty minimal, and we're both tired. Let's just find a hotel and go over there in the morning. The hotel will have an ADS system. We'll know if we get any unwelcome visitors.'

As they walked quickly to the car Julie's mobile rang. She answered and then passed it to Fuller.

'Fuller? Colonel Hilton here. It's taking ages – pretty awkward to work in those cramped conditions. My chaps are telling me they're almost in but it's been raining all day and it's flooded the passageway. Besides they're all pretty exhausted. We're getting the pumping equipment set up to run overnight so they can start again first thing in the morning. But strange thing though. Where they've started to break through the rocks a shaft of light is coming from inside the cave.'

Chapter 34

'But we've never had any of them die before,' Sam protested. 'And Forrester was one of the most susceptible – he could go across almost at will. What chance do any of the others have of finding Naylor?'

'But we know why it happened,' Lambert insisted. 'Had that idiot not forgot to connect the cable Forrester could have found Naylor.'

'You don't know that. He could have ended up turning into a tree again anyway, even if we had kept them in contact. You have no evidence that they would end up in the same place and now that you have a death on your hands we need to stop and re-think. I'm putting the project on hold. Sheena's not going across. Not until we do some further analysis on all of this.' Sam threw his clipboard on to the desk angrily.

'It's not your call as to whether we stop the project,' Jenkins butted in. 'And besides. Just think about it. OK, so Forrester was in obvious difficulties when he went across...'

'Difficulties?' Sam blurted out, red-faced. 'Difficulties? He turned into a bloody tree! That's a little more than just 'difficulties'. He had a heart attack. It killed him.'

'Whoa,' Lambert put his hands firmly on Sam's shoulders and looked him in the eye. 'What Bob is trying to say is that Sheena's scenario is different. Her environment is friendly, with birds and monkeys and waterfalls and stuff. It's got to be psychological. Forrester obviously had some issues to end up where he did. Sheena is a much more balanced individual. And she wants to reach her father so she's desperate to try again despite what happened to Forrester. We won't be forcing her to do anything she doesn't want to do.'

'Her jungle is where she jumps from. The environment there – granted – appears to be friendly.'

'She even dealt easily with that snake last time,' Lambert offered.

'But that doesn't tell us what environment she will find on the other side. What about where she ends up – assuming she crosses over?'

'What she will find on the other side, Sam, is the same environment that Naylor went to, and you've just confirmed to us yourself that his readings are normal. Heart rate fluctuating a little from time to time but still healthy, right? And he's been gone a lot longer than Forrester was.'

'Agreed,' Jenkins said. 'We go ahead in the morning. But we make sure the two are wired together this time. No more accidents.'

Jenkins and Lambert stood looking at Sam waiting for his confirmation. Eventually Sam sighed in resignation. 'OK. But any sign – any sign at all – that she's in trouble and we shock her back. Right?'

'Right,' the two said in unison.

Chapter 35

Sheena recognised the song was a Led Zeppelin track but couldn't think which one. She'd sneaked into the studio and stood watching Tom perform. He was good, she thought. Very good.

The fingers of his left hand moved crab-like up and down the frets while those on his right deftly picked at the strings. The volume was high and his body swayed to and fro to the beat of a backing track providing bass guitar and drums. Headphones hung limply over a microphone stand. In a small glass-panelled room banks of switches and knobs lay untouched, two neon displays showing graphs of red and green that danced up and down in time with the music.

Tom gritted his teeth as he stretched to reach a series of high notes, wheeling the guitar into the air as he did so. He opened his eyes again and stopped playing as he saw Sheena at the door.

'Excellent,' she called across to him smiling. 'Bravo!'

'Well, I'm no Jimmy Page but I try.' He lifted the guitar from around his neck and put it down on a stand. He walked slowly over to Sheena. 'So you accepted my invitation then? I don't give access to this room away lightly you know.'

'I know.'

'So you're going across then?'

'I've got to, Tom. You know that. We've talked about it loads of times. It's the opportunity I need to try to put things right.'

'With your Dad?'

'Yes.'

'And what happened to Andy doesn't faze you? Jeez – I can't look after the parrots if you don't come back. I wouldn't have a clue.'

'Don't worry. I've made arrangements. I've got people from the zoo and the RSPB ready to come in. Lambert's OK with it.'

'I bet he is,' Tom said frostily. 'He needs you to find Jim and bring him back. That's why they're being so good to you.'

'How do you know about Jim? I thought they only told Andy and me.'

'I know my way around this place, love. I haven't been here this long without working out how to keep abreast of things.' He reached out and grabbed a can of beer from the shelf and took a swig. 'Oh sorry. Do you want one?' he nodded towards the can.

'No thanks. No alcohol before a trip. You know that.'

'Yeah I know. Don't take much notice of that though. You've still got to enjoy life, haven't you?'

A minute or two passed as they stood in the dimly lit room, him taking the occasional sip from the can, eyes staring at the floor. She finally posed the question that she'd been wanting to ask him for days.

'So why don't you get included in their tests any more? Why do you never go across?'

His eyes met hers briefly. He transferred the empty can to his left hand and crushed it before tossing it into a bin. 'Great for stretching the hand,' he laughed. 'Helps to keep it supple for reaching those difficult chords. Really must drink more beer,' he laughed and danced back to the stage.

She ran after him, put her hand on his shoulder and wheeled him around to face her.

'I mean it,' she said sternly. 'I want to know. When I told you about my father the other day you were upset too. And not just for me. For you.'

He looked at her for a moment and then jumped on to the stage, lifting the guitar around his neck again. He carefully placed his fingers on his left hand and strummed loudly and the sound vibrated around the room. He changed the finger position again and strummed. And then again and waited for the sound to fade away.

'There you go,' he announced triumphantly. 'The three basic chords for rock and roll. Simple but so powerful. You can do so many of the great songs with just those three.' He started to pound out some rhythmic blues to prove his point.

'Talk to me Tom,' she shouted.

He started to make up and sing his own words to old rock and roll numbers.

... the Three Wise men ......Three Sides of a Triangle ......the Holy Trinity ......the Sun, the Moon, the Stars.........Air, Fire and Water.......

He stopped suddenly and gazed into the distance. 'There are so many clues, Sheena. Three is such a powerful number. It's there for those who want to see it.'

'Tom,' she started, exasperated. 'Tom, please talk to me. I don't understand what you're saying. You're talking in riddles.'

His face turned towards hers and he sat slowly on the edge of the stage. As he did so he brushed the strings of the guitar and a howl echoed across the room. He eased the jack plug from the instrument and let the cable drop to the floor. The sound died and they sat for a minute in silence, his guitar across his lap.

'I've been across, Sheena, and there's no way I can do this any more,' he said suddenly. 'I'll keep stringing them along. I know they want me to go across again so I feed them titbits of information from time to time about my 'trip',' he laughed. 'Yeah – and what a trip.'

Over the time she'd known him she'd guessed he was a drug addict. A junkie. He'd been secretive and defensive most of the time she'd been there. He'd been caught taking something on more than one occasion and threatened with eviction from the programme. She saw the dark humour in his reference to his 'trip'.

'So why do you stay? I mean, if you're not planning to go across again?' she asked.

'Oh Sheena, my darling, I will definitely go across again. Besides, do you think it's the same wherever you start your trip – in here or out there? Do you seriously think you only go across when you're in this place? You could be anywhere out there – and with no safety net.'

'I never really thought about it. But why only once more then? I don't understand.'

'They can help you on your way, and they've got all sorts of gizmo's to monitor you when you get there. But they don't have any magic potions. And, as we know now, they sure as hell can't guarantee getting you back. But – on the other hand – they do bring people back. I know from bitter experience. The difference is that they will not have the opportunity to bring me back again,' he wagged his finger in Sheena's face, 'even though I'm taking a punt that I'm better off here when I go, with so-called experts, than out there with no family or friends around me.'

She guessed his addiction had driven a wedge between him and the people he would normally have expected to rely on in life, as happened in that scenario so often. Must be a lonely existence when you reach that state she thought to herself.

'Aren't you married or with anyone?' she asked.

'Married? No. Never been married. Got a kid out there somewhere though. Little boy.'

'Let me guess – Tom junior?'

'No. She wouldn't agree to calling him Tom. Poor kid had no name at all for a while and then got christened Heath after some American that she moved in with.'

'I'm sorry. Must have been hard. Do you see him?'

''Fraid not. She managed to get a restraining order against me. Meant she got custody and I got to see them fly off to Texas or somewhere.'

'But you should fight it!' she exclaimed indignantly. 'You've got rights.'

'No chance,' he said quietly. 'Anyway, don't have a lot to offer him really. He's better off where he is. Could teach him the guitar I suppose but that doesn't get you anywhere unless you get lucky and stay straight. I was lucky for a while – never that straight though. And after the split in my relationship I was a wreck. The others in my band felt sorry for me, sure, but couldn't carry me any more. I was screwing up at all the gigs. Couldn't stay focussed. Ended with a huge argument after we turned up as a support act to one of the big bands at the time at Wembley Stadium. I was pissed as usual – well, most of us got a little merry before a show. But I was really out of it. Forgot the songs. Played the first chorus like this,' he nodded at his guitar, 'without the bloody thing plugged in. A right mess. Don't blame them for turning on me. Wrecked their best chance of making it that night I can tell you. I ended up whacking the lead singer over the head with an empty vodka bottle and spent the night in the cells. Would have probably still been there if he'd pressed charges. So my best mates were now gone and I had no money.'

'What about your family? Didn't you have someone - mother and father? Brother? Sister?'

'Nope. Never had brothers or sisters. My parents divorced when I was little and went their different ways. Dad was always in trouble with the police and eventually Mum got fed up with it and left him. I spent most of my childhood in foster homes.'

'Have you tried to find your mother and father?'

'Loads of times. And I knew where each of them was once. But the bottom line is that they don't want to know. Been too long – too much water under the bridge. They've got new lives…'

He tailed off and stopped suddenly.

'What's the matter?'

He looked at her for a second. 'Shouldn't you be getting prepared for the big journey?' he changed the subject, and brightened. 'You want to be your best if you're going to meet your Dad, right?'

'No, I'm not going until you tell me more. Why are you only planning one more trip? And what's special about the number three?'

He lifted the guitar slowly from around his neck and placed it on the stand. He pointed to the control room. 'Got some tracks of my own in there on CD. Probably crap but keeps me amused. Do you sing? Could do with some good vocals.'

'Tom!' she shouted at him.

'OK, OK. I should probably tell someone anyway. Stop me losing it completely.'

'Good, so tell me,' she said defiantly.

He slumped down on the edge of the stage again. 'I've only managed to get across once. Didn't quite make it the first time when I nearly died of an overdose. Shortly before the Wembley fiasco when Angie left me I ended up in hospital. Didn't mean to do anything stupid - just didn't know what I was doing. Drink and drug cocktails kept me going so that day blurred into night, night blurred into day, et cetera, et cetera, until I overcooked it in the corner of a dingy pub one night. Weird thing was I could see myself asleep in the pub as I floated off, speeding up until everything was a blur and I was on stage at a gig. But playing well – not like Wembley. The crowd were going wild and there were thousands of them. Indoor arena somewhere but I didn't recognise it. I was playing the encore apparently – we'd been off twice and the crowd still called out for more. Don't ask me how I knew all that, but I did. I found myself playing in a band belting out one of my own tracks as the very last number of the show. And I knew that the crowd was the key to me getting to somewhere important. To where I needed to be. So I decided to do the old stage leap into the crowd. As I landed in their outstretched arms I could see the floor and it was glowing. Like - luminescent. I wanted to reach into it but the audience threw me back on the stage so I threw myself off again. Every time I landed in their arms I tried to reach the floor but they tossed me back on stage again. I was so frustrated I could have screamed. But then I was suddenly rushing somewhere else and I woke up with a jolt with doctors around me in hospital.'

'So what was through the floor?'

'Well I found out while I was at this place,' he said looking all around him. 'The first time they put me under I floated off again to this same gig, playing the same venue and belting out the same song. Except this time when I leapt off the stage into the crowd I seemed to pass through their hands and as the light from the floor rushed up to meet me, getting brighter and brighter, I put my hands in front of my face to protect myself. A split second later and I was now in a living-room of a house. I seemed to haven fallen in through the open patio doors. I suddenly realised it was where I lived when I was young. Hearing the noise my mum came in from the kitchen and asked me why I had come home from work. Was I ill? It was really weird. But,' and he grabbed Sheena's hands and held them tightly, 'I was there, Sheena. I was really there – no dream. I made up some excuse for being home and my mum made me some soup. I ate it and we talked all afternoon. It was as if she'd never left me. Dad had always wanted me to work at his place and that's where I worked in this 'other world'. Mum expected Dad in from work around 6-ish. And then it dawned on me. What would happen when I walked in from work with Dad to find me talking to Mum? But I couldn't care. And there was no way I was ever walking back out of those patio doors. Even when the doorbell rang I wasn't bothered. I was too happy. But I needn't have worried because Mum called out that it was just Angie and Tom. Sheena - my little boy walked in and ran up to me and threw his arms around my neck. And Angie hadn't run off with any American. She walked into the room, kissed me and told me what a great day she'd had and that she'd found a fantastic dress to buy to wear at my sister's wedding.' Tom stopped. His voice had become croaky and his eyes moist. He took a while to continue.

'At 6pm the clock in the hallway chimed and I heard keys in the front door. I was so excited but still very wary. Dad came straight into the lounge, looked at me and told me that I should have said I wasn't feeling well and had to come home. He'd have driven me if he'd known rather than me getting the train. He hadn't even noticed me arriving at the office, never mind leaving. But how did I feel now? Better, I told him. I still wondered what had happened to me or rather to the other 'me' but I didn't seem to care that much. We spent the evening as a family around the table eating the meal Mum had cooked for us all, admiring Angie's new dress, little Tom sitting on my knee and Dad telling jokes about the people in his office.'

'Oh Tom. It sounds…it sounds wonderful. But I thought you said you didn't have a sister? And your dad was always in trouble.'

'It's true. I don't have a sister and my dad *was* always in trouble. Actually, a bit more than just trouble. But it was different in this place, Sheena. He had an office job, for

God's sake. Dad – in a regular job? No way! He was in prison so often I hardly recognised the man on the odd occasion that he came home. No, the only time he would have been in an office was at midnight to burgle the safe. But you're right – it was wonderful and different in this place. Better than that,' he said. 'But then it all ended. I'd been gone too long, and that Sam bloke had zapped me. I came back to the couch in the laboratory with a dread that knocked me sideways.'

'Jesus,' she said, 'no wonder you've been down. But where does 'three' come into it?'

'It's generations, Sheena. The previous generation – your father and mother. The current generation – you, your brothers and sisters. And the future generation – your children. The power of the three generations – it's the lifeblood of human existence. Will always be the way. I didn't realise until I went across but having my Mum and Dad and my son and being able to see them when and as often as I liked. And somewhere close there was a sister too! And all the while I knew that I didn't want to come back here. And that they'd had to shock me to drag me back kicking and screaming. I can't take that again. It tore me apart. So, no, Sheena – when I go again I will stay. Forever in that wonderful place.'

'But how? They'll just bring you back. How will you stop them?'

'By topping myself, love. By the only way I know to guarantee dying in peace with my family around me, and not of another overdose alone in a gutter somewhere.'

Chapter 36

'Idiot man!' Fuller shouted, slamming the mobile down on the table.

'Coffee or tea?' the waitress asked them.

'I'll have coffee,' Fuller barked.

'Don't take it out on her,' Julie said. 'I'll have tea please,' to the waitress, who wobbled off inviting them over her shoulder to help themselves to the breakfast buffet laid out in the far corner.

'The guy won't listen,' Fuller continued. 'I told him to wait until I get there before breaking through into the cave. I really need to question Jenkins before I go up there. He may have some information. But Hilton insists he has dead soldiers in there and he needs to have the bodies retrieved as soon as possible. If that arsehole just blunders in he could have more dead bodies than he can cope with before long.' Fuller seethed as he took a sip of the steaming black liquid. It wasn't coffee as he knew it but it was hot and wet.

'But those creatures can't be indestructible – nothing is. Maybe the light is coming from something else. Maybe sunlight. The explosion may have brought down the ceiling.'

'I got Hilton to take another reading on the magnetometer. It's still off the scale. That means they're still in there.'

'If they can pass through walls then that's probably how they escaped the explosion. They'd have been blown to pieces if they'd stayed in the cave.'

'Julie – when you pulled me out there were only split seconds to spare. I actually felt the heat on my feet. Hell, you saw the state of my shoes yourself! There was no way they were going to get out of that cave before the explosion happened. They're not that quick. And they certainly didn't come through the portal after me.' He shook his head slowly.

'There's got to be something else. Perhaps a defence mechanism of some sort.'

'Like a shell maybe? Armadillo, kind of thing?'

'Maybe,' he said, staring at the tablecloth. 'Or a forcefield? We need to find out. But first,' he grabbed her hand holding her teacup and moved it to her lips, 'we need to get to the Research Centre. Come on, drink up.'

The building was as he remembered it when Lambert drove Naylor to meet Jenkins. Except here Jenkins and Lambert wouldn't recognise him. He didn't even have a decent reason for them to see him yet. He did report to the PM though – should be good enough, he thought.

'Please tell Mr Jenkins that Mr Fuller is here to see him from the Ministry,' he announced to the security guard, who bent to look at his passenger. 'With my assistant, Ms Furness.'

He guard returned to his hut and made a phone call. Within a couple of minutes he was back with two plastic badges, each bearing a nondescript blue 'V' for visitor with a number underneath.

'Park in Area D and report to the security desk inside. Mr Lambert will be waiting for you.'

As they entered the building a man that Fuller recognised welcomed them. Fuller managed to restrain himself as he went initially to call him Chris which would have raised awkward questions since they'd not actually supposed to have met before.

'Mr Jenkins wasn't expecting a visit today,' Lambert said, more in the way of a question rather than a statement.

Fuller glanced quickly at Julie and then, 'We're just entering the budget cycle now. We need to know what we're planning on spending next year.'

'Not an issue is there?' Lambert sounded concerned.

'No, not at all. Relax. It's just a new system that we've introduced and I have to ensure all programme details are recorded. Scope, forecast and actual costs, resource requirements, anticipated close dates, et cetera, et cetera.'

'I would have thought you guys would have all that information regarding this facility,' Lambert questioned.

'We have it, but we insist on having experts verify it from time to time, and we're using those experts – myself being one of them – to take the opportunity to complete a verification as we add the details to the new system. To ensure we start with clean data, so to speak.' Fuller was quite pleased. For an off-the-cuff excuse for being there he thought he'd done pretty well, although he wasn't sure Lambert was totally convinced.

'OK, sign in and I'll take you to Mr Jenkins' office. You were lucky to catch him. He's meeting someone in London later this morning.'

Martha's face suddenly appeared in Fuller's – or rather Naylor's - mind, and he grimaced.

The meeting with Jenkins' proved fruitless. Fuller already knew most of what they were doing in the facility – at least the official version. He asked for a tour of the labs in case he could learn something there.

'Once through these doors and into the lab all of the activity will be monitored,' Jenkins was saying to Sheena. 'You'll be sent to sleep on one of the couches as you've been before, the only difference being you will be connected by a couple of wires. Nothing painful or dangerous, trust me. If you go across and you locate Jim scratch yourself or prick yourself on the top of each thumb and make sure you draw blood. Your recognition of your changed physiological state should be reflected in the 'Eye' and the fact you've done it on both thumbs at the same time will be specific enough to give us confirmation that you've made contact.'

'And through these doors are the labs where most of the study is undertaken,' Jenkins was saying to Julie. 'I don't like to call them experiments because that expression tends to carry some sinister undertones and there's absolutely nothing sinister in the work that we do here as you'll see. In fact, I'm sure you're going to find it very interesting indeed.'

'OK, so you're ready for this?' Lambert asked Sheena.

'Ready as I'll ever be,' she replied slightly hesitantly as they walked towards the door to the lab.

'OK, so you're ready for this?' Lambert asked Julie.

'Ready as I'll ever be,' she replied slightly hesitantly and they walked towards the door to the lab, ahead of Fuller.

Lambert moved in front of Sheena, took a plastic card out of his pocket and swiped it against a green box on the wall next to a door that hissed open quickly and caught an overall standing on the other side off-guard. The door crashed into him and sent a yellow folder he was carrying flying into the air, its contents spewing across the floor. The overall apologised for getting in the way and knelt to quickly retrieve the papers.

Lambert walked ahead of Julie and took a plastic card out of his pocket.

'Wait!' Julie shouted out, too late. He'd already swiped the card and the door had opened quickly, banging into an overall and throwing a yellow folder into the air.

'What's the matter?' Fuller asked her. Lambert stood looking at one of the technicians who was now apologising and collecting sheets of A4 that had scattered across the floor.

Julie turned to Fuller. 'I knew that was going to happen. I knew that guy was going to be there and that the door would hit him.'

'Interesting,' Lambert looked now at Julie. 'Déjà vu. Have you experienced that before?'

Julie thought back. 'A couple of times, I guess. The last time was a while ago when I drove into a lorry reversing out of a factory when I was taking my father to hospital. Couldn't stop it happening but somehow I saw that it would.'

'Were you both OK?' Fuller asked, concerned.

'Oh, sure. Just dented the car. And my pride a bit too I guess. Got a rollicking from the old man but no real harm done.'

'And – Julie – you say there have been other times?' Lambert was interested.

'Yes, a few actually,' she confirmed.

Lambert glanced sideways at Jenkins who now gave Julie a smile and put his arm across her shoulders. 'You know Julie,' Jenkins said, 'the study of the causes of déjà vu is one of the streams of work that we are focussing on here at the moment. It's an interesting point regarding whether people who experience it appear to see things a split second in advance or a split second afterwards, or actually appear to live the same event in parallel. You may be able to really help us out a lot with this.'

'No!' she shouted, twisting to push his arm away. The three men looked at her in surprise, as her face started to blush with embarrassment. 'Sorry. Er, no thanks,' she now continued more quietly. 'It's really not something I'm interested in doing right now.'

As they walked back to the car after the tour Fuller asked eagerly, 'What was that all about? You nearly broke his arm.'

'John, there is no way I'm getting involved in any of that stuff. You saw those couches and all that equipment in the lab – freaky, or what? Especially after all that Bill went through. But sorry if I over-reacted.'

'No, don't be sorry. That's OK,' he said. 'No problem. And as for the déjà vu – I've been there myself. Episode with that bank raid. Can be scary.'

'Yes, but this was strong, John. I really felt this – as though I'd been in the same situation before. Same when I hit the lorry when I was taking my father to the hospital. But I guess we didn't get any clues this morning to help with the Stabu did we?' she said. 'A bit of a waste of time.'

'Yeah, 'fraid so. I need to get to that cave to see what's going on. I'll drop you back at the hotel and shoot over to the airstrip.'

Chapter 37

Sheena lay on her back on the couch, the liquid from the syringe coursing through her veins. She was vaguely aware of the activity around her but was only now wondering what would really happen if she came face to face with her father. And she knew damned well that if she came across Jim Naylor first that there was no way on earth that she'd be giving them any indication. No scratches, no pricks, no nothing.

Giant ferns were brushing against her bare legs as she walked. A small brown scorpion scuttled ahead of her and then disappeared into the undergrowth as a bird wheeled and squawked overhead. She saw it swoop and dive through the branches of the trees and then climb again but even though she cupped her hands over her eyes the strong sunlight prevented her from being able to make out what type it was. She vaguely realised as she moved on that she needed to find two people this time, not just one. To meet her father had always been her goal but she felt she'd someone else to find now although she couldn't quite think who that was. She turned quickly as a crash in the undergrowth prompted the tops of some tall grasses to dance and jump about in a wave that moved away from her and into the jungle. Three small birds in its path flew up in the air but then slowly settled again as it passed.

The heat was intense. Rivulets of sweat ran down the back of her neck as she hacked down two tall bamboos and suddenly saw the glint of a waterfall high on the hillside across the valley in front of her. Below her and to her right was a rope bridge slung across the valley. She started to follow a rough track leading down to it.

'Anything?' Lambert asked.

'Not yet,' Sam replied tapping a dial with the end of his pen. 'Give her time.'

After a few minutes she reached the bridge. It started to sway precariously as she stepped carefully on to it. She looked down through some broken slats and peered at the valley floor hundreds of feet below. Flies buzzed around her head.

She trod carefully but the bridge swayed wildly with every step. She let her eyes follow the bridge to the other side of the valley and then up to the waterfall and the pool of water beneath. She knew she had to get to that pool but was becoming daunted by the challenge lying ahead of her.

She moved her feet from the middle to each end of the slats and moved forward slowly. It seemed to steady the bridge considerably. She slid each foot forward, one after the other, and over the supporting ropes. Gradually the chirping of the crickets behind her grew fainter, and she was aware that a cooling breeze had got up and was tossing around some strands of her hair that had come free from inside her bush hat. She had to spit some ends from her mouth from time to time and others stuck to her cheeks. She was now at the middle of the bridge, still sliding her feet along the edges. The bridge had started to sway again but gently this time in the breeze. She held on tight to the ropes.

'What's happening?'

'Mr Lambert, when anything happens I'll tell you,' Sam said, irritated that the man kept interrupting his readings.

Something darted forward over her right shoulder and up high into the sky. The bird she'd been watching earlier was now soaring above her. As she looked up it dived and disappeared under the bridge in a long, majestic sweep, appearing again almost in slow motion, ahead of her and away to the left until she lost it in the haze.

Another ten steps and it suddenly reappeared from under the bridge, screeching sounds emanating from its large, open, pointed beak as it swept up past her to her left, with sharp talons outstretched and dark eyes encircled with yellow staring at her as it passed.

Her heart started to pound and the involuntary movements she'd made to avoid the bird had set the bridge swaying to and fro. She dropped slowly to her knees and started to crawl as fast as she could. After a few yards one of the slats snapped suddenly as her left hand pushed down on it and she found herself reaching out into space. She fell forward with her face pressed down on to the wood. The bird moved quickly towards her and grabbed at her outstretched arm tearing a small piece of flesh from her wrist. She screamed and pulled her hand back, rolling over and cradling the injured wrist to her chest. Blood trickled against her shirt.

'What's that?' Lambert said pointing to the screen. Sam was already peering at the image of Sheena's wound. He instinctively looked at Sheena lying still on the couch with both left and right arms completely intact, and then back at the screen.

'I don't know. Heart rate is up. REM up.'

'Is she through?' Lambert demanded.

'No signal yet – I don't think so,' Sam said.

Sheena pulled the hem of her shirt from her shorts and began to rip off a wide strip. She wrapped it around the cut and tied it tightly. She got to her feet unsteadily and scoured the sky desperately trying to locate the bird. She found it high and to the right and plunging down towards her. She squatted quickly to try to retrieve the machete but the bird was on her too quickly. It slashed out viciously and as she ducked it caught her left shoulder, and in the same motion ripped her hat from her head diving off to the left. The hat fell tumbling and swaying in the air, reducing to the size of a pinhead before disappearing into the tops of the trees below. As she felt her shoulder with her right hand, blood seeped up through her shirt and the sight of her bloodied hand as she withdrew it made her heart beat even faster.

'Look!' Lambert was shouting at the screen.

'I can see it!' Sam shouted back at him. 'I'm bringing her back. She's not where she's meant to be. I told you,' he fumed. 'Some friendly environment this turned out to be.'

The bird screeched loudly as it came round again. Its huge wings now blocked out the sunlight as it slowed to a hover for another attack. Its two talons stretched down towards her and she could almost smell the creature. She fell to the ground and a split second felt like an eternity as her good hand scrambled at the slats on the bridge trying to locate the machete. Her palm and fingers closed around its handle and with a scream she rose up and swept the blade first across one of the bird's legs and then deep across its breast. Blood gushed and flowed and feathers fell around her as the bird shrieked and then gurgled as redness trickled out of its beak before it fell first on to and then over the side of the bridge. The black mess, so majestic a few minutes before, fell like a huge wet rag and crashed into the greenery below. A small stream of blood dripped from the raised machete on to Sheena's face. She wiped it on the cuff of her shirt and then started to run. She no longer feared the swaying of the bridge or the rotting of the slats. She ran as fast as she could until she reached the other side of the valley where she leapt off the bridge and collapsed by the side of the pool, exhausted.

'Wait!' Jenkins bellowed.

'You said at any sign of trouble .....'

'I know what I said, Sam.'

'What are the readings?' Lambert asked.

Sam slowly moved to one of the consoles glaring at the two men. He checked one read-out and then another, surprised. 'Her heart rate is dropping towards normal. REM down.' He turned to the face the men. 'Seems like whatever trouble she was in has gone now.'

'She's a strong 'un. Not like Forrester,' Jenkins said. 'We need her to carry on so leave her.'

Sheena sat staring at the sunlight glinting off the waves in the pool as she gradually regained control of her breathing. She could hardly bear to think that she may have made it this time and she needed to compose herself. Across the other side of the pool gallons of water fell from above in steely, silver strands into misty clouds, and then thundered into the depths below. The roar of the falls almost drowned out the birdsong chattering around the clearing. Huge dragonflies in greens and blues and reds darted this way and that around the edge of the pool. Over to Sheena's left the ground around the pool rose up into a rocky outcrop about fifteen feet high. Protruding from this mound was a ledge that hung out over the pool. Small pink flowers were growing in tiny groups on the rocks and on the ledge. A couple of minutes later she was standing on the top of the mound looking down at the ledge. She removed her boots and socks and kicked them away. With a little difficulty she took off her shirt and threw it behind her. She undid the buckle of her belt and let her shorts fall to her ankles. Stepping out of them she then slipped off her panties and stepped naked on to the ledge, letting the warm sun bathe her lithe, young body.

After a few minutes more, with a single skip she launched herself off the ledge and into the pool.

Chapter 38

'Great that you found them, and I haven't seen hide nor hair of them in the last 48 hours,' the Prime Minister was saying on the phone. 'Hilton says he got them. Believes they've been blown to pieces.'

'And how does he explain the strength of the magnetic force still being recorded there?' Fuller responded from his seat in the private jet.

'He says it's probably something to do with the minerals in the rocks.'

'Sir, those minerals in the rocks brought down a 757. Besides if it was something in the rocks why would it suddenly happen now? That flight path has been flown thousands of times. Did he tell you there was a glow still coming from inside the cave?'

'Yes, he did.'

'And?'

'He doesn't know but his team should be through in about an hour and he'll investigate and report back.'

Fuller glanced at his watch. 'OK, well I'll be touching down in about twenty minutes. I'd appreciate it if you could tell him not to do anything more until I get there, sir.'

'OK. But I want confirmation one way or the other as soon as possible. If those bastard things are finally gone I can start getting my life and this country back on track again.'

Fuller replaced the phone in the seat-holder.

'How's the boss?' Julie asked from the seat next to his.

'He's nervous but wants to believe there's an outside chance he's clear of those things now.'

'And you don't think so, do you?'

'No. Unless I'm mistaken we've still got a serious problem on our hands.'

'Nothing compared to the serious problem you'll have if the PM finds you've sneaked me on to this plane,' she sucked her cheeks in mockingly.

'Cheeky bitch!' he laughed. 'I was the one trying to throw you out of the car back at the hotel. I lost that battle, didn't I?'

'Don't think you fought that hard,' she smiled.

'Maybe not,' he conceded.

She leaned over and kissed him gently. 'Thanks.'

'For what?' he asked.

She didn't answer straight away but sat returning his smile and thinking through the events of the past few days. 'For not turning into someone I wouldn't love any more.'

'I didn't have a lot to say in that,' he replied. 'I – that is Jim Naylor – kind of fell into me – that is John Fuller - and this is the result.' He pointed with outstretched palms at his chest and cocked his head in mock egotism.

'But Jim Naylor could have been anyone - or anything. John Fuller interested me from the time he first came to my house' she said.

'Interested you?'

'Don't tease. You know what I mean. But supposing your alter ego Jim Naylor had been a right villain, even a murderer? What would that have made you now?'

'Someone looking for a young victim probably,' he said as he slowly reached for her neck with both hands, and stared at her wide-eyed for a moment. She thumped him in the chest and he dropped his arms, spluttering and laughing.

'No, seriously. Maybe it means,' she continued, 'that whatever the attributes of an alter ego in one world, all the alter egos in all other worlds are the same. Good guys are good guys, bad guys are bad guys.'

'Hey, I'm only just getting my head around this myself. Maybe you're right but I wouldn't count on it. The theory goes – and it's got lots of eminent supporters - that there are so many points at which another universe is created there is bound to be some in which 'good guy goes bad'. Imagine starting at the trunk of an old, established tree and working up along every bough and every branch and every twig and every leaf – so that each leaf is a different universe. And the growth of every new twig spawns opportunities for many new universes. You just got lucky with me!'

'I'll drink to that!' she said, taking a sip of her orange juice.

But Fuller had started to think through what this actually meant for him. In his tree analogy the lab where he still lay as Naylor, presumably, with Sam and Lambert and Jenkins watching over him, was in a world represented by a single leaf somewhere else on that tree. He had no idea how to jump from this leaf to another, and even if he did, which leaf should he target?

Hilton stood next to one of his men who held out protective clothing and a helmet and rope for Fuller as he pulled up in the jeep.

'You'll need to find some for me as well,' Julie called out.

'I can't allow any unauthorised civilians in there,' Hilton barked, irritated that he'd had to wait in the rain for Fuller to turn up.

'No, it's OK,' Fuller said to him. 'She'll stay in the control room.' He looked sternly at Julie as she glared defiantly. This would be no place for you, he thought as he roped up.

'And can we proceed now?' Hilton asked sarcastically, fuming. Fuller didn't answer but led the way to the hole in the ground and switched on the torch on his helmet. The rain tapped incessantly on his headgear and cagoule as he eased himself down into the hole and after a few minutes dropped gently to the floor of the tunnel. Water splashed up as both feet landed in puddles. He looked around until his eyes gradually started to become accustomed to the darkness. One of Hilton's men dropped lightly on to the tunnel floor behind Fuller, who positioned his head so his torchlight shone on his right arm and hand which he held up to motion the soldier to stand still. Fuller stood listening. There was no humming, just loud trickles of water and the constant plink plink as droplets fell from the roof and ledges into the puddles below. The air was cool, and the dampness seemed clogging making it difficult to breathe.

As Fuller moved his head towards the cave where the Stabu had been, shadows danced and fell on the walls of the tunnel. The ground underfoot was slippery and Fuller took a couple of careful footsteps before he found drier, flatter rock to stand on.

'Where are the others?' he asked.

'Over there,' the soldier pointed. 'Around the corner at the entrance to the cave.'

As they got to the corner an area of light projected on to the wall, and the shadows of men's heads moved across it. The source of the light was a small gap in a rock fall that had almost completely covered the entrance to the cave.

As the group by the entrance saw Fuller approaching one of them came to meet him and his torchlight briefly exploded in Fuller's eyes.

'Sorry,' the Sergeant whispered. 'Can we carry on digging through now?'

'Wait. I want to know what you've heard and seen since you've been down here.'

'The only thing any of us have seen is the same light that you see now. Can't tell where it's coming from. We put a small probe through the gap in the rocks but the camera just shows an empty cavern, lit up by something that we can't get to. No sounds whatsoever.'

'Can I see?' Fuller asked.

'Yeah, on the screen over here.' The Sergeant directed him to a flickering rectangle of light showing an infra-red image of the cavern beyond. It took Fuller a few seconds to realise the floor of the cavern was now under water forming a large lake. The light coming from beyond the cavern reflected on the surface of the water and up across the ceiling and walls. As Fuller manoeuvred the cable through the gap in the rocks the screen showed the different parts of the cavern. A huge stalactite hung from its ceiling and Fuller recognised this as where the throng of Stabu hung down last time he was here. He moved the cable around some more but found no trace of any of the Stabu. Some dark shapes floated in the water. Fuller reeled as he realised they were the bodies of dead soldiers. He guessed also that one or two mounds around the edge of the lake were what remained of others.

'No humming or droning noises?' he asked.

'Nothing,' the Sergeant answered. Fuller continued to study the screen and move the cable around.

'OK,' he eventually said. 'Carry on digging. But be quiet. And I want to check every few minutes so be prepared for my signal.' But every time activity stopped there was no sound at all and nothing on the camera. No indication of any life in the cavern whatsoever.

Eventually sufficient rocks had been removed to allow Fuller to scramble up and over into the cavern. A few armed soldiers followed. Fuller knelt at the edge of the water and peered in. The water was crystal clear and about fifteen or twenty feet deep, and the lake floor was clearly visible in the beam of the torchlight. As he scanned the floor he could see no debris to suggest the creatures had been destroyed. Just the bodies of the soldiers. He raised his head and shone the torch around the edge of the lake. Again no sign.

'So where are the creatures?' the Sergeant asked.

'Good question,' Fuller replied, shining the torch towards the source of the light. 'Bring a couple of your buddies.'

Fuller started to lead the way around the side of the lake. He pressed his back against the cave wall as he reached a point where there was hardly any ground between the wall and the lake. His hands clung on to small outcrops on the walls to stop him falling into the water as he eased slowly around the curve of the cavern. The slippery surface underfoot, and the wetness of the walls, made progress difficult.

Suddenly his right foot slid and shot out in front of him over the water, and his body fell away from the wall the fingernails of his right hand scraping rock as he instinctively sought some safe purchase. He felt a hand grab his left arm tightly and pull him back.

'Go careful,' the Sergeant whispered. 'That water looks cold.'

He eased onwards towards the source of the light. At each step his feet were standing on small stalagmites and nodules of rock that glistened with moisture. His hands and arms started to ache with the pressure of holding on to the walls.

Eventually the ground widened and he was able to walk forward for a few yards. The light coming from the next cave now made the torches unnecessary so he switched his off. The Sergeant joined him and did the same.

Something's definitely happened here, Fuller thought to himself. The portal's gone. Last time he would have fallen through the walls rather than being able to cling on to them.

'Explosion must have opened that up over there,' the Sergeant pointed across the lake to where an underground river was now gushing in. 'We'll need to move quickly if we don't want to get trapped down here.'

'OK. Get some of your men to take the bodies out. But I need you and two others with me. We need to check where this light is coming from.'

Julie stood shivering at the mouth of the hole, both hands clasped around a plastic cup filled with tomato soup.

'Sure you don't want to go inside?' Hilton asked her, pointing to a wooden building erected as the control room. 'I need to check on a few things.'

'No, I'm fine here thanks,' she answered and then watched Hilton disappear over to the hut.

Stretchers and harnesses started to come up from the hole one after the other, their contents covered in blankets and small tarpaulins. Each of them were placed in the back of army ambulances and then driven away.

'Any word from Fuller?' she asked one of the soldiers. He didn't answer. She guessed not.

The last stretcher was unhooked from ropes as a stream of soldiers came out of the hole like ants from a nest. One of the younger ones stood and pulled off his harness and helmet and gloves, threw them to the ground and then ran into the bushes to throw up. Moments later another soldier had his arm around his shoulder and was helping him stumble away from the site.

Julie looked back at the hut. She pulled some wet hair away from her face. Through a window in the hut she could see in the brightness that Hilton had a telephone to his ear and was mouthing something animatedly as one of his men stood listening to the conversation. She stood now in silence apart from the spatter of rain and took another sip of soup as she gazed into the hole. Several minutes passed as the sky darkened and the rain started to fall even more heavily.

Her feet slipped as she eased herself over the edge of the hole. The harness was a little big for her but she'd tied the rope around her body a couple of times to secure it. She could do nothing about the helmet which wobbled precariously on her head, the torchlight dancing crazily. Although she was light, the gloves had already been used and were muddy making it difficult for her to grip the wet rope. She descended slowly into the darkness.

After about five minutes she came to a halt as she felt the end of the rope beneath her.

'Shit,' she murmured under her breath. She peered down and the light from the torch found the ground about ten feet below her. She carefully untied the rope from around her body and dropped. The thud as she landed echoed around the tunnel and she bounced to the side landing safely on her back in a pool of water.

'Shit again!' she hissed.

The light was coming through the hole in the rocks and as she clambered through she nearly fell forward into the icy water of the lake. She edged around carefully to the right keeping her body pressed against the cave wall. She could hear distant footsteps of men clambering over rocks coming from the direction of the light. Water lapped around her boots as she moved on, step-by-step shuffling sideways around the wall, gripping on to cracks and nodules for support. Gradually the ground rose and she found herself easing up on a very narrow ridge that eventually stooped at a point about fifteen feet above the surface of the water. Finding nothing for her right foot to move on to she looked down and saw in the torchlight that the ridge just fell away at the side of her.

Anxiously she looked around but could see no way forward. Her hands and fingers hurt from having to grip so tightly to the cave wall. She looked down at the water which she could see was deep and cold. Rivulets of rainwater were running down the wall behind her and into her collar and down her neck.

She could only just hear the footsteps now as they moved further away.

'John!' she suddenly cried out, exasperated. 'John, help me!'

The footsteps stopped. Her heart was now pounding in her chest as she felt her grip start to weaken. Her heels were on the ridge but her toes were overhanging the water and her knees were shaking from the effort of standing in such a precarious position.

'John!' she shouted, louder. Her ears strained for a response but heard only silence.

Her right hand slid from the wall as the ground under her right heel gave way. She twisted in mid-air to try to grab something to save her but there was nothing and she plummeted head first into the icy water.

Her ears were filled with the sound of bubbles and a roaring noise was accompanied by shock as the coldness hit her face and hands. She involuntarily opened her mouth but managed to avoid taking in water as a severed arm, charred at the shoulder, danced in front of her face. She kicked hard to get away from it, wide-eyed and terrified. She kicked once more and the roaring and the bubbles stopped as she broke the surface.

John Fuller watched in amazement from the edge of the water as Julie came to the surface, arms flailing and spluttering but with a shimmering image of another female figure coming up with her and all around her, identical in appearance but hazy, ghost-like and naked.

Chapter 39

An overall ran into the laboratory. 'Quick! He's in a coma!' he shouted breathlessly.

'Who is? For God' sake, can't you see we're busy,' Lambert called back not taking his eyes off the monitor.

'That Tom guy. He's taken something and is out cold.'

'I'll stay here,' Jenkins said to Lambert. 'Go and see what's happening.'

Lambert trotted behind the overall as he scampered back to the accommodation block. The overall pushed open the door to the dormitory to allow Lambert to squeeze past into Tom's room. The young man lay on his bed, tourniquet around his arm and a syringe still buried in his vein. Small clouds of blood were collecting in the chamber. A red plastic card lay half in and half out of the pocket of his jeans.

'Shit, how did he get hold of that?' Lambert hissed.

'He must have raided the drugs cabinets.'

Lambert removed the syringe carefully. 'Tom? Tom? Can you hear me?' He slapped the young man's face once, and then harder a second time. No reaction. A dribble of spit glistened and ran from the corner of Tom's mouth tracing a line under his chin and on to his collar.

Tom's right hand came down hard across the strings and he knelt on the stage as the crescendo of sound boomed out of the banks of speakers behind him. The other three members of the band were energetically beating at a drum kit and crashing cymbals, plucking hard at bass strings, and screaming into a microphone with eyes tightly closed. Tom could see the faces of those near the front of the audience, some in serious appreciation and others in happy adoration, all lit up from the stage lighting. As he peered over their heads hundreds of other faces gradually disappeared into the gloom of the arena, but flickered in and out of sight as they jumped and danced backwards and forwards to the sound of the music.

The singer turned and nodded to Tom. This was the signal for the big finish both to the song and to the show. Tom was squeezing out the high notes, his left hand deftly dancing across the frets only a few inches from where his right picked at the strings like a spider in panic. He slowly stood up again and he played even faster as the drum beat got progressively louder and the cymbal crashes more frequent.

This was it - the final notes of the song. He crashed his right hand down on the strings four times in succession as the chords emphasised the last high note the singer screamed out for a full thirty seconds. The audience were going wild and the drummer was now beating at his drums standing up, ready to come down hard to end the song. As he did so, Tom crashed out one more chord then swung the guitar around the back of his body and leapt out off the stage and into the eager faces. The floor was awash with bright light and he floated through the arms of the audience and down past their legs and through the parquet blocks.

Tom's body spasmed. 'What was that?' the overall said.

Lambert didn't answer, but instead pushed a button on a microphone clipped to his collar. 'Bob? I think Tom might be across. Can we rig up another table in there?'

Tom looked ahead puzzled. The house wasn't in sight but he knew the address having lived there for a lot of his childhood. He just needed to figure out where he was now. The scene was vaguely familiar. The road ahead was narrow with dry stone walls lining each side. Around him were fields and hills that looked bleak in the fading light of the evening. A stream babbled along parallel with and to the right of the road. There was no sign of any buildings or lights of any kind, and no vehicles using the road he was on. He started to walk, pulling his jacket collar up around his ears.

The overalls busied themselves setting up a third couch and attaching cables and monitors to Tom's prone body.

'Can we retrieve this?' Jenkins asked Sam.

'Should be able to. Just means he went on a DIY trip instead of us doing it for him. He obviously didn't expect us to find him before he came back. But we should still be able to monitor his progress.'

'But why go it alone? I don't understand,' Lambert said. 'We know the guy's a junkie but Jesus, I'd want to know people were around to look after me if I went across.'

'Like we've looked after Naylor, Forrester and Furness so far?' Sam said sarcastically. 'With our record the guy probably felt he's better off alone.'

'But why go at all then? He knows it wouldn't count towards his credits. Why bother?' Jenkins asked to nobody in particular.

Tom had been walking about fifteen minutes and drizzle and poor light were now making him squint as he searched for clues as to where he was. He stopped and looked around. He felt comfortable, as if he knew the area, but he couldn't pinpoint exactly what road he was walking along or where it led to. There were no road signs of any description and no houses or buildings of any sort to ask the way. After a few more steps he suddenly noticed a single pinprick of light on a hill ahead and to his left. As his eyes focussed on it he realised there was the dark shape of a building surrounding it, and one or two others sticking up against the horizon close by. A farm.

He walked faster now and could make out a gate in the wall a couple of hundred yards ahead of him. Within a few minutes he was over the gate and beneath some trees on a track leading up to the farm. It was awkward to walk between the tractor ruts, which he could only just make out in the area beneath the trees. As the track came out into the open it became easier, although darkness was setting in quickly and the farm was quite a way ahead still and up on the side of a hill.

Eventually he could make out that the light was from one of the rooms on the ground floor. It reflected off two cars that were parked in the open close by, their normal three axles enabling their weight to be distributed more evenly to cope with this sort of off-road terrain. A four-axle 8x4 was parked in a carport, used to get over sharper inclines further up into the hills.

Tom approached the farmhouse ready to disclose the address of his home and get directions. He could hear muffled voices. If they were friendly enough maybe he could even cadge a lift. He felt sure it wasn't too far from here.

The wall of the house he faced had no door in it so he started to make his way around the side. But as he did so his foot caught in the metal of an old plough, invisible in the darkness, and his knee cracked against the frame with a clang.

'Shit!' he shouted in pain, and grabbed at his knee, pulling up his trouser leg. As he rubbed he could feel blood. He hobbled away from the plough to try to get a better look and fell back on to the ground. The voices stopped and the light from the room disappeared. He peered around in the darkness and listened to the silence.

'Blood coming from his knee. Looks like a cut,' Sam announced.

'We really need to move this scanning equipment to the next level,' Lambert said in frustration. 'We don't know if he's fallen, if he's walked into something, or what.'

'Maybe just walked into something,' Sam offered. 'His heart rate's steady so he's obviously not in any danger.'

From somewhere nearby Tom heard a door crash open with a thud on to a wall, and heavy footsteps of three or four men running on shingle.

'Bernie, put that fucking gun down!' someone shouted. It was the voice of Tom's grandfather, Harry 'Jacko' Jackson.

Torch beams danced across the plough and then on to his face and he froze as he suddenly found himself staring down the barrels of a shotgun. The footsteps stopped and Tom could make out the shapes of two tallish men and one smaller, squatter one.

'Tommy?' His grandfather's voice came from the direction of the smaller man.

'Shit, it's Tom,' Bernie Jackson said. 'What the fuck are you doing here? I thought you were down south with your mother.'

'Uncle Bernie? Granddad?' Tom said timidly as the men roughly picked him up off the ground.

'Get him in the house. Quick!' Jacko ordered the others.

Inside the kitchen of the house Ray Dean stood at the sink and threw a wet rag at Tom. 'Here you are kid. Wipe your knee. You're not hurt bad,' he said, laughing.

'So how did you find us?' Jacko asked. 'You're supposed to be home looking after your mum. Not all the way up here.'

'I d-don't know,' Tom stuttered. 'Just kind of stumbled across you.'

'Well, you can't stay here.'

'Leave him,' Bernie Jackson said. 'He's like his dad – a chip off the old block. A real Jackson. He won't say anything.'

'Dad? Where is Dad?' Tom asked. 'And what are you all doing together - in this place?' Tom looked around at the old, stained Butler sink and the cupboards almost falling off the walls.

'Well your Dad is still helping the police with their inquiries,' Deano said, 'although you know him as well as we do. He won't want to stay banged up for too long. He knows where to find us. We'll give him another day or so.'

'Banged up?' Tom said without thinking.

Bernie Jackson looked at him with a puzzled expression. 'Why have you heard from him already?'

'Er, no. I just thought he'd be out by now,' Tom lied. He decided to take a chance on his next question. 'So, are you guys going to tell me what happened? Mum won't tell me anything.'

The three looked at each other, and then relented. 'Ah, so that's why you've come. Hope you weren't followed. Well, I suppose it is your dad and you're old enough to understand. You deserve to know,' and Jacko started to explain about the bank raid that went wrong.

'...and that's why your dad is where he is. And as soon as he gets here we're all off for a holiday somewhere.' Jacko finished. Tom's eyes were moist and his voice quivered as he risked another question.

'Can Angie come with us?' he asked.

'Sure,' Bernie Jackson said smiling, and Tom's eyes lit up just for a second. 'But who the fuck's Angie?' Jackson asked, looking firstly at Tom and then at the other men for answers. Getting nothing but blank looks and upraised palms from the others he continued. 'Hey, don't worry, your dad'll be here soon trust me. No need to get upset about it. Your dad'll be fine.'

Tom's tears were for another reason all together. This was not the world he was supposed to come to. This was a nightmare. No mum and dad as he remembered them. No

Angie. No Tommy junior. He suddenly realised he needed to try again. He needed to go back.

Chapter 40

The water bubbled, hissed and steamed as the two women battled for ownership of their body. Sheena's ghost-like image solidified into her naked body as Julie vaporised around her, and then the whole process reversed again. Arms and legs whirled and flapped and smacked the surface of the water as the two women fought firstly for breath, then to stay afloat and then to stay in existence.

The three soldiers had caught up with Fuller and were witnessing the spectacle with open mouths. 'Do we go in and save her? Them?' one asked but didn't press further when Fuller stayed silent, transfixed.

Sheena was suddenly solid again and rose high into the air, arms spreading wide in an arc around her head. Julie's blue-white 'ghost' shot up through Sheena's body and they fell together beneath the surface again.

Fuller waited for them to reappear. Seconds ticked by. The splashes and waves on the surface of the water slowly receded, turning into ripples which in turn slowly calmed as the surface grew completely smooth and still again. Silence.

'Jesus,' Fuller cried out, ripping off his boots and throwing his helmet across the floor. He tugged at the clasp for his harness, which fell away behind him as he dived into the lake. He was a strong swimmer and reached the spot quickly. He kicked his legs up behind him and pressed his face under the water peering into the depths. He watched as Sheena's naked, outstretched body drifted slowly downwards away from him towards the floor of the lake. Her eyes were looking into his, pleading but apparently helpless.

He pulled his head up, and took a couple of gulps of air. He was vaguely aware of a first splash, followed by a second behind him before he took a huge mouthful of air and started to dive downwards.

His powerful arms pulled against the weight of the water and propelled him down towards Sheena. Eventually he reached her as they neared the bottom. He swam underneath her and put her arm around his neck holding firmly around her middle. With his free arm he went to push them up and away from the pebbly lake bed.

As he pushed down his hand felt mush and then disappeared up to his elbow for a moment. With the shock he blew out air bubbles and water flooded into his lungs through his nose. He struggled to resist the urge to breathe as he realised he'd discovered another portal. He pulled his arm back quickly and kicked hard for the surface but could feel himself becoming lethargic and blacking out. He felt the strong arms of the soldiers grabbing hold of him and Sheena, as they were dragged back to solid ground.

He lay on his back and coughed loudly as water spilled and spluttered out of his lungs and mouth. He turned on his side and coughed out some more water. His head ached ferociously. He opened his eyes slowly and saw Sheena gazing back at him smiling, her wet hair falling in long strands on the side of her head and shoulders. Her prone body had been partly covered with a couple of khaki camouflage jackets.

'My father's a doctor living in Oxford, still happily married to my mother, and they are looking forward to seeing me for his sixtieth birthday celebrations in a month's time,' she said, smiling happily with a single tear rolling down from the corner of her eye. Sheena didn't expect him to understand the importance of the information that Julie had just shared with her, but in her joy she didn't much care if he did or not.

An overall frantically mopped up the water on the couches and on the floor around Naylor's and Sheena's prone bodies. Their mouths were open and gurgling, although the monitors showed nothing in their lungs to cause any breathing difficulties. The overall captured some of the water in two small containers, labelling each before placing them in a storage box.

'She's found him,' Jenkins announced. 'Brilliant!'

'Looks that way,' Sam said. 'There's no physiological damage that I can detect. God knows where all that water came from. Both seem to be OK though.'

'Right,' Lambert insisted, 'let's get them back.'

'The water's still rising sir,' one of the soldiers said to Fuller. 'If we don't get out soon we could be trapped.'

Fuller sat up slowly trying to clear his head.

'You OK?' he said to Sheena.

'I think so.' She raised herself unsteadily on to her elbows. 'Jenkins and Lambert want you back,' she suddenly blurted out. 'They've sent me – er, Sheena – to get you. I'm supposed to give them a sign that I've found you.'

'I take it you won't be doing that? And how's Julie?'

'Julie's glad she didn't stay in the hotel and, no I won't be doing that,' Sheena smiled.

'In that case we can assume they don't know you've found me.'

'But did you know they tried to kill you?' she asked.

He stopped rubbing his head and looked at her. 'Kill me? How, why? How do you know?'

'Tom told me.'

'Who's Tom?'

'It doesn't matter. They gave you two doses of the drug in the lab. You weren't supposed to make it.'

One of the soldiers became more insistent. 'Sir? We have to go. The water's risen in the tunnel as well. We need to get the pumping gear in here again. There's no way we can go on towards that light now.'

'Damn. OK, let's get out. But first we need to protect the lady's modesty. Drop your trousers, soldier!'

'I hope that isn't one of your regular chat up lines,' she laughed.

They clambered out of the tunnel into fresh air again and walked towards the control room. Sheena stumbled a couple of times as she struggled to avoid treading on the bottoms of her trouser legs.

'OK, so tell me,' Hilton said to Fuller as they assembled around a table. Fuller still didn't fully understand how the Stabu used the portals and so didn't have an answer for the new one he found. He decided not to tell Hilton about the portals yet.

'Well, there is definitely a light source emanating from somewhere in the cave system. I don't think it's natural light and therefore there must be something generating it.'

'Phosphorescence, probably,' the Colonel said dismissively. 'But the Stabu – any sign?'

Fuller hesitated. He didn't want to set any high expectations but had to admit, 'No, no sign. But no dead carcasses either.'

'Blown to pieces, no doubt. So will you tell the PM or should I? Then we can pack up and leave this to the boys from the Air Accidents Investigation Branch.'

'We can't go yet. We need to check out that light source,' which was true, Fuller thought, but he also needed to understand the implications for the new portal he'd just discovered. 'Phosphorescence is normally triggered by a light source and is weak, and can often only normally be seen when under laboratory conditions. What we saw was a strong light coming from a cave system that has no access to natural light at all. It wasn't phosphorescence.'

'So what you're trying to say is that you think the Stabu could have escaped further into the caves?'

'Yes,' Fuller said, lying. The glow was not the same as he'd experienced from the Stabu. It was different.

'So we get that water pumped out and get back down there,' Hilton announced. 'If those things have managed to escape from us the first time, we'll get them at the second attempt. We lost some good men. They're not going to have died for nothing.'

'You won't pump that water out,' Fuller said. 'It's flooding too fast. The explosion's blown a hole in a wall and diverted an underground stream into the cave.'

'OK, so we'll block it up again or divert it somewhere else. I'll make some excuse to get the guys from the Royal Engineers down here. Their divers can dam the stream and check the place out for any other problems before we go back down.'

'And we'll need a guide - someone who knows the cave systems around here. We need to get an idea of where that light might be coming from.'

Chapter 41

'None of them?' Lambert was calling down from the observation deck above the laboratory.

'You've seen for yourself. I've tried all three of them now, and we can't get any of them back. We'll have to wait for them to do it themselves,' Sam replied, standing next to the couches.

Jenkins pulled roughly on Lambert's sleeve, spinning him round out of the earshot of Sam and the rest of the overalls. 'Find a way!' he hissed at Lambert, fuming and red-faced, their noses almost touching. 'We need to find out what the fuck's going on in whatever world they've ended up in. If we can't do that we're finished. We'll be closed down, especially after the episode with Forrester. I can't keep that quiet much longer with his body stored in a makeshift deep-freeze. There's got to be something we can do to get these people back. Think, man!'

Tom woke fully-clothed and stared at the ceiling for a minute trying to work out where he was. The artex swirls above him were yellowed with cigarette smoke and there was a hole where he guessed a ceiling rose once fitted. His back ached and he was aware that the mattress was folded in around him. He winced as his nose picked out the smell of urine and as he moved quickly to get out of bed a spring jabbed him sharply in his side. He realised he was still at the farmhouse. Removing the point of the spring delicately he swung his legs slowly over the edge of the bed, which creaked loudly, and eased himself up. Hearing voices outside he moved to the window and looked out over a courtyard, scratching his head and rubbing his side. The courtyard was strewn with weeds poking up through the gravel, and a rusty metal plough lay half buried in the earth at one of its corners.

Two men – Bernie and Harry Jackson – each put an arm around the shoulders of a third man and led him, all three laughing, into the kitchen below. Even though the man had bandages around his head and a patch covering one eye Tom recognised the man to be his father, Frankie Jackson.

'Tom? Tom, are you up?' Bernie called. 'Your Dad's here. I told you they wouldn't be able to keep him long, didn't I? Granddad's cooked some eggs and bacon. Come down before it gets cold.'

Shit, Tom thought. He didn't want to see his Dad. He just wanted to get back to the laboratory. He'd decided he'd stand a better chance finding his way back in the light rather than in the middle of the night so he'd stayed. But he'd planned to sneak away at first light. Exhaustion must have led to him sleeping for longer than he'd intended.

'Tommy! Come on, son,' his father called out. 'Come and see your old man.' Laughter echoed downstairs.

Tom examined the wall outside the window and saw to the right dropping vertically a clay drainpipe painted dark green but mostly covered in moss and ivy. The paint was flaking in several places. The pipe changed direction just below the window going across the wall underneath the window to a point about ten feet away to the left, and then turned and dropped down again to the ground. As he followed it across the bottom of the window he saw that it had split almost completely a few feet away to the left and the two parts of the cross pipe lay resting against each other at a precarious angle, water dripping out of the gap in between. Certainly not strong enough to hold his weight, he thought.

Where the pipe dropped to disappear into a drain on the ground it run down the corner of a lean-to. Above the lean-to and level with Tom's window was the window to another room. If he could reach the window next to his he could drop on to the lean-to and hope it didn't collapse. But the window was at least eight feet away. He couldn't reach it. The only way would be to sneak out to the landing, find the room where the other window was and climb out on to the lean-to. He turned to leave the bedroom but the door suddenly burst open.

'Ah, you're up,' Deano beamed. 'Your dad sent me to get you.'

As the two walked into the kitchen, Frankie Jackson was standing next to the stove with his back to them, his head swathed in dirty bandages, watching as his father turned some bacon in a frying pan. As he heard them come in the room he turned and looked at Tom with a smile on his face and a sparkle in the eye that was not covered by the patch. 'Can't keep a good man down,' he said.

Tom suddenly had butterflies in his stomach. As his father gazed at him Tom had the feeling he'd always had, even as a child when he last saw him, that there was something very unusual about this man, something dangerous. For some reason this man knew him like nobody else could ever do. But as he stared into the face of a man he hadn't seen in years, despite all that had gone before and all the misgivings he was having now, he realised he'd missed him. He found himself smiling back, not understanding why, but with tears welling in his eyes.

'Oh, for fuck's sake,' Bernie Jackson said. 'Don't start again. You were bad enough last night.'

Tom's father hugged him briefly before Harry Jackson thrust a bacon sandwich into each of their hands. 'So what the hell happened to you?' Harry Jackson said, pointing to the bandages.

'The guy that eyeballed us at the bank? His name's John Fuller. He was at the police station where they were holding me giving a statement.'

Tom suddenly started to recall a conversation he'd overheard at the laboratory when Lambert and Jenkins had brought in the new guy. Tom had used the red access card that he'd stolen from one of the overalls to get in, to try to break into the drugs cabinets. He'd had to hide behind the cabinets when they'd walked in. His memory was a little hazy but hadn't that new guy recently witnessed a bank raid? But his name was Jim Naylor surely, not John Fuller.

'Was he shot? At the scene?' Tom found himself suddenly asking. 'The witness – did one of you shoot him at the bank?'

'Shoot him? No,' Deano said. 'Maybe we should've done. If he'd have gotten in the way though he'd be history now.'

Frankie Jackson stood staring at Tom, puzzled, no longer smiling. He was clearly trying to work something out.

'But I hate to think what he looks like now, judging by the state of you,' Deano continued.

'They got to me before I could get him,' Frankie Jackson said quietly, still looking at Tom.

'So if he was going to give the police descriptions of any of us,' Harry Jackson said, 'he's probably done it by now. So no more talk of John effing Fuller, right? So it's great to have Frankie back but we need to move now. We're all clear on the plan, right? Or do I need to go over it again?'

Nobody spoke. 'OK, good,' he continued. 'We'll leave at ten.'

'Dad,' Frankie Jackson suddenly piped up. 'We'll take Tom with us.'

'No way. He goes home.'

'He comes with us Dad,' he said again, firmly and more insistently this time. Then softening a little, 'Our women will always be OK. You know that. But the boy's older now. The police could decide to give him a hard time. Besides, he needs to learn sometime, right?' and he playfully punched Tom on the shoulder.

The men climbed into the cars. As Deano went to get in with Frankie Jackson and Tom, his brother pushed him away. So Tom and his father started down the track together. They turned out into the road heading back the way Tom had walked the previous evening.

'You won't get back by yourself, Tom,' his father suddenly said. Tom sat gobsmacked for a second and his father continued. 'I called your mother on the mobile after breakfast. You, or my son – at least in this world – are safely tucked up in bed at home. Always was a lazy so-and-so. He wouldn't have bothered to try to find me anyway so I knew something was up. I didn't tell her about you being up here obviously. Don't want to completely blow people's minds.'

'So you know about crossing over?'

'Know about it? I wrote the book,' Frankie Jackson said, smiling. 'And – apparently – so do you. Why did you ask whether Fuller was shot in the raid?'

Tom explained about the overheard conversation.

'I lost Naylor after we met in hospital – at least in your world. Couldn't track him down after that. You know Naylor and Fuller are the same person? Well, that is to say they were two separate existences of the same person but in different worlds, and now are one and the same person living in this one.'

'I did start to piece that together,' Tom said.

Tom suddenly shuddered violently as if the car had hit something. Shocked, he looked out of the car at the road and the sky and the walls and the fields beyond. But saw nothing. He found himself pressing his hands all over his body convinced that he'd somehow been injured but everything was intact.

'Feel that?' his father asked. 'That's where you came in yesterday. Just back there on the road. But no gateway to pass back through. No door, no lake, no gate, no hole, no nothing. Which is why – old son – you're stuck here. With me.'

'That's OK,' Tom said. 'I'm not sure I want to go back now. Maybe I belong here.'

'Don't think so. Your alter ego is tucked up in bed at home. Could get tricky. Especially as the rest of the guys,' he nodded back towards the two cars following them, 'have no idea about any of this stuff.'

'Going to tell them?'

'Can't. I need to do a little more 'travelling' and a few more jobs before I retire.'

'So – how's it work?'

'What – the crossing over? No idea, old son. But I can do it and others can't. And if I can do it and see things a few seconds or even a split second in one world before they happen in another then there are certain benefits that accrue to being a traveller.'

'Kinda cool life, huh?'

'Has its perks.'

'So is this really you? Or are you asleep in a coma in some other universe.'

'Hey – you really do understand this crap, eh? So you know it is of no consequence whether I'm asleep somewhere else or not.'

'I guess unless your alter ego lying somewhere in a coma is killed. In which case, presumably, you die too.'

Frankie Jackson looked at Tom and winked. Tom suddenly realised. He was also sitting in another universe in a coma. He had no control if someone – Jenkins or Lambert for example – wanted to 'pull the plug' on him in the laboratory.

If he died there, he'd die here too and he couldn't get back to do anything about it.

They sat silent for a few seconds.

'And so this John Fuller or Jim Naylor character. Where does he fit in?' Tom asked.

'Getting to the heart of things now, Tommy boy. When we first came across Mr Naylor sitting in a car blocking our getaway the only issue when Danny blasted him was whether he was going to live to identify us. But of course as a result of Mr Naylor's near-death experience he acquired the ability to cross over into other worlds. Now firstly he has the irritating habit of getting in the way of my ambitions in those other worlds. But secondly – and more importantly – whether he realises it or not at this point, he will eventually be in possession of information and means to track down every traveller and destroy them. That means the end of me, Tommy old son, and now that also includes you. Funnily enough it also includes Naylor himself but he's one of these selfless sods who doesn't care about his own well-being. Unfortunately we are a virus, Tom. We can spread diseases across universes and therefore Mother Nature needs to put an end to us. She's already tried a couple of times with me. There are these creatures here, Tom. You wouldn't believe it unless you saw them. Flying things that can shoot acid at you. Like the formic acid that ants can throw out at you but a hundred times more powerful and a lot more of it. You and I are an unnatural phenomenon – something that breaks the laws of nature. So we need to enjoy it while it lasts. Make hay while the sun shines. We'll be gone soon enough Tom, you and me. But I'm damned if I'm going to let Mr Naylor step in and finish us off any earlier than necessary.'

'I know how to find him,' Tom said, in deep thought.

Frankie Jackson looked at him at first puzzled, and then excited. 'You do?'

'There should be a Research Centre down south run by a Bob Jenkins. We need to start there. I bet they'll know where he is.'

Chapter 42

Bright torch beams danced below the surface of the water and across the walls of the cave as divers from the Royal Engineers busied themselves around the edge of the lake where the underground stream had now stopped rushing in above their heads. The faces of two wet suited figures appeared from the other side of the hole in the wall where the breach had occurred as a result of the explosion. They were handling a large reel of cable, unwinding it as they moved back into the hole.

The man from the Engineers had told Fuller and Hilton there would be no way they could drain the lake sufficiently by pumping the water out to allow them back down within the next twenty-four hours. They would have to use explosives to divert at least some of the water away.

They'd brought in an expert and he'd laid out a map of the local cave system for them all to follow. He'd worked out where the cave with the lake was on the map, and had drawn it on the map in pencil. He traced his finger down the route of the stream, and where it met with the pencil mark. 'This is where the wall between the stream and your cave was breached by the explosion. You can see where the original stream runs. Your men need to route the stream back on its original course. And after that, the most likely points to be able to drain the lake water away are here,' he stabbed at a point at its north-easterly tip where another small cave was outlined only a few metres through the rock, 'or possibly here, where an old underground river bed runs. It's dry now because the water was diverted naturally years ago into the stream that we see now. But it should allow the water from the lake to flow out into a meadow over here,' he tapped a point about ten inches away on the map. 'You should go for the second option,' he said, 'otherwise you're just moving the problem elsewhere not solving it. The walls don't look too thick there either.'

But Fuller wasn't listening. He was trying to work out his bearings and the likely source of the light in the cave. 'What's this?' he finally asked, finger pressed against a red shaded area.

'That's our next project,' the man said. 'We found indications a week or so back of the possibility of a new cave. One of my colleagues stumbled across a kind of natural bore-hole leading down from the surface.'

'Can you climb down it?' Fuller asked eagerly.

'No, it's only a few inches wide but there are definite signs that it could lead to something interesting, especially as there appears to be daylight at the bottom of it. The bore-hole is quite symmetrical – strange really – very smooth as far down as we could reach. You can drop pebbles into it and they fall maybe a hundred feet or so. We're starting this weekend searching for ways into it.'

Fuller looked at Hilton. 'That's the direction the light was coming from when we were at the lakeside, I'm sure of it.' And then to the caver, 'I think we've found your other way in.'

Dark shapes glided through the water on the lake's Western edge. Trails of small bubbles on the water's surface traced the divers as they set submerged charges next to the wall leading to the river-bed on the other side.

Thirty minutes later and a muffled explosion shook the ground around the lake. Surface water bubbled and hissed at the site of the explosion and after a few seconds boulders and rocks tumbled slowly into the lake from above. A cloud of dust and debris started to fan out across the lake but was then suddenly sucked back again as a hole appeared just below the waterline and the lake started to empty, its waters gushing into the riverbed and then a few minutes later out into the sunlight.

Chapter 43

Fuller looked suspiciously at the floor of the cave. He guessed the portal may still be there but if it was the escape hatch for the Stabu he didn't feel the urge to follow them through it so he gently guided Sheena around the side of the cave towards the light.

Two armed soldiers followed but kept their distance as Fuller had requested.

The lake had made the wet floor even more treacherous to navigate, but eventually they clambered over a final ridge and stood staring ahead.

The cavern was enormous, like the inside of a sports stadium. It was filled with pumpkin-sized globes of light that floated in the air from wall to wall and floor to ceiling. The light balls gently bumped into each other like helium balloons.

Fuller and Sheena gazed at the sight. 'Amazing,' was all she could find to say as she tried to take in the enormity of what lay in front of her.

Fuller took a few steps towards the nearest globe and reached out to touch it. His hand passed though it.

'It's some form of hologram,' he said. Then glancing around, 'This one's not as bright as the others.'

They both noticed movement within the hologram and leant forward together to see better.

'It's a video,' she said. 'Looks like people working.'

Fuller looked around the cavern. 'But if it's a hologram or a video recording, where's the light source? It must be being projected from somewhere.'

'Maybe something to do with the electromagnetic pulse that brought the plane down. Could it be residual energy of some kind?' Sheena was examining the globe intently. 'It's a video of lots of versions of the same man. All doing different things. Some of them look like they're preparing something but I can't make out what.'

Fuller peered into the ball. 'That's because you can only see the man, not his surroundings or what he's holding. It's like a mime show. His name is Julio Rossi. He runs a restaurant in Rome. Probably whipping up some pasta.'

Sheena turned to him obviously expecting an explanation from the expression on her face. He gave her a condensed version of his – Fuller's – visit to Rome but was keen to explore the cavern. He moved on to the next ball of light. This one was brighter. 'Same thing,' he said. 'Lots of the same person - a young woman this time. I don't know her. If I had to guess I'd say she was a hairstylist. Most of them appear to be cutting someone's hair.'

He scanned the walls of the cave and turned to face Sheena. 'They're not videos and they're not projected holograms – at least not as we know them. There's no light source.'

'So what are they doing here? Who are all of these people?' She looked around at the myriad of orbs filling the cavern. She got out her torch, flicked it on and shone the beam towards the ceiling to get a better idea of how many holograms there actually were in such a massive space. As she gazed upwards she didn't notice some movement to her right. Slowly at first but then quickening, a sphere floated towards her torch and stopped as it hovered over the bulb.

'They're attracted to light,' Fuller gasped. 'That's why they stay together in this place. They're each attracted to each other's glows.'

Sheena shook the torch hard as if the orb was stuck physically to it. As she did a group of three others struck by the torchlight started to levitate towards her. She flicked the torch off. 'Spooky,' she said under her breath.

Fuller put his hand again inside one of the orbs, trying to touch the people inside. His fingers passed through the images. He pushed his face forward into the hologram but the small pictures just disappeared or danced around his head. 'Hello?' he said, feeling a little stupid. The images still danced around his head in silence. No response.

'Sheena, you remember back at ParrotWorld when I came to see you and you hypnotised that African Grey?'

'Of course I do.'

'Do it to me. Hypnotise me.'

She laughed involuntarily. 'I can't hypnotise you. That was a bird. You're a human. It's different.'

'Try. I'm a great subject because I want to go under. I need to go under.'

She looked at him in disbelief. 'John, I wouldn't know how. I don't know what to do with a human subject – what to do, what to say or how to say it. It won't work.' She turned away to look at another orb.

He grabbed her shoulder gently but firmly and turned her around to face him. 'Try,' he said again. 'I need you to put me into a trance and get me to step into one of the holograms. I need to try to contact one of these people to find out what's going on here. Maybe the subconscious is the key.'

She could see he was determined to try. 'Alright,' she said reluctantly. 'But I'll need to relax you first of all. I can't do that while you're standing up.'

'You have to. I can't reach the holograms otherwise – unless you want to try to catch them with the torch again.'

'No, I don't. OK, look at me and don't take your eyes off mine. Stand with your feet together.' She gently put his arms down by his side and started to stroke them with both her hands pressing his body from the top of his head, past his ears, past his neck and down to just above his elbows. She repeated it four more times and started to speak firmly but softly to him, giving him instructions and ending the process by giving him the keyword that would bring him out of the trance.

He stood gazing into her eyes. 'I told you I couldn't do it,' she said in a resigned tone, dropping to her knees. Fuller didn't move, and stood staring into space.

'Wow,' she said quietly, looking up at him realising she'd succeeded. She jumped up.

'OK,' she addressed Fuller again in a mellow voice. She really wasn't sure what instructions to actually give him. 'Keep your mind clear. The only thing that concerns you is the light of the hologram in front of you. When I tell you I want you to step forward into the hologram. You will find a person. I want you to make contact with that person.'

They both stood there for a few seconds, neither of them moving. 'OK, John, now gently move forward. Trust me, I'll be here to look after you. Put your face into the light.'

Gradually – slowly – his head eased into the hologram and as it did so Sheena gasped. First the tip of his nose disappeared completely, followed by the rest of his nose, his forehead, cheekbones, and lips and eventually his whole face and most of his head back past his ears. Where his head had been visible when he placed it into the hologram the first time, now the part that had penetrated the orb was gone.

Fuller realised he now existed in a white, bright space surrounded by hundreds of people who had stopped what they were doing and had turned to look skywards as if expecting something important to happen. All of the features of the faces were similar except that one face here had antennae, and another one there had yellow skin. But they were all the same man in his late fifties looking quizzically into the air.

'What do you want?' they all asked in unison. None of them seemed to realise that there were others of themselves all around, apart from one. One of the man was turning to look quizzically at each and every one of his other instances.

Fuller was aware he was communicating with this one man, although he didn't hear any words from his own mouth when he 'spoke'.

'Yes, that's right. It's me,' as his face turned towards Fuller. 'But I've only crossed over once. I didn't expect to. I expected to be dead after the accident.'

After a second the man spoke again apparently answering a question from Fuller. 'Yes I think I probably could do it again. Not sure I want to though. All those people turning into trees. Nightmare.'

'Well?' All of the other instances of the man called out together sternly, looking around their heads. 'I said what do you want? I know you're there,' they all demanded, as if each of them was the only person talking to Fuller, oblivious to every other one of their counterparts and deaf to Fuller's words.

'Sorry,' the traveller continued to Fuller. 'I can be a bit rude sometimes.'

Then after another inaudible question from Fuller, 'Me? Oh, yes, I guess I'd also like to know why you're here.'

Again, a pause. 'Lots of travellers? Thousands? Wow – I had no idea. Thought I was the only one. Thought I was going a bit mental, if I'm honest.'

Fuller communicated again. The man's shoulders dropped. He responded slowly, 'Yeah, sure, of course I'll help. I'm not a young man but I was planning on being around a while longer yet. What do you need me to do?'

All the other instances stood hands on hips staring angrily upwards. 'I won't ask you again!' they said in unison.

Fuller apparently barked something at them. They all jumped back, shocked and wide-eyed.

'Jeez, I thought I could be blunt,' the traveller said. Then after a few seconds listening to a comment from Fuller, 'No, you're right. No time for niceties.'

Stabu.

Fuller awoke suddenly and was looking at the images around his head. All of the instances of the man were looking around them with puzzled expressions, apparently straining to listen. Gradually, when they heard nothing more they each resumed what they were doing. He eased out of the hologram to face Sheena. 'Stabu?' he asked drowsily, rubbing his eyes.

'Well, that's the first thing that came into my mind as a keyword. I had to have a trigger to get you back and that obviously works fine. You know,' she said hesitantly, 'that something weird happened there. Your face disappeared inside the orb.' She examined him closely. 'But you seem to be OK. No reaction that I can see, so let's do it.'

'Do it? Do what? We've done it. You did great.'

'I don't mean a trial,' she said. 'I mean the real thing. You wanted to…'

'Wait. I've done what I needed to do. Five minutes was all I needed.'

'Five minutes? Ten seconds more like – fifteen tops. Look, I'm sorry but I wanted to make sure I could get you back. Didn't fancy doing all this on my own. So as soon as your hand hit the hologram I gave you a few seconds and then called out the trigger word. You certainly weren't gone five minutes. Are you OK? Did you find out anything? Who are these people?'

'Did I say anything while I was under?'

'No.'

'Well, I was talking to one of the instances of the man in that hologram,' he said. 'He's a traveller. He can cross over.

As I talked to him I started to understand everything. Everything that's going on. The hologram seemed to be like some form of communication device. A video-phone if you like, except I didn't have to speak. The traveller understood my questions without me having to talk. As for the rest of them in there, they each seem to be an exact – or very close - copy of the traveller. But only the traveller and I could see them all – and they were aware of me but not, it seemed, of each other.'

'So it was a kind of interactive response you were creating by being there. Like those computer games where the characters respond to your movements and actions. It could have been that you and the traveller were the players and the others were for you to use somehow.'

'But it wasn't a game. And my impression was that any one of them could have ignored me and gone about their business. They were individuals not programmed to respond to me in the way you're suggesting. No, each and every one of them was like a separate and distinct person – although they were all the same person doing different things at the same time.'

'Maybe not at the same time. Maybe they are recordings of the same man – the traveller – taken at different times.'

'Except there was one with antennae and one with yellow skin. I even saw one with claws instead of hands. So unless this guy goes through a series of wacky metamorphoses as the video clips were taken…No, these were different versions of the same man at the same time.'

'So you could communicate with all of them?'

'Yes.'

'And with the traveller?'

'Yes,' Fuller looked at her, eyes narrowing. 'You got an idea?'

'Talk to them again.'

'Are you going to hypnotise me again?'

'No, I mean – talk to them now. See what happens.'

Fuller drew himself closer to the hologram and eased his face inside. It stayed whole. 'Can you still hear me?' he directed the question to the instance of the man who was the traveller but the man continued about his business, ignoring the question. Fuller looked around at the other instances and they did the same. They clearly hadn't heard him. He moved away from the light.

'So,' she continued, 'it's the hologram that gives you the ability to communicate with whoever is inside. In fact, under hypnosis you tapped into communication lines that are already there. But why are they there? Who are those people on the other end of the line?'

'I think I know,' Fuller said suddenly starting to realise. 'Each hologram represents a person and has a label. The label is the video images you see of that person and the information about the person on the video images is stored inside the hologram. Each person represented here by a hologram is someone who has the ability to cross the bridge between parallel worlds. Maybe just one bridge, maybe many. And this ability was never meant to exist.

'Bill Goldsworth, Jim Naylor, Tom Jackson, Sheena Furness, the banker from Boston, the woman from Helsinki, the Vietnam veteran, the Italian restaurateur and hundreds of others originating from hundreds of universes all over our multiverse. They all have holograms here.

'Every universe has a form of bridge to each and every other universe. But these bridges have not been accessible previously. They probably grow when a new universe is created like the umbilical cord of a baby to its mother. Except they are never cut. The experience called déjà vu is a sixth sense channelled along one of these bridges when a kind of short-circuit happens. It's rare. A person in one universe experiences an event at exactly the same time as there is a kind of short circuit in a universal bridge which accidentally passes a signal to the person's alter ego on the other side of the bridge. This alter ego receives the message a millisecond before he has the experience for himself and therefore imagines he's 'been there before'.

'But the bridges were never meant to be crossed on a regular basis and certainly not intentionally or at will. They exist to keep the multiverse 'in balance'. To keep the universes separate but linked. So when people from a particular universe – John Fuller's and Julie Furness's and Bill Goldsworth's universe – started to get close to being able to use the bridges to cross into other universes, as a result of their near-death experiences, Mother Nature stepped in and evolved the Stabu to stop these trespassers. But why here? Why in this place and in this universe? My guess is the Stabu evolved here because this is where the first person developed the ability to cross over.

'Unfortunately over time these bridges' defences started to break down and the bridges were able to be crossed from any universe to any other universe by people with the 'gift'. Mother Nature would put hurdles in their way but eventually those hurdles would be overcome. She could have evolved Stabu, or their equivalent, in other universes - in every universe if necessary. But evolution takes time. The Stabu had outlived their usefulness. She needed to do something more drastic. A kind of 'big bang' was required.'

'So are the Stabu still around somewhere?'

'Maybe, maybe not. We may never know. If they're dead we may never find a carcass before it rots away. If they even have carcasses. Of the millions of birds flying around how often do you find the body of one that's died, especially one that hasn't met a violent end by being hit by a car or mangled by a cat? And I can't see a Stabu falling into either of those two categories, can you? Alive or dead, I doubt whether we'll see any of them again.

'Now the interesting bit. The holograms are keys. Each key opens a link to every single instance of the person depicted in the hologram. It's showing an image of that person as he or she exists now in every single universe. Whatever they're doing at this moment, whatever they're wearing, wherever they exist. That's what you're watching. The ultimate voyeuristic adventure. But the image is just of the person, not their surroundings. Their surroundings aren't important to what happens to them next. So every moving image looks like a mime without any props.'

Sheena suddenly shrieked and jumped back, eyes wide and hands cupped to her mouth.

'And in some universes,' he explained, 'the people will exist in a form that you're not necessarily familiar with.' He looked into the hologram that she'd just inspected and smiled. 'Yep, even including tentacles.'

'What do you mean when you say it's not important to what happens to them next?' she asked, still intently examining each hologram.

'As I said, these holograms are all keys. Some appear blank or opaque and you can't see the images of the person very clearly or even at all. In those cases the hologram is in an early stage – it's still developing. The 'key' is locating and identifying each instance of the person across our multiverse and creating a link – a kind of connection - to that instance. Those connections are what I have just tapped into.'

'Connections?'

'A kind of route map. Like you get in a satellite navigation system in your car. You key in where you want to go – the address of a hotel, for example - and the system locates it, determines the route for you and displays it on the screen. Imagine such a route being created within each hologram between every single instance of that person in whatever universe the person is living.'

'And why are these holograms over here brighter than the others?'

'The clearer and brighter the images in the hologram, the closer the process is to completing the mapping for that person.'

'And when the process is finished? When every 'route' is mapped?' Something made her turn quickly to her left. 'Hey, that one just disappeared. There was an old lady inside it.'

'When the mapping is finished then every instance of that person in every universe is destroyed. It's done at exactly the same time to stop any escapes between universes.'

She turned to face him, mouth open. 'You mean killed? That old lady is dead?'

'Their heart is literally stopped. That's the point. Each hologram represents someone who has the ability to travel between universes. Not every instance of that person can do so, but at least one of them can. And in some cases, like you and me, when they cross over they merge with an alter ego so now two of them can. Et cetera. Et cetera. That old lady is now dead in every single universe in which she existed.'

'And this is Nature's way of stopping people crossing over, once and for all.'

'You got it.'

'But more people could have near-death experiences like you did and gain the 'gift' to cross over in the future?'

'Well presumably the barriers are strengthened again in the meantime. Maybe the whole process is started again.'

'But why so many holograms?' she looked around at the myriad orbs floating in space from wall to wall and floor to high ceiling. 'There can't be that many people that have the ability. We would have known, surely.'

'Don't forget we're not just talking about this universe. A person could have developed the ability in any of the millions of parallel universes. Nature still wants to eradicate the problem that person causes. In our world, they may be just an ordinary man or woman – no special power at all.'

'But if all of these thousands of people die then it would be mayhem. There must be all sorts of people here; teachers, doctors, scientists, farmers. And all will suddenly stop existing.'

'And that would happen in all worlds. Every single world would experience a form of Apocalypse. And look around you again, Sheena. Not thousands – millions. Even our Prime Minister is in here somewhere.'

'It can't possibly be worth it to create such devastation and turmoil.'

'To restore the balance? It probably is. Remember the dinosaurs?'

'So all of this is generating massive amounts of magnetic activity. It wasn't the Stabu at all. Bad planning then to bring that plane down, open up the ground and let us into the secret?'

'Normally I'd say that Nature doesn't 'plan' anything, Sheena. She has never had any real impact on mechanical objects like planes. Most people would just say it was coincidence that we got involved with this. But I don't like coincidences. And I still have this lingering thought that I'm here for a reason. I hate to say it – like it was planned.'

'And me? Why am I here then?'

'In the nicest possible way, Sheena, it beats the hell out of me.'

'Maybe you can tell all the people in the holograms. Get them to agree not to use their ability. Or threaten them somehow. If they know they're about to die that would certainly incentivise them, right? It's just that they don't know, and we do.'

He suddenly beamed and held his hands up in front of his chest and clenched both fists. 'That's it,' he declared triumphantly. 'You clever, beautiful lady. That's exactly why we're here. You and I are the only ones who know about all of this. We're being given a second chance. To save all of these people. To save ourselves.'

'I don't understand. There's a problem and Nature has the solution. Why doesn't She just use it?'

'Because it would be destroying Her own creations needlessly if there is another way. So there must be one. We just need to work out what the other way is. Every minute of every hour more people are acquiring the power to cross over.' He put his arm around her shoulder and pressed the side of his head gently to hers so that they were staring together into the mass of holograms. After a few seconds a dark shape appeared about twenty feet to their left.

'Look!' He pointed it out. 'A new one. Somebody has just acquired the 'gift'. Something has to happen quickly or the multiverse will be overrun with a kind of virus. A growing network of travellers causing chaos. We have to find an answer because we are part of the problem. And if we can't find an answer quickly we become part of Her solution.'

She thought about what he was saying, and then 'But all this means…' she hesitated as she looked around wildly. 'This means there are two holograms here somewhere with pictures of you and me in them.'

Fuller had already found both of them, floating next to each other ten feet above their heads. Both shone brightly.

Sheena hadn't yet noticed them and continued to search frantically walking quickly this way and that. She stopped suddenly in front of one of the larger orbs and peered into it. Tom's face shone back at her. 'I've found Tom's,' she called to Fuller. As she looked closer she realised there were two different men in the orb. 'This is weird,' she called out. 'There's another guy in Tom's hologram.' Fuller started to move towards her to take a closer look but she realised with a start that the two men weren't actually inside the orb at all. Tom and his father passed through the hologram and grabbed Sheena's arms tightly. She shrieked as Frankie Jackson pulled out a scalpel and held it to her throat.

Chapter 44

'Let her go,' Fuller demanded. 'We're dead anyway, you and me, unless we do something.' He motioned towards the holograms. 'There's one of you and one of me, Jackson. Admittedly mine's almost at its brightest.' Sheena gasped as he said it, realising he'd kept the fact from her. 'But there's an inevitability about it all, Jackson. You'll be gone soon afterwards.'

Jackson looked around the cavern at the dancing orbs, still clinging tightly to Sheena. 'Fucking wonderful,' he said. 'Hey, Tom. Isn't Nature fucking wonderful?'

Tom Jackson was also studying the holograms. 'Am I in one of these then?' he asked.

'We all are,' Fuller continued. 'We've all done the dirty and so the dirty will be done to us.'

'How long have we got to stop this?' Jackson asked.

'Not long. And you assume, of course, that we *can* stop this,' Fuller replied.

Jackson laughed. 'Johnny, Johnny. I happen to know that you can definitely stop it.'

Fuller looked surprised.

'And more importantly you can therefore allow me,' Jackson went on, 'to continue on my way, travelling the multiverse and making my fortune.'

'Stealing and killing for your own selfish goals.'

'And what do you call this then, if it's not old Mother Nature herself slaughtering millions for her own selfish goals,' Jackson sneered. 'Ask anyone in any of these hologram things whether they want to die and, I would hazard a guess, most would say 'no'. There's no right to life, Johnny. You survive because you make sure you do. Nobody else cares – really – whether you do or don't. It's your life – and you'd better make the most of it. And if you can't look after your own life then you don't deserve to keep it. That's fair, right Tom?'

'That's fair Dad.'

'So this is the father you longed to share your life with, to even die with?' Sheena asked Tom. 'Not quite the picture you painted for me.'

'Things change,' Tom Jackson replied. 'Anyway, where's that precious father of yours when you need him most. Not here is he?' and he tightened his grip on Sheena.

'That's right, son, you hold her. Take the scalpel. I need a chat with Mr Naylor or Mr Fuller or whatever he calls himself nowadays. Still got that piece of spaceship? I could have finished you then but I received some information that convinced me to let you go. You've got the key to stop this apparently. God knows why you have, but you have.'

Fuller looked at Jackson with a puzzled expression.

'No, really,' Jackson continued. 'The same story across hundreds of universes. You're the Daddy! The only one who can make all of this go away.'

'So what do I have to do?' Fuller asked.

'Fuck knows what you have to do,' Jackson said indignantly. 'Haven't you worked something out by now, you moron?'

Fuller's face reddened and he took a step towards Jackson who motioned quickly to his son.

'Don't do anything silly, Mr Fuller,' Tom Jackson said putting the scalpel blade closer to Sheena's throat.

'If you kill her, you'll get nothing from me,' Fuller warned.

'Oh, we won't kill her, Johnny. Just a little facial surgery should be enough to convince you how dedicated we are to helping you find an answer.'

Sheena struggled at the words, and Tom Jackson placed the flat of the blade to her lips. She stopped moving, wide-eyed in panic. They all shielded their eyes as an orb of intense light floated between them and then suddenly disappeared completely.

'Another one bites the dust,' Jackson quipped.

'OK, OK. You don't need to harm her. I'll do it. I'll tell you what we need to do. But we have to move quickly.'

Fuller went through his conversations with the traveller. 'First we need Sheena to hypnotise us so we can make contact.'

'What? You think I'm fucking stupid?' Jackson said, laughing. 'No way.'

'But it's the only way I know,' Fuller explained.

'Then find another fucking way,' he said, almost spitting the words out. 'If you put me under you'll finish me off.'

'But Dad, maybe it's the only chance we've got,' and as Tom Jackson momentarily moved his hand carrying the blade away from Sheena's lip, she stamped hard down on his shin, freed herself and ran past Fuller.

'Come on,' she cried, and Fuller followed not knowing where they were supposed to be running to.

'Tom, you arsehole!' his father shouted, grabbing the scalpel and giving chase.

As she ran she struggled to re-fit her harness and headed for where the ropes still hung down at the entrance. Fuller stopped. He knew they wouldn't make it. They needed a diversion.

'Run on and get help!' he shouted to her, and he headed for the hole in the cave wall leading to the stream. He stopped for the Jacksons to see him and follow, but cursed as his father sent Tom Jackson after Sheena.

Fuller scrambled up the rock-strewn track and threw himself through the hole, falling headfirst into the stream. As he got up the full weight of Jackson came flying through the hole. Knocking him back into the stream. He got up again to run but Jackson took a huge swipe and slashed at Fuller's leg, slicing through tendons behind his left knee. Fuller collapsed, grabbing his leg and screaming in pain.

Jackson's face was breathing hard and close to his now as Fuller held his knee tightly with both hands to try to stop the flow of blood. The pain was excruciating. Jackson held the sharp tip of the scalpel – still bearing drops of Fuller's blood – a couple of inches from Fuller's right eye. He moved it to his left eye and then back again, and laughed maniacally.

'Which one first, Johnny?' The knife glinted in the light from the brightening orbs. 'Left,' he placed the blade on Fuller's left cheek, 'or right?' He put the tip on his right cheek and pushed gently until it broke the skin. A pinprick of red appeared and Fuller winced. Jackson laughed again.

Jackson left the scalpel resting on Fuller's cheek as he looked down at the damage he'd caused to Fuller's leg. With his free hand he slowly cupped Fuller's hands protecting his knee, smiled broadly into Fuller's face and then, with all of his strength, yanked down hard on his leg. Fuller screamed and his back arced as pain surged through his body. He fell back again and Jackson's attention went back to the blade.

'I think left first,' he said, and moved the knife to rest on Fuller's left cheek again. He traced a line up to the skin just under the eye. 'Eventually you'll think of a way, believe me.'

Fuller was staring at the blade. In its reflection he could make out the rocks in the cave wall above and behind him.

'Enough fun now,' Jackson said. 'We need to move things on,' and he shifted his position to get a better purchase on the scalpel. As he did so the blade turned slightly and Fuller's view in the reflection now was of two long, thin stalactites hanging from a ledge just over his right shoulder.

He suddenly swung his right arm up and behind him with as much force as he could muster, crashing into the bigger stalactite and snapping it off about ten inches from the tip. Jackson's face registered surprise as he looked up to see the ragged, sharp point of this natural dagger plunge itself deep into the side of his head in an explosion of crimson. The force of the blow knocked Jackson sideways and he screamed obscenities, grabbing at the shard of limestone, pulling it from his head and tossing it across the cave.

Shit, thought Fuller. Anyone normal would have been dead.

He pulled himself quickly up and through the hole in the wall and fell and tumbled head over heels back down into the cave, bouncing off rocks and spikes and ledges. When he stopped on the cave floor his chest felt like it was exploding and he cursed as each breath was like he was being stabbed. He guessed at two or three cracked ribs but he had to carry on. He started to pull himself towards the middle of the cave floor and pushed hard down. The earth was solid. He moved his hand to the left then to the right then just ahead of him. Everywhere he tried the ground didn't give at all. He banged his fist down in frustration again and again and swore loudly. Just in front of his prone body a stalagmite of dark orange and grey stood about three feet high. He wrapped his arm around it and pulled himself up to enable him to see across the cave to the centre of the floor. He examined every inch of the ground between him and the centre and eventually picked out a faint brown-green ring about ten feet from the middle of the floor. The earth inside the ring was a silvery grey appearing at first to be simply a combination of slurry and limestone. But as his eyes focussed more clearly the silvery nature of the earth seemed to be more luminescent, giving off a tiny glow.

A trail of blood threaded out from behind his damaged leg as he dragged himself across the ground. He felt nauseous and was fighting the urge to throw up. The pain was screaming inside his head that he should stop and rest, but he knew that to stop would be to die at the hands of a madman.

He could hear ponderous footsteps clambering down rocks behind him, scattering stones and pebbles that clattered and pinged across the cave. He turned his head to see a blood-soaked, partially blinded figure stagger towards him. Fuller dragged himself closer to the ring in the middle of the cave as he caught sight of the bodies of two soldiers on the far side laying at crazy angles across rocks, rivulets of blood from their severed throats drenching the ground beneath. Their rifles lay beside their bodies but there was no way Fuller could get to them in time.

One more heave and Fuller could reach inside the ring. He could hear Jackson's laboured breathing now and knew he was only a few yards away. He plunged his hand beyond the ring and it disappeared into the ground. Electricity suddenly surged up his arm and through his body and he shrieked in pain and pulled it back quickly. He turned on his back and looked down over his chest to see Jackson, scalpel raised and maniacal smirk on his face. Fuller just had to hope his hunch would prove to be correct in that the portal would do for Jackson what it did for him.

Jackson lunged. Fuller straightened his good leg and raised it, reached out and caught Jackson's sleeve. He pull him hard firstly on to his foot and then up and over his body. Jackson fell over Fuller's head and into the ring, but as he fell he instinctively released the scalpel and grabbed at Fuller's shirt to try to save himself. His body sunk through the entrance to the portal. For a split second Fuller was elated, but then he felt his shirt tighten around his back and his chest, and then his body being dragged along as Jackson's weight pulled him in. The two men disappeared into the ground.

Chapter 45

Sheena leapt at a rope without stopping to strap into the harness, and started to shimmy up it. Tom Jackson lunged at her but she just managed a heave upwards as his outstretched hand swept just below the soles of her boots. She climbed a few more feet but as she looked down Jackson was picking up a rock the size of his fist. He threw it hard at Sheena and it caught her in her kidneys. The force of the blow took her breath away and she almost lost her grip on the rope. She took a couple of shallow breaths and continued to climb. She felt another rock hit her calf and then noticed the rope next to here start to dance. He was starting to climb too.

'Help!' she screamed up towards the sky. 'For God's sake, someone help me!' Nobody came. She climbed another fifteen feet, but she was finding it hard to breathe and needed to stop. The rope next to hers continued to jump about and she looked down to see Jackson climbing up quickly only a few feet away. She looked at the sides of the hole but she couldn't reach. She looked up and she still had thirty feet to go. She started to sob in frustration.

'What's happening down there?' Hilton bellowed. 'Sheena, are you OK?' She looked up and saw the Colonel with four of his men standing around the top of the hole. Suddenly Jackson was on the rope next to her and she screamed. Two gunshots echoed loudly around the hole and Jackson's shoulder and chest exploded in red sinew and bone. She looked into his eyes as his expression changed from one of aggression to one of surprise and despair, and he fell with a sickening thud on to the floor below.

Chapter 46

Fuller dropped to his knees crouching on the tiled floor, and looked around nervously. His head jerked behind him to the left and then to the right. His eyes darted to the ceiling and then to the floor to the left and to the right. There was no sign of Jackson.

He was in a room with white walls and ceiling and a black, shiny floor speckled with grey. A green leather couch sat in the middle of the room. On one wall a single, solid door was set next to a window through which two faces stared at Fuller.

'What the fuck?' one of the faces mouthed as the words echoed from speakers set in the corners of the ceiling. The young man's face was white and his mouth remained open. He'd given up writing on his clipboard. Long wavy ginger hair was tied in a ponytail and green eyes continued to stare through a sea of freckles in Fuller's direction.

'Open the door,' the other, older man said.

'OK Professor Elliott.' The young man pushed a button under a console and the older man in a white overall rushed into the room.

'Where the hell did you come from?' Elliott asked.

'Did you see another guy in here?' Fuller asked, looking beyond Elliott and out of the doorway.

'No, just you. How did you get in here?'

'It's a long story. Where am I?'

'Where are you?' Elliott repeated angrily, 'Where are you? You're in a restricted area, that's where you are. In a locked containment cell that I keyed shut myself. I'll ask you again – how did you get in here?' But then he slowly brightened and a resigned smile came to his face. 'This is CERN. You're a physicist, right? Is it still called CERN where you're from? Conseil Européen pour la Recherche

Nucléaire, right? And you have just beaten me to it. Damn.'
But he didn't seem disappointed.

'CERN? The Geneva, Switzerland CERN?' Fuller
asked.

'Yes.' Elliott started to circle Fuller looking him up and
down.

'Professor Elliott? You OK?' the young man asked from
the doorway.

'Yes, fine. Go get some lunch.' As the young man
disappeared he turned back to Fuller and noticed the blood on
his leg. 'How did you do that?' He went to the wall and
pushed some buttons on an intercom that Fuller hadn't
noticed up until now. 'I'll get you fixed up. You look OK
apart from that. An almost perfect teleport then?'

Fuller looked at Elliott puzzled. Did this professor know
about the Stabu and the portals? And why did the portal lead
here?

'I work for the government,' Fuller decided to be honest
- at least up to a point. 'I don't know why I'm here. I'm on an
assignment to try to avoid something pretty dreadful
happening to the Prime Minister of the United Kingdom.'

'Not a physicist?'

'No.'

'Involved in experimentation on teleportation? You
obviously got here somehow and it wasn't through the door.

'No, not involved in experimentation. Just a victim of
it,' he lied. 'Look, have you been using this room for while?
Have you been here over the past few days? Seen anything
strange flying around here? Flapping wings and long snouts?'

'Was something else sent though then? What was it –
birds?'

'Kind of.'

Elliott had obviously not seen any Stabu. This was
clearly their next target but they'd not made it here. What or

who was such a threat here that it needed the attention of the Stabu? And where the hell had Jackson gone?

A few minutes later Fuller's leg had been treated and bandaged. He had two choices. He wasn't sure he had time for the first - to try to find out why the portal had been opened and why the Stabu were going to come to this place. The second was to go back through the portal and try to stop the annihilation of much of the human race. But something told him the first would lead to the second. The nurse left the room.

'So, Professor Elliott. My assignment has led me to you. I can share some of the background with you but I don't have a lot of time so why don't you tell me what you're working on here? You guys at CERN study particle physics, right?'

Fuller's confidence and his own eagerness to learn more had Elliott talking quickly.

'Einstein called it 'spooky action at a distance'. It means that you can change the properties of one subatomic particle by doing something to its entangled twin wherever in the universe these two particles are. This is called 'quantum entanglement'. And physicists are starting to believe that there are lots of these entangled twin particles spread across our universe. We have taken this several steps further. In fact, we have found there are a great many more properties of particles than has ever been thought possible so far.'

Fuller was interested but clearly struggling with the concept.

'OK. Imagine all of the information that exists to build two entangled particles is divided into two, and held by each particle. Think of a jigsaw of a thousand pieces where one of the particles holds four hundred and fifty of the pieces and the other particle the remaining five hundred and fifty. All of the thousand pieces representing all of the properties, or information – the 'quanta' - are held between the two, just not in equal quantities. Because the particles are 'entangled' this information stays consistent when all of the pieces are put together, but any change to the pieces of information held by one particle is automatically compensated within the other particle so that, once again, the total information between the two is the same. In the jigsaw scenario, if the first particle 'lost' fifty pieces so it now held only four hundred, those fifty pieces would be automatically transferred to the other particle. The 'entanglement' acts as a sort of communication line between the two. The tricky bit is that by simply observing one of the particles you change the information held by that particle, its 'quantum state'. Some of those jigsaw pieces the first particle retained have changed their shape and also now display a different part of the overall picture. The particles are still 'entangled' but now the information you have on particle A is changed, and so is obsolete and useless in being able to match directly against particle B to create a 'clone' of particle A. Again, using the jigsaw analogy, particle A may now have only three hundred and eighty pieces after you've observed it, but you wouldn't know that. Particle B would hold six hundred and twenty pieces and you would still be trying to add the four hundred held by A before it was observed, without knowing about the changes in number of pieces, or in their shape or that they now display different parts of the overall picture on the face of the jigsaw.'

'So the information – the 'quanta' - about particle A.' Fuller offered, 'would constantly be changing every time it was measured. This would automatically result in a compensating change to particle B but the information you have after the measurement is useless to you.'

'Correct. You could never hope to use particle B as a basis for cloning particle A. But instead, 'quantum entanglement' allows you to introduce a third particle C so that now you can take some measurements from particle A, and use particle B as a form of carrier to transfer the 'missing' information to particle C, and then create a clone of A now from C. Cool, huh?'

'But particles A and C haven't gone anywhere.'

'Exactly. The teleportation is actually of information, not matter.'

'And this has been proved? Been done?'

'Absolutely,' the physicist beamed. 'Initially with only subatomic particles. Photons specifically.'

'Initially?'

'Once the theory was proved out – like many theories – advances were significant and quick. In parallel with our work on teleportation we were also keeping close to the results of the experiments made possible elsewhere at CERN. Experiments that were suggesting the existence of many more fundamental particles than had been discovered so far. This enabled us to find ways of escalating the teleportation process into the macroscopic world. Four months ago we teleported some plant cells, and then an actual flower – an orchid - from this room to the other side of the campus. Brilliant! There will probably be a Nobel Prize in it once we issue the papers and make it public. But we had higher ambitions. We repeated the experiment successfully on firstly insects, and then smaller animals and then on a dog – a Labrador - each time over larger distances.'

'So you were actually teleporting objects and animals?'

'Teleporting – yes – but as I said, not teleporting matter. Teleporting information. And in a way that left the originals exactly where they were. Intact. Just using the transported information to re-create them elsewhere. Certainly a couple of steps up from photons.'

'That's fantastic. Very impressive. But I'm not sure what it has to do…'

'Oh, Mr Fuller, I'm not sure you understood what I meant when I mentioned our higher ambitions. If we are conducting these experiments here and succeeding,' he jerked his thumb towards Fuller with a questioning look, 'and if parallel worlds exist, it is probable that in at least one of those worlds – maybe in many of them – the same localised successes are also being experienced.'

'Parallel worlds?' Fuller was anxious suddenly. 'But we were talking teleportation. How does your work on teleportation suddenly skew into the field of parallel worlds?'

'There had been reasons to believe parallel worlds exist. A great many of my colleagues at CERN spend all of their waking hours studying the possibilities. What do you know of anti-matter, Mr Fuller?'

'I seem to remember reading that there should be lots more of it according to the Big Bang theorists. There should have been equal measures of matter and anti-matter thrown out after the Big Bang but we can't seem to find any of it in our universe. It can be created, but only in very small quantities. Perhaps it's better that way, right?'

'A common misconception, Mr Fuller. Anti-matter is not dangerous or evil or malevolent. It's not like the 'anti' in anti-Christ, for example. It simply means particles with opposite spin values to those we find in matter. And as you rightly point out, Mr Fuller, it should exist all over the place and providing it doesn't come into contact with matter then it should be fine.'

'And if it does come into contact?'

'Annihilation of the particles within the matter and the anti-matter in a huge release of photon energy. Bright lights, the works. But the point is, although there is some strong theories supporting the potential existence of anti-matter, there has been none supporting anti-energy. In fact, there have been lots of theories put forward as to why anti-energy could never exist. The one force of energy that keeps flummoxing the physicists in almost all of their formulae supporting this, that and the other, is gravity. And some say that gravity, instead of being a force of energy is actually one of anti-energy. We have found that anti-energy exists, Mr Fuller. And in a very different form to gravity.'

'What form?'

'Early on we lost some of the subjects, a couple of mice and one of the rabbits. We couldn't get over the problem that the cloning process always seemed to destroy the original subject. But since the LHC was commissioned into service...'

'LHC?'

'Large Hadron Collider. It's a particle accelerator. By setting particles on a high speed collision course – in fact a very high speed collision course, it takes 90 microseconds for a proton to travel around its 27 kilometre circumference - we've been able to study properties of subatomic particles – protons, neutrons, quarks, bosons, neutrinos, et cetera, et cetera - that have previously been unattainable. And, as I say, discover some new particles too.'

'You did say twenty-seven *kilometres*?'

'Yes. Buried beneath us, circular and spanning the French-Swiss borders. It's given us some clear indications that anti-energy exists. And in building equipment to measure anti-photons we recorded an unusual event. As I was saying, we lost some of the subjects, a couple of mice and one of the rabbits, in the experiments. Afterwards, when re-running the files from the monitoring equipment, we identified the same signs of anti-energy as we found from the LHC tests. We established that as living things die, some of them emit a last, brief series of pulses of anti-energy. Like a 'pull' from somewhere on their body, or maybe their soul. I guess theologists might argue it was evidence of the existence of the after-life.'

'For animals?'

'For all creatures, Mr Fuller. Did you also know that matter and energy are interchangeable? Well, the theory follows that therefore so are anti-matter and anti-energy. And if there is supposed to be lots of anti-matter in our universe, but there is actually very little, then where's the rest? The answer is in other universes, Mr Fuller. Other universes created at the time of the Big Bang. Other universes containing lots of anti-matter. And anti-energy too.'

'Wow. But being able to prove any of this is impossible, right? Nobody has been to a parallel world or even seen one. And then I suddenly materialise today and you're hoping I can help you develop this further, right?'

'True. I've come to a point where I wanted to test out a theory that I, myself, have developed. I'm calling it 'anti-energy teleportation'. Teleportation works – we know that. Anti-energy exists. The logical receiving station for teleported anti-energy is not in this world, Mr Fuller. It is in some other.'

'But you still need some form of transportation mechanism, right? Like particle B when we were discussing entanglement. And one that travels between universes – assuming they do, indeed, exist.' Fuller was trying to keep an air of innocent interest whilst desperately searching for some answers.

'You know about photons, Mr Fuller. These are elementary or fundamental particles thought to be responsible for electromagnetic phenomena. It has been thought that an anti-photon is exactly the same as a photon. No difference in its properties at all, and therefore probably doesn't exist. Well, it does. At least some of the evidence from the LHC experiments suggests that it does. And the level of electromagnetic activity resulting from these particles is on a hugely different scale compared to their photon counterparts.' Fuller briefly glimpsed the wreckage of the 757 in his mind again. 'But it breaks all the laws of nature because it's a particle, or anti-particle, that appears to fluctuate pulse-like between existence and non-existence.'

'Breaking the law of conservation of energy? Energy can neither be created nor destroyed, it can only be converted from one form to another.'

'Excellent, Mr Fuller. Anyway the guys that discovered it spent a lot of time coming up with a name along the same theme as protons, electrons, neutrons, leptons, photons, positrons, et cetera – and decided to call it a 'beacon' – clever really. And they are saying there is no form conversion going on – just 'being' or 'not being'. Except that I believe, Mr Fuller, that it is actually 'being' all the time. Just in different places. Specifically in different universes. So symmetry is maintained. Matter existing in this universe – anti-matter in others. Beacons existing in the same form but in different universes at different times, and only existing in any one universe for such a brief period of time that reaction and annihilation with their matter counterparts – photons – doesn't occur. Look,' Elliott changed tone. 'Can't you just tell me how you got here?'

'Soon. This is pretty amazing stuff. So, if what you are saying is true, this could presumably change the world of quantum theory completely. But how do you possibly get any evidence?'

'First I need to make something clear. The human body is made up of – shall we say – a rather large quantity of atoms. Obviously it varies between individuals but if you and I could be classed average human beings, Mr Fuller, we would each contain around seven billion billion billion of them. Mostly – about ninety-nine percent - hydrogen, oxygen and carbon, but even some more unusual or exotic ones like gold, uranium and arsenic.'

'And oxygen, hydrogen and carbon are the chemical building blocks of everything organic, right?'

'Correct. Now within the carbon elements there are isotopes. Isotopes are simply variants of the element differentiated by their atomic mass, caused by different numbers of neutrons present. For example, each atom of the normal form of carbon that we are aware of across our universe has six protons and six neutrons. Hence, it is called Carbon 12, or C-12. Another isotope of carbon is Carbon 14, C-14, so named because each atom contains the 'standard' six protons for carbon but eight neutrons. Have you heard of carbon-dating?'

'Yes.'

'Well then. That technique uses the fact that throughout its life a tree or an animal, or whatever it is that we want to date, contains a certain proportion of C-14 versus C-12 atoms. C-14 is radioactive – meaning it has an unstable atomic nuclei releasing energetic subatomic particles – with a half-life of around 5,700 years. The quantity of C-14 is extremely small - maybe one in a trillion carbon atoms are C-14. C-14 decays but is replaced naturally so the amount is constant throughout a tree's or an animals' lifetime. However, at death carbon is no longer taken in – through eating, breathing and suchlike - and therefore C-14 is no longer replaced, although it continues to decay whereas C-12 does not. Because we know C-14's half-life is around 5,700 years we can compare the proportions of C-12 to C-14 during life and now, after death, and work out when the subject died.'

'All very interesting, Professor, but…..'

'Yes, sorry. I digress. The point is that we've discovered a new carbon isotope.'

'With a different number of neutrons?'

'Er, no. That's the strange thing. It appears to be a derivative of C-12. Six protons, six neutrons, as you'd expect, but with one of these 'beacons' attaching to, and then detaching from, the nucleus. We've assigned a working nomenclature of C-12-B – for 'beacon'. There's some discussion going on as to whether in fact it's a different isotope at all.'

'So how did you discover it?'

'Well, you know I said we had developed equipment for measuring the presence of anti-photons – what we now know to be these 'beacons'. We have found out that the bodies of all animals – including humans – contain small traces of C-12-B isotopes. But on the animals we lost, at the point of death our equipment picked up a brief but hugely disproportionate amount of C-12-B atoms compared to C-12.'

'They were saturated in 'beacons'?'

'Exactly. There was a spike that went off the graph but then returned to normal once they'd died.'

'Have you worked out why?'

'No. But a surge of electromagnetic energy happened at the same time.'

'Meaning?'

'Again, Mr Fuller, I don't know. Maybe this is a point of contact with another universe. Maybe a transfer of information – as in the entanglement scenario. These things take time to analyse and understand.'

'How much time?' Fuller was nervous.

'This project kicked off many months ago. I suspect it yet has many months ahead of it. Funding for our projects here has to be ratified by the Research Board chaired by the Director General of CERN. Recommendations go in to them from the various CERN Experimental Committees but it helps if you've managed to get some external subsidy or additional funding from the world of commerce. I'm lucky in that I'm negotiating a form of joint venture with the Jenkins Institute to support the work that I'm doing here.'

'The Jenkins Institute?'

'You know of it?'

'Yes, I know the guy who runs it. Has he seen the work you're doing?'

'I've met him in London a couple of times now, and taken him through some of the basics. Doesn't pay to give everything away. He's coming here tomorrow. Maybe you can stay over?'

'Not a chance I'm afraid. I hate to disappoint you, Professor, but I've travelled here today only from England - not from another universe. I think I may have found some significant concentrations of your 'beacons' in a natural environment. If I don't work out how to tap into their energy then bad things are going to happen. Across many universes. I need you and your colleagues here to share everything you've learned about them and I need you to do that for me now. We don't have long. For some of us – probably including yourself I'm afraid – tomorrow may not exist.'

Fuller now realised why this was to be the Stabu's next port of call.

'When you think about it, as I have been doing constantly without a wink of sleep over the past few days, you could not help arriving at the rather obvious conclusion that there is a significant probability – close to one hundred percent – that in at least one other parallel universe there is a physicist, me, talking to a government agent, you, about how to teleport something from one universe to another, to prove the other's existence. That would mean that simply because we existed in parallel universes and wanted to prove out the same theory my alter ego would, at the same time, send across to me exactly the same item as I sent to him.'

'OK, I can see that. But it does beg the question. If you teleport an apple and an apple arrives here at the same time, then how do you know anything has gone anywhere? There's no point in writing a message – the same message in the same ink on the same section of the apple would also be transmitted here. There's no point in defacing the apple – taking a slice out, for example. The exact same slice will be missing from the apple transmitted here. You could try a random event – for example, you could close your eyes and select a coloured pen and put a mark on the apple. But there would be no randomness – not in relative terms across universes. The same 'random' colour will appear on the apple transmitted to you. The only opportunity would be either to observe the departure of your apple, to notice some subtle change as it goes, or in the arrival of the apple from the other universe.'

'There is an important factor here that you haven't mentioned, Mr Fuller, although you've actually used it before to explain the phenomenon of déjà vu. It just needs a slight time difference in the activities in different universes and we could see the effect of the apples arriving and departing. Even a split second caused perhaps by curvature in time and space within a universe and then across them would give us what we need to confirm the teleportation. And this is exactly how it happened and why I'm moving on to the ultimate phase of the experiment.'

'You've done it?' Fuller asked incredulous. 'You've sent an apple to another universe?'

'And received one back – just as I predicted. Someone out there has my apple and is as ecstatic as I am with these initial results.'

'And you were saying about the animals that died?'

'Oh, yes. We discovered that the pulses of energy emitted at the moment of death bore the exact same properties as a stream of beacons.'

'What does it mean?'

'I don't know yet. If the beacons are available as transport mechanisms then, and I hate to conjecture too far, maybe their 'passing on' meant actually moving to another world. But, then again, their arrival in another world would then be – as far as I can see – in their dead form.'

'As ghosts?'

'Maybe. Or maybe as angels, or even perhaps as 'living dead' like zombies.' He laughed.

'Charming. But,' Fuller suddenly had a thought, 'supposing the energy pulses happened and the animals didn't die?' And then, pushing his luck, 'And what if they were people not animals? If people were only close to death when they experienced the energy pulses, but didn't actually die?'

'Hey, I thought I was the scientist,' he laughed. 'Well I guess since C-12-B isn't radio-active and it doesn't decay, and especially with the size of the increase in C-12-B atoms it is possible that they don't revert to C-12 atoms again. That they stay with the people instead. You wouldn't notice any real difference in the macroscopic world – carbon is carbon, reacting with oxygen to generate carbon dioxide, et cetera, et cetera.'

'So these people would then have significant quantities of permanent 'beacons'?'

'It's possible.'

'And these 'beacons' could exist in entangled pairs?'

'Again, it's possible.' The Professor was deep in thought now.

'Across universes? Which would mean that … ?'

'….. that, in theory at least, those people could teleport across parallel worlds,' the Professor suddenly blurted out excitedly, smiling broadly.

'Professor, I don't have time to give my reasons but I think I may be full of your C-12-B atoms. You need to get your measuring equipment on me – now, quickly.'

'That's easy. We're standing in a containment cell. There is measuring and monitoring equipment galore in here. I'll need to shut you in here and start the checks from outside.' The Professor disappeared through the doorway, slamming the metal door shout after him. Fuller guessed that it, as well as the rest of the room, was probably lead-lined.

The Professor appeared at the window looking in at Fuller and gave him a thumbs up sign. 'Are you ready?' his voice boomed from the speakers.

'OK, go ahead,' Fuller replied warily.

The Professor pushed at some buttons and then started to tap on a screen. A few seconds later and he disappeared and the door flew open again.

'Full of them!' he shouted, excitedly. 'Your C-12-B count is off the scale. How do you feel?'

'No different than I always did.' He was telling half-truths. He was after all the product of two men but he didn't have time to explain. 'Professor, to avoid the deaths of many, many people you have exactly one hour to provide me with some help and some instructions.' He slowly placed one hand through the back wall of the room and felt the coolness of the cave beyond. He withdrew it quickly. 'And then I need to go.'

Chapter 47

The twin Honeywell T55-L-712 SSB engines throbbed loudly as nineteen tonnes of Chinook thundered across the crash site, the six gigantic blades on its two hubs stirring up dust and debris that exploded and swirled and dived back to the ground. Trees swayed and saplings danced and twisted as leaves and grass ballooned into the air like a green fountain, partially covering the eight tonnes of crated machine slung below the helicopter from the three load hooks.

Fuller and Hilton shielded their faces as the blades whipped up earth and small stones and the helicopter manoeuvred into position, hovering about thirty feet away.

'I checked as you suggested Fuller. The chopper's definitely had shields fitted so if we get any more electromagnetic pulses emanating from the cave they'll be OK.'

Slowly the Chinook's cables started to unwind and lower its cargo. Inches from the ground a strong gust of wind suddenly battered the crate which swayed violently, the helicopter rising in the air to avoid fouling its load. A minute later and the crate was safely on the ground.

Sheena came running up to the two men. 'What is it?' she asked, breathless.

As Fuller turned to answer he caught sight of a black Mercedes speeding towards them.

'Let's wait for the PM. I'll fill you all in together.' The three of them walked back to the Control Room as soldiers worked to unhook the cables and open the crate.

A few minutes later the Prime Minister sat together with Sheena and Colonel Hilton around a table sipping coffee and listening to Fuller's report. All three were engrossed as Fuller explained what he'd found out from Professor Elliott at CERN.

'So that's the science behind it – at least as best as we can guess at this point. We now need to solve the problem,' Fuller continued. 'There is some form of link between each orb in that cave and each instance of the person whose information is contained within the orb. It seems probable that the instance of the person who is able to cross over into other universes – let's call them the 'targets' – and all of their counterparts in other universes have been mapped through the use of their 'beacons' and that map is stored in each orb. You can call it a 'multiversal network' if you like, joining the orb to each 'target' and to each of the 'target's' counterparts across all universes. The best we can do in the time we have left is to remove the 'targets' and hope to leave the rest of their counterparts intact.'

'Remove?'

'Kill them. I wish there was another way but look at the numbers of people we saw in each orb. By killing only the 'targets' we'll be saving all of the other instances - millions of people across the universes.'

'We therefore need to infuse each orb with something that gets automatically transferred out to its 'target' and counterparts across its 'multiversal network'. That something needs to destroy the 'target' and leave the other instances of that person alone. So we're going to bombard the cave with X-ray photon streams so that each orb will automatically trigger the link and send the rays to all of the instances of the man or woman in the orb wherever they may be across the multiverse.'

'X-rays?' the Prime Minister was intrigued.

'I've had an industrial X-ray machine flown in – one of the biggest. It's used to detect cracks and other points of potential weakness in metal structures. We know X-rays are basically the same as normal visible light rays except they are a different wavelength – much higher energy level. They're made up of streams of photons produced by the movement of electrons in atoms. Electrons occupy orbits within an atom – the higher the orbit the stronger is that electron's energy level. They can move from a lower orbit to a higher orbit and vice versa. When they move to a lower orbit from a higher one they need to release some energy – this process creates a photon. X-ray machines heat up a positively-charged cathode to discharge electrons at great speeds in a vacuum across to a negatively-charged anode which is usually made of tungsten. This is because tungsten has a high atomic number – its atoms are large and distances between its electron orbits are relatively significant. When an electron shoots across from the cathode and collides with and displaces an electron in a Tungsten atom's lower orbit, one of the atom's electrons from a higher orbit drops to replace it. This drop is significant enough to release excess energy in the form of a high-energy photon. An X-ray photon. The X-ray machine is cased in lead to stop the photons escaping in all directions, and uses filters to direct the photons in a narrow beam through whatever is being scanned – a human body for example, or in the case of the machine I've had delivered here, thick steel sheeting – on to a camera on the other side containing appropriate metal films to create the image.'

'And X-rays,' Sheena interjected a little smugly, 'we know are harmful. You're going to destroy the orbs with X-ray beams.'

'X-ray beams can be harmful. This is true. Which is why we're only exposed to short, controlled bursts if we have X-ray images of our bodies taken in hospital. The problem is that X-rays are a form of ionizing radiation, meaning when they hit an atom they can knock off electrons causing an imbalance and creating ions – which are electrically-charged atoms. These ions can cause damage to human tissue, breaking DNA strings that can lead to cells becoming cancerous. This is radiation poisoning. But unfortunately this wouldn't affect the orbs. But in analysing its suitability it did seem to offer another solution.'

'You're going to use the 'beacons', right?' the Prime Minister jumped in, excitedly. 'You're going to somehow transfer the radiation poisoning to the 'targets' and destroy them that way.'

'That's exactly what I came up with in my discussion with Professor Elliott,' Fuller said. 'But there were a few problems. Firstly, we don't know the make-up of DNA strings in human beings in other universes. We've already seen some pretty different looking people in one or two of the orbs. Different colour skin. Double eyelids. A third nostril. We can't be sure how or if X-rays would cause damage to DNA strings to people in other universes. Secondly, using the orbs as links there is no way to stop the X-rays going to all instances of each person, not just the 'targets'. We could effectively be consigning all of the instances to a slow death, not just the 'targets'. We discovered a useful filter might be built based on the numbers of 'beacons' that the target contained compared to his counterparts across the multiverse. But even so, if we could work out a way to filter it to the 'target' only, death would not be immediate. So the risk would linger on. There would therefore be no reason for Nature to stop the path that it was currently following in using the orbs to remove that risk.' He took a few seconds for effect then continued. 'But then we discovered something much more important. The Professor had already established that 'beacons' reacted strongly with the particular wavelength ascribed to X-ray photons. The reaction results in immediate annihilation of the 'beacon'. Small numbers of 'beacon annihilations' in a person's body will cause some sickness, headaches and nausea. Nothing too dangerous. But for the 'targets' with massively increased numbers of 'beacons' the effect should be fatal.'

'Perfect. So we attack the 'targets' through their 'beacons',' the Prime Minister enthused, but then suddenly stopped and stared at Fuller. 'But then again, what about you? Aren't you a 'target'?'

'Yes, I am. And so are you and Sheena.'

'So what do we do?' Sheena asked.

'Firstly, we'll deploy three of these lead-shielded containers,' Fuller pointed to six metal boxes that had just been delivered and were sat at the doorway, 'to isolate the orbs for the three of us. We then bury the lead boxes containing the orbs in concrete deep into the earth. That will give us the best chance of stopping our orbs finalising their process on us, as well as removing them from the cave and the path of the X-ray streams.'

'Bury them? How far down? How will we do that in the time we have left?' the Prime Minister asked, agitated at having to raise his voice against the throbbing of the engines of a second Chinook that suddenly appeared from around the hillside.

'The drilling equipment and experts to set it up and use it have jus arrived on that second helicopter,' Fuller confirmed.

'But why six containers?' Sheena asked.

'There are thousands of orbs. If we stumble across other people while we're securing our orbs that we feel we also need to protect....' Fuller's mind fleetingly went back to Bill Goldsworth. Although he was dead in this universe could he have become a 'target' in another? He glanced at Sheena and wondered what he'd actually do if the opportunity to save Goldsworth arose in reality.

'OK, and the machine on that first Chinook?' the Prime Minister asked.

'It's an X-ray generator, based on an industrial type used for inspecting large steel or heavy metal components producing millions of electron volts. This one is one of the most powerful.'

'But how do you intend getting that thing into the cave?' the Colonel asked.

'We don't need to. We'll use fibre optic cables fed into the cave from the generator. We'll channel a short sub-second burst of X-ray streams along the cable and on to a strategically placed set of crystals within the cave to act as diffraction grids to disperse the rays amongst the orbs. Almost like a cloud rather than a beam. As the rays come into contact with each orb its 'multiversal network' will channel the rays directly into the 'target' and his or her counterparts across the multiverse.'

'Are you sure this will work?' the Prime Minister asked. 'I don't mind holding this thing back from the World Leaders' Group, but holding it back and then explaining why I did when tens of thousands of people have died – maybe even including one or two of the Group – could be a little tricky.'

'Absolutely. I had the boffins at CERN confirm it,' Fuller lied. He had been trying to convince himself since he left the Professor. There was so much conjecture and theory in this plan that in reality he and the Professor had come to the conclusion that it was more likely to fail than to succeed. But they couldn't come up with anything better. 'There is, however, one unknown in all of this,' he continued. He took a sip of his coffee gazing back at each of them one at a time. 'It's a biggie,' he said lamely, not knowing how to confront them with the enormity of the potential worst-case scenario. Eventually he started. 'The effect of the X-ray bombardment spreading out to people in all of the universes in the multiverse will be to destroy a large proportion of 'beacons'.

In fact, there is a chance that they will all be annihilated or otherwise become radio-active and decay over time.'

'Isn't that the whole point?' the Prime Minster asked quizzically. 'Destroy the 'beacons' and we destroy the 'targets'. Destroy the 'targets' and we save millions of people and possibly civilisation as we know it to use a well-worn phrase, right?'

'The boffins at CERN believe that the 'beacons' by jumping backwards and forwards across universes provide the attracting and repelling forces between them. The stability of the multiverse may depend on the 'beacons'.'

'So?' Sheena asked eager for an explanation.

'They are what hold universes together. Destroy those bonds and parallel worlds could drift apart.'

'Which would be a good thing, right? Makes it even more difficult to cross over and saves Nature having to take any further corrective action,' the Prime Minister said. 'She can keep the Stabu in permanent hibernation and extinguish the orbs. Anyone who would have gained the ability to cross over in the future would find it more difficult or impossible to do so. I don't see the downside.'

'Or universes could drift together,' Fuller said slowly, for emphasis.

'What, you mean collide?' Sheena asked, concerned. 'Then what?'

'We don't know,' Fuller said. 'Science isn't that far advanced, I'm afraid. Nobody at CERN or any of their colleagues across the globe seems to have the faintest idea of what would happen if universes actually touched, never mind collided.'

They sat in the Control Room in silence for a few moments. The Colonel was first to speak again. 'Maybe we should just bury the containers. At least the PM would be safe.'

'Probably not,' Fuller was confident. 'If we can't destroy the 'targets' then Nature would have no reason not to continue to remove all of the risk and so let the orbs carry on their work. New orbs would simply be created for the three of us – probably starting at the same point they are now. And if we used three new containers, three new ones after that. And three more after that. There would be insufficient time to keep protecting ourselves. Eventually our orbs would still destroy us.'

'No choice then,' Sheena eventually broke the silence.

The three men looked at each other. 'No choice,' they said in unison.

Forty minutes later after maps had been studied a bore-hole to take the three metal containers had been drilled to a depth of a hundred and fifty feet. Fuller had used the time to get further treatment on his damaged leg. He'd insisted on being lowered into the cave again to work on containing the three orbs, alongside Sheena and some of Hilton's men, although he'd also insisted on being armed when he went back in. He had no idea where Jackson had disappeared to, and nervously circumvented the cave floor where Fuller had re-emerged a couple of hours earlier after meeting with Professor Elliott at CERN. He knew Jackson went into the portal ahead of him. But he certainly hadn't arrived the other end at CERN and neither had he been waiting for Fuller when he came back through the portal into the cave.

A technician was in the centre of the mass of orbs directing some Engineers in the placement of the crystals. Fuller nodded to him briefly. The light from the orbs made Sheena's face almost luminescent as she gazed again in awe at the hologram spheres hovering in space. The soldiers following Fuller each carried one of the heavy containers. They placed them carefully on the floor next to Fuller and looked at the orbs floating all around them from the floor to the ceiling high above their heads.

'Sir?' one of the soldiers said. 'Excuse me for asking, but how do you intend getting these things into the containers? And how do you know which three we need?'

Sheena turned her gaze towards the man and then at Fuller. 'It's OK. We've kind of done this before.'

Fuller was already standing next to two orbs containing figures of him and Sheena. In each orb he could see that at least one figure was looking intently around them. He suspected the figures were in a cave surrounded by holograms. He started to wonder what would be the likely consequence of him going into hypnosis and making contact through his orb with himself. Shit, he thought. This is blowing my mind, I'm not clever enough for this – and anyway we're running out of time.

He carefully directed his torch, flicked it on and watched as Sheena's orb slowly floated towards it. He walked to where the containers were on the floor as one of the soldiers slipped the catch on one of them and opened the two halves held together with heavy metal hinges. Fuller guided the orb into the container and switched off the torch. The soldier brought the halves of the container around the orb and sealed the catch. Two other orbs that had started to follow Fuller's torch beam now floated away and upwards now that it had been switched off.

'That's me done,' Sheena said. 'You're next.'

A minute later and Fuller's orb was captured and sealed in a container.

'OK, so where's the Prime Minister?' Sheena asked.

'I don't know,' Fuller replied looking around the cave. 'That's why you're here. We'll have to search for him. Hilton's men can help. Direct your torch beams around the cave. The orbs will come to you.'

A heavy rubber tube was being dragged into the cave. On its end was a short nozzle. The technician was directing the Engineers to line it up with the crystals.

Sheena looked at Fuller and motioned towards the nozzle with a quizzical look.

'It's one of the fibre optic cables. It's covered in a form of rubberised metallic substance with the same qualities as lead. It's there to stop the seepage of X-ray photons,' Fuller said as he directed his torchlight up and across the cavern. 'The nozzle will direct them at the crystals which will disperse the beams around the cave and into the orbs.'

Sheena and the soldiers held their torches out in front of them pointing in different directions across the cave. As the holograms floated towards them they checked the contents, switched their torches off to release the orbs and then on again and directed their beams elsewhere. Fuller noticed that one of the soldiers was stood transfixed by one of the orbs he had 'captured' on his torch. His facial expression was one of disgust.

'Soldier!' Fuller barked and shone his torch directly across the cavern and into the man's face.

The soldier jumped and looked at Fuller sheepishly in the torchlight. He switched off his own torch to free the orb and after a few seconds switched it on again, pointing it in another direction.

Fuller smiled to himself and went to reposition his torch when he caught sight of Sheena, herself studying an orb held in her torch beam. She was clearly in some distress, tears starting to roll down her cheeks.

He walked over to where she stood. 'Sheena?'

She continued to stare into the hologram. 'We need another container,' she said between sobs. 'For my father.'

Fuller looked at the middle-aged men in the orb, and put his arm around her shoulder. 'Don't worry. He'll be safe,' he said, hoping to sound confident. He kissed her gently on the cheek. 'Put him in the third container and ask one of the soldiers to bring another container in here.'

Another ten minutes passed before one of the soldiers spotted the Prime Minister's hologram. It was captured and sealed in the fourth container just as the technician called out to Fuller. 'Sir, the equipment's all in place now. We're ready to go.'

On the surface, concrete slurry had been poured in to cover a few feet at the bottom of the bore-hole.

'We'll drop in the containers and then fill the rest of the hole. The containers will be completely encased,' a man in a yellow hard-hat was saying to the group comprising Fuller, Sheena and the Prime Minister, each of whom were peering into the hole. Colonel Hilton was hurriedly directing his men away from the entrance to the tunnel leading to the cave.

'OK, let us know when you're done,' Fuller said. 'We'll be in the Control Room. The number of orbs that are exploding and disappearing is increasing. We need to do this now.'

Chapter 48

The Colonel shook the rain from his cagoule as he joined them in the Control Room. Professor Elliott had arrived from Geneva and had insisting on helping by checking on the set-up of the X-ray equipment. He needn't have worried. His instructions had been followed to the letter.

'OK people,' Fuller announced, 'let's go through the list. We have the X-ray machine powered up and ready to go, the cables attached and the nozzles directed at the crystals, right?'

'Right,' said the technician and Professor Elliott in unison.

'And this button is the remote activator,' the Colonel said pointing to something on a control panel on the wall next to him that looked like an office stapler but with a red circular knob.

'Good,' said Fuller, starting to move towards the panel.

'Sorry Fuller. I need to take charge of this,' the Colonel stood rigidly next to the panel, almost apologising. 'Regulations in situations like this.' Fuller cast an eye at the Prime Minister who nodded his assent.

'OK,' Fuller went on. 'The containers are in the bore-hole, one hundred and fifty feet below us and the concrete is hardening as I speak.' The hard-hat nodded.

Fuller looked around at the faces. 'Have I missed anything?'

'Could I make a suggestion?' Professor Elliott said. 'We have no real idea what will happen when the Colonel here pushes that button to start the machine. There will be an immense amount of heat and energy generated and passed through those orbs. We've already experienced the size of the electro-magnetic power emanating from them. Can I suggest just looking now at where the entrance to the cave is,' the Professor pointed out of the window to the hole in the ground where the fibre optic cables now fed into, 'that we all move a little further away. Maybe a couple of hundred yards at least?'

'But the activator is here. We can't move that,' Sheena said.

'I'll stay. You chaps go,' the Colonel insisted, placing his finger next to the button in readiness.

They all stood and looked at each other for a second.

'Go!' the Colonel shouted. 'I'm still in charge here.'

'Give us three minutes then start the machine,' Fuller said.

The technician and the Prime Minister went out of the door, followed by the Professor and Sheena.

Fuller walked out with the hard-hat and they joined at the back of the procession towards the perimeter gate. Fuller turned to him and asked, 'Where did you put the spare containers?'

'I had one of my team put it back on the helicopter.'

'It? What do you mean 'it'?' Fuller put his hand on the hard-hat's shoulder to stop him.

The man turned to face Fuller. 'It's on the helicopter.'

Fuller's eyes widened. 'How many containers did you bury?'

'All five of them. The soldiers that came up with you and Ms Furness brought four over to us. Then the other soldier bought the last one.'

'What other soldier?' Fuller was starting to panic. The hard-hat described Frankie Jackson perfectly. Fuller turned and started to run, limping back to the Control Room, pain searing again from his leg and dread etched on his face. 'Colonel!' he screamed, as he fell to the ground clutching his leg. 'Colonel – get out!'

A blinding white light filled the air. A split second later a thunderous explosion heaved the Control Room into the air and ripped it to pieces. Green tongue-and-groove wooden slats splintered and broke and sailed through the air. Some caught fire and hissed and crackled as they fell on the ground around Fuller and the others. A rain of glass and metal and mud and stones spattered into the earth. Grey dust and debris ballooned high into the air as if in slow motion over where the Control Room used to stand.

Then silence.

'Fuck me,' the hard-hat whispered, staring at the cloud of dust. 'What the hell happened?'

Sheena came to stand over Fuller who was looking around feverishly. He stared at every soldier he could find in his line of sight. He looked intensely but he didn't see Jackson.

'Close the gate!' Fuller called over to the guards, who didn't respond at first. They were still as shocked as anyone.

'Close that fucking gate!' he shouted at them as he rose to his feet. They almost fell over each other as they clanged the gate shut and slid the two bolts. 'Nobody goes in or out!' Fuller ordered. 'Do you hear me?'

The Prime Minister rushed up to him. 'It's Jackson,' Fuller said breathlessly. 'He's here. Dressed as a soldier. He wants to stop us. His orb is buried alongside ours so he's safe for the moment but he'll realise he's failed to kill me and that I can still throw the switch on the X-ray generator without a remote. If he loses the uniform he'll stand out like a sore thumb in here.'

'So he'll go for the generator. Destroy that and we fail.'

'No. We can just bring in another one. What he needs to do is kill us. You, Sheena, the Professor and me. We know what to do and why we need to do it. Kill us and he kills our knowledge and our solution. And he's free to roam the multiverse.' Fuller collapsed to the ground again.

'So – we throw the switch,' Sheena said. 'At least if we do that we've achieved our main objective. Then we only have one man to worry about.'

One of the Prime Minister's men called over two of the soldiers and ordered them to give Fuller cover as he went to the X-ray generator.

'Look at you,' Sheena said, as Fuller clasped his leg, a trickle of blood oozing though his fingers. 'You can't do it. I'll go.'

'Wait!' Fuller said. 'You'll be too near the cavern. You could be injured.'

'Is that supposed to be funny after what just happened?' she said.

He didn't laugh. Instead he examined the faces of the two soldiers and then, satisfied, told them, 'You're not to let anyone – and I mean ANYONE – near to this woman. If anyone comes near then you shoot them. Dead. Understand?'

'Yes sir,' the two men said together, and then started to run after Sheena as she sprinted towards the generator.

Army medics appeared out of the back of an ambulance that had screamed up to the scene. Two dashed towards the remains of the Control Room whilst a third knelt next to Fuller.

'Give me morphine and then bandage the leg. Tight. Understand?'

The medic nodded and hurried about his business.

Sheena stood panting in front of the control panel on the generator. Her two bodyguards looked around nervously, rifles held out in front of them. She found the button to start the machine and looked over her shoulder at Fuller for his signal. As she did a loud crack echoed across the moor and one of the soldiers' chests exploded in crimson. His arms flailed outwards as he toppled back and fell to the ground.

Sheena was already diving behind the generator as the second soldier, bent to grab his dead friend. As he did a second bullet ricocheted with a whine and a ping behind his head against the protective casing on the generator. He swung round peering into the rocks on the hillside, rifle to his shoulder. The third and fourth bullets found their mark and the soldier fell forward, blood oozing from the holes in his chest and forehead, firstly on to his knees and then face down across his comrade.

The ambulance roared into life and Fuller threw it into first gear. The terrain was rough and as he sped towards the generator the ambulance bucked and reared up as it hit mounds of earth and hidden rocks before falling heavily back to earth and bouncing on its suspension. Fuller was being thrown around like a rag doll as he heard muffled cracks above the sound of the engine and the thud of bullets burying themselves in the bodywork.

The ambulance left the ground again around fifty yards from the generator as the left front wheel found a rock jutting out of the ground. As it landed a bullet screamed through the windscreen which shattered and sprayed Fuller with small pieces of glass. He raised his right hand to protect his face and instinctively pulled hard down on the steering wheel with his left just as the right wheel found a mound of earth and stone. The vehicle lurched violently upwards and to the left and fell on its side sliding towards the generator. Mud, grass and rocks were thrown up in its path as its wheels spun crazily before it came to a stop a few feet from where Sheena crouched. Fuller fell from his seat on to the side of the ambulance and dragged himself forward out of the hole where the windscreen once was and around to Sheena. He sat on the ground, back braced against the generator next to her, out of the line of fire.

Two jeeps full of soldiers pulled up about forty feet away. Their human cargo all jumped out quickly. As they took up positions behind the vehicles a sound rose up like bubble wrap being crushed as they cocked their rifles and pointed them into the hillside.

Silence fell. Rain started to fall again as Fuller noticed the brightness of the glow from the entrance to the underground tunnel.

'What now?' Sheena whispered. 'Most of those orbs must be ready to do their worst judging by the light coming out of that hole.'

Fuller didn't give her an answer. He didn't have one for her. He sat for a few moments trying to get his breath back.

A voice broke the silence. Jackson shouted down from somewhere in the undergrowth on the hillside. 'Johnny,' the sound echoed eerily across the rain-sodden site. 'I know you can hear me. I can't let you stop this - sorry about that. You did your best. You and that girlfriend of yours.' Fuller and Sheena glanced at each other as Jackson continued. 'You see I'm kind of different to you guys. It's the schizophrenic in me I'm afraid.'

'What about the psychopath in you?' Fuller called out, as he noticed the rifles above the bonnet of the jeep slowly trying to locate Jackson's voice.

'Now John. That's not nice. A guy's got to eat, right? But you know the funny thing about being a schizo? People feel sorry for you because you keep hearing voices inside your head. 'Must be awful' they say. That's all I ever got as a teenager at school. 'Poor boy. Fancy having to go through the rest of his life like that'. It took me a while to understand John. Too many days feeling sorry for myself, I'm afraid. But then it came to me one day. When I listened to the voices

– I mean really listened, John – I suddenly realised it was actually a gift and not a curse. I can communicate with people in other universes, Johnny. I speak to my own alter egos and to other schizos all across the multiverse.'

Sheena was staring at Fuller in disbelief. 'Could that be true?' she whispered. Fuller put his fingers to his lips to urge her not to say anything else.

'If what you say is true,' Fuller called out. 'You could make a fortune. Do you realise that? You wouldn't need to rob banks, for God's sake. The governments of the world – and of other worlds for that matter - would pay you royally and more than likely arrange a pardon for you in return for the information you could give them.'

'Pardon me? Yes, you're probably right, Johnny. But unfortunately even if they did, they would still want to keep me secure, locked up somewhere for their boffins to study. It'd be like living in a test tube. No, I prefer to stay free. A wild spirit. I just need to do things from time to time to get a little money in, that's all. You can't live on fresh air.'

Fuller looked towards the jeeps. The barrels of the rifles were still pointing at different angles. Damn, he thought. They can't find him.

'Was your boy a schizo too?' Fuller called out.

There was a long pause.

'No. Just careless. Maybe he did have some of my genes in him given his persistence in trying to finish off your girlfriend. Got what he deserved. No loss anyway – his counterpart in this universe is at home with his mother. And there are plenty more of him across the multiverse if I need him.'

'I feel sorry for them having to live with a psychopath like you,' Fuller called out. 'Maybe your boy actually wanted to die. To get away from you.' There was no answer. Thirty seconds ticked by. Fuller carried on, 'You had your chance to finish me, Jackson. As Jim Naylor in the hospital and as John Fuller in the police station. Hey,' he laughed, 'you didn't even have the sense to be able to use the firepower you had in that spaceship. And now you've even screwed up with your attempt to blow us up here. You've had your chances before and screwed them up. And you'll screw up again now.'

No answer. Silence reigned for another thirty seconds as Fuller glanced at Sheena who was looking at him quizzically, palms upwards, as if to ask what Jackson was thinking, and then across at the jeeps. There was still no activity.

Then a twig snapped behind them. 'I don't think so.'

Fuller and Sheena turned quickly to face Jackson squatting with a pistol pointed at Sheena. The side of his head was a swollen mass around a central blackened patch of congealed blood, two thin dried streaks tracing down to below his ear. His left eye was completely white and blood-stained, useless. Their hearts started to pound. In the position Fuller was sitting, his left hand was pressed against the holster on his belt. His thumb started to move across the leather towards the handle of the pistol.

'Johnny,' Jackson said mockingly, a wry smile on his face. 'You wouldn't draw it half quick enough. So don't bother.'

'You kill us and twenty soldiers will tear you to pieces,' Sheena spluttered.

Jackson pointed the pistol into the air and pulled the trigger. In the rain the gunshot through the silencer was a quiet thud. Jackson motioned towards the jeeps. Fuller and Sheena glanced across. None of the rifles moved.

'I don't think so,' Jackson said for a second time, training the barrel back on Sheena's forehead.

'So Jackson. Where did you go when we fell through the portal?' Fuller asked. 'When I materialised in CERN none of the boffins there had seen you.'

'So that's where it led, was it? Makes sense. Those scientists were too close to finding out how to use those 'beacons'.' Fuller looked surprised. 'Oh I know everything, Johnny. Don't you think the same CERN chappies are close to the same discovery in other worlds?'

'You didn't answer my question,' Fuller persisted, angrily. Out of the corner of his eye he could see Sheena's right hand edging closer to a heavy spanner sat underneath the housing for the cable connection. He needed to keep Jackson's attention. 'Did you screw that up as well? Why didn't you come with me to CERN and finish me off? Maybe scared of me now, huh? Didn't have the balls?' he was almost screaming at Jackson, who suddenly whisked the pistol around from Sheena's head to his, face contorting into rage. 'No more fucking questions!' Jackson screamed back at him and started to press the trigger.

The spanner caught him solidly on the side of his head, burying itself in the middle of the mound of congealed blood and knocking him off balance as he screamed with the pain. Fuller quickly jumped to his feet and grabbed Jackson by his collar with two hands. Two thuds sounded. Mud and grass flew up from the ground as the first of Jackson's shots went astray. His second went through Fuller's left arm, trailing blood and sinew as it passed through.

Fuller winced as his left hand fell away from Jackson but he grabbed even tighter with his right. He pushed hard at Jackson who stumbled backwards and turned to see the gaping hole and the cable leading into it. Too late he tried to lift his feet to avoid the cable but instead fell over it and down into the hole.

'Push the button!' Fuller screamed at Sheena.

She rushed to the front of the generator and threw her palm at the starter knob. The engines kicked into life. Fuller pulled Sheena away and dived to the ground laying over her with his good arm held on top of their heads.

In the cavern the stream of X-ray photons smashed into the crystals. Piercing white light beams shot across the cavern forming a huge framework like a thousand spider webs. Caught in the webs were the orbs.

In each orb the majority of the figures now stopped, some rubbing their stomachs and some mopping their foreheads, but otherwise continuing with whatever they were doing. But the expression on the face of a single figure in each orb – the 'target' - changed from surprise, to shock, and then to pure despair as its body exploded in the annihilation of their 'beacons'. After the annihilation each orb grew dimmer and then disappeared.

The burst of energy provided by the generator stopped almost as quickly as it had started.

'Look,' Sheena said pointing to the hole. 'The glow's fading. I think it's worked.'

They lay together and continued to stare in the direction of the hole. The light grew weaker and finally vanished altogether.

But as they continued to look there was a movement at the point where the cables entered the hole. Crawling up one of the cables was the shape of a man but its limbs were brown and soft and moved like a slug. As it emerged into the rain it raised its head and a grotesque face peered over at them.

Sheena screamed. 'What is it?' she shrieked in horror.

The head had a hole in the side, and a spanner protruding out from it.

'A DNA mutation of Jackson,' Fuller whispered, screwing up his eyes to focus as he started to lose consciousness.

The figure crawled a couple of feet away from the hole towards the pair. It pushed itself up on to its legs and then stood at its full height, slime dripping from its body. Where raindrops hit the figure small puffs of steam ballooned upwards.

Sheena reached for Fuller's pistol but before she could remove it a thunder of automatic weapons exploded from the jeeps. The figure jerked violently as tens of bullets found their target. Jackson's ruined body staggered backwards momentarily. The firing stopped. It raised its head and glared at Fuller. Suddenly, its mouth opened and with a primeval scream it lurched towards Fuller. Gunfire burst out again and the figure was thrown back, its torso and limbs torn off by the ferocity of the onslaught falling backwards into the hole.

A soldier ran towards Fuller and Sheena, followed by half a dozen others together with the Professor and the Prime Minister. As they got close they stopped in their tracks. A couple of the soldiers rubbed their eyes in disbelief, trying to clear their vision.

Fuller still lay over Sheena. Jim Naylor's ghostly form hovered and shimmered around Fuller's body and then solidified, as Fuller seemed to vaporise into a human-shape mist. Below Naylor lay Julie Furness, her Sheena alter ego floating like a heat haze around her outline. Seconds later the process reversed. Fuller and Sheena turned into flesh and bone and their counterparts' apparitions lingered around them for a few seconds more then disappeared.

'What the hell was that?' the Prime Minister asked after a few seconds.

The Professor said nothing, but his thoughts had drifted back with some trepidation to some discussions about the potential downsides of the plan. To the destruction of so many 'beacons' and the breaking of bonds between universes. To the potential for instability that might result.

Chapter 49

Sheena sat next to Fuller's bedside as the Prime Minister and the Professor strolled into the hospital ward. Some large men outside in dark suits pushed journalists and photographers away from the doors. As he reached Fuller's bed the PM pulled the screen around them.

Fuller was sat up, with a drip in his right arm and with his left arm and leg bandaged.

'All gone?' he asked.

'The orbs? Yes, not a sign.'

Fuller turned to the Professor. 'Nice plan,' he said smiling, although he did think he caught sight of some level of doubt in Elliott's eyes. 'Why don't we de-brief over dinner sometime.'

The Professor caught Fuller's drift. 'I think we should definitely do that. And soon,' he agreed.

'And Jackson?' Fuller directed his question to the PM, who looked nervously at the Professor before replying.

'We didn't find his body. Any of it. Not a trace.'

'I'm not totally surprised,' Fuller said with a sigh.

'Probably blown to pieces in the gunfire,' Sheena offered, not really believing a word she was saying.

'I think you should also come to dinner with the Professor and me when we meet,' Fuller said to her.

'Right,' the Prime Minister said. 'Well done. I need to attend to a few things so I'll be off. I'll need your report, of course,' he said, but then looking towards Sheena, 'but it can wait if you two want a few days break.'

'OK,' Fuller said, and turning firstly to the Professor and then to Sheena. 'How about Geneva?'

'Great,' she agreed, smiling. 'Any particular one?'

Made in the USA
Charleston, SC
09 March 2012